EARTH COLORS

Also by Sarah Andrews

Killer Dust

Fault Line

An Eye for Gold

Bone Hunter

Only Flesh and Bones

Mother Nature

A Fall in Denver

Tensleep

EARTH COLORS

Sarah Andrews

ST. MARTIN'S MINOTAUR NEW YORK

www.minotaurbooks.com

Library of Congress Cataloging-in-Publication Data

Andrews, Sarah.
Earth colors / Sarah Andrews.—1st St. Martin's Minotaur ed.
p. cm.
ISBN 0-312-30197-9
EAN 978-0312-30197-2
1. Hansen, Em (Fictitious character)—Fiction. 2. Remington, Frederic, 1861–1909—Appreciation—Fiction. 3. Painting—Forgeries—Fiction. 4. Forensic geology—Fiction. 5. Women geologists—Fiction. 6. West (U. S.)—Fiction. 7. Poisoning—Fiction. I. Title.

PS3551.N4526E26 2004
813'.54—dc22

2003058683

First Edition: April 2004

10 9 8 7 6 5 4 3 2 1

For my beloved pal Tanya,

a porch of her own

Acknowledgments

A great many people gave liberally of their time and expertise to help me prepare this story. Principal among these was Pennsylvania State Geologist and mystery reader Jay B. Parrish, who spent two years campaigning for an Em Hansen novel set in Pennsylvania, and then took me into the field, fed me Whoopie Pies, opened the Pennsylvania Geologic Survey to the ravages of my free-ranging curiosity, and read a draft of this book for technical accuracy. At the PGS, Robert C. Smith II tutored me regarding Pennsylvanian mines, and James R. Shaulis introduced me to the marvels of the Big Savage Tunnel.

I offer a special nod of appreciation to Maureen Bottrell, Geologist/Forensic Examiner, Federal Bureau of Investigation, for showing me the FBI's forensic labs from A to Z, including the most marvelous Duct Tape Archive and Geologic Reference Collection.

I am as always deeply appreciative of the continued support and enthusiasm of Kelley Ragland and Deborah Schneider.

Others who provided key pieces of this puzzle were Jonathan G. Price, Nevada State Geologist and member of the Cosmos Club; Elizabeth Price, chemist; Karl Kauffman, chemical engineer, FMC Corporation, Baltimore; Les Brooks, Professor of Chemistry, Sonoma State University; E. Dorinda Shelley and Walter B. Shelley, dermatologists; Anna Kay Behrensmeyer, Paleoecologist, Museum of Natural History, Smithsonian Institution; Bill Kayser, consulting armature builder; Thure Cerling of the University of Utah, who taught me about stable isotopes; Robert B. Kayser, Spur Ranch Company; and the entire Pennsylvania Geologic Survey, who gleefully brainstormed means of demise during their 2003 staff retreat, namely (in the order they appear on their Web site) Jay B. Parrish,

Samuel W. Berkheiser Jr., Lynn M. Goodling, Elizabeth C. Lyon, Richard C. Keen, Lewis L. Butts Jr., Christine E. Miles, Caron E. O'Neil, Anne B. Lutz, Kristen L. Reinertsen, Jaime Kostelnik, Kristin J. H. Warner, Cheryl L. Cozart, Karen L. Andrachick, Janice Hayden, Joseph E. Kunz, Lynn J. Levino, Michael E. Moore, John H. Barnes, Thomas G. Whitfield, Stuart O. Reese, John G. Kuchinski, Sharon E. Garner, Jody R. Zipperer, Gary M. Fleeger, Thomas A. McElroy, Jon D. Inners, Gale C. Blackmer, Helen L. Delano, Clifford H. Dodge, William E. Kochanov, James R. Shaulis, Viktoras W. Skema, Robert C. Smith II, Leslie T. Chubb, Antonette K. Markowski, Rodger T. Faill, Leonard J. Lentz, John C. Neubaum, John A. Harper, Christopher D. Laughrey, Joseph E. Tedeski, Kristin M. Carter, and Lajos J. Balogh.

The art community was marvelously supportive of this effort. I wish in particular to thank Sarah Boehme, curator, Whitney Gallery of Western Art; Ross Merrill, Chief of Conservation; Sarah Fisher, Head of Painting Conservation; Michael Skalka, Conservation Administrator, Conservation Division; and Deborah Ziska and Mary Jane McKinven, publicists, of the National Gallery of Art; George Gurney, William Truettner, and Quentin Rankin of the American Art Museum, Smithsonian Institution; Peter Hassrick, former Director of the Buffalo Bill Historical Center and former curator of the Whitney Gallery of Western Art; Gary Brown, computer whiz; the faculty and staff of the Department of Geography, Southwest Texas State University, especially David Butler; Walter Whippo, kinetic engineer, lifelong pal, and painter of flying fruit; and last but in no way least, Paul Rest, bon vivant, art raconteur, and Man with a Rolodex.

My understanding of efforts to preserve the open spaces of Pennsylvania were greatly helped by Kerri Steck, Lancaster County Information Technology; and June Mengel, Director of Farmland Preservation, Lancaster County, Pennsylvania.

None of this work would have been possible without the enlightened generosity of the American taxpayer and private patrons who support the Smithsonian Institution, the National Gallery of Art, the Whitney Gallery of Western Art, the Pennsylvania Geologic Survey, and the other fine museums and institutions that protect, conserve, and interpret our irreplaceable wealth in American artworks and natural history.

Two artists in particular taught me about art: my grandmother, Dorothy Warren Andrews, and my dear old dad, Richard Lloyd Andrews.

Thanks to Tanya Gjerman, for caring about this book.

The reading list and references cited for this episode of the Em Hansen forensic geology mysteries includes the following volumes, in alphabetical order:

Art Restoration: A Guide to the Care and Preservation of Works of Art, by Francis Kelley.

Artist Beware: The Hazards in Working with All Art and Craft Materials—and the Precautions Every Artist and Photographer Should Take, by Michael McCann.

The Artist's Health and Safety Guide, by Monona Rossol.

Artists' Pigments, by F. W. Weber.

Artists' Pigments: A Handbook of Their History and Use, volume 1, edited by Robert L. Feller, especially "Chrome Yellow and Other Chrome Pigments," by Hermann Kühn and Mary Curran.

Artists' Pigments: A Handbook of Their History and Use, volume 2, edited by Ashok Roy, especially "Chapter 2, Ultramarine Blue, Natural and Artificial," by Joyce Plesters; and "Chapter 3, Lead White," by Rutehrford J. Gettens, Hermann Kühn, and W. T. Chase.

Artists' Pigments: A Handbook of Their History and Use, volume 3, edited by Elisabeth West Fitzhugh, especially "Chapter 5, Gamboge," by John Winter and "Chapter 7, Prussian Blue," by Barbara H. Berrie.

The Brandywine Tradition, by Henry C. Pitz.

Color and Meaning: Art, Science, and Symbolism, by John Gage.

Color: A Natural History of the Palette, by Victoria Finlay.

Colors: The Story of Dyes and Pigments, by François Delamare and Bernard Guineau.

Conquering the Appalachians: Building the Western Maryland and Caroline, Clinchfield & Ohio Railroads through the Appalachian Mountains, by Mary Hattan Bogart.

Conservation of Paintings, by David Bomford.

Dana's Manual of Mineralogy, Eighteenth Edition, by Cornelius S. Hurlbut.

Fisher's Contact Dermatitis, by Robert L. Rietschel and Joseph F. Fowler, Jr.

Frederic Remington, by Peter Hassrick.

Frederic Remington: The Color of Night, Nancy K. Anderson, curator, with contributions by William C. Sharpe and Alexander Nemerov, including "Appendix: Notes on Conservation," by Ross Merrill, Thomas J. Branchick, Perry Huston, Norman E. Muller, Robert G. Proctor, Jr., and Jill Whitten.

Gamblin Color Book, by Robert Gamblin and Martha Bergman-Gamblin.

The Geology of Pennsylvania, edited by Charles H. Shultz.

George Catlin and His Indian Gallery, edited by George Gurney and Therese Thau Heyman.

Girl With a Pearl Earring, by Tracy Chevalier.

The History of Chromite Mining in Pennsylvania and Maryland, Information Circular 14, Pennsylvania Geologic Survey, by Nancy Pearre and Allen Heyl.

Letters and Notes on the Manners, Customs, and Conditions of North American Indians, Volume II, by George Catlin.

Living Colors: The Definitive Guide to Color Palettes Through the Ages, by Margaret Welch and Augustine Hope.

The Materials and Techniques of Painting, by Kurt Wehlte.

The Mineral Pigments of Pennsylvania, Report Number 4, the Topographic and Geologic Survey of Pennsylvania, by Benjamin L. Miller.

My Life and Love for the Land, by Amos H. Funk.

Nature's Building Blocks: an A-Z Guide to the Elements, by John Emsley.

Painting Materials: A Short Encyclopaedia, by Rutherford J. Gettens and George L. Stout.

Pennsylvania Dutch Cooking: A Mennonite Community Cookbook, by Mary Emma Showalter.

Preliminary Report on the Chromite Occurrence at the Wood Mine, Pennsylvania, Progress Report 153, Pennsylvania Geologic Survey, by Davis M. Lapham.

The Remington Studio, Buffalo Bill Historical Center, by Peter H. Hassrick.

Soil Survey of Lancaster County, Pennsylvania, by Boyd H. Custer.

Treasures from Our West, the Buffalo Bill Historical Center.

Whitney Gallery of Western Art, by Sarah E. Boehme.
Zinc and Lead Occurrences in Pennsylvania, Mineral Resource Report Number 72, Pennsylvania Geologic Survey, by Robert C. Smith, II.

Finally, and with love and admiration, I wish to acknowledge that this work would not have been possible without the patient support and interest of my beloved husband, Damon F. Brown, and our delightful son, Duncan.

EARTH COLORS

As I walked down Sheridan Avenue, I felt a mixture of nostalgia and dread: nostalgia because I had spent the embryonic beginnings of my career in geology in the oil fields nearby, and dread because of the reason I had returned.

The air was cold and dry, and the great backdrop of Rattlesnake Mountain loomed like a frozen wave on the western horizon. It was late March, too early for campers (the crush of summer tourism would not begin until May, when the snowplows opened the east entrance to Yellowstone National Park), so the wide streets of Cody, Wyoming, were visited only by a smattering of vehicles, mostly pickup trucks.

I shifted the backpack child-carrier, redistributing the weight of the baby girl who was riding in it. "This town was named for Buffalo Bill Cody," I said, as I continued along the sidewalk, trying to dispel my anxiety by chatting with her in the habit I had developed when I took her along on my walks. "Buffalo Bill was a scout who became the first and last of the great Indian Show hucksters. He made a lot of money and built that hotel over there, and named it after his daughter." We were passing the Irma, a classic Victorian-Western confection that fronted proudly on Sheridan Avenue, Cody's main drag. "But when he died, he was flat busted broke, and the story goes that his widow sold his corpse to pay the bills; true or not, his burial shrine down in Denver is something of a tourist trap. Imagine living your life as best you can only to have your grave become a roadside attraction. But of course, the Buffalo Bill Historical Center was later named after him, and if he hadn't already been dead, he could have held his head up over that."

The baby gurgled conversationally as she bobbed along behind my shoulders.

"I'm going to take you to just one of the five museums housed in the Center," I told her. "The Whitney Gallery of Western Art. It's time we started on your cultural education. You just stick with Auntie Emmy. I'll start you out with some cool cowboys and Indians stuff, like Charlie Russell or my all-time favorite, Frederic Remington."

Of course, I didn't expect a seven-month-old baby to know a Remington from a gum wrapper. My real reason for taking her to the art museum was so that her mother could take a much-needed nap. Her mother was my dear pal Faye Carter Latimer, although Faye didn't use the Latimer part, out of rage. The baby was Sloane Renee Latimer, the most cheerful half-orphan you've ever met. At least, once we got her past the colic she was cheerful. The colic was dreadful. When Sloane Renee screamed, the world stank.

I truly hoped that Faye was getting some sleep. It had been a long drive up from Salt Lake City, and the purpose of our visit was worrying her even worse than it did me. Faye was here to meet with a potential client. I was just along to fill in the cracks between single motherhood and her career.

I had left Faye staring at the wall in our room at the Pawnee, a good old girl of a hotel, but many rungs below what Faye was used to on the great ladder of hostelries. My choice in booking the Pawnee had brought on one of our small but deadly fights.

"Why didn't you book us a room at the Irma?" she had inquired, keeping her voice eerily neutral.

"This was cheaper," I had replied, trying to sound matter-of-fact.

"Is this some kind of a joke, or are you trying to tell me you think it's time I began to live within my diminished means?"

She had given me the opening I had longed for, but I had dodged the issue. "I'll just take a walk while you get some rest. You'll want to be fresh for your meeting."

"Fine," she said, a sharpening in her tone telling me that it wasn't. "I'm not sure I can sleep in a place like this, but we'll see if fatigue can prevail where my silver spoon dumped me off."

Now, as I continued down Sheridan Avenue, passing shops that sold Western wear and Indian trinkets made in China, I scrutinized her words. Uncomfortable as the confrontation had been, it was the most direct communication we'd had since before the baby was born, and that could be seen as a positive thing. I told myself that trying to function in the outside world might pry her out of the brooding silence she had dwelt in since her husband's death.

Farther down the street, as I again shifted the baby's weight, it began to hit me that I was at least as tired as Faye—after all, we had gotten up at four and had been on the road since six, and I had done most of the driving—but I pushed this awareness down into the murk from which it had arisen.

I passed a saddlery and cast a longing glance inside. *When I inherit the ranch, the first thing I'll do it buy another horse*, I told myself, but I increasingly wondered if there would be anything left to inherit. For a moment the thought froze me to the sidewalk, but I forced myself back into motion.

In the next block, I sniffed at the heady scent of cinnamon rolls that spilled from a café. I stopped, realizing I hadn't had lunch. "Do you smell that, Sloane?" I asked the baby. "Just as soon as you grow more teeth, we'll try some. You're going to *love* cinnamon rolls." I knew that I should turn around and make myself a peanut butter and jelly sandwich from my stash of ingredients in Faye's car, but instead I followed my nose into the café saying, "But as your mother always says, there's no better time than the present."

I bought a roll and a cup of coffee and settled down with Sloane on my lap. The roll was fresh and sweet, without being cloyingly so, and rich in the spicy liquor that oozes so delightfully from the swirls of that pastry. I shared my prize frugally with the baby, giving her tiny bites and making mine last too, then dawdled over the coffee, relieved at the way the sugar and caffeine revived me. But no matter how slowly I savored the treat, it was soon gone, and someone else was waiting for the table, so I got up and prepared to leave.

As I pushed open the door I about collided with a man who was just coming in from outside. He had his collar turned up against the cold and his head tucked down, so I didn't see his face at first, but something about him was instantly familiar: the thickset torso, the wild brush of hair, the humble clothing designed for manual labor. Recognition registered in my gut even before it hit my brain, and when he looked up, ready to dodge me, his eyes widened as he recognized me, too.

It was Frank Barnes, my old oilfield boyfriend. I had not seen him since I left Wyoming for a better job in Denver. How many years had it been?

I started to step back, unsure of my welcome, but he grinned, so I did, too. I said, "Frank! How are you?" His hair had gone silvery gray. How old was he now? Fifty?

He clasped my shoulders with his thick, rough hands and stared happily into my eyes. Then his gaze slid sideways. As he took in the little creature that was riding papoose on my back, his mouth sagged open. "Em! You've got a . . . a baby!" His eyes shot next to my left hand, checking for a wedding ring.

My stomach tightened. "She's . . . I'm babysitting for a friend." Immediately I wished I had lied and claimed her as mine, because Frank had left me for—*No, I left him*, I asserted to myself—*or more precisely, I left town to take that job, and while I was gone, he—but I suppose I never really was going to come back . . .*

We were being jostled now by other people who were trying to come into the restaurant, so Frank let go of my shoulders and stepped to one side, but his eyes stayed locked on Sloane Renee Latimer, his face spreading into a delighted grin. "She's beautiful," he said, offering her a callused finger to grab. He leaned his big face close to hers and said, "You certainly is. Yes, you certainly is."

The baby was totally enthralled by his big, grizzled smile. Over my shoulder, I could see that she was giving him her best drop-dead gorgeous, dimpled grin.

I smiled too, grateful that he had focused on the baby, as it gave me a moment to collect myself. Frank had passed on into the ranks of the married people, and I was still single. I was beginning to wince, now that I was almost thirty-nine, when headlines of supermarket tabloids trumpeted grim statistics about women finding partners after thirty-five.

Too quickly, Frank's gaze shifted back to me. "You're just leaving. Can you stay? I was just going to grab some—"

"Ah, sure."

Beaming with delight, he led me back toward one of the tables and helped me off with the backpack. He set it down expertly, flipping the bail out to steady it. He offered me a quick, *May I?* glance and then undid her shoulder harness. Lifting her expertly with one arm, he opened his jacket with the other hand and nestled her inside against his flannel shirt.

Sloane laid her little heady right down against his neck and patted his chest with one tiny hand. She gurgled with glee.

I was engulfed by the memory of how secure I had always felt in Frank's embrace.

The woman behind the counter boomed, "Hey there, Frank! Who's your buddy?"

Frank sauntered over to the counter. "Pretty little thing, huh? She's with my old friend Emmy here." To Sloane, he said, "What you having, little one? Some nice salami and Swiss? Cup of coffee? Hm?"

The woman laughed. "Your usual."

"Yeah."

She reached out and tickled the baby on one ear. "That'll be up in just a few. I'll call ya."

Frank brought Sloane back to the table and sat down. The two of them seemed lost in a love fest, he kissing and caressing, she settling down and looking drowsy for the first time all day. "What brings you to town?" he asked, his lips lost in the soft down of her hair.

"The baby's mother is taking care of some business here in Cody."

Frank raised an eyebrow in question.

I said, "She's a pilot. She uses her airplane to transport things that need . . . um, discreet handling. She calls her business, 'Special Deliveries.' " I laughed nervously. "It's nothing too complicated, really. She's got a potential client here—some old guy, a family friend or something—who's here to meet with some specialists at the art museum. He has some artwork that the museum wants to include in an exhibit. Collectors can be fussy who handles their treasure." I smiled, thinking of the days I first knew Faye, of all the mischief we'd gotten into. "The fact is that she doesn't really have a business. It used to be that her biggest problem in life was figuring out how to use her trust fund to dispel boredom. She bought a hot twin-engine plane and got to tooting around with expensive stuff, like jewels. Growing up with the trust fund set, I guess she knew a lot of people who needed things moved on the quiet. It was a good day when it covered her expenses."

"But then she became a mother."

"Right. Then she got pregnant. The good news was that she truly loved the man, so she married him. The bad news was that her trust fund turned into a pumpkin the instant she got hitched." I shook my head. "I don't know how well her flying service is going to mix with motherhood. I picked up a pilot's license myself along the way," I said, slipping a little personal success into the discussion.

"Really?" he said, obviously impressed.

"It's nothing as fancy as Faye has; just the basic single-engine rating. I can't fly by instruments or carry people for hire, much less fly a high-performance, twin-engine plane like Faye's, but it taught me that you've got to stay sharp and concentrate or you shouldn't be at the controls. The baby doesn't seem to need as much sleep as most babies, and when she does konk out, Faye often lies awake."

"Sleep deprivation," Frank mumbled. "Worry." He grunted empathetically. "Well, Em, you always did get yourself involved in interesting things."

I smiled uncomfortably. Frank had always said that I traveled in strange circles, going places and hanging out with people he was unlikely to meet. He had never left Wyoming, except to go to Vietnam. Now he was married, and had a son. How old would that child be now? "How's your wife?" I asked.

Frank turned and looked at me squarely, the pleasure in his eyes suddenly extinguished. "She drinks," he said. "I'm just in town to attend an Al-Anon meeting."

I made a quick study of my boots. "I'm sorry to hear."

"Yeah. Well." Suddenly he laughed. "Hey, that's what I get for foolin' around. Ya knock the lady up before you know her, and ya take home what ya catch."

I gave him an embarrassed grimace. "Tell me about your son."

Frank glanced away. "He's fine," he said, too quickly. "Growing gangbusters. Great kid." His voice caught. "A couple of challenges. School stuff. But what did he expect, with me for his dad?" Fighting his way out of his emotional logjam, Frank said, "How long you be in town?"

"Just until tomorrow, I think."

"You gotta meet him."

"I'd like that."

Now his gaze once again dropped to my left hand. "You married?" he asked, trying to make it sound like an idle question.

"No."

"Seeing someone?"

I met his eyes. This was a new Frank, a blunter, more inquiring Frank, not the reclusive soul I had known and somehow left so long ago. But the turbulence was still there, and the pain, now mixed with new agonies and the joy his son had brought him. Had fatherhood blown the restraints off his personality? "Yes, I'm seeing someone," I said, steeling myself for his reaction. "He's overseas. The Middle East. Military reservist who got called up with this current fracas. You know the pace."

Frank gave me a compassionate stare.

I couldn't stand his caring. "I'm doing great, Frank. I've been working on my master's in geology at the University of Utah. I've almost got the coursework done."

His stare eased. "That's great, Emmy."

"Thanks. I've been living at Faye's so I can help with the baby while I go to school." Realizing that this sounded pretty shiftless for a person my age, I added, "The baby's dad was killed, and . . . I figured she needed a friend."

"Killed?"

I closed my eyes. This wasn't going well. Each time I tried to divert the conversation away from myself, I managed to open another door into a room I did not want to enter. "Tom was an FBI agent," I said, picking the version of the truth that was easiest to say, and easiest to understand. "He was killed in the line of duty." This wasn't precisely accurate: It avoided certain facts such as that, with the baby coming, Tom had left the Bureau so that he wouldn't have to take on risky projects. That there had been "just one more" risk he felt he had to take. That I had been with him when he died.

When I opened my eyes, Frank was staring at the baby, his face raw with emotion. He kissed her hair. Nuzzled his nose against her scalp. Clung to her as if she were a life ring cast off a boat in a storm.

She began to fuss.

"Oh, there, there," he whispered. "There, there. I'm just your old friend Frank. I don't bite."

The woman at the counter called his name, and he handed me the baby while he got his sandwich. Back at the table, Frank ate quickly, taking in huge bites without tasting his food. The coffee he bolted after adding three little tubs of cream. As he set down the cup, he asked, "Where you staying?"

"We're just down at the Pawnee."

He nodded. His kind of place—cheap, comfortable, and unpretentious. "I'll walk you there."

I said, "Actually, we're on our way to the museums."

"My truck's parked halfway."

We loaded up and left the café. I toted the backpack over one shoulder and he carried Baby Sloane. A block down the sidewalk, Frank asked, "So your friend has an airplane?"

"Yes. A twin-engine turboprop job, goes like spit. But it's been sitting in a tie-down in Florida since before the baby was born, and she wants to bring it home to Utah. She worries about corrosion from the sea air. So if her client has the bucks, I guess she'll be doing some flying again. But in fact I'm hoping ol' Mr. Krehbeil says no, and she gets reasonable and sells the plane."

Frank stopped dead in the middle of the sidewalk. "Who'd you say her client is?"

I slapped my hands over my face in embarrassment. I couldn't believe I'd spilled the client's name. Did I think that just because Frank never left Wyoming he wasn't part of the world? "Oh, nobody," I said lamely. "Just some old geezer Faye knows."

Frank's face had gone dark as a storm cloud. "Krehbeil's not a common name."

"Please forget I said that! Look, Faye's supposed to be real discreet about this stuff, you know?"

Frank's face tightened. "You don't want to get mixed up with that bunch, Em."

"No, wait! Listen, this guy's from back East somewhere. The contact was some dude Faye knew in college, and this is his dad or something. It's got to be a different Krehbeil."

He shook his head. "Dude's the right word. You know full well there's a lot of fancy people from the East who come out here for the summer, especially that artsy set." He jerked his head to the west. "The Krehbeils got a hobby ranch outside of town here, up beyond the reservoir."

I winced. "Old money?" I asked, knowing the answer.

"Yeah, if you mean the guys who have it didn't make it. Miz Krehbeil was in her eighties, and the place goes back a generation or two."

"What do you mean, '*was* in her eighties'?"

Sloane had begun to twist in his arms.

Frank said, "She died."

"That's not unusual for someone in her eighties, is it?"

Frank had begun to hunch his shoulders like he always did when something beyond his control was making him half mad and half worried. He said, "No, but there's rumors that everything wasn't quite right. Hell, Em, it was just a month or so ago."

I stared at the sidewalk.

Frank shifted the baby into a one-armed grip and reached out with the other hand to touch my arm. "Em, I know you. You wind up right in the middle of every fight that's going down. It's an instinct of yours."

Sloane was now working her way into a good fuss. I reached out and took her into my arms, shaking my head vehemently. "No way, Frank. I was a headstrong little twit when I worked around here, but I've grown up a lot, I swear it. Hey, this little baby here has taught me a lot about covering my butt so I can be here for her and be responsible. It's Faye that's out chasing trouble this time, not me. And the job won't go through anyway. Even if the old guy does want her to do it, he won't pay enough to cover the avgas it would take to fly the plane, let alone what it would take to make the plane legal to fly. It has to go through its annual airworthiness check and there are always expensive repairs, and Faye's annual FAA flight review to fly commercially is overdue. She's kidding herself. She doesn't even have a current medical clearance. Hasn't flown since she was seven months pregnant." I started moving down the sidewalk again, as much to escape Frank's words as to arrive at my destination.

Frank hurried to keep up, his scowl deepening. "She was flying an airplane at seven months?"

"That's another part of why your pal here was a preemie." On cue, the baby broke into a full bawling cry.

Frank stopped again. "Here's my truck. Get in. I'll take you to the Pawnee and we can talk to the baby's mother, find out for sure if there's really no connection."

I said, "No. Thanks for your concern, Frank, but I'm sure it's unwarranted. I'd better keep moving, rock her to sleep. You just lift her into the backpack." I turned a shoulder toward him.

He said, "Let me bounce her."

"I should go." I didn't want Frank to be there watching if I failed to settle Sloane down. I knew her every mood, knew what made her smile and what made her cry, but that did not make her mine, and at times like this, she let me know it. "I'm sorry. I think just walking quietly is the best thing, with as few distractions as possible."

"Then I'll stop by later," Frank told me, and to Sloane he said, "You're a lucky baby. Auntie Emmy's a very good mom." He gave me a look of longing. He started to walk away, but turned back. "I . . . About the Krehbeils. There's really been some talk, Em."

"See you," I said, heading resolutely toward the museums.

A block farther along, I heard him call to me again. I spun around to hear what he was saying. A passing truck swallowed his words, but his lips said. "Take care." A common-enough phrase, and yet the look on his face spoke of farewell.

THE FATES AND THE FURIES BEING MARGINALLY ON MY SIDE FOR the moment, Sloane did settle down as I lengthened my stride, but she did not fall asleep. By and by, we passed out of the business district, and dead ahead, I could now see the statue of Buffalo Bill on his horse that stood in the middle of the north parking lot of the museum complex. The statute showed him in a bizarre rallying pose that suggested as much as anything that he was falling off his horse.

I felt a bit like I was falling also. Frank was a fine man who was wonderful with children. I couldn't help but wonder what might life be like if I had not been so career-oriented.

As if reading my emotions, Sloane let out a cranky whimper. I got going with my monologue again, hoping that between the sound of my voice and the rhythmic swaying of the backpack ride, she would fall asleep.

"I used to come here with my dad," I told her. "We'd stop by on our annual fishing trip to Yellowstone. The first time I saw the museum, I could barely cast a short rod, and as I grew up, so did the museum. Now it's five museums and a library: there's the Buffalo Bill Museum, of course; and then there's the Cody Firearms Museum; the McCracken Research Library; the Plains Indian Museum; the new Draper Museum of Natural History; and—this is the best, Sloane—the Whitney Gallery of Western Art. It's quite a place. The Louvre might have its *Mona Lisa*, and that joint in Amsterdam might have Van Goghs by the truckload, but it's the paintings at the Whitney that make this cowgirl's heart sing."

I found myself smiling. In the quiet rooms of the Whitney, I could open myself to a state of reverence for the Western experience. In those rooms, I would find the American West as it appeared before the advent of interstate highways and burger stands, back before Model T Fords and steam locomotives crossed the plains, back when travelers wore buckskins and weskits, back when travel itself was on horseback or even by foot. From the gallery's walls opened scenes by George Catlin, William Tylee Ranney, and John Mix Stanley, dating from the days of the great artist explorers and the Emigrant Trail, when whites and Indians first met and then clashed over the bare resources of survival. There were vistas of Yellowstone as it looked before it was a national park, or even a part of our nation, painted by Albert Bierstadt and Thomas Moran. There were visual narratives by the great magazine illustrators, such as Frederic Remington's and Charlie Russell's depictions of harsh light across dusty plains and craggy peaks where hard men fought a love affair over land and cattle. And there were more recent additions: arresting portraits of the last few cowboys and Indians painted by such longing romantics as James Bama. Art is, after all, history.

At the museum complex, I trooped up the lawn past a collection of teepees. Inside the main entrance, I dodged the admissions kiosk and instead spoke to the man who sat at the desk to the right. "There should be a pass waiting for Faye Carter," I said, letting him think I was her. "It's for a meeting here later this afternoon. I was wondering if I could go in early, and then return at the appointed hour."

"Certainly, Ms. Carter," the man said, rising politely from his chair. "The curator and his party are expecting you at four, but I can issue that pass now." He had me sign in.

I scribbled something illegible.

He gave me a pass marked VISITOR, winked playfully at Sloane (who was now doing her Perfect Baby act), and settled his bones back into his chair.

"Thank you so much," I said.

The man nodded and wiggled his bandy fingers to the baby.

I gave him my most sugary smile and then zipped through the turnstile. To Sloane Renee, I whispered, "Sweetie-pea, it's not that museums overcharge—trust me, they don't—but your old Auntie Emmy is sorta short on funds, so it was necessary to use some of the moves your daddy taught me. Your daddy was a very ethical man—don't get me wrong—but he was one of the best agents the FBI ever had, and that means he knew how to be slippery at times. I was his respectful protégée, which is a big word that means he was teaching me the business, and out of respect for his memory, you'd want me to keep in practice, now, wouldn't you? So you see, using your mama's free pass was not exactly deceitful, but more like . . . misdirection, and . . . an homage." I cut straight for the Whitney, which opened just a few strides off to my right.

Ah . . .

I took a quick look at the first two rooms as I hurried through to my formal pilgrimage to the works of Frederic Remington. His gallery, quite appropriately, took up the far western corner of the museum. Here I would find not just his grand renderings of cowboy-and-Indian fare, but also the smaller landscapes that he apparently had considered little more than oil sketches. The first always filled my Wyoming cowgirl heart with pride, while the second seemed a dance of the veils, luring me in past the bravura of Remington's commercial presence to the subtle magic of his personal hard-focus spin on American Impressionism. As I strode down the gallery, I told the baby, "An Impressionist he truly was: Look! He put the most improbable colors next to each other. He could evoke everything from the blinding heat of a prairie summer to the brilliant shadows of a desert night." I was waxing poetical, and impressing even myself. "But let's start at the source: his studio."

I took a right turn at the end of the gallery and pulled up next to a barrier. Beyond it waited the reconstruction of Remington's wonderful room, with its giant fireplace, now tucked intimately into this quiet corner of the gallery. How surprised I had been, the first time I'd seen it, how filled with awe. I wondered what the baby was making of it through her innocent eyes. Did she have any idea what she was seeing? I held out my arms, presenting the room to my tiny charge. "Check this out, m'dear. It's filled with the raw stuff of Remington's inspiration—Indian tomahawks and beaded moccasins, a cavalry saddle and canteen. . . . And look: even an early Mexican straw sombrero."

It was all of ten seconds before Sloane began to wiggle. Now that I was standing still, she had decided it was time to get up and party. Erupting from her contentment, she dug her little bootied feet into the space between the frame of the backpack and my spine and began to shove herself skyward.

I knew this signal well. It meant she wanted down. No more backpack for her. She wanted to get down on that board gallery floor and move, zigging and zagging about like a demented moon-rover.

From the way Sloane was arching her back, it seemed that this might even be her moment to rise up and walk, even begin to run, using her sticky fingers to grapple all things that museums label DO NOT TOUCH.

I greeted her kicks with a jagged sense of frustration, still tense from my meeting with Frank, and—not for the first time—wondering how a child I so deeply loved could snap me over the brink from frustration into seething annoyance with such terrifying speed. I stuck a finger back over my shoulder for her to grab, but she rejected my feeble maneuvers and instead leaned in the opposite direction, attempting to launch herself over the top of the frame. I tried the old bouncing up and down gambit, but she continued to fight against her shoulder harness, and in the process managed to grab herself a good handful of my hair and give it a yank.

"Sloane, honeycup," I gasped, "that's not how to put Auntie Emmy in a nice mood, now, is it?" I reached back with both hands and tried to loose my hair from her grip, but she managed to work her hands free of the little mittens that were clipped to the cuffs of her snowsuit and had twined her sticky little fingers tight against my scalp.

"Sloane . . "

The baby answered with something that sounded like a miniature motorboat trying to find its way through mud as she twisted her handful, this time putting particular stress on a few hairs, which hurt much worse than an even strain across a fistful.

"Sloane!" I screeched, my voice rising in pitch despite all attempts to keep in mind that the source of my agony was an infant who had—through innocence and curiosity—got her neurologically immature fingers stuck in my hair and not a demon from some parallel dimension who was systematically probing for the one stimulus I found most irritating.

"Let me help," came a man's voice from behind me. "Tickle, tickle, tickle," he added, before I could turn to see who was speaking.

Sloane giggled and let go of my hair with little more than a parting tug.

I glanced over my shoulder so that I could see my saviour. And jerked with surprise, because the man was standing only inches from me, staring at me through pale gray eyes that flashed like ice.

Overwhelmed to find anyone that close, especially someone with such a disconcerting gaze, I turned around and stepped back, moving away from him.

He stepped forward, continuing to play with the baby.

I did not like this. Strangers fiddling with one's baby, or one's buddy's baby was not all right—a phrase that, as a newly minted childcare-giver, I had recently added to my repertoire. I gave Gray Eyes a look that said *Back off*.

Instead of backing off, he shifted his gaze to me, and studied my face just as candidly as he would have done if I were a piece of sculpture on exhibit, his lips relaxing into a dreamy smile.

Okay, if you won't back off, I will, I decided, and eased my weight onto the leg that was farther from him. I clicked down a mental list, assessing him: *White. Male. Moderate height and build. American. Northeastern, judging by his accent. Upper-class preppie, judging by his clothing and mannerisms. And not quite on the planet, judging by his presumption in staring at me like this!*

He continued to stare at me, so I stared back. I had met a great variety of strange people in my day, but a presentable, well-to-do white male who stares fixedly at women and children in art museums was new to me. He appeared to be in his early forties (about five years older than me), and had the first smattering of gray hairs amd lines around his eyes and mouth to prove it. His grooming was impeccable, right down to the perfect haircut and subtle scent of expensive toiletries. He was dressed in a comfortable-looking tweed jacket, a nice flannel shirt and blue jeans. He was not local: cowboys do not wear that kind of jacket, their jeans fit a darn sight tighter, and they do not wear flannel shirts—even expensive Abercrombie & Fitch jobs like this one—to visit museums. *No, I decided that rig suggests that he formed his sense of style within striking distance of the East Coast boarding school from hell I attended for two miserable years.*

I do not like to admit this prejudice, but sadly, it lives on in my crooked little heart. Indeed, during my two-year tenure in boarding school, I had formed a marked allergy to preppies. I had found them too often vain and presumptuous, given to a sense of entitlement that built a wall across the places where empathy needed to grow.

This guy was like that, only somehow worse. *At least other East Coast snobs have the gentility to ignore me, not examine me like I'm some kind of specimen under glass; and, as far as I know, they leave each other's babies alone.*

"Sweet baby," he said. "About seven months?"

I did not reply.

He made a genteel bit of kissy-lips at Sloane and stuck a finger over my shoulder for her to grasp, which she was pleased to do, showing precociousness in more ways than just an early crawl.

I shifted farther away from him, breaking contact.

He smiled, just a glint of perfect white teeth. He let his gaze linger on me like he knew something important that I did not, and then moved on down the gallery.

More shaken than was reasonable, I watched him go, wondering what a damned Easterner was doing here off-season anyway. Had his personal jet been forced down by a storm, or a need to refuel? I wanted to spit: So great was his condescension that I found myself placing him and his patrician bearing high above the clouds, enjoying the heights of existence.

A second man hurried to fall into step beside him. His attire was less specifically genteel: gray flannel slacks, white shirt, a necktie. The two stopped in front of *The Sentinel*, a painting of a Westerner standing guard in front of a Conestoga wagon by moonlight, rifle cradled in his arms. The gray-eyed man leaned back, arms folded in refined contemplation, a strange postural echo of the rough-cut guardian in the painting he was observing. "This one?" he asked.

"Yes," said the man with the tie. "We crate it up tomorrow and ship it east. It's going to be a great show."

The man with the necktie must be the curator of this gallery, I decided, belatedly concerned that he might have seen Faye's name on my visitor's pass. I glanced at it, double-checking that it said only VISITOR, and exhaled with relief. *Whew! Faye will be meeting with this guy and her old geezer later this afternoon.*

Then a new worry bloomed: *What if the gray-eyed man sticks around? What if he's part of the group that's meeting here today? Might he hassle Faye the way he hassled me?* On further contemplation, I decided, *She can handle someone like this. She grew up in the smart set. She'd dispatch this guy with a glance.*

The two men stared at the masterwork awhile before either spoke again, then the gray-eyed man said, "Hooker's green."

"Ah," said Necktie.

"Yes. That's the color Remington typically used to get the effect of moonlight," Gray Eyes continued, his voice growing sonorous with erudition. "It's an odd pigment, a combination of Prussian blue and gamboge. An interesting choice, don't you think?"

Necktie nodded.

The gray-eyed man continued his scholarly dissertation: "It's simultaneously dark and light, even though he grayed it out. Intense, particularly against the warm white of the moonlight on the wagon's cover." He shook his head. "I would never have thought of it. Never. The man was brilliant."

Hooker's green. I was surprised to notice that much of the painting was, in fact, green. The picture depicted nighttime underneath a bright moon, with deep gloom under the wagon and just a smattering of bright stars like buckshot in the far sky. The guard's eyes were lost in the depths of shadow.

The gray-eyed man continued to stare at the painting, and I continued to stare at him. Now that he had taken his icy gaze off of me, I noticed that he was in fact quite good-looking. I wondered if I had been too quick to turn a cold shoulder toward him. As I watched, he shook his head absently and made a small clicking noise in the corner of his mouth, an odd gesture, but one as familiar to me as the unguarded moments after sex. Perhaps it was because I had just seen Frank, and had been pried open by the ghosts of my love life, but in that instant Gray Eyes evoked my boyfriend, Jack Sampler, and in spite of what had transpired between us five minutes earlier, I felt a shock of attraction for him.

Dismay whizzed through me; it seemed it was my afternoon to be upset by men. I studied this man's face, trying to reassert my earlier wariness. I concentrated, trying to analyze how I could simultaneously dislike this man's behavior and find him attractive. I assured myself that it was only that he reminded me of Jack, no more. I told myself firmly that Jack was a far better man than this, and berated myself for even noticing anyone else. But Jack was far, far away, and it had been a long, long time, and I could no longer quite remember exactly what he looked like. Was this how my brain let me know that far had become too far, and long had become too long?

Then it came to me: *Like Jack, this man's both here with me and not.*

But Jack is in the Middle East doing brave things for this country, I reminded myself. *Of course he's not here. It's his mission to defend—*

Face it, quick, before you stuff it out of sight again! whispered a voice deep within me.

Face what?

The room seemed to tip, as if I were wrapped in tissue in a box that someone was dumping out onto the floor. I grabbed for the wall to steady myself.

I had managed these long months of separation from Jack by keeping my feelings where they couldn't hurt me, but in jagged instants like this, I missed him so terribly that an almost physical pain shot through me. To say that I was worried about him was a gross understatement. He was not a young man anymore, and even young men got killed when they put on uniforms and carried guns, and he had gone right to the place where the newspapers told me that men were dying.

I did not know when I'd see Jack next. But that was the way it had always been with him, because he flew even higher than this guy did. Jack was a creature of the heavens, a comet so fierce that the night sky had shone with his intensity, if only for a short while.

As if reading my thoughts, the gray-eyed man turned and looked at me again.

I decided that it was time to leave. I hurried through the gallery and the lobby, and out the front door.

Outside, the cool, crisp air mercifully slapped me awake, and I sucked in great lungfuls, congratulating myself on slipping through the cracks of my loneliness one more time.

3

I STARTED BACK DOWN THE STREET. IT WAS TIME TO WAKE FAYE anyway.

I was within a half-block of the Pawnee Hotel when I saw her hurrying from its entrance. She closed on us quickly, her long legs cutting the distance with staccato strides. "Em, good," she said. "The client just called on the cell phone. It seems he's already at the gallery. Shit, I didn't expect him until later. I guess you can come along . . . um, if you like."

The only thing I wanted less just then than to return to the gallery was to explain this to Faye. Trying to sound casual, I said, "No, I'll just take the baby back to the hotel. I think she's getting fussy. You know, hungry . . ."

On cue, Sloane leaned toward Faye and made one of those insistent *Feed me!* noises that can simultaneously motivate a mother and piss her off.

Faye's forehead crumpled in frustration. She was trying to be diligent about the breast-feeding, but life was beginning to get in the way. She reached out a hand to touch her daughter, but then dropped it to her side, defeated. Pain danced across her face. "Give her some cereal," she said. "Do you have your cell phone?"

"Uh, no."

"Take mine, so you can reach me. He's carrying one, and I've got his number punched into it already." She leaned forward and whispered, "It's under *K* for Krehbeil." She pulled the instrument out of her pocket and handed it to me. "I'll be an hour, maybe two. I'll—We could get together at dinner . . ."

I said, "Gotcha covered, Faye. You go have dinner with your client. You can't be Mom and Amelia Earhart simultaneously."

"Thanks," she said nervously, then shook her head, turned, and hurried off down the sidewalk toward the museum.

"Take the car," I said. "The museum is almost a mile from here."

Faye pivoted and headed in the other direction, toward where the battered sedan she had inherited from her late husband waited.

I went back to the room and fed the baby, then gave her a bath and laid her out on the bed and tickled her. She flailed her arms happily and giggled, then twisted around onto her hands and knees and spent several minutes trying to dodge past me so that she could experiment with gravity by making a kamikaze dive off the bed. I lay back and scooped her up in my arms and sang to her awhile, then bundled her up with a fresh diaper and jammies and began the long process of walking her to sleep. I did not have the magic spell that only Faye could weave on her: a nice drink of breast milk.

The evening proved very long. The baby simply would not take a nap, even when I put her back in the backpack and walked her down the street in search of a pizza, my PB&J ingredients having gone to the museum in Faye's car. At long last, at eight P.M., I had just gotten her to sleep when Faye's cell phone rang, waking Sloane right back up. The only thing worse than a baby who won't go to sleep is a baby who's had a five-minute nap and won't go to sleep *again*. I knew that at least another half-hour of walking the little girl up and down inside the tight confines of the room lay ahead of me, so when I grabbed the phone and answered it, I was unable to keep the irritation out of my voice. "What?" I snarled.

The male voice on the other end of the line was not familiar, nor was it sober. "Faye?" a man said, thoroughly drunk. "I'm sorry to call you li' this, bu' he's got his phone switched off, and you've got to *stop* him!"

"Who's this?"

"S'me. Oh, Faye, don' let him *do* it!"

"Who's 'me?' And 'do' what? And who's 'him'?"

" 'He' is precious *Willie*, tha's who! If he messes with tha' painting, it'll *kill* her, it'll simply *kill* her! Jus' like it killed Aun' Winnie!"

"Listen, mister," I said. "You just woke the baby, and you sound like you're about a quart into your cups. Why don't you call back another time, okay?"

The man's bawling shifted to a different register. "Oh, Faye, I'm so *sorry*! I didn' *know*! 'Course, it's *late* there, innit! I forgot about the time zones. You're two hours *behind* me, aren't you? No, wait, tha' would be two hours *earlier* than me, right? No, *ahead* . . ."

I hate drunks. In fact, I detest them. "Whether you're ahead or behind would depend on where you're calling from, now, wouldn't it?" I said nastily. "And if you drink any more, you'll not only be *behind*, you'll be *late*."

"Pennsylvania," he replied, managing to make the word sound like a tire going flat. "I have a nice li'l apartment now in Moun' Choy. You should come and *visit*. It'll be like old *times*, back in *college*. And you bring that husband of yours. And ohh . . . you're a *mommy* now! Bring the *baby*. I'd jus' *love* to see the baby. You know I *love* the li'l babies." He started to blubber. "Bu' I'll never have one of my own, *will* I, because they don' let *faggots* adopt!"

"Listen, this isn't Faye. And Tom's dead."

"Faye, *honey*? You didn't *tell* me!"

I was sorry I'd brought up the subject. "She's not here right now, so call back—"

"Oh, Faye, now *you're* not even talking t'me? And I though' we were *friends*."

"Okay," I said, "we're bosom buddies. Now, how about calling back tomorrow, okay?"

"Really, Tom died? I never even *met* him! *Every*body's dying! Daddy, Aunt Winnie . . . Mother looks *awful* . . . God knows whether Cricket's alive or dead . . . but you have the baby! The only one of *us* who's produced an heir is *Deirdre*, you know *that*. The end of the 'dynasty.' " He broke into mawkish sobs.

Sloane Renee was now standing up in her Port-a-Crib, yanking on the upper rail like a prisoner planning a breakout. She was winding up to a good fuss, I could tell. "I'm going to switch this phone off now," I said. "Whoever you are."

"No, wait!" the voice said, suddenly sounding almost sober. "I'm not shitting you, Faye, something's really wrong with Mother. The doctor calls it pneumonia, but then why isn't it clearing up? Answer me that! And she's got lesions on her fingers, and she's seeing things funny. I tried to get her to the hospital, but Deirdre wouldn't let me move her!"

I picked up the baby and began to walk her. "Give me your number, okay? I'll have Faye call you. This is Em Hansen, her roommate, do you understand?"

I heard the sound of a phone clattering into its cradle. The connection went dead.

I stared at the illuminated screen at the top of the phone and considered throwing the instrument out the window, or flushing it down the toilet, but settled for switching it off. Then I began again the laborious task of getting the baby to sleep.

◇

IT WAS 9:06 p.m. when Faye showed her face again at the Pawnee Hotel, exactly eight minutes after Sloane Renee had finally drifted back to sleep. Still waiting for the twitching that would herald deep slumber, I had not yet even put her down in her crib.

The Faye who returned was not the Faye who had left. This one was glowing with vitality and good humor. Quickly undressing and going about her evening tooth-brushing with a light dispatch, she hummed a jaunty tune.

I asked, "What's put the roses in your cheeks, Faye?"

She snorted, a quick dismissal of my question. "Give that girl to me," she told me. "It's late. I got some nursing to do, and it's sacktime for all of us." She took the baby, checked her diaper although I always kept it clean, lay down on her bed, swathed the child in the folds of her arms and the blankets, presented her a milk-swollen breast, closed her eyes, and smiled a private smile.

How I missed the days when Faye shared her heart with me. I watched her *Mona Lisa* smile, wondering not for the first time what had turned the tide between us. Was it the stresses of motherhood, or losing Tom? Was she so tightly bonded to her child that there was no room for me? Or was I forever cursed for having been with her husband at his death when she was not?

I turned out the reading lamp over my bed and stared up into the darkness, listening as Faye's breathing deepened and grew slower. I thought she was long asleep when she murmured, "There might be a job for you."

"Oh?"

"Time to be getting back into the working world, don't you think?"

"Yes . . ."

"Nice little mystery, just your kind of puzzle. It involves a missing painting."

I said, "Tell me more."

I listened for an answer, but it was lost to sleep, or perhaps hidden behind a charade.

◇

THE PLAN, WHEN we had left Salt Lake City, had been to drive up to Cody starting early on one day, arriving as we had done by midafternoon, and, if Faye's business could be concluded quickly, driving home the afternoon following. Aside from the fact that I needed to get back to my classes, this would save the cost of a second night's stay, part of my campaign to teach Faye to live frugally. Food, apart from that glorious cinnamon roll, the not-so-glorious pizza, and whatever Faye could mooch off her client, was to be something we got out of paper sacks stored in the trunk of the car. So the next morning, having taken a quick trip out to the car, I sat on the edge of my bed eating that peanut butter and jelly sandwich, wondering how soon Faye might be ready to leave.

She opened one eye. "What time is it?"

"Six-thirty."

She closed her eyes again. The baby stirred. She drew Sloane to her breast.

I said, "Everything go okay yesterday?"

She smiled without opening her eyes. "Yes. Very well."

I waited. When she said nothing more, I said, "So you got the job?"

"Well, not yet. We're sort of discussing terms."

Sort of. "Oh. Good." But that wasn't good. It meant that she was being encouraged to persist with the airplane game. And it meant we would be staying longer. "Well, um, you know I have things to do back in Salt Lake City."

Faye didn't answer. I watched her and the baby in the dim early light. If we did stay another night, she might lend me her pass, and I might get an uninterrupted visit to the Whitney Gallery, even a glimpse of the Natural History Museum. I reminded myself also that mine was the easier part of the job. All I had to do was hang out with the baby and tour interesting exhibits while Faye jollied the client. I imagined some arrogant, retired captain of industry with clicking teeth and presumptions regarding Faye's availability. I shivered. I wanted out of here for all our sakes. Then I remembered the strange phone call and said, "I forgot to tell you: Someone phoned last night while you were out."

"Who?"

"I don't know. Some drunk who wanted you to keep somebody named Willie from messing with a painting. He told me all about his family. He said he was a 'faggot' and he lives someplace in Pennsylvania."

"Mount Joy?"

"I think that's what he said."

"Oh. That would be Hector."

"That would fit," I said. "Perfect name. Typecasting."

"Right. He's an actor."

"A bad one," I said. "Hector the actor. What a name. Was the painting the same one you mentioned when you came in last night?"

She didn't answer for a moment, then said, "I quit trying to keep up with Hector's hallucinations years ago. He sees a lot of pink elephants."

"In college. That's where he said he knew you from."

"Right. In college."

"He said he made you a connection. Is this how you know the Krehbeils?"

"Sure. We had a class together."

"And who's Willie?"

Faye glanced at me sharply for a moment and then closed her eyes again. The baby's lips relaxed as she fell back asleep. Faye disconnected and rolled over, putting her back toward me. "Wake me again at eight, will you?"

I gritted my teeth. That meant she wanted me to watch the baby while she slept. I took a breath and said, "No, Faye. I want to take a walk."

"Take the baby?" She made it sound pitiful.

I thought of all the times I had nearly fallen asleep in my classes from being up too late or too early with the baby.

A soft gray light was filtering in through the window blinds. It had been at about this time in the morning that Sloane Renee had been born, though closer to the fall equinox than the spring. I had been with them both, holding Faye's hand, and had watched her little treasure, her little life-changer, slide out into the world. How much more could I do for her?

I gazed at Sloane, who was doing her cherub impersonation, and decided, one more time, that it wouldn't hurt me to show kindness to this little person and that big person. I said, "Deal, long as you give me an hour in the museum without her later on."

"Deal."

So I finished my sandwich and took a shower and dressed, shifted the sleeping baby into the carrier that doubled as a car seat, bundled her up with extra blankets, then hoisted her, the car keys and the backpack, and headed out into the cold.

It was a clear, crisp morning, the kind of air that freezes the hairs inside your nostrils. Just a few high clouds traced the sky. Watching the ghosts of my breath, I loaded the baby into the car and headed up Sheridan Avenue the opposite way, toward the road to Greybull. Soon I had left behind the tourist traps and strip malls and was rising onto the mesa that stood above Cody to the east.

The road swung eastward then started its climb onto the vast, desert outcropping of the Willwood Formation, a soft, striped shale that fills the middle of the Big Horn basin. The Willwood had been laid down by the events of the Eocene Epoch: Fifty million years ago, as the earth began to heave the Rocky Mountains upward and wind and water and ice began simultaneously to wear them back down, the rivers carried away the eroded muck and dumped it here. Then, the climate was cool and humid, and the clays that settled in the lakes and on floodplains oxidized into vibrant hues.

In their labor of birth, the mountains had rested awhile, and then had heaved higher again, and the climate had shifted as well, becoming arid, with cold winters and hot summers. With the further uplift, the great-granddaughters of the earlier watercourses had ceased depositing mud and grit and had instead begun to erode channels forming broad bottom lands that were now dotted with ranches. Most of the Willwood Formation now sat like a custard in the center of the basin, surrounded by a ring of mountains that stood high like a knuckly old pie crust: Starting from the northwest and continuing counterclockwise to the northeast rose the Absarokas, the Owl Creeks, and the Big Horns, a great circle of ranges raised high by the titanic forces of the earth. Only to the north did the ground lie lower, and through this portal flowed the waters of six counties.

Thus, as was Nature's whim, the bones of ancient lakes had become a desert sculpture. Time and water and wind had eroded the Willwood into an array of hoodoos and pagodas and pyramids and temples, a badlands in bold horizontal stripes, a desert paint-box of purple and gray and red. It was a no-man's-land, good for nothing but hunting fossils and rattlesnakes, searching for oil, and taking long walks to clear the mind.

I was driving along the upper edge of the valley cut by the Shoshone River—the aptly named "Stinking Water," as it smelled of sulfur. My intention was to search for cobbles, a miscellaneous passion of mine. The rivers had occasionally been so vigorous that they had carried not just mud and grit, but also cobbles, and it was their whim to leave them here and there, laced through the shales. In places, these cobbles formed great boulevards, like Parisian streets run wild, a pirate's sampling of every kind of rock that had stuck its nose to the air as the mountains shoved their ways skyward. The Shoshone flowed east from the Yellowstone Plateau, and thus carried volcanic rocks from the Yellowstone eruptions.

I pulled the car over on the first bench in the badlands and got out to look around. I got the baby into the backpack and began to walk, turning over gray and black volcanic cobbles; dark, smooth orbs speckled randomly by angular feldspar laths. Farther afield, if I could remember where to look, waited lovely pearl-white quartzites—metamorphosed sandstones—carried clear from Idaho, that would display the interlocking circles of percussion fractures, a mute record of the violence of their turbulent ride downriver, rings within rings within rings. To anyone else these oddities might be less interesting than hockey pucks, but to me they were beautiful, a fascination of form and parentage.

The sun was well up now, and the day was perceptibly warming. Thin traces of snow lurked in the shadows behind the nearest mound of stripes. "This is a desert," I told Sloane, picking up our one-sided conversation where I had last left off. "That means it doesn't rain or snow much here. In fact, the snow you see hiding in that shadow over there is probably the only snow that actually fell from the sky this winter. The rest of the time, it's just the same stuff blowing back and forth. And it never really melts. It just finally wears out."

Sloane Renee leaned toward my left ear, making a noise like a miniature steam engine. So much for telling tall tales to an infant.

I stooped to pick up a dark gray cobble about the size of a small cantaloupe. "See this? As the ol' Stinking Water River cut down from

Yellerstone Plateau, she left me some nice chunks o' basalt and rhyolite. Any higher up into the Willwood we won't find these, so I'm a-gonna walk us on around the hill here, just following the curve like a cow does. Got it?"

Sloane's little gurgling noise now filled my right ear.

I turned to the right to see why Sloane had turned her head. Along the road, right next to where I had parked, was another car, and its driver was just stepping out. The driver was a man, and the car looked like a mid-sized rental, all shiny gray and blandly medium. He stood and stared at us for a moment, then he began to walk toward us, picking his way though the cacti. He took his time, stopping repeatedly to look around at the scenery.

Tourist, I thought. *Can't figure out what to do with himself, so he's going to ask what I'm looking at.* I stood and waited, a subtle tension rising within me. The openness of the western landscape was my solace and my refuge, but, having grown up on a ranch, I had always greeted the arrival of another person in that openness as a rare chance for a little socialization. My father had taught me that it was good luck to run into a neighbor: What if I'd fallen off my horse, or had a broken axle in a truck? But this time something didn't feel right. There was something about this man I didn't like. And this time, I had a tiny soul to protect. This time, I was carrying Sloane Renee.

I scanned the terrain, checking for the clearest route between the man and the cars should I need to run. There was only one obvious path, and the man was on it. I glanced left and right, trying to choose an alternative. To my left, the ground rose to a crumbly slope of clay; not good. To my right lay a long downslope leading to a sharp drop-off, and I knew the same topography wrapped around behind me. I stood my ground, wondering why this man had stopped his car here and what he wanted with us. I kept a good grip on my cobble, in case I needed to hurl it at him.

The man wore an expensive jacket, and, with the hood up and his head bowed slightly so that he could carefully read the terrain, I couldn't see his face. He was within fifty feet of me before I realized that I had seen him before, and where. It was the gray-eyed man. He closed to within ten feet of me, still taking his time, now gazing here and there as if appraising the landscape as a subject for a photograph, studying it, occasionally squinting his eyes and furrowing his brow in concentration, as if I had nothing better to do in the world but wait for him. This presumption added annoyance to my list of emotions stirred in me by his approach.

"Hello again," I said, when he was so close that something had to be said.

He stopped and leaned his head backwards, hands in pockets, back arched, and looked at the high reach of the sky. Finally he looked at me, and smiled. "Beautiful here."

"Yes," I replied, wondering, *Why did you stop?* Remote places like the badlands have no pathways through them, no burger stands or hardware stores to which one might be on one's way, so the idea that this guy thought he could make it look like he was "just happening by" simply did not wash. But the situation was even more confusing than that: Most tenderfoots—and this guy certainly wasn't from around here—find the badlands an oddity at best, if not downright forbidding. They floor the gas pedal as they head up this road, not wanting to tarry an extra moment for fear they will wind up like the faked mummified corpses of prospectors on the postcards labeled BUSHWHACKED. But this man appeared to be drinking in the scenery like a fine wine.

Sloane Renee wriggled in her backpack and gurgled coquettishly at him.

He shifted his focus to her ever so briefly, just long enough to send her a silent kiss, a quick pucker of his lips. Then he fixed his eyes on me. "What are you doing out here?" he inquired. Belatedly, he chased the question with a smile.

What am I *doing?* Digging around in my mental knapsack for a suitably abrupt rejoinder, I chose the obvious and said, "Collecting rocks."

He peered at my cobble, austerely keeping his hands in his pockets. "You are a geologist," he said.

"Yes." Did it show? Was he being funny? Or was this more of his condescension?

"What's your speciality? Oil and gas? Mining?"

"Oil and gas."

He said, "I hear there's a lot of oil production from this area."

My arm ached to throw the rock at him. I began to ease around him, instinctively keeping up the chitchat so he wouldn't know how nervous he was making me. "Well, yeah . . . right over there behind you, maybe a couple miles south, is Oregon Basin Field. Then, farther south, Little Buffalo Basin Field. To the east, Elk Basin. Torchlight. Manderson. There's bunches of them."

"Have you worked in the oil fields?" He took a few steps, once again positioning himself between the cars and me.

I stopped, assessing my options.

He opened a pocket, took out a packet of dried fruit and nuts, offered me some. When I shook my head, he took a nibble himself. "Did you go out on the oil derricks?" he inquired.

Drill rigs, I wanted to say, but this wasn't the moment to be correcting his jargon. "Not anymore," I said, stepping around him and now resolutely strolling toward the cars. "Oil and gas kind of cratered. It's hard to find work."

He nodded and fell into step beside me. "Not much work in petroleum back where I come from either."

"Where's that?"

"Pennsylvania."

I had been right: He was from the East. Somehow this was comforting. A man who put me ill at ease might pop up in the middle of nowhere, but I had at least gauged him accurately. "Been awhile since Pennsylvania was much of a threat for oil or gas." We were now halfway back to the cars.

He stopped and stretched and stared back out across the badlands, taking in the high dance of the Absarokas. "Or coal. Or any other geological resource."

"You got other resources back there?"

"Oh, yes," he said. "Pennsylvania had a little bit of everything, if not a lot. It was once the mineral resource capital of our budding nation." His tone was ironic, but also nostalgic, even longing.

Why was I continuing the conversation? This was the type of chat I had with strangers at parties, when men got stuck making small talk with me and found out that I worked in a so-called "man's profession." The exchange usually continued through two or three more volleys before they suddenly spotted someone they needed to talk to on the other side of the room. But this was no chat-filled room, and I was carrying something far more precious than a gin-and-tonic. I moved closer to Faye's car.

The man tipped his head to one side, as if this was what everybody did on early mornings in the middle of nowhere. He said, "But you don't go out on oil derricks anymore. What do you do now?"

I was still trying to assess what I did not like about this man. He was part of an elite of which I had never felt a part, and even after all these years, I still reacted to the sense of alienation such specimens raised in me. The countersnob within reared up and I answered his question with a statement meant to intimidate him right back: "I have a ranch."

"Oh?" He didn't smile. He fixed a probing look on me, as if testing for something.

I wondered if he didn't believe me. It was not precisely true that I owned the ranch. I had been raised there, and I expected to inherit it one day, so, in a manner of speaking, it was mine. But I had not been there in years, and the rash act of speaking these words out loud, here in the open lands that were so beautiful to me, was like tugging at a self-inflicted wound. "I—I grew up there. Mostly I work as a geologist." I realized that I was getting rattled, so I corrected that. "Sometimes I work as a forensic geologist."

This seemed to sharpen his interest.

"Oh? What does that involve?"

I had arrived at Faye's car now, and I stood with my hand on the door handle. I hadn't locked it. I had only to open it now, duck inside, and drive away, except that to do so would be difficult with the baby on my back. I couldn't imagine why this man was asking me all these questions, or why I was answering them, but I didn't feel I could stop without signaling that I was getting uncomfortable. Slipping into "cool" mode, I said, "I do the Sherlock Holmes thing; you know, dig dirt out of people's shoes and analyze where they've been. But also, it's more a matter of understanding the world of geology. What geologists do, if the murder involves a death within a professional community. What geologists search for, if it involves how geologic resources are used or abused."

He nodded. "The big picture."

I began to feel oddly naked. He seemed to be recording me inch by inch, collecting words to go with the image he had mapped the day before. "Sure," I said. "The big picture."

He said, "And you do analytical work as well."

"Yes . . ."

"I might have a job for you. Are you discreet?"

I gave him a dirty look. Who was he to question my integrity?

He turned his gaze on the badlands hills. "These are ochers, I suppose."

"Huh?"

"Earth colors." He made a gesture toward them, as if painting them with a sensuous brush. "The colors of the hills there."

I stared at the multicolored bands of mud. "I suppose. . . ."

"You see, I am an art dealer. I handle very valuable work, and sometimes there is question as to its authenticity."

"Forgeries."

His gaze probed deeper. "This is work that has to be handled in the strictest confidence, so it would be convenient to have an analyst who isn't even connected to the rest of the art world."

"Well, I . . ."

"How's your color sense?"

Sloane was beginning to twist around in the backpack. I said, "I'm not color-blind, if that's what you mean."

"The question for the artist is how to portray these colors. What would Remington have used?"

"I'm sure I have no idea."

"You saw his paintings yesterday. He would have played the warms against the cools to show the harshness of the land."

I said nothing.

He said, "He had magic on the tip of his brush. The Academicians never understood him; they thought his colors inharmonious. Imagine: They must never have seen the Western lands. Vivid, his effects of light and shadow. Contrast him, for example, with Catlin, whose landscapes are barely more than cartoons by comparison. Dead, naïve renderings of color. But Catlin's portraits on the other hand . . ."

Sloane made a screech right in my ear.

I said, "If you'll excuse me, I need to take my little friend here back to town."

He pointed sharply at a middle band of color. "That purple: How would you paint that, do you think? It's like the war paint in Catlin's portraits." Turning back to the west, he held out his hands, as if to wrestle the far peaks of the Absarokas. His face hardened with frustration. "How would he portray those colors?"

Ever so casually, I began to load the baby the car. When I had put her safely into her seat and climbed in and locked the door, I turned and looked back.

The strange man was still there, lost in contemplation of the Western mountains.

Bone black is a pigment made by the charring of bones in closed retorts. It is blue-black in color and fairly smooth in texture.

—*from the files of Fred Petridge*

WARMTH HAD FOUND ITS WAY SLOWLY TO THE FARM THAT MORNING, and Deirdre's hands were cold. She rubbed them against each other, cursing the dead numbness of her fingers. It did not suit her that she could no longer feel them. They and her feet were almost entirely without sensation now. But the lack of feeling had nothing to do with the temperature of the air. She made a clicking sound at the corner of her mouth. Foolish doctor couldn't diagnose her problem, a fact which both enraged and pleased her. He called her symptoms "idiopathic," probably thinking the term would impress her. Did he also think that she couldn't read a dictionary? *Idiopathic* was just a five-dollar way of saying that they did not know what was causing it.

She looked around the room. Same tables and chairs she had known all her fifty years. Same books on the shelves, save for a few recent additions. The woodstove crackled as a log rolled, spitting sparks. She'd have to remonstrate her son for bringing in green wood again.

At dawn, she had sat in this same chair with a cup of coffee, watching the darkness beyond the windows change into the vague notion of trees at the foot of the lawn, and from that into a tracery of black lace, the leafless winter branches backed first by an icy indigo, then briefly a fiery red before the clouds swept in and closed the landscape into another harsh winter day. It was a cold winter, the worst in recent memory for Pennsylvania. Now, at the foot of the lawn by the trees, the mists rose off the spring into dispirited gray air. A duck took off briefly and landed again, deciding to tarry in the perpetual warmth of the limestone-fed waters.

Easy living for you, duck, Deirdre thought, and gave a humorless grunt. She would have had to admit a certain jealousy toward the bird if such insights were within her nature.

The clock in the kitchen struck ten, reminding her that it was time to heave herself onto the remoteness of her feet and mount the stairs, grasping the creaking banister with her dying hands, and head toward the room where her mother lay sleeping the residue of her life away. Time to deliver medicines and make her drink. Listen to the old woman sigh, and ask again where William was. *Precious William*. Well, she'd tell her again that she didn't know. The feckless drifter had gone off somewhere with his dreams again, and God knew when he'd show his face around here once more. He got away with murder, that boy.

Boy. He was almost forty now, and making plenty of money, judging by the car he drove, but Mother always gave him pocket money and begged him to make her another picture. His fantasies in paint were all over the walls in Mother's room. Another failed artist in the family. Deirdre felt her stomach lurch with anger at the thought. She had been so sure he'd amount to nothing, but it seemed he was doing just fine with his damned business dealings. He was out there swinging deals while she stayed behind and looked after the ancients.

She swilled the last gulp of her coffee, grasped the arms of her chair, and pulled herself resolutely to a standing position. One foot in front of the other. Keep busy. Life goes on. Too much to do anyway. The running of the farm took a full twelve hours most days, between feeding and watering the animals, doing the books, and caring for her mother. And feeding her own brood. Getting them off to work. It made her blood boil that they did so little to help out around the place, but screaming at them seemed to get no results these days. They just crammed their breakfast in their mouths, hopped in their cars, and headed out into the bloody world each day. But she'd make quite certain that they were not as spoiled as precious William. Now that they were of age, she made them pay rent, and they ate their lunches and dinners away from home. Which was a filthy waste of money.

They could pay her to pack their lunches and come home for dinner, and save thousands of dollars each year!

The old wooden stairs creaked with her weight as Deirdre worked her way up to the second floor. At the upper landing, she found the black dog curled up on the braided rug with his nose stuffed under his tail. The animal looked up at her as she passed, raising his canine eyebrows in a quick display of submission. She considered kicking it, but did not; she might injure her toes, and with the numbness, wouldn't even know it. Instead, Deirdre continued down the hall to her mother's room and pushed open the door. The scent of illness hung in the unstirred air. "Mother?" she said. "Time for your meds."

"William?"

Deirdre sighed angrily. "No, Mother, it's me. William is out entertaining himself. I am here. Me. Your idiot daughter Deirdre."

"Oh. Deirdre, sweetie. How nice of you to come by and see your old mama."

"I didn't come by, Mother. I live here."

"Oh. Oh, of course. Silly me. I was just thinking of other things, I suppose. Will William be here for dinner?"

"How would I know, Mother? He hasn't come by for weeks now, and I don't suppose he'd condescend to tell me what his plans are. Come on, sit up and take your pills."

"Certainly, dear." The old woman did not move.

Deirdre leaned over and pulled the frail body of her mother up off the pillows, plumped them up, and settled her down again. It was a motion she had made countless times in the months since her mother had taken to her bed, and she was good at it. She took satisfaction in her expertise at caretaking, even though she'd been trained for better, more interesting work in her years at the university. But she reveled in effort, in the accomplishment of any task. The brute, forward motion of each day was integral to her self-definition.

And, in these moments, she felt a closeness to her mother that was all hers to enjoy. No one else had a piece of it, and it was real. She had earned it. She gently touched the corona of soft, thin hair above the old woman's scalp and smoothed it back. "Here, Mother," she said, putting the little cup that had the blue and yellow pills in it and the half-filled water glass into her mother's fragile hands. "Knock it back, gag them down. That's the ticket." She watched to make sure she didn't drop them or spit one out. Then she took another vial out of her apron pocket and shook out a gelatin capsule. "And here's your vitamins."

The old woman smiled sweetly as she tipped the glass first for the prescription drugs, but she hesitated over the capsule. "Deirdre, darling, must I take these? They make my stomach hurt, and they are so difficult to swallow."

"Yes, goddamn it!" Deirdre snapped, her composure shattering under the weight of her frustration. "How many times must I tell you? If you want to lie there and rot without even trying, you go right ahead!"

"Yes, dear," said the old woman. She put the capsule into her mouth, once again tipped the glass to her dry lips, and swallowed. Her eyes darted this way and that, glazed to the world. She coughed, choking slightly on the capsule.

Deirdre's hands jerked toward her mother's mouth as she braced herself to catch the capsule, but it went down the ancient throat instead of coming back out. She took the glass from the trembling hands and set it down on the bedside table, then helped her mother settle back among the covers. When she was sure that her mother was once again asleep, Deirdre retraced her steps out to the hallway and closed the door.

Instead of heading back down the stairs right away, she went first to the window at the end of the hall and looked out across the fields. One hundred forty acres of the most productive soils in America, and she was going to keep it that way even if she had to drag every last member of her family by the hair to do it.

5

WHEN I GOT BACK TO THE HOTEL, FAYE WAS UP AND DRESSED AND filing her fingernails with an emery board. I had never seen her take preening past a vigorous brushing of her hair and the odd touch of lipstick, so I stopped for a moment and watched her. Faye was a tall and graceful woman, blessed with the kind of looks that make men stop and stare, but not the kind that is applied with dyes from a bottle or pigments immersed in pastes and lotions. Her beauty was bone deep, served up at the moment of conception, the external expression of lucky chromosomes and a radiant soul.

She looked up at me, then at Sloane. "Hey, baby, come to Mommy," she said, holding out her hands to receive her child. She hugged the baby to her tightly and covered her fuzzy scalp with kisses.

"So what's our plan?" I asked.

Faye looked adoringly into her daughter's eyes but spoke to me. "Why don't you head on down to the museum, and I'll stay here awhile."

"Aren't you meeting with the client again?"

"Yes, but not until lunchtime. And I can take the baby with me. It's okay, he likes children."

I raised my eyebrows in surprise. Faye's hard, cold hurry of the day before was nothing but a memory. I said, "So we're staying another night. . . ."

Faye spoke tersely but politely, like a diner ordering from a menu. "Yes. I'll need you to take Sloane most of the afternoon, please." Still she kept her eyes firmly on her daughter.

"Certainly." I waited for further comments, but none came.

It had been only eight months since Tom's demise. Now Faye was primping for a meeting with an elderly man with money. Was this what single motherhood did to women? Did it make calculating pragmatists out of one's formerly adventuresome chums?

I bit my lip, trying to be charitable, trying to rationalize what was happening. *After all*, I reminded myself, *Tom was almost old enough to be her father. Perhaps she has a thing for older men. And maybe this one can support her in the style to which she was accustomed, and she can enjoy all the conveniences of live-in help and . . . and I can . . .*

My heart tightened into a knot. I had stuck around to help Faye with the baby. What if she didn't need me anymore? I suddenly felt a bit faint. *I'd go on about my life*, I told myself firmly. *And about time! Faye won't need a live-in baby-sitter forever. So how about this job, then?* I said, "Last night, you said something about a missing painting."

Faye had lain down on the bed with the baby in a sitting position on her stomach, her knees up to form a backrest for Sloane. She glanced at me. Returning her gaze to her daughter, she said, "I was wondering when you'd bite on that."

"Oh, come on. I asked last night, and again this morning."

Faye had Sloane's tiny hands in hers, and was dancing them back and forth. The baby laughed with delight.

I said, "Faye?"

She said, "A group of specialists at the gallery meet a couple of times each year with patrons who have paintings they believe to be by a certain Western artist. The specialists examine the works to decide whether they're authentic or perhaps just wanna-bes, painted in the right era but by someone else."

"Or forgeries." I thought about the gray-eyed man. Did he know something about this?

Faye's lips curled. "Sure, forgeries exist, I'm sure, and it was not uncommon to copy favorite paintings. But the story on this particular one is that it has been in the client's family since it was painted. So the question becomes, if it isn't an original, then where'd the real one go?"

"You mean someone might have swapped an original for a fake right under the owner's nose."

"That's the concern. But it could have been done anytime over the last couple of decades."

"Who's the artist?"

"It's a Remington."

My stomach tightened. A Remington was high stakes, enough to kill for. And the way Faye was choosing to spring this information on me worried me. *Is this why she brought me up here? A little bait-and-switch of her own? Tell Emmy she needs a baby-sitter when what she really wants to do is pimp me as a detective?* I took a deep breath. "No," I said.

" 'No' what?"

"No, I've hung up my spurs."

"Spurs?"

"The Sherlock Holmes kit. The magnifying glass and deerstalker hat. Whatever you want to call it. This cowgirl ain't doin' that nonsense no more, nohow." To emphasize my vehemence, I made a slicing motion through the air.

Faye trained her now overly innocent eyes back on her fingernails. "How you do mix your metaphors, Em. But really, what nonsense. What gave you the idea I'd—"

"I know you, Faye!"

"And I know *you!* Who do you think you're kidding? You're getting a master's in forensics. Or at least, you will if you ever get a thesis project. Hell, maybe you can use this. That way you'd even get your thesis paid for. That should please you. You sure are hung up about money these days!"

A surge of anger flashed through me, leaving in its wake a cold, shuddery feeling. I said, "Yes, I have every intention of staying in forensic work if I can just do it without the level of risk that's damn near gotten me killed several times already."

"Gotten *you* killed!" Faye spat.

She was thinking of Tom.

The shakiness increased. My ears began to ring and I became oddly faint. I sat down on the bed and propped my head on my hands, trying to get the ringing to leave my ears. Softly, I said, "It's just too dangerous. A Remington could be worth hundreds of thousands of dollars."

Faye's lips went into a stiff, straight line. "Try millions of dollars, Em."

It felt like Faye was miles away from me. "Well," I said, "I'll just go to the museum now."

Or go home to the ranch, said a little voice in my head.

Faye grabbed the visitor's pass off the bedside table and threw it at me. It came half the distance and slewed onto the carpet.

As if watching myself from across the room, I registered pain that Faye was talking to me like this. I just wanted to leave, go, be by myself for a moment, not have her or the baby or any of these art people depending on me. I bent to pick up the pass. Bending brought some of the blood back into my head, but as I rose I still had to steady myself, which I covered by putting my hand on the doorknob. *I used to be able to handle stress*, I told myself. *I hate this; when am I going to get my life back? Frank went through this after Vietnam; he must have. I should have asked him how to handle it. It can't still be happening to him or he wouldn't be able to hold a job.*

As I turned the knob, I heard Faye say, "And when you come back from the museum, you'll find us at the Irma."

I turned and faced her, as if swimming in molasses. "That's double or even triple the money."

Faye made a sound in her throat that sounded like a growl. Baby Sloane lifted her face from her mother's breast and stared at her, goggle-eyed.

I felt an urge to take the baby from her quick before the little tyke could learn such spendthrift habits. Which sent another jolt through me: I had no right to do that. Sloane was her baby, not mine.

I left the room and the hotel, and walked back out through the town toward the museum, trying to breathe deeply. As I passed the Irma, I stopped for a moment and stared, viewing it from the opposite sidewalk.

The door to Irma's saloon swung open and a man sauntered out, lighting a cigarette. Beyond that door stood the Irma's famous, ornately carved rosewood bar. My dad had taken me there once when I was a child, ordering a cup of coffee for himself and a chocolate shake for me. It had been an extra-special treat, because we were always so poor, getting by on second-hand pickup trucks and bailing-wire fixes. My mouth watered at the memory of that chocolate shake. I realized that the peanut butter sandwich I had eaten for breakfast had long since turned to ash in the blast furnace I called a stomach.

I turned and headed resolutely to the west, toward the museums. When I got there I headed back into the Whitney Gallery of Western Art. I had a brand new reason for looking at the Remingtons.

Gritting my teeth at the thought of anyone messing with one of my hero's paintings, I studied his work. How could anyone possibly mimic his style and techniques sufficiently to create a forgery good enough to effect a switch. I stopped by the painting of night, with the guard leaning on the Conestoga wagon. The odd, grayed green of the wagon bed and grass and the moonlit white of the canvas played games with the receptors in the backs of my eyes. Almost all of the man was rendered in shades of green. When I began to wonder how exactly the materials in the paints could be analyzed, I turned and headed out of the room.

I wandered disconsolately through the main part of the gallery to the Koerner studio. There, I paid homage to *Madonna of the Prairie*, then, feeling a bit better, headed around a corner to ogle a Bierstadt and a Moran, smiled at Rosa Bonheur's lively portrait of good ol' Buffalo Bill on his horse (no self-respecting equestrian should be painted any other way, and besides, the horse was a darn sight handsomer than he was), sighed over the rich colors in Maynard Dixon's *The Medicine Robe*, and checked out an exhibit of genre paintings from the mid-1800s, which featured highly narrative tableaux from the days of the frontier. I was heading back toward the twentieth-century stuff when I passed the row of Catlin's landscapes. What had the gray-eyed man said about them?

That they were cartoons, naïve . . .

I stopped in front of one that depicted an Indian chief standing on the roof of his mud-and-stick dwelling. He was shouting at the sky, while the rest of the tribe stood watching. *Rainmaking. Mandan*, it was titled. CIRCA 1855–1870. OIL ON PAPER. Catlin was one of the artist-explorers of the nineteenth century, those restless few that rode out with the early surveys of the West, or, as in Catlin's case, rode out solo to discover the West on their own. He had painted the Mandan just before almost all of them died of diseases unwittingly brought to them by whites. I wanted to dismiss his work and keep on walking, but a growing sense of discomfort held me to the spot. Was I shouting at the sky?

Suddenly, my stomach cramped with hunger, wresting me from the downward spiral of my thoughts. I exited the gallery and headed in the direction of the museum coffee-shop. *A little food will clear my head*, I told myself. *What am I thinking, letting my blood sugar drop like this? Surely that's all that's really the matter. . . .*

I transited the lobby and turned left into the coffee shop. I was thus strolling toward an imagined greeting with a bagel and cream cheese when I saw Faye, seated at a table by the windows. With the baby. And the gray-eyed man. He was holding Sloane Renee on his lap; she was eating something from his hands.

Faye turned her head and saw me. She rose and faced me. She spoke, her face designedly blank. "I believe you've already met, but let me formally introduce you," she said. "This is Tert Krehbeil, my client and friend. Your client, too, if you want."

Friend. Client. He could be the latter, but not the former.

The three of them looked quite happy together, and quite natural.

They looked like a family. Complete in three; they didn't need me.

6

I LEFT THE MUSEUM WITHOUT SAYING ANYTHING TO EITHER OF them, and when Faye and I next met—at the hotel, where I had gone to hide—I allowed as how I needed to get back to Salt Lake City as soon as possible.

"That's just fine," she said, "because Tert offered Sloane and me a ride back with him. It just happens he's going that way."

This was not what I had in mind at all. I said, "Tert? His name is really Tert?"

"Yes, Tert Krehbeil. Tert for 'Tercius,' as in Latin for 'the third.' "

I could not stop myself from making a very unpleasant face. I had pegged Gray Eyes as a preppie and had had my usual phobic reaction to that, but a preppie with a preppie nickname and a preppie pedigree was a thousand times worse.

Returning a disapproving glance to my reaction, Faye said, "So, yes, it would be a convenience if you would drive my car home."

Convenience. Now I'm a convenience. I said, "But I thought the client was *old.*"

Now she laughed. "Well, yes, the artworks do belong to an old man. Or, more accurately, a dead man. They belong to the estate of Tert's father, Krehbeil Secundus. In fact, they were purchased by the great scion of the family, ol' Primus."

"You're making this up."

She declared rather stiffly, "East Coast nicknames were often quite fanciful. Do you have a problem with that?"

"No . . ." *But I have a problem with my best friend consorting with people who make me break out in hives.*

Faye closed her eyes and put a hand to her forehead as if she had a headache. "Listen, I didn't realize at first when Hector contacted me that he was talking about his brother and not his father. I didn't even know his father had passed away. It's been that long since I've heard from Hector."

The thought of three Krehbeils all lined up—Primus, Secundus, and Tercius—had jammed unpleasantly in my brain. I wondered if they all had eyes as cold and gray as ice. "I suppose he's good-looking," I said, "but isn't he kind of . . . remote?"

Faye straightened her spine and gave me a look. It was a look that said everything: It said, *You're jealous*. It said, *You don't want me to be happy*. It said, *Go to hell.*

So I drove home wondering what kind of lightning had just struck my not-so-safe little world. Wondered, in fact, if it was indeed still my home. Since Tom's death, I had been staying at Faye's, first to nurse her through the final weeks of her pregnancy, then to help her as she adjusted to the new life she had brought forth. Somehow, weeks had become months. I had been chief cook and bottle washer, marketer, and devoted nanny. Now I was just chauffeur.

It's about a nine-hour drive between Cody and Salt Lake City by the route I took, so by the time I got back there, I was sufficiently tired that all I wanted to do was eat about five peanut butter–and–jelly quesadillas and go to bed, which is exactly what I did.

I did not sleep well, and awoke early. In the first pale fingers of daylight, I got up and began doing a few chores before starting to study for my classes. By daylight, the night's self-pity dissolved into acute embarrassment at having reacted so strongly. Faye was right; I should want her to be happy. I was just jealous because Jack had been gone so long.

And yet I had real misgivings about this man Tert Krehbeil. There was something about him that genuinely gave me the creeps, and it wasn't just the clash between our backgrounds.

As I went to plug in my cell phone to charge it up, I realized it was Faye's. I had forgotten to give it back to her after her hurry to meet her . . . friend. I reached deeper into my duffel bag and found my own phone, which meant Faye had neither one. I couldn't call her. I felt very much alone.

I stared at the phone in frustration, recalling the call from Hector the actor, the man who had brokered the connections between Faye and his brother Tert. I dug through Faye's desk for her address book, found a phone number for Hector and dialed. I knew better than to rely on the opinions of a drunk, but I wanted to know what Faye was getting mixed up in, and I told myself he might be able tell me something about his brother that would put my anxieties to rest. *In fact, you're so put out that you want to hear something awful*, I told myself as the call began to ring through.

A groggy voice answered on the other end. "Hello?"

"Oh, I'm sorry," I said. "I thought this might be an East Coast number. I'll call back at a more reasonable hour."

"No. Wait. It is a reasonable hour here. I'm the one who isn't reasonable. Who did you say you were?"

"Em Hansen. Hello, Hector."

There was a pause. "Well, Em Hansen, I have absolutely no idea who you are, so if you'll forgive me—"

"Wait, don't hang up. I'm Faye Carter's roommate."

There was another pause, then, "Ohhhhhh . . ."

"You phoned Faye a couple of days ago, and I answered."

"Did I? I don't recall. I must have been bombed."

"Yes, you were quite magnificently blotto."

"I am so sorry. Will you forgive me?"

"Certainly."

"Well then, if I was my usual excruciating self, to what do I owe the kindness of this call?"

"I'm trying to help Faye with a few things. Er, you *are* Tert Krehbeil's brother?"

"The one and only."

"Then, um, can you tell me something about him?"

"Miss Hansen, you are asking me to air the family laundry."

"I don't know. Am I?"

"Listen, dear lady, I may be the black sheep, but I know which side of the bread gets buttered. And other metaphors as appropriate. I have a devil of a headache, and I should get off the phone before I make a worse ass of myself."

"Is he . . . Would he be a good friend to Faye? Does he treat women nicely?"

"Oh no . . . so that's happening, is it? Well, Miss Hansen, my brother *is* an unusual person. I cannot say that I approve of him in every way. We are siblings, and siblings are known to have their differences. Tert is an accomplished businessman, respected by his peers. He has never married, perhaps because he has trouble showing a woman half as much attention as he shows to his own image in the mirror. But they said that about Narcissus, too, and his name is still on the lips of the well-to-do and erudite. He doesn't beat women or stand them up on dates, to my knowledge, if that's what you're asking."

"Thanks. That helps, I suppose." I fished around for something short of his favorite shot of whiskey that would get him to open up a bit more. "The other night you said something about concern for your mother's health. Is everything okay?"

This prompted a lengthy silence, then, broodingly, "I was probably just raving."

"Can I ask about the painting?"

"What painting." It was not a question, it was an answer.

Now I paused. I had already skated too close to breaking Tert's confidence, and while I had no interest in working with him myself, I did not want it on my conscience that I had ruined a deal for Faye. "I'm interested in . . . your family's artworks."

"Are you an art historian?"

"No."

"Conservator?"

"No."

Irritably he said, "Well, what, then? Private investigator?" He meant it to be an insulting joke.

"No," I said stiffly. "But you're not far off. I am a forensic geologist."

"What's *that*?" he said, mocking me.

I was so annoyed at his tone that I said, "I work with trace evidence. In the case of a painting, I can perhaps discover whether the minerals used in the paint pigments are what the artist would have used. I can—"

Hector's response was swift. "I do not recommend you do that, Miss Hansen!"

"I—I didn't mean . . . Hey, listen, I'm just Faye's friend. I'm trying to understand what she's gotten herself mixed up in, you get me?"

"Look, if you ever get to Pennsylvania, look me up. We'll have some drinks and some laughs. I'll tell you the story of a family that used to be more than it is today, and we can all look out over Lancaster County and sigh. But I really can't say anything else that would help you."

I let him go and broke the connection. But I copied down the phone number, just in case, putting it with my own papers.

Then I sat staring at the phone. I did not like what was happening. Faye had been through a lot in the last year and a half. She'd dealt with an accidental pregnancy, a sudden marriage, the loss of her trust fund, widowhood, and the adjustment to motherhood. She had gone from being a highly attractive, single, wealthy, independent woman who had the world by the tail to a highly attractive, highly obligated, highly vulnerable single mother who missed her former life just as much as she loved her child.

I got up and paced for a while, then booted up Faye's laptop computer and checked for e-mails from Jack, hoping to find a little comfort in his virtual embrace. As the computer went through its starting-up ceremony, my attention came to rest on one of Baby Sloane's teething rings, and I thought of her sitting in Tert Krehbeil's lap. An unseen hand formed a fist around my heart. Seeing the three of them sitting there in the museum had been a terrible shock. Woman, man, and baby. The full complement of personnel. Tert had been holding Sloane as if she were his, all comfortable and easy, Mr. Composure, just dropping in to stay a couple hundred years.

It's not Faye I'm really worried about, I realized, *it's the baby. Could this man replace the father she would never know? Or would he in fact be worse than no father at all?*

And it was clear to me now, in the harshness of an empty house, that the idea of being made extraneous in Sloane's life was part of what had panicked me.

The computer made a jungle roar at me, a sound Jack had programmed in as its wake-up noise back when he was around enough to capture my heart. *Back before he ran off to Florida to help someone other than me.*

And I followed him.

And Tom followed me, and got himself killed. . . .

The room tilted slightly at the memory of Tom's stiffening corpse. I fought the sensation, forcing myself to tap in commands and downloaded my e-mail.

I stared at the results. Tucked in among the spam that pushed on-line Viagra, mortgage re-fis, make money at home schemes, penile enlargements, and red-hot farmgirl "cams," there was in fact a message from Jack. I told myself this was a good omen. Until I read it.

Hey there Em

Looks like no luck on my request for early release. It's a tough job out here but they say somebody's got to do it, so why not this old pinniped. Sorry to disappoint you. Can't say much else as I'm on someone else's machine and that's a no no, so give that baby a squeeze for me and I'll write again soon.

Love always, Jack

I read it again and then closed the message. Then I opened it up again, hit REPLY, and wrote:

Hey there Jack

Just back from Cody, where I was with Faye as I explained before. I came back early because she's gotten tight with some

I erased the second sentence and tried again.

Hey there Jack

Just back from Cody, where I was with Faye as I explained before. Had some nice moments with baby S out on the badlands looking for rocks. Surprise surprise I found some, pretty strange considering I'm a geologist and that's what the world is made of, huh? Well, I sure miss you and

And what? It was getting harder and harder to write to Jack, and I could not sort out why. The fact that we had not seen each other since a month before Sloane Renee was born was certainly an issue, but that couldn't have been avoided. It was best that he did not come around just after the baby was born, because after all, it was Tom's death that put Faye into early labor. Jack was a walking reminder of that tragedy. And Jack had lived. Jack's absence had seemed reasonable at the time, because I did not want to be reminded, either. We had expected to see each other after, at most, perhaps a month. But then he had been called up from the Reserves, like so many others. Off he went, a forty-one-year-old Navy

SEAL sent out to do what the spooky boys do in a time of war, and my discomfort over what was unsettled in our relationship had been conveniently swapped for discomfort over the adversity he was facing.

And now I faced another communication that felt like no communication at all. I wanted him home. I wanted him safe and sound. And I wanted to see him through his assignment. I couldn't stand the idea of being the girlfriend who could not take the strain, who couldn't get her brain around the simple task of writing a few messages, who quit writing, who failed to support him as he supported all of us.

I settled for typing some more newsy bits, then sent off my e-mail and closed down the computer. I had no sooner gone off-line, thereby clearing the phone line, when the telephone rang. I glanced at the clock. It was seven A.M. Wondering who would call this early, I picked it up and said hello.

A familiar voice filled the line. "Hi, Em." It was Ray, the man I had been nuts over before I met Jack.

I sat there with my mouth hanging open for some good ten or fifteen seconds, because I had not heard from Officer Thomas B-for-Brigham "Ray" Raymond in quite some time. Not since the night all hell had broken loose and he had tacitly chosen his family and his religion over me. Funny how these interfaith engagements can go. I had thought I would never hear from Ray again, and decided that was just fine, but it seemed that this was my forty-eight hours for emotional jolts.

"Em? Am I calling too early?"

"Ray. Uh . . . hi. No, I'm up. But uh . . . *why* exactly are you calling?"

"Because I want to talk to you." From the tone of his voice, he thought this was funny. As in, *Duh*.

"Uh, okay. So, uh . . . talk."

"No, I mean get *together* and talk."

This did not compute. In part because Thomas B. Whutzisname Raymond was not a talker. But I said, "Okay." Why? Because sometimes I just don't know how to say no, such as at moments like this, when I am in fact curious to know what is motivating a pig to take up the habit of sprouting wings and flying.

"Meet me for lunch?"

"No."

"Dinner?"

"No," I said, more firmly. "I'm willing to talk, Ray, but I don't think I can mix it with food."

He chuckled. "Fair enough. Go for a walk, then?"

I thought this through a moment. Sure, in broad daylight in a public place, we could walk and talk. "Where and when?"

"How about right now?"

"Mm." I was trying to sound noncommittal, because I was in fact free, but did not want to sound easy.

"I'll park in front of your house, and we can just walk from there."

"Okay . . . but, wait, you don't know where I'm living."

He laughed again. "Yes, I do. You're staying with Faye, in that house she bought with Tom . . . before he died. By the way, I was sorry to hear about that."

Hearing his condolences was more than I could handle. If he wanted to get together, then fine, but not on my turf. "I'm coming downtown anyway. I can meet you at Salt Lake Roasters," I said, venting my annoyance by asking a strict Mormon to meet me at a coffee shop. "And make it ten o'clock." I did not want him coming to my home, and I'd be damned if he was going to see me this disheveled. I needed time to take a shower and dig out a clean pair of jeans. *Why am I so annoyed?* I wondered. *I've moved on with life. Ray is in the past. But there's something not right about this!* I said, "How the hell do you know where I live, Ray?"

"Oh come on, Em. I'm a cop. Remember?"

I HAD TO admit, Ray looked good. I mean *good*, not just his usual handsome self. He had a certain glow about him. He was smiling, and his gait seemed easier, more open. As I joined him on the sidewalk, I decided that he had come to tell me that he was getting married or something.

He was wearing one of those nice pairs of blue jeans he filled so athletically, his usual pristine white running shoes, and a nice fleece-lined jacket. His indigo-blue eyes were bright, and his cheeks were rosy in the crisp air. He gave me a slight bow, but kept his hands in his pockets.

I bowed, too.

He indicated that we could start walking to the east, uphill toward the trace of the Wasatch Fault. We walked. We had gone perhaps a block and a half before he spoke, which seemed more like the Ray I was used to, the one who spoke ten paragraphs in body English for every word that passed his lips. But then the words started, and it seemed he had quite a bit to say.

"I wanted to talk to you about what happened between us, kind of clear things up. That okay with you?"

"Sure," I said.

"We were engaged, and then all that business with my family happened, and I didn't handle it well. So I wanted first to apologize."

Huh? He was referring to a falling-out of titanic proportions. He was a Mormon and I had precipitated an event that resulted in the incarceration of two of his family members. "I figure you could be forgiven for just about anything that night, Ray. Uh, I think even it's the other way around. Maybe I should be apologizing."

He smiled, a bit more shyly this time. "No, it's definitely my turn. If you want to make amends to me, you can call me and make an appointment." He kind of danced his shoulders about as he said this, trying to be funny, keeping things light.

"Well, fine. I accept your apology."

"Thanks."

We walked on for about another block or so without saying anything. Gradually, his words sank in, and not just what he had said, but how he had said it. *Amends?* "Uh, Ray, are you going to Al-Anon or something?"

He blushed crimson. "Does it show?"

"What the—Your family are all Mormons. Not a one of them drinks a drop. What are you doing in Al-Anon?"

Suddenly all the frivolity was gone from his face. "It's a good program. Surely you know that from your mother."

"Well, yeah, the Twelve Steps is part of how she got sober. But she was a drunk, Ray."

"And I am part of a . . . It works for me. That's all that needs saying."

I kept walking, studying the pavement just in front of my feet with great concentration. "I'm impressed, Ray."

"Well . . ."

"And I'm glad for you." In fact, I was jealous. Apart from his current embarrassment, he looked jubilant, downright happy, and I was not.

"So as long as I'm making amends, I'm supposed to be specific about it. I am sorry that I was so hard on you, Em. I'm sorry I asked you to give up what was true for you to try to be with me. I judged you very harshly, and that wasn't fair. I wanted you to change yourself so that I wouldn't have to face myself. That was cowardly."

I tripped, and there wasn't even any broken pavement to trip on. My feet just got in each other's ways, and I stumbled. "Ray—" In the movies, this is where the guy is supposed to reach out and take the girl in his arms, and it's all sweetness and mush and the music swells and off we go to la-la land. But this was Em Hansen and Ray Raymond on a sidewalk on a brisk morning in Salt Lake City, and he kept his hands stuck in his pockets while I found my footing and lurched forward, hurrying to keep out of range just in case he got his hands out. I did not think that physical touch from another human being would help me get my bearings just then. I opened my mouth and closed it several times, trying out sounds that did not quite emerge from my throat, and then finally managed to say, "Thank you."

"Thank you for listening."

We walked on for quite a while, he with his head up, me with my head bowed like I was pressing into a high wind. We must have looked quite a pair. *So this is the gag*, I was thinking. *He did not phone me up to say, "Let's get together," or "I still miss you terribly and will pine for you forever." No, he's rattling my cage just to free his self. Well, I can't fault him for that, but I must admit—*

Admit what? That I'm a vain idiot who can't see that life is marching on without me?

Ooo, I scolded. *Here we go again, arguing with ourself!*

Ray broke the silence. "You're a good person, Em. A good friend. I've missed your company."

Ah. Now it starts.

Suddenly his throat sounded tight. "I'd like it if we could get together now and then, or talk, just on the phone if that's okay."

"I don't know, Ray."

"I know, I know. When you blow someone's trust like I did with you, well . . . you've simply blown it, and they're not going to trust you again all at once, so you have to earn it back in tiny bits. This isn't a boy-girl thing I'm trying to press on you, so please relax. I just don't like to leave it like it was. I want to be worthy of your trust, because you're someone I admire."

My brain had now reached full boil, and I wondered if steam was pouring out of my ears. I did not feel admirable in the least, or even trustworthy, let alone someone whose trust should be sought. I felt like a prize idiot who had been mistaken for a woman with sense. I wanted simultaneously to mount a valiant steed in my Joan of Arc suit and to turn around and kick this man in the shins, and I could not explain either urge to myself.

We walked on.

Eventually we turned right, and then right again, passing between the square Victorian grandeur of the City and County Building and the ultramodern curves of the new city library, and by and by we were back at Salt Lake Roasters. "Everything going okay with Faye?" he asked. "Or at least as well as might be expected?"

I clenched my teeth. "Oh, she's doing just fine," I said, a bit too forcefully. I was thinking that right now, she was on the road with what's-his-name, laughing and preening, preening and laughing, and that Sloane Renee was probably strapped into her little car seat all by herself in the back, all lonesome. I imagined her crying, unheard, ignored. I tried to erase that thought, not wanting her to feel an instant's pain, then I decided that I was going insane as I felt a sharp urge to grab Ray by the wrist, give him a yank toward me, and say, *Want to make a baby? Right now? Right here?*

But I did not, because who'd want to get it on with a nut case?

Oblivious to what was going on inside my head and heart, Ray gave me a final smile, or perhaps he gave it to himself. "Thanks for meeting with me," he said. "I've got to go."

And he left.

7

YOU'D THINK I WOULD HAVE FOUND IT PLEASING TO RECEIVE AN apology like that, but something about it did not stick to my ribs. In fact, I felt quite annoyed at Ray, and the longer I thought about it, the stronger that annoyance grew. So I did the only reasonable thing: I pushed the conundrum of the meeting out of my mind and stormed into Salt Lake Roasters in search of a cup of coffee, muttering to myself that if there were a twelve-step program for caffeine addicts, I'd make a good poster child for it.

I met a pal at the counter: the incomparable Tanya, the woman who managed the local FBI office, the one where Tom Latimer worked before he married Faye.

Tanya was her usual appallingly cheerful self. She was just purchasing a latte and a chocolate cookie, and she invited me to join her for a tour of the roof of the new library.

I liked the new library. It is the only library I have ever known that has a coffee shop on the main floor, lounges featuring chessboards, fireplaces, and stunning city views on every level, a newsstand inside its five-story glass atrium, and a garden on its roof. So I said yes, paid for my jolt of java, and followed her down the sidewalk and up the elevators to the roof of the new building. We settled on a bench that had a nice view and I started into the ritual of small talk, which was about all I was good for at that moment. "What brings you out on a workday?"

Tanya was just placing the cookie between her lips for rapturous nibble. Efficient in her sensuousness, she waited until she had chewed and swallowed before answering me. "I took the morning off to run some errands. And then I decided to play hooky from doing the errands."

"Well, it's nice to see you. Been ages."

"Hey, you too. Where's your papoose?"

"Faye's up in Wyoming for a few days," I said, my tone of voice more glum than I had intended.

Tanya's eyebrows jumped ever so slightly. Nothing got past Tanya, not even the FBI spooks that worked with her. "Had a spat, have you?" She put down her cookie and attended to some crumbs she had dropped on her blouse.

One thing I had to hand to Tanya, she could make the third degree sound like light, impersonal chitchat. Almost. I clenched my teeth, vowing that I would not say another word about Faye or her reasons for being away. I buried my attention in taking a long draw on my coffee while I collected myself.

Tanya took a demure sip of her latte and studied me frankly. "Strange marriage you two have."

"What?" I snapped.

She made a dismissive gesture and plucked another crumb from her shirt.

I gripped my coffee with both hands. *First Ray and now Tanya. Hey, it's open season on Em. Let's just line them up, and everyone take their best shot.* I said, "Sure, just laser-search my psyche, make a couple of wild leading remarks, and move on. Nice to see you, too, Tanya."

Tanya pulled back her head and made an elaborate job of blinking at me. "My, my, but didn't *you* wake up feeling a bit defensive this morning."

"Yes, I did. The baby is with Faye. I miss the baby. You got a problem with that?"

"What's Faye doing in Wyoming?"

My self-control vanished. "What's Faye doing? Oh, just screwing around with some swell who puts Narcissus to shame for rank self-involvement. Which leaves me here in Salt Lake feeling like a prize chump for taking off a year from my life to help her with her adjustment to motherhood, as it seems she's done with me now, thank-you-very-much-goodbye. And just to add sunshine to my day, Ray Raymond looks me up to do a twelve-step dump job so he can feel just great while I feel like a retard. Just what the hell do you mean, 'marriage?' "

Tanya put down both cup and cookie and raised her hands in mock surrender. "Hey—mortgage, baby, arguments you don't talk about; some people call that a commitment."

"Very funny," I said irritably. "I'm just waiting for Jack to come back. And I'm finishing my master's."

" 'Finishing'," she said, almost making it a question. "So sorry to intrude. So, what are your plans, really?"

I wanted to snarl, *You sound just like Faye!* but the reality was that I did not have a plan. I was winging it, waiting to see what happened with Jack. I said, "I am willing to help Faye as long as she needs me."

Tanya patted me on the arm. "Are you still feeling responsible for Tom's death?"

"Oh, great. First Ray with the Twelve Steps, and now you're a full-on shrink. Fine. Call it 'survivor's syndrome' if you want, but I keep thinking that I could have prevented what happened to him."

Tanya shook her head. "He was in the wrong place at the wrong instant, Em. The life of an agent hangs on split-second timing. Tom could have gotten it a hundred times before you ever met him."

"So, I should have seen that he was slowing down. I pushed him."

"No one pushed Tom Latimer. He was the one that did the pushing. We all miss him, Em."

I was babbling now. "Jack can't even talk about it. I can't talk to him about it. We were both there with him, together. Whom better to talk to?"

Tanya let silence sit for a moment, then said, "You think that might have had something to do with Jack going active?"

I froze. This was the thing I had not wanted to consider. Had Jack run away when his feelings overwhelmed him? Did he run to war when I'd have preferred he'd come to me with his pain?

Tanya changed the subject. "So, back to this Ray Raymond. Is that the Ray Raymond with the nice buns who's a cop on the Salt Lake force?"

"That would be the one."

"What do you mean, 'twelve-step dump job'? He take your inventory or something?"

"Inventory?"

"That's when someone who's sworn off the sauce figures he's so smart he gets to go around telling everyone else what's wrong with *them*."

"No, that would be what *you're* doing. No, Ray was much cuter than that. He gave me the old 'Here I am apologizing for my folly in having known you' job. 'Things were sweet. Things were, in fact, *so* great that I'm getting a life. I was a turkey, now I'm an eagle—*see* ya.' "

Tanya rolled her eyes. "I agree that twelve-step amends can be more for the forgiven than for the forgiver, but aside from that, Mrs. Lincoln, how did you like the play? I mean . . . it's quite a view from up here, isn't it?" She gestured out toward the rocky wall of the Wasatch range, which today arched its spine above Salt Lake City with particular pride. The view from the roof of the library was nothing short of stunning: The Wasatch front reached south to hold hands with the Oquirrhs, and the curving sweep of the library's daring architecture completed the geometry like a circle of young maidens embracing the coming of spring.

As always, Tanya's reasonableness had its effect, and I began to calm down. It was true that Ray's apology had been more for his sake than for mine; nothing had changed, everything was still on his terms, still lacking in the mutuality I craved. Seeing Frank up in Cody had bothered me, too. He was as kind and gentle and caring as Jack was romantic and funny and . . . well, thrilling. I wanted a man who was all that and more like Ray, possessed of a healthy dash of self-interest. And wanting all that made me emotionally dizzy.

Tanya cleared her throat. "So what do you hear from Jack?"

I tried to bury my face in the task of taking another sip of my brew, but managed to choke on it.

"That bad?" she inquired.

"He's doing fine," I rasped.

"But you're not," she said affably. "You look like somebody swiped your birthday cake."

"Tanya, let's change the subject, okay?"

"Okay. How's the thesis going?"

"Nowhere. Faye's got a hot idea for me, but—"

Tanya put a comforting hand on my shoulder. "Tell me about it."

I began to crumple under her sympathy. "Maybe it's not the stupidest idea anyone ever had, but I'd need a lot of help with it, because the thing is . . . Well, hell, the problem is that there really is no place to go to get a degree in forensic geology. The curriculum does not exist. I've been taking courses that other forensic geologists have taken, but when it comes to doing a thesis, it's darned hard to come up with something. My advisor is supposed to help me with this, but she's not a forensic geologist. In fact, there aren't any theses to use as guides, even."

"But people do the work. We have three forensic geologists on staff back at the labs in Quantico."

I fought the urge to lean against her for strength. "Can I take you into my confidence on something? I mean, pick your brains a bit?"

Tanya arched her own spine and offered the bronze skin of her face skyward to the kiss of the sun. "Pick ho; I'm not sure what you'll find in there, but if there's anything, it's all yours. I surely wouldn't want to get stuck paying the storage fee."

"Well, the fact is that the reason Faye's in Wyoming . . . Well, she has a client . . . And well, I've been asked to do a little private investigation work. I don't like the sound of the job, but Faye's involved in it, so I have to convince her that it's best to turn it down."

"What don't you like about it?"

"It would require a lot of analytical work, for starts."

Tanya cocked her head to one side. "Analytical work? You mean hard evidence? You're right; that's not you."

"What do you mean?"

"Tom always told me you fly seat-of-the-pants."

"Ye-es," I drawled, "Tom always loved me for my intuition, not for my hard science, but that's because—"

"I thought he said it was your hard *head* he liked."

"Tanya, you are so far out of line today, I—"

"So what is it you need from me?"

"Like you say, there are geologists working in the FBI forensics lab. I've been meaning to contact them anyway to ask them . . . well, for help with the thesis. But it's kind of tough, phoning someone I don't really know and saying, 'Hey, help me.' But I'd also like to ask them about the work. Kind of do an informational interview. Find out where I might apply for work if I ever—*when* I get this master's finished."

Tanya said, "Oh, I get it, you want to work in the lab in D.C. so you can be near Jack when he gets home. Why didn't you just say so?"

I closed my eyes and counted to ten. "Tanya, I swear, can you take just one little thing I say at face value?"

"Just one."

"Good. Okay, so I need to talk with this woman who's a forensic geologist in the FBI lab. Tom was just trying to put me in touch with her when he—" My voice caught in my throat.

Tanya tucked the last bite of her cookie into her mouth and chewed it quickly. "Noreen Babcock. Sure, no problem. She's a real smart lady, and almost as much of a loner as you are. You two would get along like a couple of stones in a rock garden. I'll write down her number."

◈

BY THE TIME I got back to Faye's house, I was in such an unstable mood that I figured it was best to avoid all contact with other human beings for as long as possible. I decided to stick my head into something intellectual, in the hope that I might push my wolf pack of feelings into a cave and roll a rock in front of it.

That something was my schoolwork. I was almost done with my coursework but it was true that to complete the degree I needed to write a thesis, and to write a thesis, I needed a research topic. Worse yet, research tended to cost money, and that was something I did not have. The tank was empty; I was getting by on fumes. I was getting free rent from Faye, and she was essentially feeding me, too. My mother was paying my tuition and sending the occasional check that covered books and bus fare and a little pocket change. Even this was a problem for me, not just because at age thirty-eight it hurt my pride to be hitting my mother for expenses, but also because she expected to be paid back.

As I opened my books to study, my brain ground once again through the problem of identifying a thesis project. I hoped to do something that involved trace materials, which meant soils and other fine sediments, the kinds of things that cling to a crime scene in such microscopic quantities that most criminals don't notice they're leaving evidence behind.

This term I was taking a full load of courses: Sedimentology, Soil Science, Meteorology, and Statistics. It was a real grind, but quite engrossing. Sedimentology was teaching me what kind of rock fragments wound up where, and why; Soil Science and Meteorology were teaching me how these sediments weathered into dirt, and why and where; and Statistics was teaching me how to put numbers and probabilities to the whole business. By the end of the semester, I'd have everything I needed to finish except the dreaded thesis. My advisor, Molly Chang, was beginning to roll her eyes every time she saw me coming.

I leaned back in my chair and stared at the ceiling. Perhaps I *could* make a thesis out of the job Tert was offering. *A painting is made of paint, which is made of pigments and a binder, and pigments are, after all, trace evidence. The key to documenting the forgery might be a matter of identifying the pigments, which were most likely ground-up bits of minerals. The trick would be to focus on the painting, and stay away from Tert Krehbeil and whatever's going on with his family.*

Little cash-register sounds went off in my head. If Gray Eyes paid enough, I could quit borrowing from my mother, an act I enjoyed about as much as gargling turpentine. Why? Because Mother was the only one left on the ranch I had told Gray Eyes I owned. In fact, *she* owned the ranch, not me, but it belonged to me in the sense that I knew each bluff and swale, each blade of grass, and each beam in the barn. The ranch was woven into the very fabric of my soul. But until Mother left, I could not be there. She might be sober now, but sobriety had not healed our relationship.

Money, money, money. The ranch was small, as semiarid ranchland went, just a few square miles of short-grass prairie, not enough to raise much beef. I knew that since my father's death and the last drought, and with the rise in the cost of feed and labor and the continued sluggish prices in beef, my mother had been struggling financially, but she had been only too willing to loan me the money to get my degree. "With a master's," she had said, "you might get a real job." I had bitten my tongue, figuring to repay her by taking over the ranch the instant she was ready to give up the charade and move to town. She didn't belong there, not really. She had been born gagging on a silver spoon in Boston. But, forty years after thumbing her nose at her family by running away to Wyoming with the cowboy who had been my father, she still spoke with a Brahmin accent as she addressed her neighbors with a dry, stinging, ironic New England wit that sailed past them like so many cow chips in a high wind.

I drummed my fingers. The ranch might have been purchased with her money (or, more accurately, her father's money), but my father had built every foot of fence and dug every inch of irrigation ditch. In my angrier moments, I blamed his overwork for his early demise, even as I longed to pick up where he had left off. But she had sent me away again and again.

I took several long, deep breaths, trying once again to let go of a past in which the milk of being in a land I loved was always curdled by the vinegar of human failings. *About now, Faye would be giving me a pep talk on the art of letting go,* I told myself. *If she were here. And if she were still talking to me.* I cringed at how truly accurate Tanya's observation had been: Faye and I now communicated with about the frequency and to approximately the depth that my parents had done, three and a half decades into the disappointment they'd called a marriage. I was playing Clyde Hansen's stoic servant to Leila Bradstreet Hansen's self-indulgence. I had re-created my family drama—and to what gain? None. If I didn't get a grip on myself soon, I'd wind up as prematurely dead as my father or as eternally self-destructive as my mother.

I stopped to calculate how old my mother was now. I reckoned sixty-three: She had borne me when she was just shy of twenty-five. She still had her looks, and was disgustingly strong, physically speaking. Her body had weathered decades of alcohol abuse, and now more than half a decade of hard physical labor. How long had it been since Daddy died? Six years? Or was it seven?

In all the months I had studied the ceiling while thinking my thoughts, I had made a pretty thorough map of the patterns in the drywall texturing. To the right of center was the land of big blotches that formed a shape like a canoe, and to the left, the isthmus of the funny guy with only one leg. One-Leg reminded me of myself, forever hopping around, never quite whole.

My eyes shifted to other figures I had traced in the plaster. A long, sinuous line could be Faye, skating toward the edge of reality, ready to date again, having been widowed now longer than she was married. The blob next to it could be good ol' Em Hansen, now starring in the supporting role as the cuckolded roommate with gender confusion. And was that jagged bit to the other side of her Tert Krehbeil? What did Faye see in him? Why was she reverting to her snob-ridden past? Would regression help wall off the memory of Tom? Better a self-absorbed bit of fluff from Pennsylvania than a man who took one last risk and was killed? And was it my job to save her from this fate, or was I, in fact, part of the problem?

Enough of this maundering self-pity, I decided. *Time to go out for a walk. Restore the body, and the spirit will follow.*

Outside, the day was warming, and I had walked only a few blocks before I needed to open my jacket. Flowers were beginning to peek out of the gardens I passed, and all but the last dirty, icy chunks of snow piled up in the deepest north-side shadows had melted away. My mood lightened, and I even got to rolling my hips a little in a sort of celebration of spring.

Which in turn immediately soured my mood again. Sensual motion in my pelvis reminded me of Jack, and where the hell was he?

I tripped over a break in the sidewalk, and as I lurched to catch myself, my head snapped forward so fast that for a moment I could see through my own self-interest. I had no idea who Gray Eyes was as a person, not really; and although no one could replace Tom Latimer, he was dead, and life went on.

Everybody's life is going on but mine! whined my nasty little brain.

Now desperate to escape myself, I leaned forward and began to jog, and then to run. I made three blocks before I got winded, at which juncture I turned right and right again and headed back toward the house. I was coming down the straightaway, slowing back to a shambling jog, when I was passed by a man who was really moving along, all fleet feet and sopping-wet sweat suit. He hoofed it three houses past Faye's and then pulled up, jogged up the front walkway, put his hands on the bottom step of the porch, and began pumping off push-ups.

Who's this? I wondered.

A Realtor's sign saying FOR SALE had stood on the front lawn for several weeks, and was now surmounted by a smaller sign that read SOLD.

I put my hands in my pockets and wandered over to make his acquaintance. "Hi," I said. "You must be a new neighbor. I'm Em Hansen. Welcome to the neighborhood."

The man pushed himself upright with one big shove, turned, took me in with a quick glance, smiled, and said, "Hi yourself. I'm Fritz Calder."

Oooo, macho . . . Much taller and more manly than Mr. Gray Eyes. And he lives right here! My mind took off like a dart, computing a much better future for Faye and Sloane that would joyously include me, now featured in the role of the savior who had found the right man for them.

Fritz asked, "Which house do you live in?"

I pointed. "The house actually belongs to my housemate, Faye," I replied, grinning at the match this was going to make. *He's athletic, good-looking . . .* "She's not here just now. Just ran up to Wyoming with the baby for a few days."

The flicker of a thought crossed Fritz Calder's eyes. He shifted his pose slightly. As his spine relaxed, I realized that until then he had been standing extraordinarily straight, almost as if at attention. He leaned over against one of the posts that held up his porch roof and began stretching the muscles down the side of his torso. "Baby girl or baby boy?"

"Girl. Sloane Renee."

"Sweet name. I like kids."

"Oh. Do you and your wife have children?" I inquired, belatedly wondering if there might be impediments to my plan. I glanced toward the front windows of his house, hoping I would not glimpse any other inmates. I calculated that he was about the same age as Faye and I were, or perhaps a bit older; if he was Mormon (about a fifty-percent likelihood in this town), that meant a wife and a passel of kids ranging from teenagers down through grade-schoolers. I glanced at the house. Not big enough for a tribe like that.

He stared at the ground for a moment, hands on his hips. "I have one kid, Brendan. He's nine years old and likes Legos and soccer. And I have one ex-wife, Marsha, and she's . . . not my wife anymore." Having gotten this off his chest, he went back to his stretches, which now evolved into broad, smooth swings of his arms.

I was indeed enjoying the show, especially now that he had relaxed around me, but I shifted into a posture that said I did not notice such things. I had committed myself to Jack Sampler, and it was best, therefore, to send the proper signals. "So, as long as I'm the welcoming committee, let me grill you good and proper. What brings you to the neighborhood?"

"Business opportunities. I have a fledgling aircraft-design and-manufacturing business, and being here in Utah puts me in the middle, between the coasts, and in dry air, where my equipment won't corrode."

Aircraft? Oh, this is wonderful! He's tall, he's good-looking, and he flies! Mr. Gray Eyes is going down in flames, his parachute is not opening, he's hitting the ground with a resounding smack. . . . *It's sad, folks, but he's been outshined by a man of action, of sagacity, of* . . . "Is your aircraft for general aviation, commercial, or the military?"

Again the flickering of thought crossed his eyes. I had used the correct jargon, and he had noticed. He said, "You fly?"

I grinned. "Yes. And so does Faye."

He matched my grin. "Great. Yes, well, I am bringing on a new general-aviation in-line twin-engine craft—that's my true love—but I also make widgets for the government. That pays the rent while I search for capital and contracts so I can bring the twin into production."

I was ready to sing odes of joy. "I have just a basic license, but Faye's a multi-engine, instrument-rated, commercial pilot. She flies a Piper Cheyenne Two."

Fritz raised his eyebrows in appraisal. "That's a nice plane. Yeager set a time to climb record in a stock Cheyenne Two."

Oh, this is perfect! He even approves of her choice in aircraft! "You two should really meet," I said. "Why don't you come over for dinner once she gets back? You can bring your son, too. Or, that is, as long as he's not dripping with a cold or something. Faye gets kind of jumpy about that sort of stuff around the baby."

Fritz gave me a little *Why not?* shrug of his shoulders. "That would be very nice of you. My son's in Germany just now with his mom, visiting her dad, so you won't need the surgical masks. I'd offer to bring something, but I'm a lousy cook. Of course, I know how to pick out wines. . . ."

I laughed. "Wine is wasted on me; I don't know it from sour grape juice. And Faye is still nursing the baby. But a good microbrew beer would be welcome."

"Deal."

"Deal."

"Well, I gotta get to work."

"Right."

He nodded pleasantly and headed up the steps to his house. I headed back down the sidewalk to mine, all but chortling with glee. *So he's a divorcé. So what? Faye wouldn't even date one before she married and had that baby, but I'll bet she's got a different attitude now. Now, what excuse can I use to slip out and leave them romantically alone as they get to talking? I could say I have a midterm, or a paper due . . . and of course I'll be such a pal and offer to put the baby to bed. . . .*

Life was once again filled with possibilities.

8

> Ochre is a natural earth color which consists of silica and clay, and which owes its color to iron oxide in either the hydrous form (limonite or goethite, the latter mineral named for the poet) or anhydrous form (hematite, from the Latin for blood). It has been universally used as a pigment since earliest history, beginning with the painting of human bodies for ceremony and battle.
>
> —*from the files of Fred Petridge*

JENNIFER NEUMANN CLOSED THE PROJECT FILE WITH THE TAB marked FRAVEL FARM and thumped it with her fist, right in the center of the color-coded manila folder where she had mounted the glossy printed sticker that read, PENNSYLVANIA OPEN SPACE HERITAGE FOUNDATION, FARMLANDS PRESERVATION DIVISION. This one wasn't going her way; any fool could see that. If she and her crew didn't get things turned around fast, Fravel would enter into negotiations with a developer, and yet another Lancaster County farm would be cut up into half-acre home sites. McMansions, she and her colleagues called them. Except that all six billion people on the planet couldn't and wouldn't be served. And yet these 'starter castles' were popping up like bad mushrooms all over the county, using up the best nonirrigated farmland in the United States to grow lawns upon which the idiot rich could cruise their ride-along mowers.

She had just returned from the Fravel farm, where she had seen the bad news with her own eyes. Farmer Fravel had lost patience with her efforts to get one of the farm-preservation bureaus to purchase his development rights, and had begun planting his last crop: sod. She always knew what was coming when she saw a farmer planting sod. It meant he no longer cared about his topsoil, and was ready to have it peeled off along with the grass, rolled up and carted off to apply to the half-acre home sites that had been robbed of their topsoil by a previous subdividing farmer when he had planted *his* final crop.

Jennifer turned her hands inward so that she could examine her fingernails. They were painted a variety of lively colors, her one bow to cosmetics. She applied not a lick of color to the Germanic bones of her face, but coloring her fingernails amused her, and added the right touch of frivolity to her day.

She was able to tolerate such frustrations as the Fravel farm project without sinking into despair or burnout because she knew how to pace herself. It was tough being a one-woman foundation, spreading her expertise and support across the heritage concerns of an entire state on an almost nonexistent budget, but she had learned that when one project went into a bad dive, it was time to take a short visit to one on the upswing.

So she put away the Fravel file (color-coded green for "farmlands") and shuffled through the other colors, searching for a project that would lift her spirits. *There's the Rails-to-Trails group,* she mused, perusing an item she had assigned to a brown folder, indicating that the project was of historical importance. She had cross-referenced it with a yellow sticker, her color for "recreation," indicating sunshine. *Rails to Trails is much more satisfying. I should call Fred Petridge at the Pennsylvania State Geologic Survey and ask where he's gotten with the latest fund-raiser.* She opened the file, slid her finger down the front page until she found Fred's number, and dialed.

A recorded message answered, informing all callers that Fred Petridge was temporarily away from his desk.

"Fred, it's Jenny," she said into the phone when the God Almighty recording beep cued her response. "Give me a call. It's about the Big Savage Mountain railroad tunnel project. Just checking up, seeing how it's going, giving you an attaboy and any help you might need. 'Bye."

She returned to her stack of files and again sifted through them, looking for something else to sink her teeth into. A red file caught her attention. *Ah. Pursuant to Fred and the Geologic Survey, the limonite project could use a little more energy,* she decided, as she came to a file marked LIMONITE

PSEUDOMORPHS. She especially liked this project because it involved a mineral that was classically used in making paints, and Jenny was an artist of some accomplishment. Even though the experts had assured her that the limonite local farmers historically had plowed up in their fields was used for iron ore rather than in making red pigment, she still held out a hope that some farmer somewhere had harvested a little of the mineral to make barn-red paint. It was disappointing that most Lancaster County farmers painted their barns white, or built them out of stone and never had need of paint except for the doors, but she had never allowed contrary dogmas to stop her before, so why start now?

She opened the file and paged through it, admiring again the photographs she had taken of the little brown cubes, which she had assiduously labeled LIMONITE (AMORPHOUS HYDROUS IRON OXIDE), PSEUDOMORPHS AFTER PYRITE. There were three of the mysterious little cubes, and they ranged in size from a quarter- to a half-inch. It was through these little stones that she had met Fred Petridge. She had asked to speak with a mineral specialist, and he had held the little cubes in his hand and told her, "Pyrite is iron sulfide, a shiny, metallic-looking mineral. Its molecules organize into cubes as it crystallizes. Limonite pseudomorphs form when iron sulfide is altered into iron oxide, changing the internal structure of the crystal but preserving the external form. Where precisely did you get these?"

"On a farm in Manheim Township. They come up in the fields when the farmer plows in the spring."

"Ah, yes. Weathering out of the soils. You'll see them in the old bricks in the historic part of downtown Lancaster. They're neat."

"Are they rare?" she had asked. "Endangered?"

The geologist had given her a conspiratorial smile. "Are you trying to find an excuse to prevent development, perchance?"

Jennifer had lowered her eyelids slyly and smiled.

Petridge had shaken his head. "They're uncommon these days, but not what you could call rare or endangered, like some kind of bird or trout. Sadly, minerals don't enjoy protected status in the same sense that plants and animals do. I say sadly because when it comes to trying to save the farmlands, you're preaching to the choir. I'll take a view across open fields any day over a whole row of two-story houses with expensive cars sitting out front. I don't know how you can tolerate working on that problem day after day."

Jennifer had said, "I feel better sticking with it than walking away. People always ask me, 'What can one woman do?' but I tell them: 'Plenty.' "

"One woman? I thought you were with a foundation."

"I am. Pennsylvania Open Space Heritage Foundation is really just me, but calling myself a foundation gets me more respect. I team up with other groups as needed. Why don't you come to a meeting sometime? We can have some laughs and lick envelopes. It's a good crew. We could use your help." She had tipped her head in a welcoming angle and given him a wink, and that had been all it took. His specialty in mineralogy was a great help, and it turned out that with a little coaxing, she had been able to get him interested in the Big Savage Railroad Tunnel, too, because it seemed he had a thing about railroads.

Jennifer now heaved a quick sigh, a habit she allowed herself more to fill her tissues with oxygen than to express any concern that she might not prevail in her tasks. She liked the limonite project because she liked Fred. This little respite of looking at the lovely pictures had helped to restore her vital juices, but it was time to get back to work on the farmlands issue.

She closed the red limonite file and opened another green one she had marked KREHBEIL FARM. On the inside left face of the folder she had clipped a phone-contact log listing every contact she had made to the Krehbeil family in her attempts to help them preserve their farm. She noted again that there had been an ominous slacking-off of contacts coming her way from them. Mr. Krehbeil had died, and his wife was ailing, but the daughter who lived with them seemed to share their interest in preservation.

She rechecked her phone log. The daughter's name was Deirdre. Had Deirdre given up? Did she need money for doctors' bills so badly that she was going for the final crop? Or was it that Mrs. Krehbeil had gotten so sick that Deirdre had no time even to think about the encroachment of developments around their farm?

Jennifer turned now to a photocopy of an aerial photo of the farm and its immediate environs. Only last week she had had to draw red diagonal lines across a farm less than a quarter-mile away, her symbol for another battle lost.

In working to preserve farm heritage, it was important to understand the dynamics of the families involved. Some followed religious principles, some played politics, and others just went after the money, letting the fur fly where it may. In the case of Mr. Krehbeil, he had gone to meet his Maker, so his patriarchal stance was no longer in play. Mrs. Krehbeil was ill, which could mean anything from abdication of power with the onset of dependency to a total logjam, if the offspring were still clinging to her emotionally. There were four grown children; an abdication would leave them to duke out who got control of the situation. Deirdre was not returning Jenny's phone calls. The older son had left to make his fortune decades ago; Deirdre had once told her that. The younger daughter had not shown her face around the county in years, a total flake according to Deirdre.

That left the second brother. His name was Hector. She'd heard stories about him that suggested that he would be of no help. *What the hell, I'll give him a try*, Jennifer decided, as she once again picked up her telephone and dialed.

9

I SPENT THE NEXT TWO HOURS UP AT THE U, DIGGING THROUGH the library for reference texts on paint pigments, so that when I telephoned Noreen Babcock I wouldn't sound like a total rube.

My search was not in vain. I found a three-volume set of books published jointly by the National Gallery of Art in Washington, D.C., and the Oxford University Press: *Artists' Pigments: A Handbook of Their History and Characteristics*. These books were filled with highly detailed information. Each chapter presented a different pigment, documenting its characteristics with laboratory analyses such as mass spectrography, chromatography, spectral absorption curves, X-ray diffraction patterns, photomicrographs, scanning electron micrographs, and a host of other analytical methods. I felt simultaneously cowed by the depth of information and heartened that there might be some meat on the bone of the idea of making a thesis project out of examining Gray Eyes's painting. Foolish me, I thought all I would need to do was fill in the gap between what the authors of the articles knew about the general topic and what I needed to know in particular about Gray Eyes's painting, write it up, and run it by Molly Chang for approval.

At lunchtime, I checked the volumes out of the library and took them home to Faye's house, where I set myself up with a comfy overstuffed chair and ottoman, a PB&J, a cup of tea, and a plate of chocolate-chip cookies. In fact I wolfed down the sandwich on the way between the kitchen and the chair, but I do mean to suggest that I was trying to feed myself a balanced diet. Stuffing the first cookie into my mouth, I picked up Volume 2 and opened it at random. I had gone through volume 1 at the library. I found myself in chapter two of *Ultramarine Blue, Natural and Artificial*, by Joyce Plesters.

I am not a strong reader. Reading is a linear sequential activity, and I have a time-space random kind of mind, built for visualizing problems in 3- and 4-D. So naturally I turned first to the illustrations. Figure 1 was captioned, "Lapis lazuli from Afghanistan. Cut and polished specimen. White veins of crystalline impurities and gold-colored flecks of pyrites are visible."

Cool, I thought. *Ultramarine-blue pigment was once ground from lapis lazuli. It's a semiprecious stone, so that must have been expensive!*

I went to my room and pulled my copy of *Dana's Manual of Mineralogy* off of the bookshelf in search of details on lapis lazuli. *Dana's* advised me that the part of the stone that was used as pigment was in fact a mineral called lazurite, which is the blue part of lapis lazuli, and that the white streaks were calcite, which, together with the pyrite and pyroxene and other silicate minerals, made up the marbled appearance. *The painter would try to remove the calcite and pyrite from the lazurite,* I supposed. *But trace impurities would persist in the pigment, and the stone would vary with its source, perhaps making it possible to identify its source. This is going to be great!*

Figure two, on the next page, was a detail from Titian's *Madonna and Child with Saints John the Baptist and Catherine of Alexandria.* "The Madonna's robe is painted in natural ultramarine," the caption informed me. *That's why the Madonna always wore blue,* I decided, in an art history "aha." *The paint was so expensive that it became an indicator of value and status.*

I was on a roll. But then I got to looking at the figures in the painting. The seated Madonna was serene, soft, and loving, and appeared tall and strong, like Faye. She even looked somewhat like Faye, her dark hair parted down the middle, accentuating a patrician brow and straight nose. The infant Christ lay supine on her lap. A woman in yellow knelt at the Madonna's knee, her face bent close to the child's, her arms around him, as if in desperate need to be near the child's tiny body.

Needless to say, this image got me thinking about Baby Sloane. Throughout the day I had been pushing away a deep sense of heaviness. Now I realized where that heaviness was coming from: I missed that baby very, very badly. Since her birth, I had not before been separated from her for longer than a few hours, and now the gap was accumulating into days.

I thought of phoning the Irma Hotel, thinking that Faye would probably have moved there, but knew that if she was there at this hour, she and the baby would be trying to take a nap, and I should not interrupt. To fill the void in my heart, I thought about writing to Jack, but that idea fell flat as well.

The book closed itself in my lap, my excitement dead.

At least it's a female saint that's bending over the child, I thought bitterly. *If Tanya was right, it would have been some guy saint, not this woman in yellow.*

I ate another cookie—or two, or three—took some sips of tea and stared out the window at the street.

A bright yellow rental van was just pulling up. I surmised that Fritz's furniture must be arriving.

I needed to be around another human being, and the sooner the better, so I got up and wandered outside to see if my new neighbor needed any help. I found him lowering a liftgate from the van, getting ready to offload some furniture. "Good afternoon, Fritz," I said, as I sauntered up the sidewalk. "Can I give you a hand?"

He turned around and smiled. "Sure," he said. He had swapped the floppy sweats for a T-shirt and a pair of jeans, and I was pleased to note that all that running and stretching had worked to good effect on his musculature. I decided again with satisfaction that he was sufficiently good-looking—not to mention classy—to turn Faye's head.

As I joined Fritz on the liftgate, I set out to make small talk. "I've just been reading a set of books about artists' pigments. In one book, half the chapters are about yellow. Now you drive up in a yellow truck."

Fritz smiled at me. "You have a lively mind, Em Hansen. You just stroll up and say, 'I've just been reading some books about pigments.' "

Pleased at the compliment, I helped Fritz untether a piece of furniture so we could move it out of the truck. "Yeah, well. Funny, the associations colors can have. I see a big rental truck this color and all I can think about is Oklahoma City and the first World Trade Center bombing. Nowadays I see as many of these trucks painted white. I guess they're trying to edge away from the negative publicity."

I looked up. Fritz was looking straight at me, and he was no longer smiling. As I connected with his gaze, he averted his eyes to the floor of the truck for a moment, then looked at me again, this time trying to smile but not quite making it. I could not tell whether he was annoyed, disgusted, or about to get sick.

I said, "Sorry. It's just the work I do. You see it's the colors, really, not the bombing. Bombs—"

"Let's not talk about bombs, okay?"

"Sure," I said, my curiosity now running rampant.

"Tell me about another color," he said firmly.

I paused, mentally jogging around ultramarine-blue and the associations with it that had propelled me away from my studies. "Well, there's verdigris; that's a nice turquoise color that hails from antiquity."

"Ah, antiquity," he echoed, working a nice blue corduroy couch loose from the stack of belongings in the truck.

"Yeah, these books are great. They list how these guys called colormen used to make some of the pigments. I can practically quote you the line for verdigris: 'According to the medieval recipes, copper strips are attached to a wooden block containing acetic acid, and then buried in dung,' " I said, daintily crooking a pinkie.

"Mm. Sounds . . . delectable," Fritz said.

Together Fritz and I hefted the couch out of the truck and into the living room. *It's not a couch, it's a love seat,* I thought cagily, as I helped him settle it in front of the fireplace. The house was an early Craftsman style, with lots of oak flooring and trim, and the big comfy couch looked nice there, inviting. I imagined a warm fire and some cozy snuggling going on, just the tonic Faye needed.

Next, we brought in some nice side chairs and an end table. "Where do you think I ought to put the table?" he asked.

I cast an eye around the room. "Over here," I said. "That way it's handy to the best lounging spot in the room, but not in the main traffic pattern. You can put your beer here and tuck your copies of *Pilot* magazine into the rack underneath it."

Fritz nodded. "I like that," he said. "Now, how about the lamps?"

"Here and here," I suggested, pointing at the obvious positions to illuminate reading. "You get good natural light for daytime reading by this chair and ottoman, but at night you'll want to be over there, facing the fireplace."

"Just so."

In half an hour, we had set up the entire living room, even putting pictures on the walls. He had some decent serigraph prints of high, floaty mountains, nothing too extraordinary but darned easy to look at, and he held them in various positions while I backed up and checked the proportions of the pictures relative to the other large objects in the room, all the time thinking how impressed Faye would be with his taste. As a finishing touch, he opened a cardboard box filled with carefully wrapped framed photographs of his son at various ages, which I helped him array across the mantelpiece. "Nice-looking kid," I said, looking at a lovely snap of the boy at about age two, showing a nice round face with big blue eyes and wild blond curls, lit by a gorgeous smile.

"My son's very special to me," he replied.

"You miss him."

"Yeah. Like I said, he's in Germany with his mom right now. When he's in the States I get him most weekends." He shook himself slightly, as if snapping himself back into focus. He looked around the room. "This looks great," he said. "So, is this what you do for a living?"

"What?"

"The colors and all. Are you an interior decorator?"

I began to laugh. "No way. I'm a geologist. The pigment books are for a forensics project I'm working on."

Fritz looked lost.

I shook my head in amazement. "Pigments are geology, get it? They're little bits of rock, finely ground up. Some pigments are animal-based, and some are vegetable, but most are mineral. Or, these days, most everything is synthetic, but when you think about it, synthetics are like minerals that are man-made, and they're derived from mined materials."

"Oh. I never knew that. But of course I never thought about it, either. Color is just . . . color. But I guess there's more to it than that."

"A whole lot. But I'd have to be a chemist or a physicist to really get into all the business about excitement of the electron levels. That part is a total mystery to me. But I can handle the literal part of pigments: A blue rock generally becomes a blue pigment. Plain and simple. Then you hand it over to an artist, who mixes it in oil or water or some other medium, and . . . then we're into art, and that's not mystery, that's magic."

He smiled and shook his head. "I took chemistry and physics in college, but I just design aircraft. Composites. Stabilities. Color is something some other guy paints on the outside of the bird to get it to look sweet." He gave me an uncertain smile. "Got a little more time? I could use your help with the . . . well, the beds."

Oh, a bit of shyness here? How charming. "Sure," I said. I helped him muscle the kid's bunk bed into the first bedroom, and then we went after a nice, big queen-sized sleigh bed that tucked nicely into the larger bedroom toward the back of the house. "Nice carving in this thing," I commented. I ran a hand along the footboard as I held it so that he could set up the rails.

"Thanks. I got it at an estate sale a couple years back. Sure beats having the box spring and mattress down on the floor."

"How long you been divorced?" I asked.

Fritz grinned at me. "I like you, Em," he said. "You want to know something, you open your mouth and ask, don'tcha."

I blushed. "Yeah, well . . ."

"The answer is three years. Three years next month, to be precise. We were separated for a year before that. Marsha is an efficient woman, and we didn't have that much to divide—except custody—so it went pretty quickly. She got the bed. I didn't want it."

"Sorry if I'm being nosy."

"You are, but I don't mind it. Besides, we might just as well get to know each other, eh?"

"Eh."

"Now you: How old is Sloane Renee?"

"Seven months."

"A nice age. Which one of you had her?"

"Huh?"

"Which one of you's the birth mother?"

My mouth dropped open. I stood there catching flies while the dime dropped and I sorted out what he was saying. "Oh! Oh, you think . . ."

Suddenly Fritz turned scarlet. "Oh, shit," he said under his breath. "I mean—oh, I am sorry. I thought you were . . ."

"A lesbian couple? A two-mommy household?"

He gave me a wilted grin, the kind that looks like a person's just swallowed about a quart of glue. "I am such an idiot. You know, that was number eight on Marsha's list of the top ten reasons why she had to divorce me: I am totally clueless about people."

My first reaction was frustration: How was he supposed to find Faye attractive if he thought she wasn't interested in men? I said, "Fritz, you're a sweet guy. But no, Faye and I are not, uh . . ." Then it hit home that this guy had thought that *I* was one of the guys, too. And he wasn't clueless. No, he'd had some clues, so what were they? Did I look a little too butch in my blue jeans and sloppy shirt?

Fritz's posture had gone oddly formal, and he was furtively looking me up and down in reevaluation. I realized that *he* had just realized he was standing in his bedroom with a heterosexual female he hardly knew. "Let's see what else needs to come in from the truck," I said, diplomatically leading the way out of the room, but deep inside, I felt sick. Something strange was happening to me, like waking up one morning to discover that I was a bug. And it was not just a matter of identity: The rules of the world seemed to have shifted. It was as if a hole was opening underneath my feet, and I was hanging over a dark, cavernous space that had no bottom.

We made short and austere work out of bringing the mattress and box springs in from the truck and hefting them into place, after which Fritz said he was certain he could get the rest in by himself and I excused myself and went back to Faye's house.

Like an automaton, I picked up the mail on the way in from the street and tossed it onto the kitchen counter with the rest of the pile that had accumulated while I'd been in Cody. I didn't even look through it. Certainly none of it was for me, because I did not have a life.

I decided that I needed a beer. I usually did not drink when I was unhappy, as booze sure hadn't fixed things for my mother, but just then I could not think beyond the look on Fritz's face when he realized that I was not what he had assumed. That look had said, *Something is wrong with this woman.*

As I reached for the refrigerator door I noticed that the envelope on the top of the stack of mail was in fact addressed to me.

It was a letter from my mother.

Another remittance check, guilt money to cover the hole in her conscience where she kicked her own daughter out, I thought bitterly.

I decided to open it, extract the check, and light a match to it. *To hell with her. To hell with Faye and her new friend and his painting. To hell with my master's degree. I'll just get a job, any job, find myself a studio apartment and a can of dog food to live on, climb the rest of the way down into my emotional hole, and pull the lid on after me.*

I grabbed the beer and a strike-anywhere match for the letter and headed down the hall to my room, tearing open the slim envelope as I went. Inside I found a check and a folded piece of paper with only one paragraph that read:

Dear Emily,

Here's a miscellaneous contribution toward your education. Let me say as always that I am proud of you for going after an advanced degree. Don't worry about paying this one back because I have a rather healthier cash flow situation than usual. This is because I have sold the ranch to the Nature Conservancy. Your father and I had to mortgage it to the quick years ago. Revenues have not exceeded costs for many years. With the rise in the value of the land, I can this way pay off the debt and have enough to retire on. I will be moving up to Douglas where I'll be closer to friends and services, so at least you won't have to look after me in my advancing years.

Sorry—

Mother

The world went numb and the open bottle of beer slipped out of my hand, hit the floor, and began to empty itself onto the rug.

She was sorry.

The hallway seemed to bend. I grabbed at the wall so I wouldn't go down, and stumbled into my room through a narrowing world.

10

Faye and Sloane Renee arrived home the next afternoon in a big, gray rental car driven by Tert Krehbeil. They came into the house laughing and giggling, all just as giddy as if they'd been having a tickle fight. I withdrew quickly before they spotted me, and stayed in my room for as long as I could get away with it.

"Em?" Faye called out at last. "Are you here?"

"Just finishing something for class," I called back. I was in fact doing nothing, unless you count staring at the ceiling as doing something. This was because I was lying on my back, which was a change from lying on my face, the posture in which I had spent most of the hours since reading my mother's note. "I'm right in the middle of an important paragraph," I added, fleshing out my lie. "I'll be out in a moment."

I heard Faye move down the hallway past my room and enter the bathroom. "What's going on, Em? It smells like a brewery in here!"

I didn't answer. Hours after the beer had gone flat in the carpeting, I had used a towel to soak up the worst of it, but had not moved past wringing out the towel into the bathtub and hanging it up over the curtain rail.

When I did finally drag myself out of my cave, Faye had disappeared into her own room with Sloane to do the things mothers constantly need to do for babies. That left me to face off with His Nibs in the living room. "Hi," I said, my voice coming out as flat as the beer now was.

"Hi."

"Pleasant drive?" I asked, meaning to be ironical. I managed to sound sullen.

"Very pleasant."

We stood and stared at each other for a while. He appeared just as peculiarly serene as ever. His eyes were so pale that it was almost as if a silvery light played constantly across his face, a sort of Charlton Heston–plays–Moses effect.

In the long hours of nighttime and daylight since I had read my mother's letter, I had moved from feeling shock to nausea to extreme self-pity, but now I felt only a deep, cold fury. Apparently this didn't show, because as Tert spoke again, his tone suggested that he found nothing unusual about the state of my composure. "As I mentioned in Cody, I'd like to hire you to investigate a painting," he said, coming right to the point. His point. The only point left in the world.

I picked up a soft fleece baby blanket and began to fold it. It had slid onto the floor next to the few items of luggage that had come in from the car. Had Gray Eyes carried it in and dropped it like this? *No*, I had to admit, *this is more like Faye, to be so casual with the baby's things. This man I do not know, not really. Perhaps he's nice. Perhaps he truly cares about people other than himself. Perhaps I'm just imploding on my empty little life, and I should just head out for the evening and leave them to the house, and to their bright future together.* I set the blanket on the back of the couch and smoothed it with my hand.

It was several moments before I realized that I had not replied to the man's proposal, which could just fund the research for my thesis, that little five- to twenty-thousand-dollar budget item that stood between so many people and their degrees. Certainly I would not cash my mother's check. I cleared my throat. "A painting," I said. "Just exactly what do you want me to do for you?" After another moment, I added, "Tert."

He folded his arms across his chest and raised one hand to his mouth. He played the fingers of that hand across his lips, as if exploring his own sensual beauty. "May I count on your discretion?"

"Yes."

"Then I am your client, and you will keep my confidence."

"Sure."

"I don't know if Faye told you that the painting in question is a Remington."

"Ah."

"So it would be quite valuable. It has been in the family since it was first exhibited at Knoedler's Gallery in New York almost one hundred years ago. Knoedler's was Remington's main outlet, aside from the magazine contracts and the occasional sale straight out of his studio."

"Mm."

He began to move in a circle around the room, arms still folded, now looking at the gorgeous Chinese silk rug that Faye had laid down, now gazing out the window or briefly examining one of her prize Acoma pots. I felt almost as if I were watching him in the museum again, taking in an exhibit, except that this time he was talking to me. His speech sounded odd, as if he were speaking from the depths of a dream. He said, "My grandfather purchased the painting. He brought it home from New York on the train to Philadelphia, thence out on the spur line that comes out to Lancaster. My grandmother met him at the station in a hired cab, and he gave it to her then. It was a birthday present, you see. She had always wanted to travel west, but had been forbidden by her parents. The story goes that they were afraid she might marry a cowboy and live a life of pain and drudgery. They had money, you see—lots of money—and they did not want their daughter to suffer. But my grandmother had read the stories in *Collier's Magazine*, and her heart was full of romance."

He paused in his recitation and stared out into the street. Cars were going past, the late-afternoon return of the working world to their little homes. I had time to think on the image of his grandmother, forbidden to visit the West that had captured her heart. I knew that love. I loved the West to the last blade of grass, craggy peak, and lost calf that dwelt within its panorama. I loved it to the very depths of my soul. I loved it to the tight spin of every last electron in my body. But the West was more than just a romance. The West was a place of simple virtues, where lines between right and wrong were more precisely drawn than in the East. Doing what is right is embedded in the Code of the West.

I wondered if that code had called to Tert's grandmother, or if she merely liked the idea of being somewhere she hadn't been. She had buried her rebellion in house and family, no doubt; here stood her grandson as proof of the fruits of her duty. And she had loved her husband, I was sure of that even without knowing the rest of the story. She had met him at the station, and he had brought her the best thing short of a train ticket west: a Remington, fresh from the artist's brush, its colors bright and true, the varnishes untouched by the grit and yellowing of time. A Remington, the genius spawn of the finest Impressionist of the American West, a burst of prairie light frozen in paint.

Softly, I asked, "What was the scene?"

He sighed, long and deeply. "It was a group of horses in the moonlight in a corral. I guess you'd call them ponies. There's a cabin in the background, just a touch of candlelight coming from it."

He paused a moment in his description, moved up close to the window of the room we were standing in, and stared outward, his back to me. "Something has frightened the ponies. They lower their heads as they shy away from something outside the frame of the picture. . . . There's something out there." He shook his head. "I spent hours staring at that painting when I was a child. Hours."

Now he turned and looked straight at me, his gray eyes locking with mine. "So you can imagine my surprise . . . my *horror* . . . when I realized that the painting was no longer the original."

I could not figure out how to respond. In reciting his drama, he had managed momentarily to jog me from the darkness of my mood; he had reminded me that I was not the only creature in the universe that suffered. I could not imagine why he had brought this to me. He did not know me. I was just a friend of a friend, and I wasn't sure how well he even knew Faye. And the experience of seeing inside him, however briefly, made me feel oddly naked.

Fortunately, Faye chose that moment to enter the room, and she was carrying Baby Sloane. The instant I saw her, I was again engulfed with the warmth and pain of my jagged heart. I rushed to her, and Faye handed her to me. I bent my body around her, snuggled her tiny head up beneath my cheek, and squeezed her as close as I could without troubling her. The scent of baby soothed me, reminding me that there were things in the world more important than land, or any particular outcome of any particular problem of the mind. I squeezed my eyes shut so that I would not cry in front of Tert or the stranger the child's mother had become.

"Am I interrupting anything?" Faye inquired of her friend.

Tert cleared his throat. "I was just telling Emily about the painting," he replied. "Perhaps we should see what you've got in the kitchen. It was a long drive, and I could really use a beer about now."

They left me alone with the little girl. I sat down in the gliding rocker Faye used when nursing her, curled her in my arms, and quit fighting back my sorrow.

11

WHEN I WOKE UP THE NEXT MORNING, I DECIDED THAT I'D SNEAK into the nursery and have some time with the baby—if she was not in bed with Faye—then grab some breakfast and make a clean escape before the happy family crawled out of their various rooms. But on opening the door to my room, I heard sounds in the kitchen. I approached cautiously, and found Faye fussing over something on the stove and Tert Krehbeil already sitting at the table with Sloane Renee on his lap, feeding her Cream of Wheat. The baby was staring up into his eyes with the awestruck glow of an Italian Renaissance saint observing an angel. I stopped short in the doorway, and was just throwing my feet into reverse when Faye spotted me.

She said, "Oh, there you are, Em. Hey, I was wondering if you could take the baby while Tert and I catch a little skiing up at Snowbird."

"Um, ah . . . sure. I can take her to class with me, I guess."

"No, I don't mean for the whole day. This is a Friday, right? You've got classes just in the morning, and besides, you already missed two days of class this week helping me out. So, no, we were thinking of just doing a half-day pass." She gave me a pleasant little smile.

"The eggs are scorching," I said, then, realizing that she was trying to be considerate, added, "Okay, I'll cover you from noon onward. Eleven, if you meet me at the Geology Department and bring the baby to me."

Faye stabbed at the mess of eggs with a spatula. She had once been a fairly accomplished cook when she put her mind to it, but with the distractions of motherhood, culinary disasters like this had become more frequent and of increasingly greater magnitude.

Tert said, "Thanks, Em. That's really nice of you. But as regards our business arrangement—"

"I need to talk to you about that," I said quickly.

The temperature of his gaze cooled. "You sound uncertain."

"I have some questions." I veered away from Faye's seared omelette toward the cupboard, grabbed a cup of coffee, and led Tert out of Faye's hearing into the living room. Once he was settled on the couch and I had room to pace, I said, "First, it's obvious to me that there are a great many people more qualified than I am to evaluate your painting. Some kind of art specialist."

"A conservator," he said.

"Okay, a conservator." I was annoyed that I hadn't even known the correct term. "But you need a private detective because the art world is a nosy place and this is a matter you wish to keep just that way—private."

He nodded. "That is correct."

"Have you taken up the matter with the appropriate sheriff's department or police?"

Tert averted his gray eyes to indicate emotional discomfort at the very thought.

I said, "Well, how do you expect me to find out when the switch was made—if indeed the painting is faked—and who did it? I can't subpoena evidence, and I can't—"

"All I want you to do is document that it is not original."

I took a deep breath and let it out. I said, "Well, I am not a licensed detective, but I am a professional geologist with some experience in forensics, and you're talking about a matter that a forensic geologist would categorize as trace evidence: artists' pigments." I paused, giving myself time to contemplate the line of B.S. I was coming out with. I was almost even convincing myself. "I've been reading up on these things. It's an interesting topic. You see, the thing is, I'd like to make a master's thesis out of the work."

Tert looked pained. "No. I'm sorry. The information would be proprietary."

"Well, then, I have a proposal. I believe Faye said you have other paintings, am I right?"

"What do you have in mind?"

"I'd like to study one of them. Perhaps one of the ones you were going to loan to the Whitney. I could go there, and—"

He nodded. "I see where you're going with this. I could probably arrange that."

"And I'll need your permission to consult with colleagues at the FBI labs. I will be absolutely discreet, don't you worry. Your name needn't be mentioned."

He smiled vaguely.

"Then I'll do it," I said. "My fee is fifty bucks an hour plus expenses, plus I get to work with another painting."

Tert did not even bat an eye. "Agreed."

"Where do you keep the family paintings?"

He paused a moment, caught off guard. "Uh, at the family farm."

"Where's that?"

"But you would see the paintings when they are hung in Cody." His smile came into focus. He seemed pleased about something he wasn't saying.

I nodded. I wasn't sure what he was hiding, but I saw no reason to go clear to the East Coast if the paintings were coming to me. "I've got exams and reports due in the next few days, but spring break starts in a couple of weeks. I can start then."

"Good."

"Where is the painting?" I asked, starting to raise my coffee for a sip now that the business was settled.

"In the car."

I stopped with the coffee halfway to my lips. "In the *car*? You left a million-dollar piece of artwork in the trunk of your *car*?"

He looked mildly affronted. "The original would be worth at least three million. But as I said, the painting in the car is not the original."

"You're pretty damned sure of that."

"I am."

Tert went out to his car, unlocked the trunk, and returned with what looked like a long, fat mailing tube. He headed into the dining room, pulled a handkerchief from his pocket, fastidiously dusted the table, then opened the tube and extracted a roll of canvas. This he unfurled and spread out flat on the table, exposing a layer of cheesecloth. He lifted the cloth, and there before me was a picture of horses in a corral at night that sure as hell *looked* like a real Remington. "It's beautiful," I said.

"Not as beautiful as the original," he said sadly.

I stared into the painting. The horses were gloriously rendered, and full of tension. But it was odd seeing a supposed masterwork without its frame and without even the stretcher bars. "You removed its skeleton," I said.

"Easier to transport this way. The stretchers are in the car. I can take it home with me on the plane."

"Take it home? Then you didn't bring it out with you from the East?"

"No."

"Where was it?"

He paused as if trying to decide what or how much to tell me. "It was near Cody."

Near Cody. My conversation with Frank Barnes came back to me. "Do you mean on a ranch?" I asked.

"Yes . . . at a summer place my grandmother owned."

"Oh. Is it still in the family?"

Tert shifted uncomfortably. "I haven't been there for . . . a number of years."

"Then you can't pinpoint exactly when the switch was made," I said.

He stood with his hands gripped behind his back, drawing himself into a caricature of a British lord. He said nothing, the gentry defending the honor of privilege.

I said, "I looked through every book on Remington I could find in the University library. I saw several other night paintings."

"Nocturnes," Tert corrected me.

"Yes. Well, some of the earlier works seemed a little cruder than others. Even Remington saw that. The text said that he routinely built bonfires in his backyard and burned paintings that he thought inferior." I knew I might be pulling my thesis project out from under my own feet, but it was essential that I approach the science with utmost integrity. If I started out with a lie, then the whole thing would be a sham. "It could be that you've got an original there that just isn't as wonderful as some of his others, and you're not remembering it as clearly as you thought. What if—"

He held up a hand. "I understand what you're saying. I at first tried to convince myself of the same thing. But, no, I am certain." He turned dismissively and moved back into the kitchen, where he resumed his seat at the table and once again began to feed cereal to the baby. Faye had put Sloane Renee in her high chair during our absence, and the baby watched us with grave eyes. Faye watched also, but more covertly.

"Then why did you bring it to the museum?" I asked, following him into the room. "You'll excuse me if I'm a little confused, but why hire me in the name of discretion if you've already shown it to the Remington committee in Cody? Why close the barn door after the horse has escaped?"

"They didn't see this painting."

"Oh? Then why were you there?"

Faye rolled her eyes at me.

Tert said, "Because I am a member of that committee."

This revelation hit me like a board with a nail in the end of it. I looked back and forth between Tert and Faye. *They lured me into this project like a rat to the cheese.* "So you're one of their experts."

"That's right." He set down the baby's spoon and stared at me.

"Then what the hell do you need me for?"

He waved a hand as if to clear obnoxious smoke. "I'm on that committee because I know Remington's painting style. His brushwork. The scumbles and glazes. We do aesthetic evaluation, not scientific documentation. I know his materials in a gross sense—the type of canvas he used, the Shattuck keys on the stretchers—but I know little of what you call trace evidence, and certainly cannot do the microscopic work. That analysis is usually done by a conservator. But as you accurately surmised, it's a small world, and I want this kept quiet. And my reasons for doing so are my own, and I will not discuss them."

I knew right then that he was lying. *I have not forgotten the first time I saw you. In the gallery, before you knew who I was. You were talking to another man—another committee member, no doubt—about the shade of green Remington used in the nocturne of the man by the Conestoga wagon. Hooker's green. You named the exact pigments that make that color—Prussian blue and something that begins with a* G*—and if you're worth your salt to that committee, you'll know all about the National Gallery's books on pig-*

ments. Yes, you know a lot more than you're letting on. And in some important way, in some critical detail, you are lying to me!

Tert and I stared at each other, neither of us blinking.

The baby let out a shriek.

I have no patience for lies. I said, "So, getting us up to Cody was all a ruse. You never had anything that needed to be transported."

Faye's spine stiffened noticeably.

For a moment Tert evinced incomprehension. Then he said, "Oh. Oh, I see what's upsetting you. No, in fact there *are* paintings that need transportation, but the Remington was not one of them."

"Most of the rest of the collection is near Lancaster at your mother's house, isn't it?" Faye asked.

He said, "I'm loaning them several Russells." His tone was now professorial, almost condescending.

"*Several* Russells." *Oh deary me.* I shifted my gaze back to Faye, who had tipped her head sharply to one side, her lips pursed as if affecting an innocent whistling.

Gritting my teeth, I said, "Fine, just fine. I think I'm getting up to speed now. Right now I need to head to class. I'll see you both at eleven. And you," I leaned forward and gave Sloane Renee a kiss on her fuzzy little head, "I will see all afternoon."

I got my book bag and got my butt on the bus to the U as fast as I could, quick before I blew my chance for a thesis project the rest of the way out the window.

I sat the baby that afternoon while the fun couple skied, and while the baby napped, I took a tour of the guest room to see what I could discover about our resident liar. He had left behind a suitcase and a thin leather attaché. There was nothing of interest in the first, no electronic gizmos such as computer or Palm Pilot in the other. About all I found of interest was a small spiral-bound book full of notes written in a tight little handwriting which I presumed to be his. They read like this:

May 3rd

*Rem to H**
Wyo / UPS (spec.)—SAC / will call
O/—ridge / hoc*
Pd. / ck + cash

June 8th
orange—no. 26
223,000 profit
split / 50.50

Aug 12th
Big One—10% to [ ]
new frame—Rocetti/Boston
Denver—van / cash
Split w/ GRR / London a/*

Sept. 30th
LA—SF—Napa
7 days
2 + 2 + 2
3 w/c—2 a*ib—1 ltr.—2*****
7 sales—1.43
3 way split / ? / 500 net to me!

Dec 8th
It's starting to look like . . .
2 b/w w/e
unframed
Por**t* Denver / Dallas
~~100K to Mother~~
NO / to me!

Feb 8th
Can R—letter
show to JST
cash or trade
trades to Scottsdate/Tuscon
Net: $15,120.—

I spent several minutes trying to dope out the entries, but beyond "Rem to H*" possibly referring to a Remington, and the few references that looked like payments and splits, I had no clue what they meant.

The next morning Tert presented me with a check for three thousand dollars (drawn off his business, Krehbeil Gallery, Philadelphia), which he suggested might cover my initial fees and expenses (I guess Faye had told him I was broke); shook my hand (although I would have preferred to stick it in a jar of eels), and caught an early flight home to Philadelphia. And that, I hoped and prayed, was the last Salt Lake City would see of Tert Krehbeil. Faye seemed a bit let-down for a day or two, but she did not broach the subject of their acquaintance, and neither did I. She went on about her life, which involved going to a lot of yoga classes and disappearing for long hours with the baby in the jogger, and I went back to my schoolbooks, or tried to. Bit by bit, I began to get over the shock of losing the ranch. Unfortunately, part of how I got over that shock was to throw myself into my work, which now included Tert's painting.

I shall be candid. I dove into the job like any other form of an obsessive-compulsive disorder, first rationalizing that I'd pick up the books I needed while studying other things, and then using my growing interest in artists' pigments as a carrot on the end of the stick to reward myself for doing other tasks—as in, *I'll read one more chapter in my geochemistry text and then I'll let myself kick back and fiddle with pigments some more.* In no time at all, I was fully out of control, taking every available moment to mess with the project, rationalizing that I was working on my thesis, but knowing full well I was digging at some kind of crime.

I hungered for another look at the painting, but alas, Mr. Gray Eyes had taken it with him, leaving only a tiny sample of each major paint color. These we had carefully chipped from the extreme edges of the painting where it had been covered by the frame. It was easy to see where the frame had lain because the colors were a bit brighter there, which suggested that the painting was not brand-new.

I kept the paint chips in little glass vials to keep them pristine. I spent an inordinate amount of time studying them with my hand lens, dreaming dreams of Remington. Had this bit of color flowed from his brush, or from that of an impostor? I laid plans for getting time with the analytical equipment in the Geology Department, and imagined hugely magnified views of my tiny charges.

As the weather was nice, I got to sitting out on the front porch with my books. That's where I was the middle of the following week, when Fritz Calder happened by on his way home from a run.

"Good morning," he said. "You're Em, right?"

"Yes. And you're still Fritz."

He wiped his forehead with the sleeve of his sweatshirt, assumed a pose of thoughtfulness for a moment, and then nodded decisively. "I suppose you're right," he said. "But then, Kafka woke up one morning feeling bugged, and it was true."

"Are you feeling bugged?"

He smiled. "Nah. It's just embarrassing that I have trouble remembering peoples' names."

I changed the subject. "Did your kid come back from Germany yet?"

His smile broadened to an expectant grin. "Two more days and he'll be home. He'll be here for the weekend." He turned and moved toward me, his running shoes scuffing the sandstone flags of the walkway. He came up on the porch and sat down next to me, his greater weight moving the swing to a different plane of motion. "What you reading there?"

"Stuff." I turned over the book so he could see the cover. It was *A Concise Encyclopaedia of Artists' Materials.*

He took the book and began to flip through the pages. Unconsciously he set the swing into a gently spiraling motion. I found this soothing. He read around in the text for a while and I soaked up the comfort of having a big, warm body near me. Trying to focus again on the book, I said, "Like I said, stuff. But fascinating, eh?"

" 'Mediums and Adhesives,' " he said, reading the chapter headings aloud as he went. " 'Pigments.' 'Solvents and Diluents.' Diluents? Huh, I thought the word would be 'dilutents.' "

"That's not a word. I looked it up. 'Diluents' looked weird to me, too."

" 'Supports,' " he read. "Is that like the canvas?"

I said, "Canvas, wood, cardboard, paper . . ."

" 'Tools and Equipment.' I can get that part. That's paintbrushes and such." When he had turned to the last page he pointed to the illustration printed on it and read the caption aloud. " 'Containers for oil paint: *(a)* the skin or bladder in which the mixed and ground paint was kept, with a tack-like piece of bone to puncture the skin; *(b)* the firm metal tube with piston and refilled with paint; *(c)* the collapsible metal tube in use today.' "

I leaned in close to get a look at that illustration. " '*(a)*' and '*(b)*' are pretty bizarre, huh? I guess screw caps are a fairly new invention."

He skimmed the adjoining text, and read, " 'The development of collapsible tubes as containers for colors occurred largely during the middle of the nineteenth century. Bladders were still listed in catalogs until 1840.' "

I looked askance at him. "You seem genuinely interested in this stuff."

He shrugged his athletic shoulders. "Sure. I read that book . . . you know, *Girl with a Pearl Earring*."

"I don't know that one."

"Oh, it's a novel about this fictitious girl who worked for Vermeer. The part I liked best was where she used to hang out in his attic grinding the pigments for him. She really got into it. Very sensual scene."

"What was she grinding? Was it a mineral pigment?"

"Some semiprecious rock," he said. "I forget the name of it. He used it to make ultramarine-blue."

"Lapis lazuli." *Ultramarine, the color of the Madonna's robe.* I thought of Sloane Renee and looked at my hands to cover my feelings.

Fritz turned to me. "Are you all right?"

"I'm fine," I lied. "Hey, I meant to get you over for a meal before this. Are you free tonight?"

"No, but I'm reasonable. What brand of microbrew shall I bring?" he asked.

He hadn't been sure what my name was, but he had remembered that I preferred beer to wine. As I noticed that, I realized that it had in fact bothered me that he hadn't been sure of my name. Why? "I like the Polygamy Porter they make at Squatter's," I said, immediately wishing I had named a different label. *First he thinks we're a gay couple. Now he'll think we're a couple of sisters looking for a sire!*

" 'Why Have Just One?' " Fritz parried, quoting the microbrewery's advertising slogan for its infamous porter.

I felt myself turning red. "It's actually pretty good stuff."

He gave me a roguish wink. "I like it, too. What time?"

"Seven."

"I'll be there." He got up and headed home to a shower and his afternoon's work.

WHEN FRITZ REAPPEARED at seven carrying the six-pack, I had completed my Geochemistry reading and started on a take-home exam for Statistics.

I looked up to appraise the candidate. He was nicely turned out in a pressed blue oxford cloth shirt and blue jeans.

I grinned, certain that this six-foot-two-inch stack of manhood would turn Faye's head. "Come on in," I said boisterously. "I told Faye you were coming and she took pity on you."

"Oh? And she exhibits this sentiment how?"

"She would not let me cook. The aroma from the kitchen is her current specialty, pizza and salad. The pizza is takeout from the Pie Pizzeria. The salad she built herself. You can't burn salad."

"Unless you put it on the stove," he said, hurrying into the kitchen. At the precise moment he yanked the wooden bowl off the burner, the smoke alarm started to shriek.

Faye spun around and stared at him. He stared at her. He handed her the bowl. His mouth opened slightly. I thought, *Music up. Close-up on hero and heroine moving helplessly into each other's arms. They kiss, they fall into bed. End of story as warm Pacific waves wash up on sunset beach.*

Unfortunately, things did not proceed quite that smoothly. On cue, the baby raised her voice from annoyed snit through basic banshee to advanced air-raid siren. Faye took the bowl from Fritz's hands, lifted to examine the damage to the bottom, and muttered, "Balls!" which caused Fritz to color slightly. Faye charged out of the kitchen and through the dining room at high speed, slammed the salad bowl on the table, and headed down the hall toward the baby's room.

Fritz turned from his position in the middle of the kitchen and looked at me inquiringly.

I said, "She's been getting a bit touchy about certain things lately."

"Such as?"

"Such as fancy kitchenwares given by her Aunt Nancy. You know, stuff you get for a wedding present but you can't afford to replace. Babies that show up six months after you get married. Things like that."

Fritz said, "And where is Mr. Faye?"

I moved up close to him so I could answer his question in a whisper. "He's dead. Died a month before the baby was born. So, you see . . ."

Fritz moved his head up and down in one long, eloquent *aha*. "Yes . . ." Then he sniffed the air, turned, and opened the oven door. Smoke billowed out. "I think the pizza's warmed up."

"Yes, so it appears."

He grabbed a hot pad and pulled it out. "Pepperoni and artichoke hearts, my fave."

"What luck."

Fritz appraised the smoking slab. "I think if we trim off the edges here it will be fine."

I let out a ragged breath. *He looks good in blue jeans, he flies a plane, he brings beer, and he knows how to say, "You're clueless in the kitchen" without it sounding like an insult. Why in God's name did his wife divorce him?*

Perhaps it was he who dumped her, I decided, falling into one of my itinerant internal debates.

He doesn't look like the dumping type, I volleyed.

What do you know? The pendulum of your life has swung way too close to forty without your ever seeing even the front side of a marriage, let alone the back, so what makes you an expert allofasudden?

About then, Faye marched back into the room carrying Sloane Renee, and Fritz went all googly over her. The baby, that is. He took her into his arms and whispered into her tiny shell of an ear. Faye might not even have existed for all the attention she got from him after that. He was pleasant, and said all the right things, but through three pieces of pizza and two beers he bounced that child on his knee, held her over his head like an airplane, played Where's-the-Baby, coddled, cuddled, cooed, and generally collapsed like a heap of mush around the amazing and remarkable Sloane Renee Latimer. Fritz Calder might be a good-looking buck and an eligible bachelor, but he was a touch too much aware of the baby and a touch too little aware of the mother to register on Faye's Richter scale. In fact, she excused herself at eight o'clock to put the baby to bed and did not return.

Fritz made no move to leave.

I offered him a brandy.

"No thanks," he said. "I got to fly tomorrow. You know the drill: eight hours bottle to throttle."

"You flying somewhere early?"

"Yeah, I have to take the prototype to Denver to show to an investor."

"Still looking for more funding?"

"Always looking for more funding. Want to come along?"

"A round-trip flight to Denver in a small plane. I used to do that with Faye. It was a blast. Skimming over the high peaks like an eagle, a sense that I owned the known universe. You mean come along just for the ride?"

He shrugged his shoulders. "Sure. I can always use a copilot. It gets lonesome up there."

I heaved a sigh. "I'd love to, but I have a lot of schoolwork to finish."

"Oh come on, you can catch up over spring break."

"I can't. Over the break I have to work for my living."

"What's the project?"

I made a zip-the-lips gesture. "Can't say more, sorry. And besides, I have the little one to care for whenever Faye needs help."

"Well, let me know if you ever decide to play hooky. It's Denver tomorrow, then L.A. on Friday, and Baltimore in about a week and a half."

"What's in Baltimore?"

"They have lots of interesting things in Baltimore. Like the east end of a railroad line that goes to Ohio. And parts for a widget I'm building."

"You got to fly all the way there to pick up parts? Why not have them shipped?"

He looked at the floor, his face clouding. "It's a design meeting. And I have to see some clients. And some money men."

I nodded. "Military stuff."

"Yeah."

"If you don't like military stuff, why do you do it?"

"You mean, apart from the fact that military contracting pays the bills, and supports my habit of tilting at the windmill of designing a new airplane? And keeps our nation strong?"

"It sounds like I've poked a nerve. I'm sorry."

He hunched his shoulders. At length, he said, "I used to fly for the military. I was a navy pilot. Jets."

He had told me he did not like bombs. Now he said he'd been a navy pilot. That sounded like an uncomfortable combination of traits. I said, "I didn't mean to pry, or to imply—"

"No, it's a legitimate question, and the problem is, I don't really have an answer for you, but I do mean to suggest that I don't disapprove of the military out-of-hand. Soldiers aren't bad things. Everyone agrees on self-defense, or almost everyone, and a lot of people believe in maintaining a standing army as a deterrent."

"I don't disagree."

"As I said. But beyond that, things get messy, because right there you move into the territory where things are no longer quite so black and white. You get into 'Who's in charge here, really?' and 'What's the agenda?' "

Trying to sound like I understood, I said, "It's like that for me as a geologist some days. We're paid to find resources, and we find them, all right, but we have absolutely no control over how it's gotten out of the ground, or by whom, and we sure as hell have no say over who's going to use it, or where, or how, or when."

He rose from the couch and shook his head. "Bottom line is, I haven't really sorted all this out yet."

"I'm sorry to open a can of worms."

"No, it's okay. Don't ever apologize to me for asking questions like that. Besides, it's me who should be apologizing. I kind of popped off on you. I—"

"Let's call it a draw," I said.

Fritz nodded and let himself out the door. I caught it before he could close it behind himself and told him good night.

Halfway down the walk toward the street, he turned around and faced me again, and said, "Thanks for dinner. I had a good time. Really."

"You're welcome any time." I shut the door against the night air, feeling like a prize jerk, not to mention a failure as a matchmaker. So I went to bed myself, carrying books about artists' pigments with me. It was time to set other peoples' worries aside, and just earn my damned degree.

THOSE OF YOU WHO HAVE WRITTEN A MASTER'S THESIS WILL BY now have begun to think, *Shouldn't Em be discussing her thesis idea with her advisor? You have to get your advisor's okay, don't you?*

Yes and yes. But I had a little problem, and that was that I had already blown one thesis project, and therefore did not want to go to Molly Chang with my hot idea until I was sure it wasn't going to cool off before the biscuits were baked. Instead I scheduled time on the analytical equipment at the University. I figured I'd spend spring break working up some hard data so that I could shove, not just an idea but full research parameters across Molly's desk. I would explain to her that I could not publish Tert's data (I would not even mention his name or the work in question), but that I had a lead on a similar set of data I could put into a thesis.

By the Monday before spring break, I had assembled quite a raft of materials. I had the National Gallery of Art's *Artists' Pigments*, volumes 1, 2 and 3, the *Short Encyclopaedia* (which I could not look at without pronouncing each and every vowel in my head), and now Weber's *Artists' Pigments*. To this stack, I had added my old mineralogy book (*Dana's Manual of Mineralogy*) and a few other texts. I also made another pass through the art section of the library stacks, adding several texts on Frederic Remington, and also two on George Catlin and one on Charlie Russell.

One morning when I again awakened too damned early, I turned on the light by my bed and read around in *Frederic Remington* by Peter Hassrick. It seemed a good survey of the life of Remington, so I got up and began tapping a summary into the computer, hoping that one day it would become a chapter in my thesis.

> Frederic Remington, born 1861 in upstate New York, was the son of a newspaperman. During the Civil War, Remington's father fought for the North and earned the rank of major, and was highly decorated for his valor. Young Frederic rounded out his basic education at a military academy in Massachusetts.
>
> In 1878, two months before his seventeenth birthday, he enrolled in art training at Yale. After three semesters, he left Yale in part because his father had died, leaving the family without income. Guardianship of young Fred passed to his uncle, who was "opposed to having any men artists in the family" and "desired to have him carry on the family tradition of writer-politician." He worked at various clerical jobs for a couple of years.
>
> At the age of twenty, he fell in love with Eva Caten and asked her father for her hand in marriage. Apparently finding young Frederic short on prospects, Eva's father sent him packing. To seek his fortune, Remington headed west.

Here I put down the book for a while and stared out the window toward the Oquirrh range, which that morning wore a fresh cap of snow tinted pink with the early light. I was liking this Remington guy. He was a restless, incurable romantic, just like me. I liked a man who was sensitive enough to become an artist yet tough enough to paint macho men and starkly beautiful scenery.

I tried to imagine the twenty-year-old painter heading west with his dreams. As the Oquirrhs turned from pink to yellow, I read further, then wrote:

> Remington came home two months later with a different sort of riches than he had imagined: His portfolio bulged with drawings, and he quickly sold one to *Harper's Weekly*, where it was reproduced as an engraving. Returning to the West as soon as he had passed his twenty-first birthday and collected his inheritance, Remington set himself up in sheep ranching in Kansas, and there he made enough of himself to finally win the hand of his beloved. When his fortunes in Kansas City failed, Eva went home to New York while Remington again traveled to collect material for magazine illustrations. Reunited with Eva a few months later, he made the rounds in New York

> City, peddling his drawings to editors to be used as illustrations for stories of the West. When there weren't enough stories, he wrote them himself.
>
> Remington would return again and again to his beloved West to collect artifacts, sketches, memories, and impressions, soaking up the fading world of Indians, mountain men, cavalry, and cowboys. Peter Hassrick wrote, "Remington had selected an exotic theme, the final act of the drama of the Far West, but he chose to portray this romantic theme in the terms of a realist, allowing few compromises with grace, beauty, or sympathy. As a Romantic Realist, then, he found a place in American art, and his stature as a painter grew apace with the advancement of his technical facility."

I got up from the computer and crossed the room to the windows. The Oquirrhs were now brilliant white in the full strength of morning. Romantic Realism; this I understood. This was the Code of the West.

But Remington had been a man's man in the closing days of the Old West, and I was a woman in the new West, hitting bottom while standing in for a man who had died too soon. I made a rotten daddy: I was more of a deadbeat than a breadwinner. In the movies, I'd be the aging spinster stuck in some dusty Western town who had discovered too late that all she wanted was to be someone's mother. I needed what Remington had had, a true love who waited patiently at home while I traveled to seek inspiration. Instead, I was in love with a man who did the adventuring while I stayed behind with no home and with growing impatience. Not for the first time, I railed against the ambiguities of being born female.

The sharp line of the Oquirrhs swam in my vision. I wanted adventure, I wanted professional satisfaction, I wanted marriage, and I wanted motherhood. And I wanted to stay home and out of trouble, I wanted to be looked after, I wanted to quit hiding in a failed relationship, and I wanted to stake my own mother out over an anthill and dribble syrup over her traitorous, ranch-selling hide.

I blinked, and the scene outside my window was momentarily sharp and clear.

In that instant, Fritz Calder jogged by. He glanced toward the window where I was standing and waved, and when I waved back, he stopped, jogged in place, and made a gesture designed to get me to open the window. When I did so, he said, "I'm still going to Baltimore next Monday. Have you changed your mind?"

I smiled wanly and shook my head. "Too much to do," I answered.

"Okay, then, will you water my houseplants?"

"Sure."

"Thanks." He paused a moment. "Are you sure you won't come? Life is short, Em."

"I'm sure," I said, absurdly complimented that he had remembered my name.

He gave me an ironic smile, and said, "Okay, but you can still change your mind. It's the final frontier, y'know." Then he threw his body out of neutral and back into forward gear and disappeared down the sidewalk.

Smiling at his jest, I fought my way back across the room and into the book, thinking, *Another adventure lost because life's just too unromantically real.*

I began to skim forward in Hassrick's narrative of Remington's life, looking for additional significant facts to decant into my computer.

> Remington enjoyed great success as an illustrator, but his longing for recognition as a "painter's painter" pressed him to stretch his skills. As a member of the American Impressionist movement, he finally did succeed, enjoying many shows at Knoedler's. Then late in 1909, at the age of forty-eight, Remington developed appendicitis, underwent surgery, and abruptly died.

Forty-eight. I was now a scant decade short of that mark, and I had little to show for my life but a handful of obscure mentions in the case files of a scattering of jurisdictions, a tattered bachelor's in geology, a few friends I found it hard to be close with, fond memories of a girlhood on the prairies of eastern Wyoming, and a painful love for a baby who was not my own. That baby now slept peacefully, cuddled against the warm body of her mother. She was over her colic. She no longer needed to be walked in the night, nor did Faye seem to need me to take her very often during the day. I briefly considered finding ways I could contract appendicitis myself, but Remington had died unintentionally, and at the center of the creative force, at the top of his form. I was in a slump, no place to quit. Such an ignominious death would hardly have people writing books about me.

So, how are you going to make something of your life? I asked myself. *Do you think it's easy to go out on top? Remington traveled west many times to collect inspiration, and wrestled with his muse. His success was hard-won!*

I decided in that moment that it was time that I took charge of my life and started to make something of it; became proactive rather than always just reacting to the next emergency. And if going west worked for Remington, perhaps going east would work for me. Fritz Calder was going to Baltimore in a few days, and Baltimore was not far from Washington, D.C., the home of the FBI labs and half a dozen world-class museums I was sure would be chockablock with specialists who could tell me all about artists' pigments. Why talk on the phone when I could visit the specialists in person?

I got up and tugged on some shoes and headed out the front door, hurried down the sidewalk, and knocked on Fritz's door.

He answered barefoot, stripped down to a T-shirt and shorts, a towel around his neck. Smiling like he already knew the answer, he asked, "What can I do for you this lovely morning?"

"I've changed my mind. Take me with you to Baltimore, Fritz," I said. "You're right. Life is short, and it's time for my next adventure."

Vermillion is red mercuric sulfide. It is found in nature as cinnabar, which is the principle ore of the metal mercury, and as such is highly toxic.

—*from the notebooks of Fred Petridge*

As Jennifer Neumann walked up the empty grade that led to the west portal of the Big Savage railroad tunnel, she opened the throat of her denim jacket and patted its heavily studded collar into place. It was a fine spring day, and she was enjoying the tight green buds that were starting to appear on the trees lining the right-of-way through the Allegheny Mountains. The Big Savage Tunnel was a wonderful challenge, part of Pennsylvania's Rails-to-Trails project, which sought to increase hiking and biking recreation while preserving the transit heritage that was such a key part of the state's history. Many miles of disused railroad grades had been salvaged for use by hikers and bikers, just the kind of people she wanted to keep happy and entertained: Well-educated people were often interested in fitness, and it was well-educated people who wanted to invest their charity dollars in the cause of preserving heritage. The 3,295-foot-long Big Savage Tunnel was the engineering masterpiece of the Connellsville extension of the Western Maryland Railway, a whole system of viaducts and tunnels that had been a marvel of engineering for that time.

Pennsylvania Geologic Survey geologist Fred Petridge walked alongside her. "It's a joy to help bring this tunnel back into use," she told him.

He smiled wryly. "I know you're a heritage buff, Jenny," he said in his soft Southern lilt, "but do you know how many men died digging this thing? Is that part of the package that inspires you?"

"It's sad that the toll was so heavy. But I like to think of it in terms of effort, not loss."

Fred shook his head and smiled. "You sure have your way of looking at things. Sometimes the dead were interred in concrete culverts and underpasses along the construction sites. They were paid eighty cents a day. At the height of construction, they had twenty-seven hundred men here, working thirty shovels, three hundred donkeys, and forty-one narrow-gauge locomotives. Construction of the west end of the tunnel was hindered by quicksand. There was a sinkhole in the Loyalhanna limestone, and—"

"That's why I love it when you come along, Fred. You tell me the geology connected to these sites."

"Flattery will get you lots of places, Jenny. But this site is all about geology. Or to take it back another notch, it's all thermodynamics. Think on it: The exchange of heat from the center of the earth to its crust sets up convective flow in the mantle. As the motion of the mantle pushes on the crust, it breaks up into sections and slides around with the flow. Of course, an alternate model says that the crust is pulled around by sinking slabs, not pushed, but—"

Jenny smiled. "You were telling me about the Alleghenies."

Fred nodded. "Part of that motion has opened and closed the Atlantic Ocean more than once, and every time it slams shut, it wrinkles up the crust and forms us some mountains. *Voilà*, Allegheny Mountains. Also, during one of the open phases, there was ocean here, and the Loyalhanna limestone was deposited."

"And I didn't even have to go to college to learn all that," Jenny said.

Fred waved an arm at the mountain that rose in front of them. "This tunnel also cuts through the eastern divide. All streams east of here flow into the Atlantic; everything west, the Gulf of Mexico."

"And we're within a stone's throw of the Mason-Dixon Line," Jenny added. "That's why we get along, Fred. We're both interested in history, it's just that you add a few zeros to the time numbers."

"More than a few, Jenny. You're dealing with hundreds of years. I'm talking about hundreds of millions."

Jenny truly did enjoy Fred's company. He was a nice sort, amiable and intelligent, and good in the out-of-doors. Too bad he wore a ring on the third finger of his left hand. She loved the causes she supported, truly she did, but every once in a while it did occur to her that it would be nice to have a man to come home to, and eventually a couple of kids. *And a dog*, she thought. *A big, shaggy sheepdog would be very, very nice*. Jenny twitched—a quick, sharp motion of her head and neck—an unconscious motion meant to shake loose the temptation of thinking about such elusive gratifications.

"Are you okay?" asked Fred.

Jenny flushed slightly, embarrassed to be caught showing her thoughts in public. "Just fine!" she answered, a bit too brightly. "I was just thinking about something, is all."

"What?"

She pointed up at the sky. A flock of geese were passing in classic V formation. "Know why one side of the V is longer than the other?"

"No," said Fred. "Why?"

"More geese."

Fred laughed appreciatively, then said, "But you were looking at your feet when you twitched. Come on, Jenny, what's up?"

As Jenny flipped through her mental files, seeking an excuse for her preoccupation, the Krehbeil farm situation hit her psychic windscreen like a fat June bug. "Well, you know I'm also working on the farmlands preservation in Lancaster County," she said.

"You have quite a reputation as a go-getter, Jenny, mixed up in all sorts of conservation projects. It doesn't surprise me in the least that you'd be involved with that one, too."

Jenny smiled. "I suppose. Well, you know how it goes: The farmers aren't making that much, and they get offered all that money by the developers to sell out."

"You're preaching to the choir," said Fred, encouraging her story.

"Well, as you probably know, then, there are two formal entities in Lancaster County that are trying to save open spaces, as well as the farming lifestyle, by purchasing the development easements from the farmers. But the county is short of funds, and can only purchase the best, most-threatened farms each year, and the private organization doesn't pay as much. In fact, they rely on the farmer being rich enough to donate the easements. And they deal mostly with the Mennonite and Amish farms. So what happens when you have a farmer who's down on his luck, the farm's soils aren't the very finest limestone-based soils, and he isn't in good standing with one of the churches?"

"I can see where that might get complicated," said Fred.

"I've been trying to help several farms. One in particular seems to be going to hell in a handbasket. One of the owners is dead and the other looks like she's about to join him. That would leave it to four grown offspring, and that's a problem."

"One or more will want their cash value out of the place."

"That's what I'm afraid of."

"Perhaps this family believes in primogeniture."

"Ah, yes: leaving everything to the eldest."

"It works for the British. They tend to be royalists, so they like the firstborn-takes-all system. But over here in Yankeeland, we like to split things even Steven. We're egalitarian, or so we kid ourselves. Things get messy very easily, because no two siblings have the same ideas about a piece of property, and it's amazing how quickly they'll get to fighting over a little bit of turf."

Jenny gave Fred a sideways look. "I didn't know you were a royalist, Fred."

"I'm not. Far be it."

"But it sounds like you know a lot about this kind of issue."

Fred gave an ironic grin and stared off into the trees. "Too much. I'm a third son, myself. Anyway, there are ways of doping this kind of problem out."

"Such as?"

"Well, where there's one piece of land in a family, there often can be two or three. If they aren't Amish or Mennonite they're probably not really making a living at farming anymore anyway, so why not carve up the farm? Or one can take cash and another takes furniture and the third takes land. Or take all but one of the offspring out and shoot them; that would help the overpopulation problem in the bargain. Or just take the brawling brats to a mediator. Or leave the lot to the Wednesday Afternoon Literary Society."

"The what?"

"Oh, it's a drinking organization my grandmother belonged to in Wisconsin."

"I like your first idea best. But how can I find out if the Krehbeils own other parcels?"

Fred cocked his head in surprise. "You don't know how to go online and run the county GIS system?"

Jenny pursed her lips. "That sounds like computer talk."

"'GIS' stands for Geographic Information System. It's one of the things that computers are truly good for. The idea is that huge amounts of data are stored in layers, like transparent maps, and you can look at any number of layers at a time, all superimposed and at the same scale. That way you can cross-correlate say, geology and landownership at a glance."

They had arrived at the portal of the tunnel, a concrete arch surrounded by a jutting rock face. Colleagues were already there, hardhats on, working on maintenance projects.

"There's my baby," said Fred. "Nothing I like better than a combination of my two favorite passions: geology and railroads. Mm-hm."

"Do you understand what caused the cave-in?" asked Jenny.

"You mean back when the tunnel was originally built?"

"Yes."

"Well, there are two limestone units in the rock sequence that makes up the rocks the tunnel was driven through, the Loyalhanna and Deer Valley limestones. They're about forty to fifty feet thick," he explained. "The rock formations were tipped up on edge by the forces that formed these mountains." He made a big gesture like he was compressing an accordion. "As you know, limestone dissolves easily in waters that percolate down through it; the groundwater comes down through the fractures in the rock, dissolving calcite along the way, so the cracks become caverns over thousands or millions of years." He had begun to use his hands to express the third and fourth dimensions of what he was saying. "So, it's speculated that one of these caverns had filled with water and silt and other materials, and when the tunnelers hit the pocket, it emptied catastrophically, killing a bunch of them."

"And a lot of other workers who came in after that," said Jenny.

Fred shrugged, the embarrassed tacit apology of the twenty-first–century man observing the sacrifices of those who built his conveniences at the expense of their lives. "I know. It's alarming how many people died building this tunnel. A hundred, or even two. No one kept good records. Nowadays, we shut down a public-works project if even one person dies, and we mire it in expensive investigations." He winked at Jenny. "Making it too expensive for projects you oppose to go forward."

Jenny tipped her head to one side and gave a prim smile. "I have been known to bring a lawsuit here and there."

"God bless the POSH Foundation."

Jenny winced. "I just hate it when people call it that."

"Then change the name," Fred kidded. "Or I'm gonna continue to josh you about naming it POSH." He turned back to the tunnel. "Anyway, it's a sign of our changing times—our greater state of civilization, if you will—that we now care so much for our workers that we do better by them than just carting their corpses up the mountain and pitching them into the hole that was formed when the tunnel collapsed on them."

Jenny wrinkled up her nose. "I know. That's the sad part of this project. Those poor men dug their own graves."

"Yeah."

The idea of graves brought the Krehbeil family back to mind. Father Krehbeil was dead, and now Mother was sick. Jenny wondered if they would be buried together out at the edge of one of their fields. The idea was so romantic that it sent surges of passion through her body. "I've seen the old limestone grave-markers out on the farmlands," she said.

Fred gave Jenny a sly look. "Yes, and those gravestones have a way of falling down, and too often get leaned up against a tree, and then the tree dies and falls down as time passes, and eventually no one knows where the old bones of Great-Granddad and Great-Grandmom are any more."

"They are united with their heritage," she said.

"Right. I wonder how many developers have kicked up an ancestor or two in the process of digging basements for all those McMansions. You ought to look into that, Jenny. That would be even better than chaining yourself to a tree or something to prevent grounds-breaking. Just go out there and watch through your binoculars and wait for a thigh bone to come cartwheeling out of the backhoe's bucket."

"Fred, you are a kidder . . ." Jenny said, but already she was envisioning herself lying patiently in a portable blind, waiting for the developer with his chrome-plated shovel to come out for the grounds-breaking ceremony. "But you were also mentioning this GIF thing."

"GI*S*."

"Of course. GIS. I can see how you could contribute a lot with that, Fred."

Fred rolled his eyes. "Okay, Jenny, I can see that you're getting me on the hook for another one of your causes."

"It's all one cause, Fred."

"However you want to dish it up. I'll introduce you to a colleague of mine at the PGS, a guy named Nigel Iago. He's a real whiz at GIS. It's a powerful tool. Anything on the county rolls is fair game."

The two of them walked into the tunnel together. Fred's mind was already deep in the earth, reckoning the history of the rocks through which the tunnel was cut. Jenny's was on the Krehbeil farm, reckoning what she'd have this Nigel fellow do for her there.

14

I HURRIED HOME FROM FRITZ'S HOUSE. NOW THAT I HAD AGREED to go east, I needed to make plans so I could use my time wisely.

I dug out the telephone number Tanya had given me and dialed. Noreen Babcock answered on the second ring. "Trace Evidence," she announced. "Babcock speaking."

I took a deep breath and jumped in. "Hi, my name is Em Hansen. I was an associate of the late Tom Latimer, and I—"

"Of course, Em," she said, her voice softer now but no less authoritative. "Tanya phoned. You were with Tom when it happened. I've been hoping you'd call."

I opened and closed my mouth several times but felt like I had something caught in my throat. Perhaps it was my heart. Finally I managed a whispered, "Yes."

"Even though he left the Bureau before his death, he was still our colleague, and when a colleague falls in action, it's . . ."

"Thank you," I said.

"So, now, please tell me there's something I can do for you."

"Well, I've been asked to work on an art forgery case, and I want to make a master's thesis out of it. That would mean that I'd need to get the details and procedures exactly right, and next week I'm flying to the D.C. area, and—"

"Next week? Then we've got to step on it. Let me see. . . . I've got time Tuesday, late afternoon. But you need to write a letter to our security clearance unit. They don't call us the Bureau for nothing. And you aren't going to believe what his name is. Do you have a fax? There's not time to dink around with the mails. Everything that gets mailed to us goes through the antiterrorism unit, and that can take months. They even stamp my post cards OPENED AND INSPECTED. Got a pen? Ready for the name and phone number?"

She gave me full instructions on how to make my visit sound essential but nonthreatening, instructed me to check with her Wednesday if I hadn't heard back from Mr. Covert (she was right, I couldn't believe that name), and said she had to ring off, citing a backlog of glass shards she had to identify from drive-by shootings.

I cranked the requisite letter out of the computer and shoved it through Tom's old fax machine, feeling a bit cocky. *That was easy,* I told myself. *Who else can I hit up for information?*

My eyes came to rest on *Artists' Pigments,* volume 1, and I thought, *I'll be in Washington; why not ask?* So I turned to the computer, surfed the Web, found a general information number for the National Gallery of Art, and again dialed the phone. "Hello," I told the person who answered. "I have some questions regarding certain books published by the National Gallery. May I speak with someone who can put me in touch with the authors?"

"I'll transfer you," the voice on the phone said. "I'm not sure who you need to speak with, but let me try. . . . " After being transferred to the gallery's bookstore, publications, and the research library, I was put through to a receptionist who mellifluously announced, "Conservation."

I repeated my question a fifth time.

"Is there anyone in particular with whom you wish to speak?"

After repeating my story that many times to people who had no real interest in it, my guard was down, so I answered too candidly.

"Uh—anyone who can tell me about the pigments used by Frederic Remington." I immediately wanted to take back my words. I had ridden too close to the fence that distinguished a curious citizen from a private eye doing a bad job of keeping a client's confidences, but as my dad used to say, once you're on the horse, it's important to keep on riding.

"I'll put you through to Emmett Jones," the receptionist replied.

"Jones," the next voice said.

Trying to pull away from that fence, I said, "I'm a graduate student in geology with an interest in artists' pigments. I'll be in Washington next week, and—" here I paused for a split second, panicked, and sank to embroidering the truth—"I'm working with a colleague at the FBI, and she suggested I contact you regarding a specific line of evidence."

Mr. Jones said he would be pleased to assist. We set a time on Tuesday morning.

Next, I went online and found a number for the Pennsylvania Geologic Survey. When I asked for a specialist on mining, I was told that Fred Petridge was my man, but that he was out in the field. The receptionist said that he would be in all the following week. I left a message asking for an appointment on Monday.

It was nearing time to run up to the U to attend a class, but I figured there was time to stop by an art-supply store on the way to school if I mooched Faye's car, so I opened the phone book, found the address of the one nearest my trajectory, picked up my books, and headed on over there.

I hadn't been inside a whole lot of shops like that, and was bewildered by the variety of supplies that were available. I walked past aisles that displayed pencils and chalks, pastels, acrylics, and watercolors, and stopped at a rack of oil colors.

The object of my desire was Hooker's green, the color that predominated in Remington's nocturnes in general and in Tert's painting in particular. I wanted to see what it looked like straight from the tube, not mixed with the other colors that grayed it down. I had come just far enough with the project to know that the colors on the plates in the art books from the library were not the precise hues that Remington had dipped from his palette. Remington had used linen canvas with a gesso ground, and had built up his colors in layers ranging from thick, painterly impasto to sly layers of glazes, a far cry from a microscopically thin layer of printer's inks on glossy paper.

But as I searched through the dizzying assortment of tubes in the store, I did not find Hooker's green. I knew that new colors had been added to the artists' palette since Remington's time, but had the old ones been discarded? Thinking that Remington might have mixed some of his own paints, I asked the man at the counter where he kept the dry pigments.

"That's a specialty supply item," he said. "There's a place in San Francisco where you can order them, and several places on the Internet."

Perplexed, I went on up to the U.

I was on my way back out of the geology building after class an hour later when I ran into Molly Chang, my advisor.

"Ah, Hansen," she said. "Just the enigma I was hoping to run into. Come into my office."

I gritted my teeth and followed her. "What's up?" I inquired.

"What's up? You mean 'Doc?' What's up is that you're almost done with your coursework, so when are you going to start a thesis project?"

"Well, I . . ."

"Come on, it's almost spring break. You could be out next week scouting a mapping area at least, or come to my field area with me and look at some of the work I've been doing. You never know, you might get inspired. Or are you still kidding me and yourself that you're going to do a forensics project?"

I grinned weakly. "Well, Molly, that's what I've always liked about you: You come right to the point."

"As my husband likes to say, 'When push comes to shove, Molly does both.' "

Well, I knew how to push back. I said, "Actually, I'll be working on a consulting job in forensic geology next week back in Pennsylvania."

"Oh?" she said, looking dubious. "What?"

The gauntlet was thrown. Answering her challenge, I said, "I'm supposed to look at the pigments in a painting and decide whether it's a forgery or not. I have appointments with a forensic geologist at the FBI, a conservator at the National Gallery of Art, and a mineral pigment mining specialist at the Pennsylvania Geologic Survey."

Molly gave me a wry smile. "Sounds like a thesis project to me."

"No, wait!"

"You'll need to do some X-ray diffraction work, and maybe some thin sections. I tell you what: You relate this to economic geology and you just might have something. Surely there's something about the mining and refinement processes that would have a bearing on pigments. So what's the painting? I have an interest in art, you know." She gestured around the walls of her office.

An arrow of panic shot through me. Staring at me from her walls were prints by Maynard Dixon, Thomas Moran, George Catlin, and other Western artists. I had noticed them before, but had always considered them decoration, not avocation. I said, "Listen, Molly, making a thesis project out of this kind of work sounds like great idea, except for one problem: The results of this investigation are proprietary. As in, no public reporting."

Molly's dark eyes turned to flint. "You're a good huckster, Hansen; with all your contacts, *surely* you can get your hands on something in the public domain."

"I have a line on a few Russells," I said, trying to sound confident, but immediately wished I hadn't spoken. Could I really depend on Tert's promise that I could see other paintings?

She leaned back in her swivel chair and stared up at a poster from a show at the Smithsonian Institution. It featured a portrait of an Indian chief. She said, "Take Catlin, for instance. The Renwick Gallery there in D.C. has a bunch of his works. And he was an interesting guy. He trained in law first, and he knew some geology."

"That's a Catlin?" I asked. It was robust and sophisticated portraiture, a far cry from his landscapes.

"Yes. So you could ask yourself, What pigments did he use? Look at that guy in the poster: His skin tone has to be some iron oxide or another, and that dark-red war paint . . . what do you think, some manganese in with the ol' Fe_2O_3? It looks like desert varnish to me."

My mind spiraled backward to my first meeting with Tert, back at the Whitney Gallery in Cody. He had commented on the pigments Catlin had used. *No, not at the gallery,* I remembered, *it was when he met me up by the badlands . . .*

Unbidden, a piece of the Tert Krehbeil puzzle turned itself upside down and laughed at me. For the first time since the stress and shuffle of those first days, I had time to wonder how he had happened upon me on that hillside. With grim certainty, I saw that Faye must have phoned him. *Go on out there and check her out. Follow her; she'll be driving my car. . . .*

Molly gave me a strange look, and I realized that I was pulling fiercely on my lower lip. I moved quickly to cover my emotions. "Sure, Catlin would be a good choice for research," I said in my most intellectual tone. "He was working long before most of the modern synthetic pigments came on the market. And he dates back to the 1830s, before the advent of the collapsible paint tube, so maybe he was carrying his paint in little leather bladders with a bit of bone to prick through to the paint. Messy. And maybe that means he had to make his own paints. Yeah, come to think of it, where would he have gotten his colors?"

"Maybe he brought them from home. Do you know where Catlin was from?"

"No." I didn't care. Anything to deflect the conversation from my client's interests.

"A town called Wyoming, Pennsylvania. And Pennsylvania has a little bit of economic geology in its history. Such as America's first oil wells, and all that coal."

"What are you thinking, Molly?"

She offered a sardonic laugh. "You're going to see a pigment mining specialist at the Pennsylvania Survey. I like the way your mind works. Maybe Catlin got his pigments locally, or even dug the stuff up in the backyard. Go see if you can match the impurities." She turned in her chair and slapped her desktop, indicating that our meeting was over. "Call me if you need to discuss your sampling technique. And get your ass in gear. I want you out of here by Christmas."

15

Time seemed to whiz by in the few days left before Fritz and I would be departing for the East. I had no time to worry about anything that had been bothering me—not the ranch, not Jack, not even how little I was seeing of Faye and the baby. I had phone calls to make, interviews to line up. I had to finish schoolwork, pack a duffel bag, line up a rental car, and figure out where I was going to stay. Luckily, most of that was settled when I finally got up the nerve to talk to Faye about my plans.

"Where in Pennsylvania does Tert's mother live?" I inquired, as I opened a highway-map atlas on the kitchen table.

"Just outside of Lancaster," she replied. "They have a farm. Why?"

"Lancaster is right here," I said, stabbing an index finger into the southeast quadrant of the state. And Middletown is . . . right here. Not far at all. Maybe a half-hour drive."

"What's in Middletown?"

"The state geological survey. I've been talking to a guy who knows a lot about mining in Pennsylvania."

"You just *happen* to be talking to a guy in Pennsylvania," she said. She was busy feeding Sloane Renee some mashed banana. Sloane kept turning her head just as the spoon got in range, resulting in a smear of goo across one cheek or the other.

"Yeah. Tert said that the rest of his paintings were at his mother's. It would help if I could see them. So I can get my damned thesis done."

"Oh? Does this mean you're planning a trip east?"

"Yes. I'm going to talk to an old colleague of Tom's at the FBI about the analytical work for Tert's painting. Strictly confidential. Tert's name and the work won't enter the conversation. The labs are in Quantico, Virginia, just outside of D.C."

"When is all this happening?"

"Next week. Know of any good, cheap places to stay in D.C.?"

Faye said, "I shudder at the thought of what you call a good, cheap place to stay. But you could call my great uncle. He has some sort of club there, and I think they have rooms. But wait, how are you going to get an affordable flight at the last minute? Surely Em Hansen is not going to pay top dollar."

"I have that covered," I said. I looked up and we made eye contact for the first time that day. She looked pettish, and that rather pleased me. *Perhaps she'll miss me,* I thought. "Your idea about making a thesis project out of Tert's job is a good one," I said. "You're right. I need to get this degree finished. Life goes on, you know?"

Faye smiled brightly. "I'm glad to hear you say that. I've been wondering if you had a plan for what you're going to do next."

"What do you mean, 'next'?"

"You know, when you've finished your degree, and you're ready to move on."

Move on? . . .

"I'm so glad to have helped by getting you this job," she said.

This wasn't going as I had planned. This was all meant as a lead-in to getting her into that plane with Fritz. "Want to come along?" I blurted.

Faye's eyes hardened. "No way! I shudder twice at the thought of going through all that security screening at the airport. And with the baby? Don't even think it. You're not getting me on a commercial flight. When I get my plane back in the air, we'll talk. But until then, I'm staying on the ground. And going into Washington? Are you mad? We're probably still at Code Orange with all this mess in the Middle East. What's *that* going to be like? I hear Washington is like an armed camp. Men with automatic rifles standing guard on the Capitol steps."

Things were going from bad to worse. Faye did not want to think about the reason airport security had become so strict—terrorism, and the wars surrounding it—and not just for the reasons that made us all tremble at the thought. Faye had paid a price most of us only visited in our nightmares: The fight against terrorism had put her husband in an early grave. I said, "It's not like that. I'm going with Fritz Calder in his plane, and we're flying into the General Aviation Terminal in Baltimore. We'd go for free. You'd have the chance to get back in the saddle without doing all the flight planning and stuff right out of the chute."

She gave me a wry look. "I'm not sure I like your choice of metaphors. Is his plane a bucking bronco or something?"

"Uh, no. It's a centerline thrust twin."

"A push-me-pull-you . . . interesting. . . ." Faye got up and began to pace.

I watched silently, letting her work off her upset. Finally she ran out of steam, turned, and bit her lip. "Pressurized?"

"Yes. Seats six, I think he said."

"How fast?"

"Cruises at two-hundred-twenty knots." I fought to repress a smile. She was going for it. "Not as fast as your plane, but c'mon, the baby's car seat would fit quite nicely, and Fritz seems quite hungry for a copilot. I mean, I'm only single-engine–rated, and if he hit weather, well, I'm hardly instrument rated. We'll be flying out of the private terminal here in Salt Lake and landing at the private terminal in Baltimore. You won't have to get wanded or take your shoes off either direction."

Faye snorted. "General Aviation, the only civilized way to fly in America."

"Amen. You can't hijack your own aircraft, and you know all your passengers personally. There's no higher form of security."

Faye glanced at me out of the corners of her eyes. "You're sure it's okay with Fritz if you bring a friend or two?"

"I asked him if you and the baby could come, and he said, 'The more the merrier.' " I couldn't suppress a grin.

Faye smiled, too, and said, "Well, I do owe a visit to some relatives who live not far from Baltimore. They haven't seen the baby." I heard a slight ring of obfuscation in her voice, but hoped that it was merely an attempt to seem cool about the trip.

It was decided that she and the baby would head north to visit relatives while I headed south into Washington. And she phoned her great uncle in D.C., who said he'd be most pleased to make a reservation for me at his club. When I heard the nightly fee for the guest room I gasped, but apparently it was cheap for anywhere near that town. I got on the Internet and found a list of much more reasonable places to stay in Pennsylvania.

So everything was settled, and very early on Sunday morning we rode to the airport with Fritz. The plane was hangared not far from where Faye used to keep her twin, so it was a bittersweet moment for her. It was a sweet-looking craft, all smooth with modern lines that spoke of computer-assisted design. As Fritz took Faye with him on his walk-around, I loaded the gear and the baby, taking the backseat next to Sloane so that Faye could sit up front with someone I trusted she would soon find much more fascinating than Mr. Self-Obsessed Gray Eyes Who Cons Geologists Into Thinking He Knows Nothing About Pigments. Fritz and Faye climbed aboard, did the run-up, talked to the tower, taxied, lined up, and we took to the air.

It was a cool, crisp morning, and the air was like silk. The ragged summits of the Rocky Mountains caught the sun with the sensual pride of a maiden showing off her charms, and I watched them roll past with pleasure, thinking that for the first time in a long time, I was doing something right.

After a while, Faye switched seats with me so she could nurse the baby, and I put on the headphones and talked to Fritz. It was the kind of chat one gets into on long trips, and the headphones we wore added their odd form of intimacy. I got to asking about his child and his ex-wife. "Didn't she like being a military wife?" I inquired. "I know it can be stressful."

"*Like* it?" He shook his head. "Being a military wife is what she wanted. Our marriage started to crumble when I *left* the military."

"I don't understand. Usually it's the other way around."

"She's the daughter of a high-ranking officer," he explained. "That's why she's been in Germany. Her dad's over there."

"So she wanted you to make a career out of it, too."

"Yup-per . . ."

This got my attention, because I was still trying to figure out how I felt about Jack's return to active duty, not to mention why he was still a reservist after all these years. "But you trained in jets. That's a big commitment. Didn't you plan to stay in?"

"Yes, that was the plan, as far as I'd thought it through."

"Then why'd you change your mind?"

He shifted uncomfortably in his seat. "Well, I was flying in Desert Storm, the first Gulf War."

"And?"

He didn't answer.

After half a minute, I said, "I'm sorry, this time I really am prying."

"No, it's okay," he said, though the look on his face suggested otherwise. "I need to talk about it. It's just hard. The thing was, I did all that training to fly those jets, but it was because I wanted to *fly*. I never thought my skills would be needed, not really. I was pretty naïve, or selfish, or . . ."

"So you didn't want to fight. Or drop bombs. Or whatever it was."

He shook his head. "Oh, I thought I was good for it. You tell yourself that you'll be able to do what's asked of you if the time ever comes."

I noted that he had reflexively switched from "I" to the more impersonal "you," an Americanism that pops up when a speaker wishes to distance himself from something that makes him nervous. "What happened? Did you refuse to fly?"

"No." He left that word hanging by itself for a while, and then added, "I flew out and dropped my bombs just as I had trained to do, and the automatic cameras took their pictures. Then, that evening, as my superiors were going over the tapes, I . . . realized . . . I mean, for the first time *really* understood, could really *feel*,"—he thumped his heart—"that it wasn't all just a video game."

I glanced sideways at him. His grip on the control wheel had tightened to the point where his knuckles had blanched. "I admire that, Fritz. It must be a great temptation to rationalize it and feel nothing."

"Oh, I felt something all right."

I let him decide how much more he wanted to say.

He took a deep breath, then said, "I went out the next day and did it again. And the next day and the next. I was lucky: Most of the time I was bombing places where there were no people. And then the war was over.

"I don't like war, Em. I don't approve of it. I don't see it as a solution. Oh, don't get me wrong—I know there are times when it's important to fight—but on reflection, I did not think this was one of them. But as soon as I started thinking that, I knew I wasn't a soldier anymore."

"Perhaps that's when you began being a warrior," I said.

He glanced my way, surprised. Then he smiled and shook his head. "I wish I could see it in those terms. Anyway, things were plenty clear to my wife. She'd signed up for a life as an officer's wife, someone her dad could approve of, and here I was taking the exit into civilian life. Our marriage was doomed from there."

"I'm sorry."

"I'm not. Not anymore. It was hard to stay mad when I realized that I was the one who changed the agreement. I just hope she doesn't find some poor sucker who wants her and my son to live on the other side of the globe."

"Got ya."

I let the subject drop. The plane cruised at two-hundred-twenty knots and we had about seventeen-hundred nautical miles to go, so with one refueling in Greenfield, Iowa ("It's the cheapest avgas," Fritz told me, to which I replied, "A man after my own heart"), and two hours' time change, we were on the ground in Baltimore by the middle of the afternoon. Faye and Fritz seemed to have a nice chat as we tore along over the Great Plains into increasingly humid air, and she again took the controls while the baby slept peacefully in my arms. I watched as the ground turned from brown to green beneath us and lost the wrinkly hide of the Pennsylvanian Appalachians under a cloud cover. I knew we were approaching Baltimore only as I heard Fritz ask flight control for vectors so he could make his approach through the soup.

Once on the ground, we loaded into three different rental cars that were waiting for us at the general aviation terminal, confirmed plans to meet on Friday morning for the flight home, and prepared to scurry off in our various directions.

Fritz gave the baby a kiss and was the first to leave, citing a dinner meeting with one of his money people. For my part, scurrying off first involved helping Faye cinch the baby's car seat into the center of the backseat of a midsized Chevy. Then I sat with the baby awhile while Faye heaved her various diaper bags and cold packs carrying juices and applesauce into the trunk.

"Hey, little one," I said, giving Sloane a finger on which to teethe. "Auntie Emmy's gonna go do some work, but I'll see you in five days. Four and a half, really. I'll miss you more than you can imagine." I bent forward and kissed her on the crown of her head.

Faye climbed into the driver's seat and indicated she was ready to go.

"Do you want to give me a number where you're staying?" I asked. "I mean, I don't know exactly where you guys'll be . . . if you need me or anything."

Faye gave me an impatient sigh. "I have your cell number, and you have mine," she said.

"Well, I'll be at the General Sutter Inn in Lititz."

"Where's that?"

"Pennsylvania."

"I thought you were going to Washington."

"I am, but my appointment's not until Tuesday. I thought I'd use Monday to get a look at some of Tert's family's paintings."

Faye gave me a strange look. "Does Tert know about your plans?"

"No. I wasn't sure until recently what my timing was."

Faye stared at me.

Okay, I thought, *she doesn't believe me. But it was sort of true*. I got out of the car and watched them drive away. Then I climbed into my own rental car, which was shaped like a Kaiser roll and about the size of a tennis shoe, scanned the overly simplified map that had been given to me by the rental car agent, fired the ignition, and headed out into the murky air of the East.

I had not been on the East Coast since my last two horrible years of high school, when my mother had insisted that I go east and "get an education." I had gotten one all right, but not the one she had expected. What I had learned was that I hated everything east of the Mississippi. Everything was the wrong colors, for one—green and brown instead of tan and yellow and red—and entirely too damp, not to mention overpopulated. There seemed to be about one hundred cars per square inch, and the roads were twisty even where there were no mountains to wind through. And all of this had somehow gotten much, much worse in the decades since I had gleefully escaped back to my beloved, dry, empty West.

I jogged around Baltimore on the beltway, then headed northwest on Interstate 83. I rolled past turnoffs for suburbs for quite some miles before the countryside opened up into dense woodlands. At about the state line into Pennsylvania, it opened further into broad, sloping farmlands bordered by the brown fringes of trees not yet in bud. At York, I turned east onto Highway 30.

It grew dark as I crossed the wide expanse of the Susquehanna River and entered Lancaster County. The highway unwound past brightly lit car dealerships and other eyesores. I wondered where the legendary Amish farmlands were. Just outside of Lancaster, I turned left on Route 501, the Lititz Pike, a narrow, two-lane road that rolled north through small towns and glimpses of cropland. I had chosen Lititz for two reasons: First, it was not far from Lancaster, and therefore presumably close to the Krehbeil family farm; and second, it offered a reasonably cheap place to stay.

The General Sutter Inn proved to be an old brick hotel right smack at the center of town. And when I say old, I mean older than most any structure built by white folks anywhere in the West. The whole of Lititz fairly dripped with early-American cachet. I pulled my little car over at the curb, got out, and took my first lungful of Pennsylvanian air. It smelled of chocolate.

I let myself into the lobby of the hotel. "Are we near the town of Hershey?" I inquired of the innkeeper. "I smell . . . ah . . ."

She shook her head as she ran an impression of my credit card. "No, we got our own factory here in Lititz. Wilber Buds. Lots of chocolate factories in this county," she informed me. "You're in room three-ten, up two flights and around to the right." She pointed to the ceiling and made a corkscrew gesture.

I thanked her, hefted my duffel bag, and headed up the stairs. At the second landing, the decor turned from early American antique to garage-sale miscellaneous, and I began to inhale the bouquet of ancient carpeting. I unlocked the door to room 310, dropped my duffel onto the floor, and sat down on the bed. Loneliness descended upon me like cold mist.

I rousted myself out for dinner at the café on the street level of the hotel, where I chomped down a hamburger and fries, but the meal hit my stomach like a rock and pulled me down. Everything seemed to be descending, most of all me.

Back up in the room, I plugged the cell phone into the charging jack, shucked off my clothes, shrugged my way into a giant T-shirt that I wore as a nightgown, and slipped between the sheets. I lay staring into the darkness for about half an hour, listening to the odd car passing in the street below. Just as I was thinking of turning on the light and getting out my notes on pigments, the phone rang.

It was Faye. She whispered, "Em, listen, you can't go to the Krehbeil farm tomorrow, okay?"

Okay? Then what am I doing here, collecting hotel ghosts? I sat up and turned on the light. I said, "Oh, so you're visiting a *relative*, are you? Put Tert on the phone!"

There was a muffled pause as Faye spoke to someone, her hand over the receiver. Then Tert's voice came on the line. "Good evening, Em."

"Hi, Tert. Surprise, I'm in Lititz. I have a date to speak with a colleague at the Pennsylvania State Geologic Survey tomorrow to get data for my thesis project. And yes, I'd like to go to your mother's to see the other paintings. Do you have a problem with that?" Even as I said it, I knew it sounded hopelessly combative.

"In fact I do." He kept his voice level, but crisply patrician and authoritative. "Your master's thesis may be a matter of public record, but your errand for me is not."

"I thought your family knew all about this," I said, Hector's drunken voice echoing in my memory. I tried to keep my voice steady, but anger seeped into it. I had delayed telling him of my plans because I did not trust him, but I was not comforted to discover just how correct my assessment had been.

"I do not wish my family to be consulted in this matter," he said firmly.

"But you said I could see the paintings," I insisted.

Silence.

I calmed my voice as best I could and said, "They needn't know that I have any connection with the painting in question. Faye can phone ahead of me, and present me as a friend of hers who is doing a paper for an art history course."

Cell phones can be damned hard instruments of communication. A lot of subtlety is lost, and sometimes it sounds like the connection is lost when it is not. I had been listening to blankness for several seconds when Faye's voice came back on the line. She was seething mad. "How dare you pull this stunt?"

"This *stunt*? You knew where I was going. And that's why Tert knows. You *told* him."

I heard Faye tell Tert, "Give me a minute," and then heard a door close. When Faye spoke to me next, she was so angry that she was stuttering. "I try to help you out by getting you a job, and what do you do? You fuck up my social life!"

Help me out? Out what? Out the door? I loaded my heaviest round and fired. "Faye, what are you doing with a man who lies?"

"What am I doing? Trying to have a life, Em. Because I haven't had one lately, no thanks to *your* wonderful boyfriend."

"You blame *Jack* for Tom's death?"

"Would you rather I blame you? God, Em, he led Tom right into that bullet!" Her voice cracked with pain and rage as she added, "*You* should know, Em! *You* were there!"

The line went dead.

I wanted to say, *I led him there*. I wanted to say, *I'm so sorry. I led Tom to his death, not Jack. Me. My cleverness. My detection of the point of danger. If I had been slower or stupider, Jack might have died instead.*

But Jack was alive, and gone, and Faye was a widow. And Sloane had no father. I hated war with all my heart and yet if it would bring Tom back, I would rip my heart from my chest with my own hands and lead the charge into battle naked.

My ears rang with shock. It had never occurred to me that Faye would feel robbed of those last moments of Tom's life. His death was hideous and still robbed me of sleep; why would she want that trauma? But to her, the scenario was different: He had died far away from her, with his ruined head cradled in someone else's arms.

I set the phone down very carefully, then turned out the light. I lay down on the bed and pulled the covers up to my chin. I did not bother to close my eyes. I knew I would not sleep.

16

At dawn, I got up and showered and dressed and packed my duffel, then checked out of the General Sutter Inn. I did not know if I'd be staying another night in Pennsylvania, and I wanted the option of leaving. I did not know if I was still working for Tert Krehbeil, and I was not sure I cared, but I had cashed his check for three thousand and would continue to work until I had spent every penny of it, or until he said to quit. Life was too short to be bullied by one's employer.

I headed out in search of a shop that would sell me half a dozen glazed doughnuts and a pint of strong coffee. I was in major need of comfort food, and something that would prop open my eyelids.

I was bone-aching tired. And I was deeply, dangerously angry. In the small hours of the night, I had reasoned the whole mess through one more time, and decided that I had not killed Tom, and neither had Jack. I had not twisted his arm or manipulated him. Tom went into the fight that had hastened his death out of an urge I could neither understand nor remedy. Nevertheless, I had helped Faye through the final weeks of her pregnancy and had nursed her and her child for almost eight long months afterward. I had done it because I felt guilty, yes, but more than that, I had done it because I loved her, and because I had also come to love her child.

I had never admitted it to myself, but I had feared that, given the chance to become a mother, I would fail to care enough. Now I knew that I could, and did. I had never known I could love anyone as I loved that infant.

And Faye had no right to accuse me of sabotaging her social life. In fact, I'd been trying to improve it.

It was bitter icing on my cake of rage that Tert Krehbeil had so breezily promised access to artwork and never meant a word of it. I wanted to see Tert turn on a spit.

I found a strip mall south of town and got what I was looking for, then consulted the local telephone directory. I opened to the *K*'s, and found several Krehbeils. One of them was in Elm, a woman named Deirdre, a name that sounded familiar. Had Hector mentioned a Deirdre? I thought back again to my conversation with him, trying to remember. *Yes, something about a dynasty*. A second number was for Hector himself, no address given, but the exchange listings in the front of the book suggested the number was in Mount Joy. The third number was for William Krehbeil II, also at the Elm address. *Krehbeil Secundus. That must be Tert's deceased father, and Tert's mother has kept the number under his name. So, that means two things: Deirdre's living at the farm and Tert's full given name is William. Then, did Hector mean Tert when he said, "Precious Willie"?* I brought up a mental image of the check Tert had written to pay my retainer. Had his name been on that check? *No, it bore the name of his business, Krehbeil Gallery, Philadelphia; and his signature was illegible.*

I looked at my map. Elm was north of Lititz. Even at this county's rate of travel—snail's pace—I could be there within twenty minutes. I looked at my watch. It was just after seven.

I was in such a nasty mood that I was inclined to screw Tert's project—something I seemed to have a knack for, according to Faye and her social life—and instead just find out what in hell's name was going on with his family. This information I would serve up to Faye on a platter. I would point out that one of them was a coldhearted liar and another was a drunk, and Faye would apologize to me. Simultaneously I suspected that I was just an overgrown adolescent who should apologize to *her*.

Hang on to your anger, I told myself. *It'll keep you alert.*

Before last night's blowup, my seat-of-the-pants plan had been to telephone Tert at his office and extract an introduction to his mother so I could see the paintings. Now that I had been told not to go there, I decided I had nothing to lose by contacting her anyway and seeing what happened. But I would wait until eight.

I glanced at my watch again. It was seven-fifteen. If they truly were a true farm family—which I doubted—they would be up already and have half the chores done; but if they were typical Easterners, they were probably still asleep, or would consider me rude to phone so early. Itching to get started with something—anything—I decided to drive out to the farm and take a look. If I saw people up and about, I'd drop in and introduce myself as Faye's pal. If they took a pitchfork to me, I'd know she'd phoned ahead. If she hadn't, and they were amenable, I might get a squint at the paintings and get out of there with little fuss. Not that the paintings would do me any good now—there was no way these people would let me analyze their pigments—but having come all this way to see the artwork, I was damned well going to see it.

As a last point of justification for my mania, I reminded myself that Tert was hiding something, and that I needed to know what that was. I had run into this kind of thing on previous cases, and had learned I could not solve the client's puzzle without first knowing why the client was lying to me, and what he was trying to hide.

I got into the car and started to drive. North of town, in the soft light of that early-spring morning, I at last viewed the farmlands for which Lancaster County was famous. The patchwork of fields rolled out from either side of the road. They were neatly tended, with crops planted right up to the edge of the pavement, not a hedgerow or boundary fence in sight. The farmhouses were closer together than I was used to in the West, two-stories tall and built of stone. The barns were likewise made of stone up to the second story, where many of them gave over to wood, painted white.

I wondered if some of the farms belonged to the Amish, a people synonymous with Lancaster County's famous farmlands. Clearly Tert was not of that persuasion, although what I knew of the Amish went about as deep as cardboard: Amish people stayed on the farm. They did not drive automobiles, or use electric lights. I dared say that their ancestors did not take the train into New York City and purchase paintings by Frederic Remington. And they did not own hobby ranches west of Cody, Wyoming. They were "the plain folk" who were "in the world, but not of this world." They wore unornamented clothing and lived simply, in order to escape temptation. The women made fabulous quilts using solid-color fabrics in fully saturated colors and no white. They were one of a list of Protestant Christian sects that had come over from Europe to escape persecution. They are easily confused with the Mennonites, from whom they had split off, and who have a similar story but drive cars, use white fabrics in their quilts, and often dress just like "the English." The Mennonites seemed a more variable group. Were the Krehbeils Mennonites?

It was not a simple matter to find the Krehbeil farm. The map of Pennsylvania I had with me showed only numbered highways, and I was looking for a farm road. Finally I stopped at a filling station and asked directions. Those instructions put me out onto a network of narrow blacktop roads that wound through shallow hills among farms broken up by narrow strips of housing developments featuring two-story mansionettes on quarter-acre spacing. Being ranch raised, it horrified me to see lines of houses backed up against such luscious croplands.

When I at last found the road and the number that matched the Krehbeils' address, I parked a short distance away and wandered along the verge to take a look.

The day was proving to be quite mild, and the scents of the land rose to meet me. Flights of seed-eating birds and the first spring flowers lightened my heart. Then a car pulled out of the drive and zoomed past me, shattering my idyll. It was driven by a hulking man in his twenties—Then I heard a door slam, and saw a young woman with spiky hair and tattooed ankles slouch down across the lawn, light a cigarette, jump into a beat-up Toyota sedan, jab it into a fast start, and skid it backwards into a smuggler's turn. She roared up to the pavement and ripped off down the road in the other direction without looking left or right to see if anyone was coming. I wondered who these two were, and whether I indeed had the correct farm. They didn't have an ounce of the patrician classiness that oozed from Tert Krehbeil.

The brick house was finer than any I had seen in the neighborhood, but the wooden trim was badly in need of paint, except the front door, which was a vivid yellow. It was two stories tall and surrounded on three sides by broad porches that sagged badly, and some of the ornamental woodwork had been broken away. In places, panes of glass were held together with duct tape. The screening on the front door was ripped. But overall, it had an imposing appearance, even in its obvious state of decline. It was a house that once had been quite grand, but was now all but falling down.

The barn was large and finely crafted but the foundation stonework bulged downhill. There were no signs of recent usage. The track that led past it was tall with grasses where it should have been bald from traffic, and there were no splashes of mud along the wall.

I checked and rechecked the address, incredulous that this was the home that had produced Tert Krehbeil.

A sound from the front porch drew my attention back to the house. I saw the front door swing wide, and the feet of an elderly woman appeared, followed by a great wrapping of quilts and then by the rest of her figure seated in a wheelchair. The chair was pushed by a middle-aged woman who moved briskly, even brusquely, making the old woman's head wobble on her narrow neck as the chair encountered bumps in the porch. She brought the chair to a stop at the sunny end of the porch and moved quickly about it, setting the brakes and stuffing loosened folds of the quilts into place around the older woman. From her pocket, she produced a knit hat and set it on the older woman's head. This accomplished, she put her fists on her hips and leaned her head toward the white-haired ancient as if scolding her. Then she turned and left her to the morning breezes.

The elderly woman looked like a nestling left behind while its parent searched for food. As the moments passed, her head bobbled with the rhythm of short, panting breaths, and she slowly tilted farther and farther forward in her chair.

Robins hopped across the lawn in search of food. I could not believe from the outward appearance of the property that these people had a fortune in Western art on the premises. Had Tert invented the story of the family treasure? I struggled with conflicting emotions: I wanted to see the paintings and yet I did not want to meet these women. I wanted to know enough about them to justify my unease around Tert and yet did not want to become involved in the unpleasantness of their circumstances and manner.

I was just preparing to flip a coin between leaving and heading up to the house to ask when something happened that precluded any other action: The elderly woman fell out of her chair.

I rushed up the driveway toward the house, leapt up over the steps and across the boards, went down on both knees in front of her, and felt her ancient neck for a pulse. At my touch, her eyes opened and began rolling around. Tiny grunts emanated from her throat.

"Are you all right?" I asked, foolishly. It was clear that she was not. Her skin was sallow and fit her like crumpled tissue paper, and her breath—even in the open air of an early-spring morning—stank of internal rot. Even after I helped her replace her glasses, her pale eyes did not focus on me, and were milky but charged with surprise. I put my hands under her head, felt for dampness and found none. *Good*, I decided, *at least she's not bleeding*. "Are you in pain?" I asked.

"Ah . . . ah . . . always, my dear," she said. "Always. Getting old is not without its trials. But don't worry about me."

Don't worry? I took her frail old hands in mine and again felt for her pulse. It was faint and rapid. Her fingers were long and narrow, very elegant, but just as Hector had said, they were ruined by painful-looking scars along the cuticles. "Can you stay like this a moment?" I asked. "I'll run and get your daughter."

"Deirdre? No, don't trouble her. She's so overworked, poor dear."

I was certain now that I had the right house, but I didn't know if Mrs. Krehbeil was displaying shock or just dementia. I said, "I'd offer to put you back in your chair, ma'am, but I don't know what your situation is. You might have injuries. I'll go fetch your daughter."

I rose and hurried to the front entrance and knocked on the screen door. No answer came. The inner door stood ajar, so I put my face to the opening and shouted, "Hello? Excuse me, but your mother has fallen from her chair!" Still no answer. I peeked inside. A gray tabby cat the color of Tert Krehbeil's eyes scowled at me from a broad, gray sofa. The room was decorated with jarringly bad paintings, sentimental renderings of dripping foliage and turgid millponds, not museum-quality masterworks of Western action scenes.

I glanced back toward the fallen woman. The quilts still moved up and down with her frail attempts to breathe. She was not making perfect sense, but she seemed reasonably stable. *But I've got to do something*, I decided.

There was a cordless telephone lying on a table just inside the door. I decided to dodge in and grab it and dial 911.

I opened the door and stepped inside. "Hello!" I shouted again. "Help! The lady on the front porch has fallen!" I took several more steps and called again, then listened.

From the far end of the house, I heard a muffled, "Shit!" and then footsteps. The sound approached none too quickly. Finally the middle-aged woman whom I presumed to be Deirdre appeared at the far end of the central hall. When she spotted me, she said, "What is it?" none too kindly.

"Your m—The old lady on the porch has fallen from her chair," I said. "I don't think she's well."

"*That's* an understatement," said Deirdre. "Okay, okay." She barged past me and out the door. As she turned and finally spotted her mother, she cried angrily, "Mother! Oh, good God!" and rushed towards her.

I know the care of the elderly can be trying, but I found Deirdre's attitude appalling. But this was a moment for action, so I grabbed the phone from its cradle and rushed out the door behind her. "Shall I call an ambulance?" I asked.

Deirdre had crouched beside her mother. At the instant I said "ambulance," she spun on her toes to face me, her eyes wide. "No!" she cried. "No, don't do that! Give me that!" she demanded.

I hurried to her and gave her the phone, expecting her to dial another number, perhaps someone who lived closer, but she snatched it from my hand and set it aside. "Just help me get her into the chair," she said. "She's fine, I'm sure of it. This happens all the time. She just wiggles her way out of it."

I moved into position and helped her lift the frail, old body of the woman, which seemed to weigh nothing. She was little more than a husk. We settled her back into the chair and covered her again.

She appeared dazed, and her breathing still came in gasps, but she smiled pleasantly and, panting between words, said, "Thank you, Deirdre. And who is our visitor?"

As Deirdre turned to second her mother's inquiry with a raised eyebrow, I got control of my mouth and said, "Um, I'm—I was just driving past and I saw her lying here."

Deirdre gave me an artful smile that stopped halfway up her cheeks. "I do so appreciate your stopping," she said, moving toward me as if to squeegee me off the porch.

"Let me help you get her inside," I said.

"I'm sure I can make it."

She wasn't going for the easy sell, so I affected a case of the vapors, waving my hand in front of my face as if I felt faint. "I'm sorry, but it seems I'm more upset by this than anyone. I need to sit a moment." I thumped myself down on the bench.

Old Mrs. Krehbeil said, "Deirdre, you run along and . . ." She stopped to pant. "Finish what you were doing." *Pant.* "I'll sit with our friend." *Pant.* "I so seldom get a visitor."

Deirdre gave me a look like January in the Arctic. Then she turned abruptly and lumbered back into the house. She had a large frame, and moved like she was carrying a piano.

I turned to Mrs. Krehbeil. "How are you feeling?" I inquired.

"Fine," she panted. "Sorry to trouble you. Won't you have a seat?"

I didn't point out that I was already sitting.

"I should introduce myself," she wheezed. "I'm Mrs. Krehbeil, and this is my husband's country home." Her frail hand trembled through a grand gesture, upsetting her quilts. "We call it 'Far Diggings.'" *Pant.* "It's a name my father-in-law gave it."

"My name is Leila," I said, giving my mother's name to obscure my identity. "Far Diggings. Was your father-in-law an educated man, then? It doesn't sound like a name a farmer would choose."

Her answer was a moment coming. "He was an industrialist," she gasped finally, and again, "This was his country home." She began to sag forward again.

I edged toward her, ready to catch her if she leaned too far over again. "Oh? What was his business?"

"Paint. Just exactly that shade." She raised a shaking hand to point at the front door.

"Ah." So it was no wild coincidence that Tert had gone into an aesthetic enterprise. In an instant, I spun a whole history for the family, putting Krehbeil Primus at the apex of an expanding dynasty of gray-eyed men who held themselves in high esteem while they manipulated their women.

Mrs. Krehbeil's breathing seemed to have eased for a moment. "Deirdre is preparing a downstairs room for me," she said conspiratorially. "My doctor said I should take the air, and we have no second-story porch. So she's moving my things. . . ."

I heard the door open behind me again, and Deirdre reappeared. "I'll take you back inside now, Mother. Clearly Doc Abram's idea was a bit premature."

"All right, dear," the old girl gasped. "Oh, but Deirdre, when is William coming?"

"He's not coming today, Mother," she said testily. Then, in a low, growling tone, she muttered, "You get sicker every time he comes. Don't you think it best he stay away?"

"My precious William. When did you say he was coming?"

"Don't wait up, Mom." Deirdre unlocked the wheels and moved around behind the chair to push it back inside. I had to hustle to make it look like I was helping her with the doors, so efficient was the daughter, but, moving from door to living room to inner hallway at a good clip, I was able to keep ahead of Deirdre, all the time taking surreptitious glances at the drizzly paintings. At the far end of the hall, there was a small maid's room with a hospital bed, sheets tight and blankets turned down.

I helped Deirdre heft her mother into the bed and arrange the covers. "There," she said, as she smoothed her white curls about her papery face, "you get some rest, Mother."

"Yes, dear." The old woman dutifully closed her eyes.

Deirdre indicated that I should lead the way out of the room. "Thank you for your assistance," she said briskly.

As I moved back into the hallway I smelled cinnamon and glanced into the kitchen, in hopes of obligating her to invite me there. "What smells so divine?" I gushed.

Mrs. Krehbeil's voice quavered from the small room. "Give her some toast and tea, dear."

Deirdre's eyes closed. "Okay," she said heavily. "Would you like some toast?"

"I'd love some!" I drawled. By then I wanted to stay, not only so I could gather information, but also in some small way to inconvenience this creature who treated her ailing mother so churlishly.

Deirdre showed me to a chair at the kitchen table and hurried about the task of preparing one slice of balloon bread, toasted lightly in an ancient toaster and spread with a niggardly film of butter and a chintzy glaze of home-made jam. I noticed that she pulled the bread out of the toaster barehanded, as if her hands were made of asbestos. Without even whacking the piece in half, she stuck it in front of me. "Tea?" she inquired.

"Tea would be marvelous," I replied. I dawdled, lifting the toast to my lips and taking the tiniest of bites from one corner.

Deirdre turned on the fire underneath a pan of water. When it had heated, she grabbed the metal handle and poured a half-cup into a mug, stuck a cheap tea-bag in it, lifted it by the sides of the mug, and set it in front of me. Then she sat down across from me and stared. I noticed that her eyes were the same cool shade of gray as her brother's, but instead of self-absorption I saw unveiled cunning.

Trying to engage her in conversation that might lead to information, I said, "You have good, honest farmwoman's hands."

"What do you mean?"

"You don't seem to need a hot-pad to handle hot things."

She made a derisive grunt. "I have a condition called peripheral neuropathy. That means I can no longer feel my hands or feet." She smiled, as if taking a bizarre pleasure in talking about it. "It's like death visiting you a little bit at a time," she said. "Gradually, the tips of you die, each nerve going out with a bolt of pain, but all portending your overall death. The numbness is just an early visit."

We stared at each other a moment. Her words had been more an assault than an opening-up. I said, "Has your mother been ill long? It can be such a trial."

Deirdre shook her head with robust bitterness. "I'm out here all alone with her." Casting me a sidelong glance, she added, "She won't go to the hospital. Why do that when I'm here to wait on her hand and foot? Insists on going to that old cadaver of a doctor. He should have retired years ago."

I smiled sweetly, but thought, *What luck! A griper. She'll tell me all sorts of things that are none of my business in the name of glorifying her martyrdom.* "Is it her lungs?" I asked, giving my voice ever-so-slight a quaver. *Martyrdom and drama, they go hand in hand.*

Deirdre bore down on her pet issues. "I get no help from my brothers," she grouched. "One is a drunk who fancies himself an *actor*," she emphasized this last, indicating her distaste for the profession. "And the other is off making his millions."

"Is that the 'Precious William' your mother mentioned?" I asked. "Your mother asked after him."

"William seldom comes to see her, which is just as well, because every time he comes, she gets sicker."

"Yes, you said."

Ignoring me, she went on with her diatribe. "But it's fine with *them* that I give up my life to nurse her. I try to run the farm, but just watching her keeps me busy, let me tell you."

"Oh, I'm sure. But you have the farm."

"Damn straight I do!"

"You love this place," I said, wondering if she in fact loved anything.

"This farm has been in the family for generations! *Nobody* loves it as much as I do, and I *will* pass it on to my children!"

"Farming is such an endless list of chores," I clucked.

"The roof's all but gone on the barn, and the porch is falling off the house."

"It's ever thus," I said morosely, getting into the flavor of the gripe session.

"But the old girl has to have her pretty things. I was just moving her pet objects downstairs when she said she wanted to take the air."

"Ah." *And what are these pet objects?* I wanted to inquire. *Perhaps a Remington bronze or two?*

"Well," she said, glancing at her watch, "I have a lot to do."

"Would you like me to sit with her while you take care of a few things? I know how this goes. My mother was ill for years with cancer, and I about lost my mind. I'll just sit by and drink my tea, and you can get about things."

She scowled at me. "I couldn't impose," she said, her brusque tone not matching the politeness of her words.

"Really, it would be a pleasure to help, and it's no trouble whatsoever."

Deirdre stared at me, taking my measure in detail, her mind turning as methodically as the escapement in an old watch. "Fine," she said. "Then you can be on your way." It was an order.

She rose and bustled from the room.

I instantly got down to the business of making observations, first making a visual inventory of the room. The refrigerator was avocado-colored and made a grinding sound, which indicated that it was quite old and as sick as Mrs. Krehbeil. The stove looked like it had been installed no later than the 1940s. There was no dishwasher. The walls once had been white, but had yellowed with the vaporized grease of five thousand dinners. Again, this did not fit with a place that might house original Russells.

Deirdre rushed past the doorway carrying an elegant fluted vase and a silver-backed brush-and-comb set. She disappeared into the room where she had installed her mother and then reappeared, hurrying back toward the stairs for another load.

While she was upstairs, I went to the door into the dining room and took a look. One small painting hung above the sideboard. It was another amateurish, inconsequential piece, and the subject was definitely an East Coast village. Hearing Deirdre returning, I hurriedly sat down again and lifted my cup as if I had not left the table. The toast was congealing on the plate in front of me. I took another bite and forced it down my throat. It stuck like the lack of welcome it was meant to represent.

This time Deirdre was carrying a small set of leather-bound books. After she had deposited them and hurried off again, I got up and cast about for a paper napkin so I could wrap up the toast and hide it in my pocket rather than gag it down. Not a scrap of paper was visible in the room, not even a roll of paper toweling. I moved across the hall and started searching for a bathroom, thinking I would use toilet paper instead, but it seemed that the house predated indoor bathrooms, at least on the ground floor. I opened the only two closed doors, but found only a coat closet and a small storage room filled with the accumulation of a hundred years of indecision about which papers and books might be thrown out. There was a pantry, but it was filled with the usual sorts of things one might expect to find, mostly dishes, and mostly chipped or mismatched.

Deirdre was fast returning with the next load, so I returned to the kitchen table but did not sit down. "May I use your bathroom?" I inquired, after palming the toast back onto the plate.

She stopped and stared at me for several moments. "Up the stairs and to your right," she said with obvious annoyance. "Hold the handle down for at least ten seconds."

I mounted the stairs, past faded wallpaper and framed photographs in black and white. One was of Deirdre as a young girl, and others were children who had to be her siblings. Tert as a boy, the gray gaze already perfected. Another pale-eyed lad with a supercilious smile and wide-ranging ears, hugging a stuffed beagle. A fourth portrait showed a very blonde little blue-eyed girl who smiled so widely that her dimples hurt to look at. *A sister?* I wondered. *No. If Deirdre had a sister, she would have made a special fetish out of griping about her, underlining her own worthiness at the expense of a female who does not assist.*

I found the bathroom and pretended to make use of it. Like the kitchen, it was greatly in need of an update. The toilet indeed needed coaxing, and the sink dripped mercilessly. The tub was a marvelous old claw-foot thing, but the enamel was far past its prime.

I ran water in the sink as if I were washing, waiting until I heard Deirdre pass by to seize another few objects, and then pass again on her way downstairs. When she was well on her way down the staircase, I slipped out the door and moved as silently as I could up the hallway, glancing into each room as I went. I found the doors to several bedrooms ajar, and checked each one. The first was a monument to the slovenly habits of the young male I had seen coming out of the driveway as I arrived; unwashed clothing lay in drifts around the bed, and the air stank of armpits. I pulled my nose quickly from this room; there was nothing of interest on the walls anyway, just posters of fast cars and busty women. The second bedroom reeked of stale cigarettes, and the scattering of clothing on its floor suggested it belonged to the young female. Again, the walls were ornamented with cheap posters, not priceless Remingtons. I moved on down the hall to the last room. It stank of the ailing woman.

This room was larger than the others, clearly the master bedroom. There, centered on the wall opposite the four-poster bed where it could be admired from the pillow, was a small watercolor that looked like it just might be a Russell.

I heard Deirdre returning. I glanced back toward the bathroom. I had closed the door so she might assume I was still in there, which was good, because there was no way I could make it back in time. I hurried down the hall, ducked into a fourth bedroom, and plastered myself against a wall, out of sight of the doorway.

This room smelled sourly of another sort of decay, something unused and fusty. The yellowed roller shades were drawn two-thirds of the way, making the room look like it was lost in sad amber. There were bookshelves all around the walls. The bed was neatly made, and some bookwork was open on a drop-leaf desk. A tattered nightdress lay across the chair. I glanced around the walls. Not a single picture graced the aging plaster.

Deirdre was making another circuit now, so I slipped back out into the hall and grasped the doorknob of the final door and turned it. Or tried to. It was locked. "Shit," I whispered under my breath. I gave it a shove, and the knob came off in my hand. I stuck it quickly back in place and, bending, took a peek in through the keyhole. I saw the shadows of some sort of small wooden structure and caught the scent of turpentine. A studio?

It was time to skedaddle. I had introduced myself as a passing Samaritan, not a friend of the family who deserved a glimpse of the paintings, and I could think of no artifice to throw out now to justify bringing up the subject. So, with regrets and frustration, I moved as silently as possible back down the hallway, flushed the toilet, and then made plenty of noise going down the stairs.

Deirdre met me in the front hall, blocking my return to the kitchen.

"Do you need any more help?" I asked.

"None whatsoever."

"Well then, I'll be off. It was nice meeting you and your mother."

She backed me toward the door by crowding me physically, and closed it behind me with a firm thump.

I found my way down the lawn and down the road, and got into my car. As I went about the ritual of pulling the key out of my pocket and adjusting my seat belt, I surveyed the front of the house, counting windows until I found the locked room. Only one blind was up, but I saw what had cast the shadow: It was indeed an artist's easel.

I put the car in gear and drove away, trying to piece together the puzzle that was the family Krehbeil.

I HEADED SOUTH INTO THE CITY OF LANCASTER AND FOUND A bookstore near the center of town and purchased an atlas of Lancaster County and a map of Washington D.C. In the atlas, I plotted my trajectory to the Pennsylvania Geologic Survey, which was just over the county line on the far side of Mount Joy. I thumped my finger on the map, wondering where exactly in that town Hector might be found; half an hour later, as I drove past that part of the county, I tried to figure an approach to visiting him. *It wouldn't be good to look him up immediately after "dropping in" on his mother and sister*, I decided. *If they talk at all, my visit would be the first thing on Deirdre's lips. Or the second thing, if she happens to mention that Ma fell out of her wheelchair.*

The Commonwealth of Pennsylvania's Bureau of Topographic and Geologic Survey headquarters occupied a modern, one-story brick building at the top of a rise just off the highway. I parked the rental car and headed up past a hunk of limestone and a big slab of sandstone, resplendent in fossilized critter burrows, to the entrance of the building, where I found a glassed-in foyer presided over by more geologic specimens and a receptionist. "Can I help you?" the receptionist inquired. She was a perfectly reasonable specimen of humanity, but the rocks held about ninety percent of my attention. "That's our state fossil," she intoned, as I bent close to a trilobite.

"I'm here to see Fred Petridge," I said, now admiring a chunk of coal half the size of a Volkswagen. "I'm Em Hansen. I'm a geologist from Utah."

The receptionist dialed a number and had me sign a registry. Then I made myself to home with the rack of free booklets that stood by the door. Geological surveys are a veritable gold mine for such treasures. I selected booklets entitled, *The Geological Story of Pennsylvania, The Non-fuel Resources of Pennsylvania, Oil and Gas in Pennsylvania*, and *Sinkholes in Pennsylvania*. I was just absorbing the fact that some of the rocks that outcropped in Pennsylvania were 2.5-billion-year-old schists, slates, and marbles populated by fossilized blue-green algae, jellyfish, and worms, when Dr. Petridge joined me.

"Em Hansen, is it?" He held out a hand for me to shake. He was a medium-looking sort who wore steel-rimmed glasses and spoke with a slight Southern accent. "Did you have any trouble finding us?" he inquired.

"No, I am a geologist. I bought a map."

Petridge grinned at this inside joke, led me down a maze of hallways to his office, and offered me a seat.

I sat down and took in the ambience of the room. It was, by my standards, quite homey, being stacked to the gills with reference texts and plastered floor-to-ceiling with maps. The desk was awash with a paper he appeared to be reviewing for a colleague. The edges of the pages bristled with colored sticky notes.

Petridge settled into his swivel chair. "So. How can I help you with your project? For that matter, precisely what *is* your project?"

That I wanted to know myself. "Well, as I think I mentioned in my e-mail, I'm searching for a possible thesis project in forensic geology. Generally, that's trace evidence, the art of finding tiny mineral clues."

He nodded. "I understand all that, but what brings you clear from Utah to Pennsylvania? Don't you have tiny mineral clues there?"

I grinned. It was fun talking with such a smart man. "Well, to be honest, I was coming this way anyway, but I've also become interested in mineral pigments, some of which are mined materials. I understand you're an expert on the mines of Pennsylvania. I've worked in petroleum, so I'm approaching this as a cross between a resource issue and a matter of trace evidence. I'd like to know how certain resources might be fingerprinted. I imagine that some ore bodies are quite distinct."

Petridge nodded. "Yes, they are. Others are not, and some pigment mines are so variable that the producers routinely mix the production from various places around the pit so that it remains more consistent. Is this a doctoral dissertation you're talking about?"

"No, a master's thesis."

Petridge smiled indulgently. "Then what you're talking about sounds pretty broad and overly ambitious. You know the distinction between a doctoral dissertation and a master's thesis, don't you?"

I smiled uncertainly.

"A doctoral dissertation is intended to be groundbreaking work, as highly detailed and exhaustive as suits the subject. A master's is just supposed to show that you can do the work with the judges watching. My advice is simple: Be selfish. Trim it down as far as possible. Get it done. Get on about your life."

I had a feeling this Fred Petridge guy and I were going to get along. "Then what would you suggest?"

He tipped his head to one side. "How should I know? I've never worked in forensics. But let me call in someone who has. Nigel Iago. He's our GIS specialist." He picked up his phone and dialed, and told the person who answered it, "Hey, come on down here a mo,' will you? Got a woman who's into forensic geology here. Yeah."

When he had put down the phone, I asked hopefully, "Does your colleague have a specialty in forensics? We're rare beasts, so it would be great luck to meet another."

Petridge shook his head. "Not exactly," he said. "Oh, here he is now. I'll let him explain."

The man who appeared through the doorway was tall and angular, and had mustaches that were brushed wildly to either side of his long, narrow nose. As he shook my hand he grinned brightly, an action that induced his mustaches to rise and spread like two wings taking flight. "Fred," he said, "who is this vision?"

"Don't mind Nigel," said Fred. "He hits on all the girls."

"Nice to meet you, Nigel," I said noncommittally.

He said, "You're interested in forensic work, are you? How marvelous. I have an inverse specialty in forensic geology."

"Oh?" I said. "Inverse?"

"Yes, it's what brought me to the Survey, in fact. When I taught at Bowling Green State, a fellow faculty member taught forensic geology there, and each term he'd declare me dead and make his students figure out who killed me and how and where it was done. Dirt in the shoes, forged securities in overrated gold stocks, that sort of thing. I got very good at lying about looking extinct."

Petridge said, "When the forensic man left Bowling Green, he came here to head the Survey. He took pity on Nigel's corpse and brought it along. We try to ignore the odor."

Nigel made a gesture that was inclusive of the whole building. "This is my new coffin. Quite nice, really, though I'd rather fancy a bit of tucked sateen."

"Nigel works the graveyard shift, usually," said Petridge. "You're lucky to catch him in by daylight. The garlic we were wearing around our necks generally keeps him at bay."

Nigel said, "I do have to stay out of direct sunlight." He threw back his head and bayed with laughter at his own joke.

"How nice for you both," I said carefully. I could see that these two guys got on like gunpowder and lightning.

Fred Petridge nodded. "Yes it is, in fact," he said, "Nigel's building up the GIS force at the Survey here and is also working with the U.S. Geological Survey to create a detailed electronic map of the state that is ten times better than the old topo sheets, a project called 'PA Map.' "

"That's a palindrome," Nigel informed me.

"The thing is," said Fred, "Pennsylvania is in fact a commonwealth. The counties have much more power than the state. They already have tremendous amounts of data on the county Web sites. Their combined budgets dwarf ours, and if the federal government were to try to replicate what the counties have done, it would cost untold millions. So, Nigel is working with me as I try to make a mine layer for the state, county by county."

"Wait, back up. What exactly is GIS?" I said.

"Geographic Information Systems," said Nigel, his eyes flashing. "Computer magic. Each 'layer' is one slice of information: land ownership, utilities, geology, mines. We have forty-four layers going for Lancaster County alone."

"You see his prejudices already," Fred commented. "Geology is just a slice. Mines are another slice, which means that he doesn't really consider mines to be geology, or geology to include mines."

Nigel's mustaches flew out wildly with a new level of joviality. "Fred, dear man, I see that you are finally beginning to understand." To me, he said, "GIS is marvelous. You can select the layers you want and cross-compare graphical information in a blink."

"So the point is, Em, that you can ask to see your mines relative to any other layer, such as roads. But keep in mind that it's actually a dark art," said Fred. "You know what they always say about computers: garbage in, garbage out."

Nigel sat down in a second side chair and put his feet up on this desk. "Fred is such a naysayer, but GIS is the new buzz. There are whole university departments that do nothing but. Big bucks. Very powerful tool. Thing of the future. Fred, old bean, you are a dinosaur, has anyone told you?"

Fred shook his head affably. "Me? I'm just a field geologist with a mineral hammer and a tiny little braincase."

Nigel said, "Don't believe a word of it, Ms. Hansen. Our Dr. Petridge here is a veritable warehouse of information on things mineralogical. Of course, he comes with no backup file, but that is the inherent weakness of your basic hominid. But getting back to your mission, my dear lady, what is it we can do for you?"

I said, "I'd like to know what artists' pigments might have been mined in Pennsylvania in the 1800s."

Fred Petridge's swivel chair squeaked as he leaned back to examine the ceiling, where he apparently kept his mental retrieval system. "In the 1800s there was plenty going on. Pigment mining was a fairly local affair, with small shops scattered around the commonwealth, mostly mining ocher and other earth colors. Of course, you had your chromite mining down by the Maryland line; that was very big from about the 1820s through the turn of the century."

"I know that the 1800s saw the development of chemically-derived pigments," I said. "Was there much pigment manufacturing here, or was it more like with the ochers, used directly?"

"Well, chromite was processed into lead chromate. That was done down near Baltimore and then richer reserves were found in Africa and the game folded and moved there. It's always thus with mining and manufacturing." He shrugged his shoulders. "Right now our nation is importing most of its mined resources, and that creates a trade deficit."

Nigel interjected, "Can't have all that mess right here in our own backyards, old man."

Fred shook his head. "I say if we're using the resources, then we ought to use our own, and avoid weakening our economy. But you're asking about the 1800s. Even the ochers were washed and sorted, and we have umbers. Come with me," he said, leading us back out into the network of halls. "We have a nice old text in our library that might interest you."

The library was a large room with low ceilings and tall bookcases crammed with texts and maps. Fred introduced me to the librarian, who hurried back into the stacks and found the text in question.

It was a slim volume entitled, *The Mineral Pigments of Pennsylvania*, by Benjamin Miller, published in 1911. I licked my chops, metaphorically speaking, and reached out to take it from the librarian's hands.

Nigel grabbed before I reached it and flipped through it impatiently, his mustaches pulling up like a moth folding its wings. "Looks very interesting, I'm sure. But how do you intend to use some old stuffy tome like this to catch bad guys?"

"I work intuitively," I said, trying to make that sound as if it explained everything.

"Ah," said Nigel. "First you fight your way into the wet paper bag, and then you fight your way back out again."

Fred said, "Oh, don't get going on her, Nigel, she doesn't know yet what a cream puff you really are. Don't take him seriously, Em. I'm sure you can't talk about most aspects of the cases you've worked on. But, of course, we'd love hearing about anything you *can* talk about."

"Thank you," I said. "In fact, yes, a lot of it is privileged information. I can tell you that I have a date at the FBI's forensic labs tomorrow. . . ."

Nigel's mustaches took flight again, and I saw almost all of his teeth. "Oh goody! Might I come along?"

I shook my head. "Sorry. I've had to survive a security screening to get cleared for the visit, and it took a week. I'm sure they couldn't do it on twenty-four hours' notice."

"Drat. But you'll give us a full report."

"I will?"

"Yes. Because you'll come back the day after next, to join us. Won't she, Freddie?"

I said, "Join you for what?"

"For *where*," said Nigel. "Fred here has pretensions of taking me in the field to show me what's actually on the ground. Imagine. It would tuck in nicely with your work, I'd say."

Fred nodded appraisingly. "Sure. We could go see some of the old chromite district as a focal point to experiment with your system. Another colleague of mine will be along, too, but that's okay, there are seats for four."

"Sounds like fun," I said. "Where else might we be going on our trip?"

Fred said, "Oh, I was figuring to run over to Manheim Township and look at some limonite pseudomorphs. They're iron oxide—right up your alley—though I don't suppose these ones were used in paints."

"Pseudomorphs," said Nigel, wrinkling up his nose in such a way that his mustaches looked like they were having sex. "What possible use are pseudomorphs to a man like me?"

"They're a mined material, first," answered Petridge, "and they're a clue to what lies beneath." He turned to me. "Here in Pennsylvania, we have a rather heavy soil and vegetative cover. It makes it difficult to discern much about the structure of the rock formations beneath, but we have our ways of figuring things out."

Nigel sneered theatrically. "GIS, my good man. I keep telling you, my GIS will make it all clear to you. Some good color infrared aerial photography with the right crop in the fields, and you're going to see all the structure you can tolerate."

Fred shook his head. "Nigel, it's remarkable that I've convinced you to look at actual data. You'd so much prefer to invent reality."

"Bosh," said Nigel. "On Wednesday I'll show you correlations between the county soils map and your geology, cross-correlated to property values and usage. You'll be on your ruddy little knees asking for more."

"Can you show how that correlates with the farms?" I inquired.

"A flick of the wrist," said Nigel.

"Well, then, we'll meet here at eight," said Fred.

"For what?" squealed Nigel. "To drive a stake through my heart? What an ungodly hour!"

I said, "Actually, it would be great if we could start a little later. I might be driving back up from Washington," I said.

Fred shrugged his shoulders. "Call it nine then."

◇

Sometimes the adventure of making professional contacts is an exercise in uncertainty, or even time wasted. I came away from the Pennsylvania Geologic Survey feeling intellectually stimulated, but wondering if I had gotten anything that would be of any use in constructing a master's thesis. As I drove south towards Washington, I felt only a brewing sense of anxiety. Fred and Nigel were very entertaining individuals and obviously knew a lot, but I did not even know what questions to ask them. I had met Tert's mother and sister, but had learned only that they were, each in her own way, as emotionally off-kilter as he was, and that the supposed collection of Western masterworks was either a fiction or stored somewhere else.

And yet Tert had wanted to keep me away from the house. Why? Was he afraid I'd tell Faye that the family fortune was on the skids? I wondered why I was making so much work for myself. *Faye is probably sick of him by now. I could just analyze the pigments in the chips he gave me, write up a short summary—or perhaps he doesn't even want anything in writing—hand over the data, and spend the money.*

But you can't publish those results, I reminded myself. *So you're off to find a painting or paintings you can analyze in public. Maybe tomorrow morning's meeting at the National Gallery of Art will pan out, or the afternoon's meeting at the FBI.*

The road wound ahead of me, a long black ribbon dotted with cars. About halfway between Baltimore and Washington, traffic slowed to a molasseslike crawl, and it took two hours to travel the next forty miles. In that time, I struggled to tease the two problems—Tert and his paint chips and the question of a Master's thesis—into two heaps, but they kept grabbing hold of each other again.

So this is rush hour, I mused. No one was going anywhere in a hurry. I inched southward along Interstate 95 to Washington's beltway, where I had to slow down even more. Illuminated signs advised traffic conditions for several exits on either side of the junction. Eventually I gained the turnoff onto New Hampshire Avenue, following the instructions Faye's great uncle had advised, and moved ponderously miles and miles down a city street through endless traffic lights. I missed several critical turns where the route took unexpected jogs, but eventually found my way to

Dupont Circle, where I dodged kamikaze Volvo and Mercedes drivers who were clearly tired of living, and missed my turn onto Massachusetts Avenue. I went all the way around the circle as cars crossed wildly to inner and outer lanes, then finally made the correct right turn and promptly overran the building I was looking for.

I had presumed that something named the Cosmos Club would be well marked, perhaps with a large marquee sign with twinkling lights or neon, but in this grove of ostentatious buildings, their signs were oddly reserved. It took me three passes involving as many twisty negotiations of a network of side streets to find the club—a three-story mansion in some sort of Baroque revival style, encrusted with pillars and pilasters and dripping with carved putti and gargoyles—and then it was only by dead reckoning.

Parking briefly on the street, I walked past the wrought iron gates and clear up the curving driveway to the door before I could read the small brass plaque by the ornate door that demurely indicated that this building indeed housed the Cosmos Club.

Next I had to figure out how to get in. It seemed that one had to ring a buzzer and be let in by a man in uniform. He showed me through the ornate lobby and into a room to the right, where a young woman from somewhere in the Middle East checked me in, took a print of my credit card, offered me an apple from the bowl on the counter, and said that Mr. Carter—Faye's great uncle—would be meeting me for dinner at eight. That gave me less than an hour to figure out where to park the car (there was a gated lot for fifteen dollars a night, highly recommended, or a long walk to a side street so I wouldn't get towed, not recommended as the car might be stolen or ransacked), take my luggage to my room (down a couple of hallways, into the world's tiniest elevator, around and down more confusing junctions of corridors, and into a room not much bigger than my car), and dress for dinner (Faye had intervened in my packing ritual just enough to persuade me to pack what little I had in the way of travel clothes that looked like city attire, which amounted to one knit skirt, a turtleneck shirt with no holes in it, a boiled-wool jacket, and a pair of dress pumps).

It was a nice room, very clean and very quiet. I ceremoniously set my duffel on the little folding table supplied for luggage, kicked off my shoes, and lay down on the bed. I closed my eyes for precisely two minutes and forced myself to take long, deep breaths. Once done with that attempt at relaxation, I toured the room. It featured a tidy set of furniture in American Colonial style, a phone, a closet, and a small private bath. Here I was in for a treat: The Cosmos Club might believe in understated signs at the entrance, but inside it regarded its name and crest so highly that it printed one or both on all consumables—on the soaps, on the cups, on the hand towels, and even on the emery boards that had been kindly supplied should I choose to smooth my fingernails. Back by the bed on the tiny writing desk, I found the Cosmos crest on the pens and the little pads of paper. I decided that Washington was not only the capital of our nation, but also of self-importance.

At the appointed hour, I made my way back down to the lobby by a route which took me through halls encased in an overwhelming amount of dark, ornately carved paneling past billiard rooms, ballrooms with Baroque and Rococo ceilings, and down curving stairways. On two levels I found galleries of portraits of members past and present, including proud displays of Cosmos members who had won Pulitzers, Nobels, and other prizes, and a nice oil of a past president of the United States who was identified here only as "Herbert Hoover, Mining Engineer." By the time I found my way back to the lobby, I was positively giddy. The man in uniform bid me good evening and gestured toward an elderly gentleman in a dark green suit and bow tie who was seated in an overstuffed chair near a row of French doors.

Mr. Carter was tall, like his niece, and equally slender—in his case, almost to the point of boniness—and blessed with the same large, eloquent eyes, although his were surmounted by an untamed array of twisting eyebrows. His pale gray hair lay in thin wisps around his sagging face. When he saw me approach, he rose from his chair with the stiffness of age and took my hand in his long, dry fingers. "Miss Hansen, is it? Welcome to my club. I trust they've made you comfortable."

"Please call me Emily," I said, slipping into prep-schoolitis. I was back in the East, inside the many-toothed jaws of my childhood, and I could not for the life of me behave as the independent woman I so fervently tried to be.

Mr. Carter led me into the restaurant, which was quietly alive with waiters in tuxedos and ancient diners enjoying lavish meals at tables heavy with linen cloths and elaborate settings. We settled in and ordered, then he said how pleased he was that Faye had befriended a geologist, and that I was to feel quite welcome at the Cosmos, which had been founded by John Wesley Powell, a giant among students of the Earth. "This is after all a meeting place for scientists, and you young women are earning your place right along with the men these days," he informed me.

I could see why Faye had sent me to him. *You're a nice old dinosaur,* I decided, *especially considering that you're paying for dinner. Or at least I hope you are.*

He asked, "So what brings you to Washington, my dear? Faye tells me you are a forensic scientist." Here he shot out his head like a turtle coming out of its shell, lowered his bushy eyebrows, and said, "Are you on a case?"

I couldn't help smiling. He was a sweet old geezer, and, like his great-niece, a bit of a rogue. I realized that I was thinking warmly of Faye for the first time in quite a while. I was, in fact, enjoying myself immensely, and felt grateful to her that she had made it possible. "Well," I said, leaning forward to meet my host with a suitably conspiratorial tone, "I can't talk about it much, but it involves paint pigments." I chose these last words carefully, indicating by my choice of terms that the paints in question were those used by artists. "Pigments are often mined materials," I added, for spice. "I'll be visiting some chromite mines on Wednesday."

His wild old eyebrows shot skyward. "Aha! Then you must meet Martin Hauser." He leaned back and beckoned to another old gent who was dining alone at a nearby table. "Ho there, Mart! Come join us." As the man arrived, Mr. Carter added, "Miss Hansen, meet Mr. Hauser, retired chemical engineer for Chromex Corporation in Baltimore. Miss Hansen is a geologist, and a dear friend to my great-niece."

Mr. Hauser fit his suit like a sausage in its casing. He bowed slightly as he shook my hand and then lowered himself into a chair, crimping his rotund body into a sitting position. "To what do I owe the pleasure of your acquaintance?"

I felt like I had both of my granddads to myself on Christmas morning. "I'm trying to learn what I can about mineral pigments," I said. "It sounds from the name as if Chromex Corporation might have interests in that area."

Mr. Hauser's cheeks went Santa Claus–rosy as they bunched up into a smile. "Why, my dear, Chromex has entirely too much interest in mineral pigments. Our site in Baltimore was ground zero for a marvelous experiment done by the Environmental Protection Agency. You see, Baltimore was the center of chromite milling and chromate pigment manufacture during the nineteenth century."

Why Faye, you sly fox, I mused. *You've used some of your pixie dust to connect me with people who can help me with my thesis*. Aloud, I said, "Wait, I'm confused: Did you say chro*mate* or chro*mite*?"

Mr. Hauser smiled indulgently and waggled a fat finger at me. "Heavens, my dear, a geologist should know these things! Chromate is the ion: CrO_4^{-2}, or one chromium atom to four oxygen. Chromite is the mineral, $FeCr_2O_4$, so you have one iron, two chromium, and four oxygen."

"And what interest did the EPA have in chromite?"

"None whatsoever," he replied cheerily. "But of course, chromate contains into hexavalent chromium, a terrible toxin when released into the wild—what the EPA calls 'the environment.' In the latter half of the twentieth century, when the EPA decided that there was too much hex chromium leaching into Chesapeake Bay—which I don't dispute; heavens, it was ruining the oyster beds!—we were required to do a clean closure of the old processing plant. We moved hundreds of thousands of yards of material and essentially sealed it in an impermeable sarcophagus. Then we all sat back and waited for the EPA to notice that the hex levels were not dropping in the Chesapeake."

"And weren't they? Why not?"

Mr. Hauser's grin broadened until his eyes were merry little dots. "Because that wasn't the only place the stuff was coming from. You see, during the mid-1800s, when chromite mining was at its height, Baltimore was also growing at a terrific clip. They needed more solid ground for building. Baltimore sits at the boggy edge of the Chesapeake, so they had some baylands to fill. And what nice, solid fill material was handy? Why, the tailings from the chromite milling! Half of downtown Baltimore is built on chromite rubble, and there's no way the EPA is going to get those towering buildings to lift up their skirts while we sweep away the floorboards they're standing on. So as groundwater percolates through the ground Baltimore is built on, it acts like one, big, nasty tea-bag spewing that carcinogen right into the Bay."

"Martin," said Mr. Carter, "Miss Hansen will think your amusement over the fouling of the Chesapeake rooted in psychopathic glee."

"No, sir," he replied. "This is how perfectly healthy scientists speak when discussing the human comedy. Certain tensions inevitably erupt around our attempts to fix errors made in prior ignorance, and a delight in irony can dispel the irritation built up while dealing with the zeal of regulatory agents who too often take the attitude that retroactive righteousness is a proper cure for the environmental woes that betide us all. In the 1800s, humanity wanted chromate, and the demand created an economic basis for mining, refining, and manufacturing products from it. Unfortunately the technology used had an unintended side effect, namely the release of toxins that were not understood until people and oysters began to show illness many decades later. Sadly, the cost of cleanup probably dwarfed the profits made in the heyday of production."

"So the chromate was made into paint," I prompted.

"Yes," Mr. Hauser replied. "Nowadays chromite is a strategic mineral used in strengthening steel, but back then, much of it was processed into lead chromate, a lovely yellow pigment. Locally it was called Baltimore yellow, although with minute variations in chemistry the pigment has also been called Paris yellow, Vienna yellow, Cologne yellow, and even Leipzig yellow, not to mention king's yellow, new yellow, Spooner's yellow, and jonquil chrome yellow."

"All those names for one pigment?" said Mr. Carter, the corners of his mouth crimping into a smile. "Really, Hauser, you'd think you chemist fellows would get together on your terminology."

Mr. Hauser raised a finger in mock schoolmaster severity. "There exists a solid solution between lead chromate and lead sulfate. The more lead sulfate you add, the lighter your tone, transiting primrose yellow to lemon yellow. And really, Carter, why be such a curmudgeon? Can't each city have its own special tint?"

"Ah, well," said Mr. Carter, "I'll go with Washington jonquil chrome yellow."

"No," said Mr. Hauser. "There are no colormen or chemists making pigments here in our nation's capital. We'll have to rely on Baltimore to defend our chromatic honor."

"What luck to meet you here," I said. "I can't imagine even knowing to ask to speak with a chemical engineer about this topic."

Faye's great-uncle preened. "The Cosmos Club was founded to promote social and professional congress between scientists."

I wondered if there was a chapter on lead chromate in the *Artists' Pigments* volumes. "So lead chromate had not only the offending hexavalent chromium, but also good old lead, a nice, toxic, heavy metal."

Mr. Hauser's cheeks went into shiny apples as his smile again brimmed with enthusiasm. "My dear, surely you've noticed that a great many of the classic mineral pigments are salts of heavy metals."

"Salts?"

"Why, yes, in the chemical sense." He picked up the saltcellar from the center of our table. "This is what most people mean when they say 'salt': Table salt, sodium chloride. NaCl. One sodium atom to one chlorine. As a geologist, you'd call it by its mineral name, halite. But chemically speaking, a salt is any metal atom joined through ionic bonding to a nonmetal. In the case of lead chromate, the chromate ion acts as the nonmetal. But take your other classic pigments, especially the reds: Vermilion, that's mercuric sulfide. Realgar, another source of red, is arsenic sulfide. Your most important white is lead carbonate. They don't call cadmium yellow 'cadmium yellow' for no reason; it's cadmium sulfide. Mercury, arsenic, lead, cadmium, all heavy metals. Other important pigments are salts of strontium, cobalt, antimony, copper, zinc, titanium, barium. A whole host of heavy metals, most of them as toxic as all get-out."

He leaned back and chuckled. "It's all chemistry. By taking the materials from their native states and spreading them on canvas, you're starting a chemistry experiment. You see, from the moment you grind your pigment—or dry it out of your washing bath, in the manufacturing plant—and expose it to air, or your wetting medium, or to the other colors you put around it, in the case of artworks, you continue your chemistry experiment. Everything attacks it. Light, heat, moisture, the sulfur in the air. And what happens? Your pigment reacts. So you want the least reactive molecule you can get that still has the color you want. It's just basic chemistry," he concluded, quite pleased with himself.

I glanced at Mr. Carter. He was starting to nod off in his chair. Mr. Hauser followed my glance and patted his friend on the wrist. "Wake up there, Carter, it's time for you to go home."

We ended our party then, and agreed to meet again the next evening, this time beginning our occasion as a threesome. Both gentlemen simultaneously tried to give me directions regarding how to travel via foot and the Metro from the Dupont Circle station to the National Gallery of Art, but could not agree. "George in the lobby can help you," Mr. Carter said, winning the debate.

"Yes," added Mr. Hauser, his cheeks turning into apples again. "Let George do it. That's what we always like to say around Washington."

On that effervescent note, we all nodded like so many penguins and toddled off toward our separate accommodations for some much-needed sleep. I had miles to go the next day, and people to see, but three steps up from the lobby floor, I turned and asked, "Oh, by the way, did the Krehbeil family have any interests in the chromite industry in Baltimore?"

"Krehbeil?" Hauser asked, standing half in and half out of the front door of the Cosmos Club. "Why, certainly, my dear. William Krehbeil founded Chromium Exporters, Incorporated."

"I don't know that company," I said politely.

Hauser smiled. "It's what we called Chromex before it was called Chromex," he said, then bowed, put on his hat, and headed down the walkway toward the street.

18

Gamboge is a transparent dark mustard yellow pigment derived from trees in Southeast Asia. An organic resin, it is soluble and therefore best suited for use in watercolor. In modern times, it has been replaced by synthetic pigments because of its extreme toxicity.

—*from the files of Fred Petridge*

DEIRDRE SPREAD A THIN LAYER OF MARGARINE ON THE BREAD SHE had purchased at the day-old store. She then spread an exceedingly fine glaze of last summer's strawberry preserves across it, took a miserly nibble from one corner, and contemplated every item large and small that filled her with rage. Such as the fact that the preserves were almost gone, and next year's crop was not yet flowering. Her feckless son had eaten nearly all of it. She would have to hide this last jar from him.

Moving on to a more perennial loathing, there was just how deeply she hated her brother William. All of her hard work had stacked itself into a towering cliff that overhung his hard-headed selfishness. *Precious William. God wasted charm and talent on you, boy. What have you done with it? Nothing. You loll about with your fancy pals in the museum set, and Mother thinks you're as clever as clever. Is she interested in what I studied in college, or what jobs I have slaved at as I've struggled to save this farm?*

And then there was that woman who had come on Monday morning. *Out of nowhere! Imposed herself on this household. Snooped all around; I know it! I'm not fooled! How much did she see?*

The two irritants became fused in the hardened muscle she called her heart. *Something has to be done!*

Having finished her breakfast and hidden the jar of jam in the back of the refrigerator, Deirdre rose and started running water into the sink to do her dishes. As she soaped the plate on which she had served herself toast, the dish slipped from her hands and broke in two against the porcelain.

"Damn!" she shouted. She picked up the two pieces and hurled them onto the floor, shattering them into much smaller parts.

Deirdre's daughter walked into the kitchen. "Ho, Ma, what's up with that?" she asked, dodging the sharp chips with her bare feet.

Deirdre's lungs heaved with emotion. She leaned on the sink a moment, then dropped backwards into the nearest chair at the table. "I can't feel the dishes anymore," she said angrily. "They slip out of my hands. My hands are totally numb now."

Her daughter put a hand on her shoulder. "Aw, Ma. You loved that pattern, too. Was that the last one without a chip?"

"Yes." Deirdre's voice came out high-pitched, pitiable.

Her daughter massaged her shoulders a moment. "Have you been to the doctor lately?"

"No," she scolded. "He knows nothing."

"I thought he wanted to test for lead."

"Where would I have gotten that?"

"I don't know . . . the old paints in the woodwork?"

"I'm hardly given to chewing the windowsills." She glared at the closest one. "It could use a little paint, though, eh?"

The younger woman nodded. "Yeah. There's lots of things that need fixing around here, Ma. Maybe it's time to hit up Uncle Tert for a loan, don't you think?"

Deirdre's voice dropped to a growl. "I will ask nothing from your uncle! Nothing!"

"It was just an idea, Ma. Don't go biting my head off." She sat down and poured herself a bowl of cereal.

Deirdre said nothing more. She sat and watched the sun rise through the leafless trees near the spring.

The elephantine sounds of her son's descent of the aging wooden stairs broke the silence. Deirdre heard the front door open and slam, heard his car start, heard the diminishing sound as it exited the driveway and moved off down the road. Silence once again settled on the room except for the clinking of her daughter's spoon against the bottom of her cereal bowl and the occasional slurp.

Presently, having unceremoniously finished her breakfast, Deirdre's daughter shrugged her way into a jacket, said a cursory good-bye, and left.

Deirdre stared down at her hands. They might as well have been someone else's.

She's right, thought Deirdre. *It is time I called brother William.*

19

I WOKE UP EARLY, SICK WITH WORRY OVER SLOANE RENEE Latimer. I knew that Faye was a good mother in all ways except one: She had taken her baby to stay with a man I did not trust, and my anxiety over her safety woke me long before the alarm.

I lay on my back, staring into the darkness, trying to figure out anything I could do that I was not already doing. I itched to telephone Faye, but waking her early was no way to convince her that I was anything but insane. How could I regain her confidence and get her and her infant away from this man who might . . .

Might what? I asked myself. *What exactly is he capable of doing?*

As it grew light out I rose and showered and put on a nice pair of corduroy slacks, but kept the dress pumps, knowing I was going to hate myself as my feet swelled over the course of the day. I didn't like torturing myself, but I was more than a little nervous about meeting with the conservator at the National Gallery of Art; and for reasons I've never understood, the thing I worry about most when meeting strangers is whether or not my feet are properly dressed. Like they're really going to be looking at my feet.

The evening before, on my way to dinner, I had stumbled across a room on the ground floor of the Cosmos Club that had a computer, and now I found my way back there and typed my way onto the Internet in search of e-mail messages from Jack. I found one:

Dear Em,

Another day here and lots to do, but just wanted to take a moment to talk to you. I have sorry news. My friend Bill who's here needs to get home, and there are just the two of us at our level, so one of us has to stay. I know you'll understand. Bill's wife had a baby just before he came out here, and he needs to be back there, watching the little one learn to walk and all the wonderful things that babies do. So I've volunteered to stay a little bit longer, just to make sure he gets clear and gets home, then I can start my release campaign again. Not much else to report. The food's lousy and my bed is lonely.

Love always, Jack

The only replies I could think of were, *Guess my life is less important than this guy Bill's,* which sounded peevish, and *Guess you have to do what you have to do,* which sounded final.

I stared into the screen for a while, then shut down the computer and quietly left the room.

I headed out the front door of the Cosmos Club and walked down Massachusetts Avenue toward Dupont Circle, passing rows of elegant old mansions, half of which appeared to be embassies. It began to dawn on me at last that I was in the nation's capital. I found the Metro. I negotiated the purchase of a ticket from a vending machine. I read the map on the wall. I got on a train. I got off and climbed the stairs back up to street level. I turned, oriented myself by a map of Washington I had purchased in the bookstore in Lancaster, and headed toward the Mall, that long, narrow park around which the principal buildings and museums of Washington were built.

The weather was brisk, and the only people that were about jogged along in tights, fleece jackets, and various descriptions of casual headgear. Not a one smiled or looked at me as they passed. I put on my city face and quit trying to make eye contact.

I glanced at my watch. Just past eight. My meeting was not until ten. It seemed that business was not done in Washington at this hour.

I reached Pennsylvania Avenue and glanced right, wondering if I could see the White House. I saw only big, important-looking buildings, looming above the street as if in competition to be the most imposing. Soaring pillars supporting carved pediments faced off against modern expanses of glass. Orienting myself by the building where I would meet at ten with Emmett Jones, I crossed into the Mall between the old and new buildings of the National Gallery. Alongside the stolid neoclassical traditionalism of the old, the new was soaringly modern, all glass and wild angles.

I hiked right past them to the center of the Mall. I turned left. I stared up toward the Capitol. Sure enough, there it was, all ice-cream white, just like on the postcards. In all my thirty-eight years I had never seen it, and it struck me as absurdly comforting to know that it was real. Turning 180 degrees, I faced down toward the graceful needle of the Washington Monument. That was real, too, and both imposingly tall, compared to the buildings that surrounded it, and laughably short by the standards of modern skyscrapers.

Oblivious of what it was going to do to my feet, I began to stride toward the needle, soon lengthening my stride with the exhilaration of moving through all the human history and achievements the museums had been built to celebrate. On my left I passed the American Indian Museum, the Air and Space Museum, Arts and Industries, the Hirschorn, the Smithsonian Castle, the Freer. To my right lay the Sculpture Garden, the Natural History Museum, and the Museum of American History.

Now I crossed Fourteenth Street and walked up the lawn to the Washington Monument. I mean I walked right up to it, passing in between the big, ugly, cement highway barriers that had been put there to deter terrorists, and, stepping right up to the base of the thing, I stuck my nose right up to it, because I wanted to know what the building was made out of. It was marble, nice, white, metamorphosed limestone with big, fat crystals all dressed to a smooth face. I stared up the edge and enjoyed the intersection of stone and sky.

From the lawn beyond the Washington Monument, I could finally see the White House. It was a nice enough view of a not-terribly-interesting bit of architecture, and I found myself wondering what all the fuss was about. Its frail grace was besmirched by a string of ugly barriers, as if in a state of siege by an unseen foe. Anger rose within me as I thought of Tom. No guards or barriers had protected him.

Confused by my anger, I got out my map and made a straight hike down the Mall toward a special destination: the Vietnam Veteran's Memorial. To add to my confusion, the cherry blossoms had burst in their ritual of rebirth and the day was warming nicely. Joggers and bicyclists sped past cars that cruised along the tidal basin, lining up to see the gorgeous row of blooming trees.

By the time I arrived at the memorial, I was thinking not only of Tom and Jack but also of Frank Barnes, and his brother and all the friends he'd lost in Vietnam. My hands balled into fists of anguish for the Frank who had left and came home caring too much. The Frank who needed someone to love. The Frank who loved babies. He had traveled to distant shores back when I was just a child because he loved his country, had suffered fear in the jungles, and had come home chased by a thousand ghosts.

The Vietnam Veteran's Memorial was not tall, like Washington's monument, but low, a slash in the earth. Before me stretched a long canyon of black stone, its polished faces incised with the names of the dead. I entered its depths in silence, and by the time I reached the middle, my face was wet with tears for an entire generation scarred by a war that had mired them in shame.

I stumbled onward to the Lincoln Memorial and climbed the steps, looking to rest for a moment by the great man's feet, and was rewarded by his immense stone likeness waiting cool and serene behind Ionic columns. Lincoln's visitors moved about quietly, as awed by his immensity as visitors to the Vietnam memorial were moved by its gravity. A woman bent over her tiny son, reading the Gettysburg Address aloud, explaining Lincoln's words to him. A Japanese tourist took flash pictures.

I read Lincoln's speech, too, and discovered that in this setting, it carried a whole new meaning for me. He spoke of the nation's grief over lives lost in war, and urged humankind to rise from its ashes.

I began to feel overwhelmed by the conflicts of human history, a sensation I had avoided in all my years of thinking in the much broader timescale of geology. I sat awhile on the steps, facing back up the Mall toward the Capitol, contemplating how far I'd come in building my life, and wondered whether life was truly just an accidental accumulation of molecules, or was in fact the big string of lessons some religions said it was.

I was in love with Jack, but loving him had led me into danger, and Tom had followed. On this early-spring morning, as I looked down the length of the Mall, I saw how much of my life was in a shambles. So much was in a state of flux. The moments of my life seemed to stretch out before me like so many stepping-stones, leading away. And yet I knew what always brought me back to center: I always followed my heart, and my heart always brought me home again to myself.

Where was home? Was it here on the Washington Mall, being American with the rest of America? Or was it something even bigger than that?

I smiled softly, enjoying the moment of clarity, even if what I saw in it was uncertainty.

The sun climbed higher in the sky, chasing the coolness of shadows underneath the budding trees. Traffic was increasing on the roads and footpaths. I glanced at my watch. It was time to head out if I was going to look at Catlin paintings at the Renwick before my appointment at the National Gallery, but yet I sat a while longer and savored a moment of quiet in all the rush and noise that was my life.

◇

I HEADED OUT across the lawns of the Mall toward Pennsylvania Avenue. Catlin's portraits had been hung at the Renwick, a small satellite gallery of the Smithsonian's American Art Museum.

I expected at most a ten-minute walk, but after ten minutes I was not even clear of the Mall, so I got out my map and plotted the shortest route, which, it seemed, would take me right past the White House. As I approached that building, I was turned away by a man in uniform. "You can't go through here," he said, indicating the public sidewalk on the other side of the street from the edifice.

"Why not?"

"*He*'s coming through," the man told me, and made one of those *Move along now* gestures that Irish cops make in B movies.

"Oh *he*," I said. "When?" As in, *Should I just wait a moment?*

The guard evaded my gaze and shook his head. "Don't know. Can't say," he replied, his voice flat, either with condescension or boredom, I was not sure which.

Anger boiled up inside of me. I wanted to tell him, *I may be just a hick from Wyoming, but all I want to do is use a public sidewalk to walk along a public street to get to a public art exhibit—all of which are supported by the taxes I pay every time I'm lucky enough to get a job. You're telling me that one man who lives on the other side of that big iron fence and the goons who handle him are so wigged out about getting shot at that they see fit to inconvenience the everyday business of hundreds of thousands of his fellow citizens! Why doesn't he go live at Camp David and have those who don't need quite such high security come to* him?

Rage rolled over me in waves. I began to tremble. *Dear God*, I thought, *this is supposed to be a center of strength and power, but it's just as shook up and scared as I am*. The urge to run home to Wyoming all but flattened me to the pavement.

The cop now made a gesture that said I should get moving, *right now*.

Moving like an automaton, I started the long detour around the White House barricades. By the time I was halfway around, I had not yet even glimpsed the façade of the Renwick Gallery. It was time to make a beeline for the National Gallery of Art and my appointment with Emmett Jones, conservator. *So much for the Catlins*, I told myself. *Maybe I'll have time this afternoon, after my trip to the FBI.*

I made it to the National Gallery by ten, but it took until twenty minutes after the hour to get all the way inside. Code Orange meant that I and a great crocodile-walk of other citizens had to wait in line, pass through a metal detector, and allow a uniformed matron to search our bags. Having made it through this screening, I then presented myself to another uniformed guard, who directed me to the security office, where I had to show identification, sign a form, and otherwise subject myself to scrutiny. Apparently deemed non-threatening, I was issued a visitor's pass on a long plastic neck chain and finally was escorted by a guard with a squawking radio downstairs into the basement. Beyond a heavy door lay the Conservation Department, where a young woman with a big smile greeted me and showed me a place to wait, as if it made her deliriously happy to do so. She offered me a seat while she rustled up Emmett Jones, whom, she explained, was, "With somebody. Being chief of the department keeps him very busy. But he won't be long."

I nodded meekly. Even the basement of the building was grand, and I confess to feeling quite intimidated. But when the Chief of Conservation of the National Gallery of Art strolled up to fetch me, he put me entirely at ease. "Hi, I'm Emmett Jones. You must be Em Hansen," he said, extending a broad hand to be shaken. "So," he said, leading me into his office, "what can I do for you?"

Taking in his soaring bookshelves filled with reference texts, I said, "I'm looking for some help understanding Remington's use of color. From a geological standpoint, that is. I'm wondering what pigments he used; which were natural mineral pigments, and which synthetic? And, if possible, I'd be curious to know where his paints came from."

Emmett pointed to a framed photograph of an artist's palette, a classic kidney-shaped blade of wood with a thumbhole. "He left four palettes, you know. Here's a photograph of one of them. He died suddenly, so you can see that the paint was still on it, exactly as he'd laid it out for use. And he left some paint tubes as well."

"Did you do analytical testing to determine what pigments he used?"

"Oh, sure," he said. "But that didn't give us the precise pigments."

"I don't understand."

"Well, we could have nailed them precisely if we had cut samples for microscope analysis, or X-ray diffraction or electron microprobe, but it was important to leave them intact. So we used X-ray fluorescence spectrometry, because it's nondestructive. The only problem is that XRF gives us the elemental analysis of the pigments—a listing of the elements that are there—but not the compounds in which those elements are grouped. This is particularly complicated because Remington was very systematic, and always put his colors in the same positions."

He pointed at the blob of red paint in the photograph. "This red, for instance. It was probably cadmium, but you can see it's sitting on the remains of another red, in this case chrome red. The reds are one thing, but how about the whites?" He moved his finger to the white. "If he put lead white here one day and then zinc white another—see, he always put white first, closest to his brush hand—then we get an XRF reading that gives us elements from which we can build lead white and zinc white. That's lead sulfate and zinc oxide, easy enough to tell apart, but they also form a paint made with half lead white and half zinc white, which was also used at that time."

"I follow the chemistry, but I'm not a painter. What's the significance of choosing one white over another?"

Emmett leaned back in his chair and tented his short, thick fingers. "Zinc white dried notoriously slowly, and tended to crack. Lead white was notoriously toxic."

"So you mix the two to combat both problems?"

"Yes. And some whites are 'cooler' than others. I mean that in the sense that yellow is a 'warm' color, while blue is a cooler one. But within a color, you can have warmer and cooler tones. Take egg-yolk yellow and say, lemon-yellow. You've handled both colors in the kitchen all your life, not thinking of them as warm or cool. But if you had to arrange the two colors between a blue and a red, you'd put the egg yellow closer to the red—that's warm—and the lemon closer to the blue—that's 'cool.' The impressionists understood this, and played it to the hilt, using cooler colors for the shadows and warmer tones for what's closest, that sort of game."

"But what *makes* those colors warm or cool?"

He shook a finger at me. "Now you're talking about chemistry and physics, and you know what? I've asked chemists and physicists that very same question, and they give me a whole lot of math and hocus-pocus and diagrams on a piece of paper before they finally admit that they don't really, *really* know what makes an atom one color or another."

"Well, there's that business about the wavelengths of light. . . ."

"But that's light. We're talking about solid matter that either reflects or absorbs certain wavelengths of light. My shirt is blue because it absorbs all the *other* wavelengths and reflects just this one. I stayed awake that day in class; I remember this stuff." He chuckled. "But you know what really makes it interesting for artists, or for people who come up with the dyes for this shirt, for that matter? Not all colors are available."

"What do you mean?"

"Say I admire a lovely tree, and I want to paint it. Do I have the right green on my palette? No. In light wavelengths, green is midway between blue and yellow, but perhaps none of the available pigments is that exact green. Most greens in nature are pretty warm, closer to yellow, but most green pigments are pretty cool. It's a real hassle, let me tell you."

"Oh."

"And even if we have the right green, we're again talking about the pigment, and the way light bounces off it or is absorbed, and not the light itself, as it plays in nature. So artists have to come up with all their little tricks to get the *effects* of color and light. Getting back to Remington, who used the Impressionist tricks and many more, let's stick with which pigments he actually had at his disposal. Lead white was a wonderful paint in the way it behaved. It went on smoothly and didn't crack as it dried. But it had a nasty side effect: It was indeed lead sulfate, and as such, was highly poisonous. That sulfate part won't hurt you—but the lead, oh dear."

Toxins seemed to be working their way into an awful lot of conversations I was having as of late. "Then artists of Remington's generation knew about the toxicity of lead," I said.

Emmett was beginning to grin like Mr. Hauser had done when talking about hexavalent chromium. "Yes, painters of Remington's era knew about heavy metals, but like I said, if they wanted to get the colors and the lighting effects, they had to use the pigments that would produce them. Nowadays, we have wonderful new synthetics that are nowhere near as problematic, and they're much more versatile. We have transparent reds and yellows to use in glazing, where we used to have mostly blues and greens."

"Glazing?"

"Yes. A painting is far more than just one layer of paint. There's the ground—usually white—and then an underpainting, and then however many layers, and then the glazes. The light passes down through the layers, bounces off the white ground, and reflects back up through the layers. Pigments are very complicated. Some are opaque; some are, to varying degrees, transparent. Some have high tinting strength—that's how much impact the pigment has per unit volume—and others don't. And you'd think the opaque ones would have the highest tinting strength, but not necessarily. And some gray out when you mix them with white, while others maintain their intensity. But, no matter; you were asking about the pigments Remington used." He opened a file and pulled out a list and showed it to me:

Leaded-zinc white
Lead white
Zinc white
Prussian blue
Bone black
Hooker's green
Vermilion
Chrome orange
Cadmium red
Mars red
Emerald green
Cadmium yellow
Chrome yellow
Chromium oxide green
Purple lake

"Vermilion, that's mercuric sulfide," I said. "Chrome yellow, that's lead chromate. Both were extremely toxic."

Emmett nodded. "The man died of appendicitis, not poisoning. But yes, there were artists who licked their brushes to make just the right point. It's thought that Van Gogh's madness might have something to do with that."

"Any of those symptoms could also be the result of other diseases," I noted. "I wonder if they knew?"

"Modern art technology is hardly toxin-free; there are some colors that can't be achieved with the modern synthetics, either. That's why cadmium is still used in reds and yellows. And then there's the problem with all the solvents. Here, come with me."

He got up and led the way down a network of hallways. We entered a large room with high ceilings. Several people sat at massive easels, conserving paintings. All around them, other paintings were laid out on broad tables. The woman nearest us was dipping a cotton swab into a bottle of liquid. She withdrew it and dabbed at a painting. The surface changed color, giving up the amber darkness, bringing vivid blues and reds to light.

Emmett gestured around the room. "See the vent hoods? These conservators are using all sorts of solvents, and sometimes they do use the old pigments, just to match lost portions accurately." He led me up to the nearest table and pointed to a painting that lay face-up upon it.

I gasped. "That looks like a Rembrandt!" I said.

He grinned. "It is. And that's a Gauguin, and over there we have a Delacroix. That woman's working on a—"

"But they're naked!" I said. "I mean, the colors are so bright! I thought the old masters used really mucky, boring colors."

Emmett shook his head, obviously amused. "No, no. What colors they had were vibrant. What you're talking about is badly yellowed varnish. That's been stripped off here, and will be replaced with fresh, transparent varnish."

"How do you get that off without damaging the paintings?"

Emmett rolled his eyes. "Verrry carefully. As you can imagine, we have to make sure we take off only the varnish. And then it's time to decide what can be done for missing paint. It gets chipped over the years, and dampness and mold can wreak havoc. Aside from providing a protective layer, the varnish gave the colors a gloss, and made the light bounce nicely. So we'll replace it with a fresh coat."

"Won't the new coat yellow, too?"

"Eventually. But our varnishes are much finer these days, as are the oil media. We have all those nice herbicides that we can put on our linseed crops—it's flax, actually; 'linseed' is short for 'linen seed'—to keep the weeds from growing. That way, our linseed oil is pure, and not a mixture of linseed and half a dozen other seeds. Pure linseed oil dries faster, too, so the modern product is nicer all the way around."

I moved to the next easel, where a man was working on a panel that had great cracks and places where chunks of paint were missing, making a rendition of the Madonna look like she had terrible acne. "How do you conserve something as beat-up as this?" I asked.

"We clean and stabilize it first," said Emmett, "and then we have to look at damage done by previous restorers. There was an era when museums would paint fig leafs over nude figures, and another when restorers used to 'touch up' the work of the masters. Imagine." He pointed to a place where a large patch of paint was missing, almost half an inch square. "What was going on here, for instance? What's missing? What if it was her hand? A gesture can be very important, even have esoteric meaning."

Emmett beckoned me toward the far end of the room. "You'll want to see this, as long as you're here." He threw a switch, and suddenly every bit of lint on his shirt glowed eerily. "Black light," he said. "It picks up the relative ages of paint. We use it to help evaluate what's been done by earlier restorers, because newer paint will fluoresce slightly. You might use this in your work with forgeries."

My ear pricked to his words. He was spending a lot of time with me, and he expected information in return. Emmett turned off the black light and pointed to a big photograph that had been mounted on foam-core board. "Here's another interesting tool for you: infrared photography. It reveals parts of the drawing underneath the painting."

I gawked at the picture. It was something from the Italian Renaissance, a standing figure draped in robes. The painting was tightly rendered, each hair in place, each fold of fabric crisp and smooth. But in the infrared photograph, I could clearly see the artist's initial sketch, and it was wild and loose.

Emmett said, "Sometimes we even find another painting underneath.

But all of this is just a sideshow for you. You came to talk about Remington. Let's go look at the exhibit while we're talking."

"The exhibit?" I said.

Emmett gave me a quizzical look. "Why, yes. The Remington exhibit. His nocturnes. I thought that must be the reason for the timing of your visit."

"I'm . . . I'm here to consult with my colleague at the FBI," I said.

He smiled. "Then this will come as a great bonus. You're in for a treat."

◇

THE EXHIBIT OF Remington's nocturnes was in the new building of the National Gallery. From the tunnel that connected the buildings, we emerged into a soaring atrium of unexpected geometry, as triangular as the old building was staunchly square. A mobile soared over my head. A tingling of delight coursed through me.

We rode a hexagonal elevator up two levels and crossed a balcony. Inside the gallery where Remington's masterworks had been gathered, everything was as muted and intimate as the atrium was bright and exuberant. The walls were painted indigo blue. The floor and ceiling were a warm, medium gray. The only light came from small spots aimed precisely at the paintings. And the paintings took my breath away.

Here were paintings of moonlight, starlight, candlelight, and firelight, all moodily set in broad, dark frames. The paintings glowed—there was no other word for it—their majesty reaching out to overwhelm the viewer in this special room where everything else in the world was eclipsed.

"Here," said Emmett, a hand sweeping out with the pleasure of serving up great riches. "This is Remington at his finest."

I moved quickly at first, drinking in paintings of moonlight on snow, of lakes at dusk, of wolves and men and horses engulfed in starlight.

Each painting spun a different trick of light and shadow. I paused by *Evening on a Canadian Lake*, which showed two hearty voyageurs and their husky dog paddling a birch-bark canoe across a quiet lake. Their canoe rode a diagonal line between water that reflected the brilliant blue of the night sky and the darker, less revealing water that lay in the shadow of the trees. "The diagonal," I said. "It has such . . ."

"Power," Emmett said. "Remington was a master of composition. That diagonal gives the composition tension, as does the play between darkness and light."

"So the tension is between the darkness and the light," I said.

I stopped next at *The Grass Fire*, in which Indian braves are standing at the edge of a burning prairie. Again the image was divided diagonally between light and dark. Spits of fire bordered the boundary between ground already burned and that which had not, and even the blackened earth in the nearest foreground seemed brighter than the looming shadows cast by the row of men who waited tensely, their faces lit from below by the flames. *In from the Night Herd* played the same trick, this time with cowboys sleeping in the glow of an unseen campfire, their bodies forming the diagonal and casting the shadows.

"They're wonderful," I said. "I've never seen Remingtons glow like this."

"We struggled to get the lighting just right, and we replaced the frames. Black, very simple, that's what Remington intended; the frames underscore the darkness. Collectors too often replaced them with fancy gilt because that's what they were used to, but that puts light around the edges instead of darkness."

"It's amazing how bright the darkness is in some of these," I marveled. I pointed at *Friends or Foes?*, which played its visual tricks with a surprisingly pale shade of blue. A lone brave has halted, alert and uncertain astride his horse, staring across a snow-covered, starlit vastness. The horse's breath forms ghosts in the frigid air. An unseen moon casts their shadows across the frozen ground. Horse and rider are lost in a world of coldness, a chilling blue, as the brave tries to ascertain what awaits him at a row of distant lights.

My eye was drawn next to *The Hungry Moon*, a dark, moody painting of three Indian women dressing down a buffalo kill in the moonlight. "The subjects form a dark hole right in the center of the composition," I observed.

"Yes," said Emmett. "You can sense their anxiety, their rush to complete the task. Why were they working in the night, and where were their men?"

The Hungry Moon was composed primarily using dark greens and black shadows. Suddenly that peculiar green flashed a message to my brain, and I turned and stared at *The Sentinel*, the green painting I had seen only weeks before at the Whitney Gallery in Cody. "This shade of green," I said. "It's . . ." I turned slowly and examined adjoining walls.

Emmett said, "Remington used the trick of juxtaposing that bluish green with a yellowish white many times; it's as clear and masterful as a signature musical riff played in concert, tossed out in bravado flourishes. Look: Here it is again." He pointed at *Shotgun Hospitality*, which used these colors to depict the nighttime visit of three Indians. They had caught one uncertain white man seated alone by his campfire. The Indians are standing swathed in blankets that make them even more massive, more imposing, and the one at the center of the scene has his back square to the viewer. Emmett said softly, "Again he's filled the center of the composition with a darkness that consumes our attention."

This was romantic realism at its most grim.

I felt the hair on the back of my neck stand up. I glanced from painting to painting, taking in each one using that green as the mask of darkness. The value of the color varied from canvas to canvas, and the degree to which it had been grayed, but in each, it was the same unmistakable blue-green. "Hooker's green," I said aloud.

Emmett turned from his own musings and looked at me. "Yes. An interesting choice, eh?"

An interesting choice. Those had been the exact words Tert Krehbeil had used when discussing the pigment with his companion in Cody.

And as I looked at this color repeated in so many of these paintings, I realized how he knew that the painting he had shown me was a forgery.

The green in Tert's painting was not correct. It was not Hooker's green.

I steadied my voice and asked questions as calmly as I could. "Hooker's green was on your list of Remington's pigments. I went to an art-supply shop before flying out here and looked all through the oil paints, but it wasn't there."

"Of course not. It's a watercolor pigment."

"Then how—"

"It was occasionally made up as an oil paint back then. The problem is that the yellow—"

"Gamboge."

"Yes, gamboge is water-soluble, and it's not lightfast. It's also extremely toxic."

"Really? Then why did he use it?"

"Well, Remington wanted that precise effect, and it took those two pigments to get it. Prussian blue is a distinct dark blue, rather less purple than ultramarine, but not as warm as indigo. And gamboge is a mustard yellow. In Remington's day, the only other pigment that even came close was Indian yellow, and it had already been outlawed."

"Why?"

"Because even then, in an era when people were much more used to using and abusing animals, the manner in which it was created was considered cruel."

"I'm almost afraid to ask."

"Cows were fed mango leaves and kept on short water rations. Indian yellow is an acid that collected in their urine. Nowadays we have a synthetic pigment that comes close, but it's not the same." He shook his head. "No, they're never quite the same."

I took a breath. "So Emmett, speaking of inexact pigments, are you ever asked to examine forgeries?"

He chuckled. "Oh, yes. Certainly. People donate paintings and want to write them off their taxes, so of course we have to look them over carefully, and occasionally we get one that's been cooked."

"What do you look for? Modern pigments in a painting that's supposed to be old?"

"Yes, certainly, but that's only good if the forger was a callow idiot. More often, he's smart enough to use only colors that existed at the time the artist was working. Then we have to look a little deeper."

"Such as?"

"The lead in the lead white. As a geologist, you probably already know this: With modern milling and cyanide processes, how pure is the lead produced at a silver mine?"

I said, "The lead is removed from the silver, not the other way around. . . . No, wait! I get it! I'm used to thinking of the silver as the product and the lead as the by-product, but either way, you're just trying to separate the two. Prior to the development of cyanide refinement systems a century ago, some of the silver would be left in the lead!"

Emmett said, "You could check the date of that development with your mining specialists. And there are other clues. If it was a supposed Renaissance painting you were dealing with, I'd say to look at the ground. There are coccoliths in the earlier gessoes. By the nineteenth century, the precipitation techniques filtered them out. You can also look at the sulfur ratio in the ultramarine; that's a way to tell the natural from the synthetic. I'm sure you can think up plenty of other little tricks, and if you do, will you please tell me?" He gave me a meaningful smile.

I smiled with chagrin. I had nothing I could give him yet, but when I did, I vowed that he'd be one of the first to know. "Most certainly," I said. "I probably won't be able to tell you much about the specific job I'm working on, but any new tools of the trade will certainly come your way. Mind if I share your techniques with my colleague at the FBI?"

"I'd be delighted. But do advise him that our shop isn't set up to do analyses at the level of rigor they require for legal evidence."

"I'll advise *her*. And what would that level of rigor require?"

"I'm sure *she* could tell you better than I. But at minimum, the chain-of-custody documentation would be much more stringent."

Chain of custody . . . The words hit me like a brick as I realized another part of Tert's deceit. *He just cut out the chips and handed them to me. . . . Oh, no. . . .* It took me a moment to pull myself together and act like I hadn't just been caught being a total ignoramus regarding documentation of evidence. *Of course a chain-of-custody would be required! Em Hansen, what were you thinking!* I said, "What is your standard chain-of-custody system?"

"Well, whenever a valuable painting is moved—say, from a collector's home to the shop for repairs, or to the museum for display—documentation is required. And insurance. Typically, our team goes straight to the owner's house and builds the shipping crate right there, and the owner witnesses the painting being packed safely in the crate. He—or *she*"—he gave me a wink—"signs the document, as do the handlers. They carry it into their truck. And yes, sometimes the owners require we use Brinks." He sighed and rolled his eyes. "Although I don't know why they'd want to call attention to the move, and the insurance is in place regardless. Heavens, I've done the blanket-wrap method myself, and the insurance was every bit as valid, and there was less banging around."

"Blanket wrap?"

"Yes. One takes a special soft blanket and just wraps it around the painting, frame and all, and lays it flat in the trunk of a car. It's perfectly adequate for a shorter jaunt, and as I say, sometimes there is less jostling that way."

"And do you sometimes take the painting off the stretchers?" I inquired. I wanted to know whether Tert's methods had any legitimacy whatsoever.

Emmett shrugged his shoulders. "It depends. For a larger work, as long as it's not painted on a wooden panel and hasn't been backed with something stiff along the way, then unmounting and rolling can be the answer. Oils are surprisingly elastic. You put cheesecloth against the paint film to prevent scraping." He gestured at the paintings on the walls. "One of these would fit into a large mailing tube, as you wouldn't want to roll it very tightly. But if it's a Remington, that would be sinful, because you'd want to take every measure to prevent the slightest chip. Although one of these would take a crate too big to fit into a lot of common carriers. He had a standard size, twenty-seven by forty inches. With crate, that's . . . let's see . . . add eight or ten inches each to height and length, and say, twelve inches in thickness. . . . You get the idea. And a crate that size is heavy!"

"You wouldn't be able to fit one into the baggage bay of a private airplane," I said, trying to keep a sardonic tone out of my voice. I tried to imagine Faye wrestling something that size or weight into her airplane. There was no way she could manage it. And if my survey of Tert's mother's house was correct, there *were* no other paintings. He had indeed been lying to Faye. He had never intended that she move a painting for him. Then why *had* he asked her to come to Cody? The whole reason for getting her to Cody must have been to engage her connections to people who could document that his painting was indeed a forgery, and do it with strict confidentiality. But why would he want to keep it a secret? And who copied the original, and where had the original gone?

Emmett was saying, "Oh, no. No, you'd need a commercial airliner, and, well . . . It's so much easier to send by surface." He glanced at his watch, indicating it was nearing time that he must address other demands on his schedule.

I slowly turned, taking in each painting one more time, letting them raise me above the concerns of Tert Krehbeil. These were real. They filled me with awe, and happiness, even as their subject matter and force of light and darkness and composition filled me with foreboding. These paintings were not jovial, nor composed for the pure premise of beauty; no, these pictures yanked the viewer in and shouted something deep and unnerving.

"I've seen a great number of his paintings at the Whitney Gallery in Wyoming," I said, "but these . . . there's something about them. . . ."

Emmett took a moment longer and stood like I did, taking in the view, his hands clasped behind his back. "You're noticing what Remington knew about himself: In his earlier work, he was an illustrator, not a fine artist."

"What is the difference between the two, really?"

Emmett sighed. "That's always hard to say. There's an intangible quality that separates the two, a line that dances and vanishes. But in his earlier work, Remington was accurately termed a 'black-and-white man.' He even painted in black and white sometimes, knowing that any colors would be lost in reproduction. Remember that he worked in the days before color printing, before television, radio, and high-speed, candid photography. We needed narrative scenes for black-and-white publication, so if you were an artist trying to make a living, that's what you created: black-and-white illustrations. Look at *The Luckless Hunter* there: It was published in *Scribner's* as a halftone. The subtleties of the color were lost, but not the strength of the composition or the narrative. Yet this was one of his last paintings, a masterpiece of color usage."

"And I can feel just how cold that Indian is, riding along in the dark, over the snow. . . ."

"And Remington was at last acknowledged as an artist, not just an illustrator. Because as you can see here, he could illustrate any story and make it so gripping that you can, as you say, feel the cold, and yet he aspired to more. He wanted to be included among 'the painters,' as he called them, so he labored hard to work with color. He had early successes, but the Academy of Art was interested in harmony. They found Remington's colors too harsh, too dissonant. What they didn't know was that he was painting the impressions of a landscape that was just that—harsh, unforgiving, even brutal. It was not the soft, dripping stuff of the Eastern scenery and lighting."

"Amen to that," I said, knowing all too well how quick Easterners could be to dismiss the West as quaint, or naïve. My West was a land of contrasts, all right, but also of clarity. "So what inspired him? What carried him over the threshold from . . . picaresque to profound?"

"Nicely phrased," Emmett said. "Well, what happened is that Remington went to war. His father was a hero of the Civil War, who died when Remington was still quite young. He must have idolized his father, and wished to measure up to his glory. So he went to Cuba. He became a war correspondent in the Spanish-American War, and it put an end to the romantic notions of his childhood. He came home in a state of shock, what we now call post-traumatic stress." His hand fluttered up with the tension of his tale. "These paintings were his struggle to embrace that ambiguity. Here is beauty, seamlessly intermixed with threat and danger.

"Look closely at the story told in each picture," Emmett continued, now almost whispering. He pointed at one picture and then another, and settled on *Apache Scouts Listening*, another tour de force in Hooker's green. "The scouts are hiding in a grove of trees, listening for the approach of an unseen enemy. The story goes that if they heard anything—a barking dog, a breaking twig—they have been discovered. But if all Remington wanted to do was tell that story, he would have shown us also the men and dogs that were tracking them. But no, he left them outside the frame. So where are they?"

"The threat is outside the frame, out here with us. That makes it so much more frightening!"

"He left the story open and unresolved," Emmett said quietly. "Because *that* is what is true."

20

As I rode the Metro back to Dupont Circle and retrieved my rental car for the drive out to Quantico and my meeting with the FBI, I felt a great weight rolling off my shoulders. I had found a missing part of myself in Remington's paintings. I had experienced art, that force which lifts us above ourselves and out into the clear air of vision.

It had been months, a year or more, since I had felt such clarity. I could now name the fog that had clouded my sight for so many months: trauma. I had been with Tom when he died, a witness to war, and it had so terrified me that I had left part of myself behind, frozen in that time and place, and there was nothing that would ever erase the grim truth of what I had seen. But Remington had shown me the deeper purpose of art: it embraces the ambiguity and tension between light and darkness, wresting beauty from the deepest pain and anger, restoring harmony to that which has been divided.

The beauty of the love I felt for Tom and Jack and Faye and her baby were forever crosscut with a memory I did not like to revisit. I felt guilty that Tom had died, because I'd had a hand in putting him in that wrong place at that wrong time, but also because I had survived. I felt a longing for him and for our lives as they had been before, back when Faye was my friend and confidante, not just an intimate in need of my help.

Tom's death was one small footnote in the war on terrorism. War in any form was hideous. It was a darkness that reached out to swallow the bright center of clarity. Everything in my being resisted that darkness, and yet Remington had embraced it, held it shimmering in tension against the light, showing me to my astonishment that the light was not complete without it. He had found power and strength in darkness which informed the light, and brought its crushing weight to force the brilliance of truth to blaze more fiercely.

It was time for me to bring light into my darkness, to cast it into the shadows that had grown around me. To do that I must face what frightened me, and shatter the ice of my grief. I had to quit leaning on a love relationship that had fizzled almost as soon as it had started. I had to start living my life by a plan that built a future, rather than as a reaction to my past. I had to figure out what I wanted to have in that life, and make it happen, even if that meant embracing the biggest ambiguity on two legs: me.

This resolution to plan ahead made me look at the puzzle of Tert's paint chips from a very different angle. The subject of toxicity in artists' paints had come up several times in the past twenty-four hours, and pointed straight at Tert's elderly mother. There were too many things about her condition that diverged from the usual decrepitude of age. Her skin was sallow and weirdly scarred around her cuticles. She was breathing badly and yet sat out on the porch, suggesting that this problem did not have its roots in infectious disease. She was having trouble seeing even with her glasses on, and oscillated in and out of being as batty as a church steeple. Did this mean she suffered from heavy-metal poisoning? And Deirdre had said that her symptoms always increased after Tert's visits. Was he poisoning his own mother and sister? And how about Deirdre's numb hands, and her incredible irritability? Could her neurological problems spring from the same source?

These thoughts made it difficult for me to concentrate on my driving, but somehow I got to Quantico, Virginia, and found my way to the new building that housed the FBI's forensics laboratories.

The FBI lab building was post-industrial-modern and had gangs of vent stacks that rose high above its top floor, making it look like the *Queen Mary* at full steam. I parked the car and presented myself for the security screening. Noreen Babcock had explained to me that I would have to go through a rather rigorous shakedown, so I was prepared when I was asked to empty my pockets into a bucket for X-ray and walk through a metal detector, but it was the first time I had weathered a full-body frisk. After that, I identified myself through a microphone to a woman who lurked behind bulletproof glass. I explained who I was and whom I was there to see, and she told me to sign a roster, issued me an electronic badge, and pointed to a telephone that I should use to phone Noreen. I clipped the badge to my collar, then dialed and got a recording, so I left a message saying I was waiting in the lobby.

Minutes ground by. By the time twenty had passed, I began to wonder if Noreen had gone home sick or been called into some important meeting, or if, worse yet, I had the wrong day. And did I have the correct hour? And she was here, and not in downtown D.C., wasn't she? Had the creature behind the glass given me the correct number?

I was just about to dial the phone a second time when a woman about my size, shape, and age popped into view right in front of me. "Em?" she said. "I'm Noreen." She wasn't smiling. Something was wrong.

I got up from the bench I had settled on. "I'm glad to meet you," I said doubtfully. "I . . . I wasn't early, was I?"

She blinked. "No. I'm sorry, there's . . . something's come up."

"I could come back another day," I said quickly.

"No. No, that's not it. Actually, it's about your security clearance."

"What?"

"Come this way," Noreen said, averting her eyes from the woman behind the bulletproof glass, who was now staring at us with frank interest.

Noreen turned to a guy with a beer gut and the remains of bad acne who was seated nearby. I had noticed him when I arrived. He had been waiting placidly, apparently in no hurry. I had examined him abstractly, short on anything else to do, and he had done the same with me. But now he stood up and stuck his hands in his pockets, an action that thrust his gut even farther forward. "Emily Hansen," he said with a slight drawl, "I am Agent Wardlaw."

I stifled a nervous giggle at the idea of an FBI agent named Wardlaw, and stuck out my hand.

He did not shake it. Instead, he kept his hands in his pockets and rocked back and forth a bit on his heels, working his lips as if he had a toothpick between his teeth. He wore a dark, conservative, ready-to-wear suit with a white, polyester broadcloth shirt and a dark tie that was a hair too narrow.

I felt an urge to give the man a pair of dark glasses and a bad hat and ask him to play the blues for me. "What's going on?" I asked.

Agent Wardlaw spoke to Noreen. "I got her a visitor's badge, but she has to stay with me," he said.

I turned to Noreen. "Uh, does this guy know I'm a friend of Tom's?"

Noreen nodded. "Yeah, elsewise you wouldn't be getting in at all today. Look, Tom was legendary, and more than a few of us knew he was training you and trying to recruit you. Oh hell, we know all about you. You underwent a security screening a long time ago, you just didn't know it.

And you passed with flying colors. The thing is, it seems that just recently, you've—"

Agent Wardlaw interrupted. "I'll take over now, if you don't mind. Ladies?" He made a gesture toward an inner door.

With misgivings, I followed him. Noreen fell into step beside me, saying, "I'm sorry about this, Em. We just had to set up a few things. . . ."

We marched in silence through a series of hallways past large displays of the results of other investigations. After several turns, we stepped into a small conference room. Agent Wardlaw indicated that I should sit in a chair that waited at a long table. There was a telephone on the table. A long cord led off toward a smaller table by the wall, suggesting that the telephone had been set there for this occasion.

I sat. I was not liking this. It was, in fact, beginning to scare me. I glanced up at Noreen for some sort of indication of what was going on, but she avoided eye contact.

Agent Wardlaw picked up the receiver, laid a small notebook open on the table, and began to dial a series of numbers that were written on the page. He seemed to be punching in an abnormally long sequence of digits. Finally he settled in and listened, unbuttoning his suit jacket and tugging his waistband up over his expansive gut. At length, the party answered. He gave some clearances. Then he handed the phone to me.

"Hello?" I said uncertainly.

A second passed, two, then a very familiar voice came on the line. It said, "Hey, babe."

"Jack?"

There was that same funny delay, then: "It's me all right."

"What the—" I looked up at Agent Wardlaw, who was not smiling. In the split second after I recognized Jack's voice, I had decided that this must be some elaborate joke the boys were playing on me, but this man still looked like he thought I was something the cat had dragged in.

"Honeybun," Jack said, "listen up, and listen quick. You're in Quantico, right?"

"Yeah . . . where are you?"

He did not answer my question directly. "I am on a satellite phone, so this is being expensive, and it's gotta be short. And there are people listening, got me? Our people. This is a secure line in the respect that everybody listening is friendly, but they don't know you like Tom and I do. So, here's the deal: You've gone and gotten yourself a client, eh?"

I said nothing. My heart beat out a tattoo. I glanced over at Noreen, who was standing half turned away, her arms folded across her chest to comfort herself. Her lips were tight with anger. After maybe five seconds, I said, "Jack, I have taken on a case, yes, but you understand that there is such a thing as discretion."

The satellite delay made Jack's sardonic laugh come a beat late. "Sure, darling, except your client is someone our guys have been keeping an eye on."

The floor felt like it was dissolving below me. The room went slightly gray. "What the f—" I caught myself, remembering that judgmental strangers were listening.

"We will deny *all* of this if you spill a word of it to *anyone*," Jack said. "And that includes Faye. You keep your lip buttoned. I am on the phone right now hoping you'll do the smart thing and sever your contract."

"Jack, I can't—"

"Yes you can, and you will. Because I know you understand what's at stake. We're bending the rules just to warn you. And if you play this wrong, you . . . know how difficult it will be to get anyone on your side in the future."

"Okay," I said weakly.

"Good. I know and you know that you had no intention of doing anything illegal when you took this guy on."

"I have not broken any laws!" I said hotly.

"Of course you haven't. But your client probably has. That's why he's on our list. You got me?"

My skin began to feel clammy. "What's he done?"

"Well, now, we lack a little evidence on that score as yet, but trust me, he's been on the radar screen for quite a while now. It's an old game called supply the guys with the strongest currency. When I first came on board, it was the Italians; then, when the mark got strong, it was the German industrialists. The mark fell and the yen came up, and it was the Japanese. Next it was the drug lords, and after them, the Arabs. They all want pretty things. We've been working with Interpol for years on these jobs."

"You're talking about stolen art?"

"Don't ask questions. Now, Emmy, Agent Wardlaw was kind enough to give me a holler when he saw your name come across his bow. He knew you'd probably take this better coming from me than from him. Am I right?"

I sat in stunned silence. "You think I wouldn't listen to him?"

"Knowing you like I do, he'd have had quite a job getting you onboard all by himself. So here I am up in the middle of the night, and it's what, two in the afternoon where you are. I got to get back to my sack, sweet thing. I wish you were . . . well, you know. It's time for me to hand you back over to Pretty Boy there."

"Do you know this man, Jack?" I blurted. "Do you vouch for him?" I was reading Noreen Babcock's body language. She did not like this fellow.

"Yeah, yeah, Wardlaw and I go way back. You ask him about the job at that bar in Cleveland sometime. Or the time he got his butt in a crack in Kansas City. Look, keep your nose clean, darling. I miss you. Wish I could say more."

"Jack—"

"I gotta go, hon."

"Jack?" I was beginning to tremble with adrenaline, and only half of it had to do with the intimidation I was feeling from being goose-walked down the hallway by one of the Blues Brothers. The rest was the shock of hearing for the first time in over half a year the voice of a man whom, for better or worse, I loved.

" 'Bye now," he said. The line went empty.

I wanted to reach out across the miles and grab Jack and kiss him and, at the same time, throttle him. I held the phone to my ear a moment longer, hoping that I was dreaming this whole thing, and that in a moment, the conference-room door would open and he would walk in and throw me on my back on the table and give me some of what I had been missing for far too long.

Agent Wardlaw pulled a small object with a wire trailing out of it from his ear and put it in his pocket. Then he reached out and took the phone back from me and returned it to its cradle. Almost amiably, he said, "That bit about Kansas City is a lie."

◇

FIVE MINUTES LATER, Noreen, Agent Wardlaw, and I were settled in a small employees' lounge with cups of coffee.

"You can leave us if you want," Wardlaw told Noreen. "Our guest and I need to have a little discussion, and then I'll bring her up to your laboratory. I'll be staying with her the rest of the time she's in this building anyway. You got work to do, don't you?"

"I'll stay," she said stiffly. I had to hand it to Noreen: She had not left my side since fetching me from the lobby. She was obviously annoyed that Agent Wardlaw had insisted on observing me for so long before letting me into the building.

I wanted to join her in kicking his butt up between his ears. "Okay, ask me whatever it is you insist on knowing," I said irritably. "I'm not even sure who we're talking about here."

"William Krehbeil the Third," said Agent Wardlaw.

My head sank toward my coffee cup. So much for my nonexistent poker face. "Okay, he is my client. But I have very little to say. Really, he's a far better poker player than I am. Cool as a cucumber. Showed me next to nothing."

"What *did* he show you?"

"No!" I said hotly. "Listen, this is not a fishing expedition. I am here because two of your best agents—Tom Latimer and Jack Sampler—have found me completely trustworthy. They like my instincts, approve of my ethics. So no, I am not going to blurt out everything I know about Tert Krehbeil to you just because you're flashing a badge at me."

"Tert?" said Agent Wardlaw. "Is that some sort of a nickname?"

I jumped to my feet. "I do not like your attitude, Mr. Wardlaw. I was looking for work when I found this job, and I can go right back to that status in a heartbeat with a smile on my face and a song in my heart. I don't need Tert Krehbeil and I don't need to answer to you. You want to serve me a subpoena? I'll get myself a lawyer. I may be flat broke and naïve as shit, but I don't go around letting people like you intimidate me, do you hear me?"

Wardlaw was grinning, his fingers interlaced on top of his necktie. "Jack said you were a spitfire. I like that in a—"

"Go to hell!" I roared. I was still shaking, but it was a different kind of adrenaline rush now. I was ready to move. "Noreen, maybe you'd better escort me back outside."

Noreen stood up, and smiled for the first time.

Wardlaw leaned back in his chair and raised a hand to calm me. "Okay, fun's over, I can see that. Jack never was no idiot, and I can see he's picked hisself a smart girlfriend. Sorry. Sit down. Please." He patted the air with his paw.

I stayed standing, but relaxed slightly. Noreen folded her arms across her chest again and looked back and forth between us like she was watching a particularly good tennis match.

Agent Wardlaw cleared his throat. "Okay, we'll do this the other way. This Tert Krehbeil—I like that nickname, kinda cute, kinda like 'Turd' or something—has got his tit in the wringer with us Feds. He's an art dealer, you know that?"

I said nothing.

Wardlaw shrugged his shoulders. "Yeah, well, art dealers are handling all kinds of dough, y'know? And it can kinda go to their heads sometimes. They start out with a little favor to a client . . . say, delivering the goods to them on the sly in-state, but shipping an empty crate to their country home out-of-state. That way the client avoids paying sales tax. That can amount to thousands, or even tens of thousands, of bucks."

I sat down again and leaned my head onto my hands on the tabletop. I felt a ripping urge to start gabbling, to tell this moron that I had known all along that Tert was dishonest. I wanted to underscore once again that I was nobody's idiot. What stopped me was that I wasn't sure whom I would be trying to convince, him or me.

Noreen said, "So he's been doing what, smuggling artworks? Defrauding the IRS?"

"Probably some of each," said Wardlaw. "These guys are like cakes of soap in the bathtub. We catch one and another one dives in and starts to get slippery. Of course it doesn't help that they're dealing to high rollers who think it's just a laugh and a half to flout their obligations to the government." He examined his stubby fingers, and took a nibble of one cuticle.

"What do you mean?" I said.

Wardlaw yawned. "Oh, the clients are a bunch of rich guys. Multimillionaires. Billionaires, some of them. So they get a hard-on for ways to show off to each other. They get to needing some new hit, something no one else has. A thing of great beau-ty," he sing-songed, lifting one pinkie like he was having tea with the Queen. "They'll buy an artwork and hide it away in some inner room in their mansion somewhere, and even the cleaning lady isn't allowed in. Only they get to look at it, see? It's like an Arab sheik having a new virgin every couple months."

Tert's missing painting began to flash like neon in my brain. "So, let me guess: A painting that hasn't been seen by very many people is worth more than one that has."

"The fewer the better," said Wardlaw. "If the image is made public, they call it 'burned.' It's like somebody else deflowered it."

"They want the piece that went straight from the artist's studio into a private collection a hundred years ago," I said sourly. *So that's it: If Tert's painting had been real, it would have commanded an especially high sum. Crying over his lost childhood picture, my eye!*

Wardlaw scratched an ear. "Or they go for the big time, and do art theft on request. They make the necessary connections, and their tricky-fingered friend goes into the museum with a mat knife and liberates a Renoir from its frame. Either way, they get their rocks off."

My stomach was lurching at the terms he was using, but I could not deny that they fit perfectly with everything that had felt strange about Tert Krehbeil. He was my age or better, and had never married, presumably preoccupied with other obsessions. He had tossed out a check for three thousand dollars as if it were pocket change. He was aristocratic and dripping in a sense of entitlement, above the law. He was . . . what had his brother and sister called him? *Precious.* I asked, "Do you have anything solid on him, or does he just keep bad company?"

Agent Wardlaw did not reply. Having made his accusation, he had folded his arms across his chest, waiting to see what I would do. For all the affect he showed, he might have been a B-movie version of the Sphinx.

I sat and pulled my lip, thinking. What *was* I going to do?

It was tempting to tell Wardlaw that apparently this time someone had put one over on Tert, and that he had gotten stuck with forged goods. But Tert had told me that the painting in question was a family heirloom. Was it, or was that another one of his deceits? He had moaned so persuasively about his grandmother and her beloved painting. Had that story been imaginary? Or had that once-proud family long since sold its treasures? Had he hired me to document a fake so they could collect insurance on a painting he'd already sold to some high-roller?

And there was the little matter of Faye's involvement with this deceitful little upper-crust so-and-so. She was staying with someone who was being watched by the FBI, and that was not good. Now I was completely certain that I should get Faye and Sloane Renee out of there.

"Your friend Faye Carter is staying with him," Wardlaw said, as if reading my mind.

Another wave of adrenaline shot over me. I had let myself believe that Wardlaw was not the crispest card in the deck. "Faye Carter is the widow of Tom Latimer," I said. "She has known Tert's brother Hector since college, that much I'll give you for free. She only met Tert a few weeks ago. I'm sure the whole thing amounts to nothing more than friend-of-the-family status, or I would have known about it. I am her closest confidante," I said, appalled at the fiction I was weaving, "and she said nothing about him until a few weeks ago, when he phoned out of nowhere and asked her to transport some artwork for him."

Wardlaw pursed his chubby lips. "Did she do it?" He actually managed to look concerned.

Heat swept up over my face as I realized that I was once again giving things away. Explaining now that the services she had intended to provide would support a show in a very highly regarded museum would sound like I was treading water, so I said, "If you've been following this guy closely enough to know I'm working for him, then surely you know the answer to that one!"

He pawed the air again. "Okay, okay, calm down. I just wanted to make sure we didn't miss something."

Through gritted teeth, I said, "Faye came east with me to take a break. It's been a long, tough adjustment for her since Tom was killed. She thought she'd visit a few friends. Look, she has the baby with her. She'd never knowingly put that kid at risk, do you hear me?"

Wardlaw spread his hands out in mock self-protection. "Loud and clear. Jesus, I didn't know what I was taking on here, or I would have brought a backup. A'right, a'right, so I've told you my stuff. So, I was wondering if you had anything you'd like to tell me. You get me?"

"I'd have to think about this," I muttered. "No, on second thought, I don't. The fact is I have nothing to tell you."

Noreen took that as a cue. "Great! So why don't we go on up to my office and get some science done, okay?"

Wardlaw opened his mouth to say something smart, but closed it again. After a moment, he said, "Okay."

"First we have to get you *both* cleared to enter the lab space," she said nastily. Then she opened the door and swept a hand toward it, showing us the way.

21

I DID NOT EVEN TRY TO FIND MY WAY BACK TO THE RENWICK Gallery to visit the Catlin portraits. I was too distracted by the weight of my heart, and I was sure that if I looked half as bad as I felt, some White House guard would shoot me first and ask questions later.

I was never so glad to see a couple of sweet old geezers as I was to see Mr. Carter and Mr. Hauser that evening at the Cosmos Club. I wanted to grab Mr. Carter by the lapels and say, *Your niece needs help. Drive up to Philadelphia and drag her away from that gray-eyed snake!* It took me until halfway through dinner to concentrate on what was being said.

"The dosage makes the poison," Mr. Hauser was saying, as he slathered butter on a second roll and I finally got my anxiety-ridden brain into the room. "Anything, even this butter, can become a poison if taken in sufficient amounts."

"What are the symptoms of butter poisoning?" asked Mr. Carter jovially, raising his astonishing eyebrows at his friend's paunch.

"A large bill from one's cardiologist," answered Mr. Hauser. "But seriously, toxic thresholds are calculated as the amount in excess of what one can take in over an eight-hour period and hope to excrete within the following sixteen."

"I have never been able to take in as much butter as you, Martin," said Mr. Carter.

Mr. Hauser smiled. "Some of us are made of stouter stuff than others, my friend."

"Ah. Just so."

I asked, "What are the symptoms of heavy-metal poisoning?"

"Oh, that varie . And it depends on the vector, of course. One has to think in terms of ingestion, inhalation, or transdermal absorption."

"Lead, for instance," I said, trying not to make the question sound pointed. "Or lead chromate; you know, ol' Baltimore yellow."

"Oh, lead is a horrible toxin if eaten or inhaled, but it doesn't move through the skin. Inhalation would cause obvious distress—painter's cough, and with greater exposure, pneumonia; but that would show up on X-ray, the lead being photo-opaque." He speared a mouthful of salad and munched it down like a great rabbit let loose in Mr. McGregor's garden.

Wouldn't Mrs. Krehbeil's doctor have taken an X-ray? I wondered.

"How does it act on the human body?"

Mr. Hauser said, "Lead is a cumulative poison; the body does not expel it well, which is common to many heavy metals. It is absorbed by the bloodstream, where it deactivates the enzymes that create hemoglobin. This results in the buildup of precursor molecules of aminolaevulinic acid, which causes the various symptoms of lead poisoning. It is taken up in the bones, replacing the calcium and forming lead phosphate. It paralyzes the gut, causing cramps and constipation; it results in excess fluid in the brain, causing headaches and insomnia; and it affects the reproductive system, causing infertility and miscarriage. Beyond that it moves to weariness, anemia, and insanity. All of these symptoms are also characteristic of other disorders. Mild lead poisoning might be easily overlooked. Long-term exposure is insidious. The ultimate symptom is death."

I said, "Would it mimic pneumonia, or senility?"

Hauser smiled and added more dressing to his salad. "Oh, certainly. It mimics many other diseases, but when a great many people develop the same symptoms, then one gets to looking closely for the cause. The Romans were the first to discern that lead caused problems, and historians point to it as a major cause of the fall of Rome. You see, their water-supply pipes were made of the stuff. But we're still using it. In very recent times we've put lead in our gasoline, belching it out into the air as exhaust. Our city streets became contaminated with it. It rose as a dust that accumulated in the lungs, particularly afflicting young children, whose brains were still developing. It was, within my lifetime, still used in the glazes on tableware, and was often ingested with one's dinner."

Mr. Carter looked doubtfully at his plate. I thought of Sloane Renee and wanted to jump up and start screaming.

The waiter brought our entrées. Mr. Hauser took a bite and chewed merrily. "Ignorance is only one problem. There is also vanity. Young ladies, from the ancient Egyptians clear up through Victorian times and in Japan, the geisha, used lead-based cosmetics to whiten their complexions. Over time, they lost their appetites and slowly swooned, all the time applying more and more of the stuff in order to keep up appearances. No, sorry to tell you, we're selectively blind where it comes to some of the things we release in our environments, despite our best intentions."

Mr. Carter dropped a dollop of salad dressing on his skin. "But you said lead wasn't transdermal, didn't you?"

"They smeared it around their mouths. It's sweet, you know. The English used to place pellets of lead in their wines for flavor," said Mr. Hauser cheerfully. "Many toxins will move readily through the skin, especially if the barrier formed by the skin's protective oils is breached. An artist clears away his protective oils by handling solvents, such as turpentine, and then off we go."

"I suppose one gets scars from that," I said, remembering Mrs. Krehbeil's fingers.

"Oh yes, a marvelous little symptom called paronychia: They're sores that develop around the cuticle. The subject hardly feels them, as the toxin also poses as a nerve deadener, but they don't heal well, and form odd little scars."

Bingo: fingers, pulmonary distress, and dottiness. Did Mrs. K paint all those not-so-great pictures at her house, or is someone . . . such as Precious William, feeding it to her? "So, artists are known to have been exposed to it," I said. "The man at the National Gallery today was telling me about Van Gogh licking his brush."

"Yes, certainly," said Mr. Hauser. "He developed insanity, after all, and those halos around the stars . . . that could be what he actually saw. Lead would have caused swelling on his optic nerve. Oh, yes, toxicologists have had a lovely time fixing twenty-twenty hindsight to some of our more famous characters. Oh, yes, great stuff. Beethoven's hair has been shown to have one hundred times the normal amount of lead. Perhaps that explains his erratic behavior, and maybe even his deafness."

Mr. Carter said, "What about that hexavalent chromium you were espousing last evening, Hauser? What lovely thing does that do to us?"

"Cancer," said Mr. Hauser. "But chromium is also necessary for the body to utilize glucose. And lead chromate itself is a carcinogen."

"Last evening you said that chromite ore was processed and manufactured into pigments in Baltimore. And you mentioned the Krehbeils," I said.

"Ah yes, William Krehbeil Primus. He was the youngest son of an old Mennonite family. His parents left their farm to his oldest sibling, so he left them and said he'd buy his own farm, and quit the church in the bargain. They shook their heads and said he'd never amount to anything because the land he bought was down in the barrens, but then it proved to have one of the hottest ore bodies. He sold out to the entrepreneur who bought up all the claims and set himself up in paint manufacturing down in Baltimore. Then, to finish the job of thumbing his nose at his forebears, he bought a very large farm back in Lancaster County and built a grand house on it."

"Did Krehbeil the second and Krehbeil the third carry on the business?" Mr. Carter asked.

Martin Hauser wrinkled his brow as if to massage his brain for further information. "Krehbeil Primus was well advanced in years when he married. Wed a lovely lass from Philadelphia, the story goes. She was a lively young thing, wanted to go west, but of course young girls didn't just travel at will in those years. He built a grand house for her, so she could have that sense of the rural and he could have his sense of grandeur. She gave him two children, a son and a daughter, and outlived the old man by many decades."

Mr. Hauser took another bite of his buttered roll and continued his tale. "The son wasn't much for engineering and such. He tried to run the shop for a while after the old man died, but the board of directors made short work of him, jacked him up and ran a man with a mind for business underneath. I've heard it said they bought him out with a bit of stock maneuvering, and everybody was happy, or so the story goes. I've heard that he went into dealing art, or some such."

"I think Faye knows the current generation," I said tentatively.

Mr. Carter lowered his eyebrows in thought. "Couldn't say."

Hauser forked a bit of chop into his mouth and chewed. "Krehbeil Secundus died recently. Your niece could know his son." He smiled abstractly.

"Yes, in fact she's staying with him in Philadelphia just now. It's a business visit, you see. She wants to start that flying delivery business of hers again."

Mr. Carter stiffened. "Surely not! Not with a baby!"

The baby. Indeed, it was the baby I feared for the most. Tert appeared to have affection for Sloane, but if he would poison his own mother—and that was what I was beginning to suspect—would he be sick enough to hurt an infant? Or might he have the stuff about? *Lead is sweet, after all . . .*

I lifted my napkin to my lips and gave Mr. Carter a sideways glance. "Um, I think you and I ought to have a talk about this situation."

He addressed his roast beef with mathematical vigor. "Yes, I agree. Are you available tomorrow morning?"

"I have to run back up to Pennsylvania, but may I give you a call soon?"

"Please do, my dear."

Mr. Hauser said, "On to lighter topics. You haven't told us anything about your visit to Quantico. Please don't hold out on us. That sounds like a most stimulating experience."

I paused with a forkful of fish halfway to my lips, my stomach tightening at the memory of my meeting with Agent Wardlaw. "Ah . . . yes, it was quite something. Noreen Babcock, their forensic geologist showed me all about the labs."

Mr. Carter's eyebrows shot up. "The whole place?"

"The whole kit and caboodle. Geology—that's trace evidence—gets the evidence first, because they're dealing with fine stuff that can easily be lost in other analyses. They work with geologic materials—dirt, dust, sand, all that—but also glass, hairs, and fibers. They have a scraping room where they hang up the evidence and knock free the trace materials for analysis. They have all the standard equipment—X-ray diffraction, SEM, mass spec, Fourier-transform IR, and such, but also the good old handlens and their quick minds."

"Hear, hear," said Mr. Carter. "No amount of machinery is going to replace the power of a good analytical mind."

"My favorite thing was the duct-tape archive," I said.

Both men chuckled. "Duct tape?" asked Mr. Hauser.

"Oh yes," I assured him, doing my best to offer entertainment when what I wanted to do was weep. "The FBI's motto is: 'No crime is committed without duct tape.' Imagine the criminal tearing off his bit of duct tape to accomplish his crime. Then, being frugal, or tidy, or both, he tosses the rest of the roll into the trunk of his car. Voilà. Ergo and forthwith, the FBI keeps on file one of every kind of duct tape ever manufactured."

"But surely duct tape is duct tape," said Mr. Hauser, his eyes dancing with amusement.

"Oh, no, no, no! Think of all the different companies that make it. There are seven or eight different adhesives, for starts. The fiber used to reinforce it varies, as does its weave, and the density of the weave. And even within your basic gray duct tape—it comes in red, and blue, and . . . well, what have you—the tape material itself varies, and the filler material in it, which, by the way, is also geologic trace evidence, because that filler is made of clay—kaolinite, bentonite—and the coloring pigments include rutile, calcite, aragonite. . . ."

Both men laughed, covering their mouths with their napkins in mirth.

I managed a smile, but it had been damned hard enjoying any part of the tour with Agent Wardlaw breathing down my neck. What I had hoped would be a discreet, exchange of methodologies was not possible with him there, and now that Noreen knew who my client was. I said, "It gets better: Duct tape does not always tear cleanly. So, Joe Criminal tears off his chunk to, say, tape the victim's mouth shut so she can't scream for help. Nasty stuff. But the tape comes off ragged, and Joe's kept the rest of the roll. Aha, our forensic expert now matches the two sides of the tear."

"Marvelous," said Mr. Carter. "And what else did she show you?"

"Oh, let's see. There was the questioned-documents section, shoeprint analysis, tire tracks, chemistry, latent fingerprints, genetics. . . ."

"And bomb analysis?" said Mr. Hauser. "I understand they have quite a lab for that."

Bombs. Yes, Noreen had shown me photographs of what was left of the yellow trucks that had bombed Oklahoma City and the garage at the World Trade Center. Bombs and yellow trucks brought to mind Fritz Calder, but they also brought to mind Jack, who was still over there, wherever "there" was, looking for the colleagues of the people who had taken the Trade Center the rest of the way down. Jack who had taken the trouble to warn me about Tert. Jack needed and deserved my support in return. How could I reject him for not coming home?

I stared at my dinner plate. The conversation ebbed. Even Mr. Hauser laid down his fork.

"You must be exhausted," said Mr. Carter.

"I am."

He reached out an ancient hand and patted mine. "Don't worry about us, my dear. You go on upstairs and get some sleep."

"Yes . . . Yes, I think I will." There was nothing I could do right now for Jack, but on the morrow, I would think up some way to better protect Sloane and Faye. It hurt like fury that they were all moving away from me, but I loved each intensely anyway, and I would care for them in my own way.

I nodded to the gentlemen who had given me closeness for the evening and produced the bravest smile I could muster, thanked them kindly for the meal, their companionship, and the enlightenment of their conversation, and found my way upstairs to my room.

22

Early the next morning, I turned my little rental car north, back toward Pennsylvania and a day in the field with Fred Petridge and Nigel Iago. Even though I left Washington well ahead of the commuter traffic, it was hard on nine o'clock when I reached the Geologic Survey. I found Fred Petridge in front of the building, packing gear into a Jeep. A woman about my age stood beside him holding a big wicker picnic basket. It even had a checkered tablecloth folded over the top.

"Ah, Em, here you are," said Petridge. "Slow down, catch your breath, Nigel isn't here yet. If it was important to leave right at nine I would have told him eight-thirty. Meanwhile, I'd like you to meet Jenny Neumann, an expert on the local farms and a colleague from various volunteer efforts I've become involved in. You asked about the farm situation here in Lancaster, and Jenny had asked to come along on one of my field jaunts, so I've taken the liberty of putting the two together. She's also interested in the limonite pseudomorphs I mentioned."

Jenny and I exchanged pleasantries. She was an interesting sort: slim, athletic, and short-haired, with striking Germanic coloring and cheekbones. She was dressed in mixture of retro-hippie, drape-and-dangle stuff and practical farm gear. Her fingernails were a vivid purple, dotted with scarlet.

Fred put Jenny's picnic hamper into the back of the Jeep and closed the tailgate. "I guess we're all ready except for our resident warlock. Ah, there he is now."

I turned to find Nigel Iago just skidding into the lot in a beat-up Austin Mini with Indiana license plates. He approximated fitting his vehicle into a slot—rather missing the center of one pew and overlapping at a notable angle into the next—and sat for a moment, possibly meditating on having survived his transit. The door opened. He unfolded himself from the driver's seat, put both hands against his spine, and leaned back, unkinking with an audible crunch. He leaned back into the car for a moment and rummaged around, producing a large black computer bag. Then, whistling the tune of a sea chantey, he headed toward us. "Morning, all!" he caroled, raking the sky with one wild, long-fingered hand. "Or at least, that's what they call this overabundance of illumination, isn't it?"

Nigel strode right past me and brought his frame to attention directly in front of Jenny. He took her right hand in both of his. "My heavens," he said, his voice dropping into a purr, "Fred, who is this vision of feminine pulchritude?"

Fred rolled his eyes heavenward. "Get in the vehicle, Nigel, you're late."

I rushed for the shotgun seat. I wanted a good view of the day, and it was clear by Jenny's blushing, smiling response to Nigel's bromide that she and he were going to be looking more inward. Besides, I wouldn't have wanted to give him the front seat and have him hurt his neck turning around to leer at her all day.

Nigel helped Jenny into the backseat, Fred gunned the motor, and we were off in a cloud of flying dung, as my mother used to say. We turned onto Highway 283 and headed southeast toward Lancaster.

Nigel crooned to Jenny in the backseat. "I have within my command—right here in this computer—all the soils maps, geologic maps, land ownership for this county, plus forty other layers of information."

Jenny bestowed a smile on him. "Oh, you're a GIS expert, right? Fred has told me *all* about you. He said how *useful* your expertise can be. I have *so* many projects that need *exactly* that kind of help!"

I fought back a snort. Our boy Nigel was in for a wild ride with this filly.

I heard Nigel unzip his satchel.

"Watch out with that zipper of yours," Fred boomed.

"Wash out your mouth, Petridge," Nigel growled appreciatively.

I glanced around at his laptop computer. It was a thick thing, obviously jam-packed with bells and whistles and lots and lots of firepower. Nigel began tapping commands into its keyboard. He said, "How may I prove my devotion to you, O my lovely?"

Jenny replied, "Give me the entire holdings in this county for one farming family. Show me the influence of the geology on the lands and the productivity of the farms."

I was liking Jenny more and more.

"Give me a name," said Nigel.

"Oh!" said Jenny. "There are so many I'm interested in."

"How about 'Krehbeil'?" I said.

Jenny's head popped forward between the seats and she fixed a round-eyed stare on me. "You know the Krehbeils?"

Oh shit! I thought. *She knows them! I should have guessed that! Even in this humid land of tiny farm footprints, most of the farmholders will know each other.* Obfuscating as best I could, I said, "In fact, I don't know the Krehbeils. I'd never even been in this county until Sunday. But I was driving around Monday and happened to go by their house. Mrs. Krehbeil was on the front porch in a wheelchair. She fell out of it, so I stopped to help her. I stayed for a bit and helped her daughter get her resettled."

"Was she all right?" Jenny asked anxiously.

"Apparently . . . although I'm a bit concerned," I said, seeing a way to turn my gaffe into a route toward gaining information. Perhaps Jenny knew something damning about the family, and I could phone Faye and tell her, and that would be that. "I mean, I don't even know these people, but it seems as if that old lady ought to be in a hospital, or a care home, where they have the equipment and staff to care for her."

"I've had the same concern," she said.

Nigel interjected, "Krehbeil. Spell that name?"

Jenny said, "K-R-E-H-B-E-I-L. That's one of the farms I've been telling you about, Fred. They've applied for an easement, but they're not on the preferred soil types, so each year I can't seem to get the Ag Board to give them a high enough rating to qualify for purchase."

Nigel said, "I thought that would be with a *C*."

"It's an old Mennonite name," Jenny said, returning to the backseat. "Many have Anglicized it into C-R-A-Y-B-I-L-E, but this family is out-Pennsylvania-Dutching the Pennsylvania Dutch."

"So then it's a Dutch name?" Nigel inquired.

Jenny leaned back out of sight again and said, "No. 'Dutch' is in this case a corruption of 'Deutsche.' They're all just as German as I am."

"Getting back to that Ag easement stuff," I said. "What's all that mean?"

Jenny shifted the volume and tone of her voice into something appropriate for a public lecture. "The encroachment of subdivisions threatens farms like the Krehbeils have. These farms have been in the families for generations, so it's not just a loss of open space, it's the loss of the heritage of small farmholders. The care given to the production of crops and dairy is not the same in the big agribusiness spreads in the flatlands of states out west. If the farms of Lancaster County die, a way of life dies with them."

I said, "You're selling rocks to a geologist. I was raised on a ranch in Wyoming, and we're seeing the same kind of problem out there."

Jenny's face popped into view again. "Oh, really? I'm very interested to hear what it's like out there. Your acreages are larger, right?"

"Well, I don't know what they are here, but it takes up to fifty acres a head out west, so a viable cow/calf operation is say, six or eight square miles."

"Square *miles*?" roared Nigel. "Hell, woman, back here in God's country, a whole *farm* is fifty acres!"

Jenny said, "That's because here we get forty inches of rain a year. We're raising crops and dairy on the best nonirrigated cropland in the nation. Back where Em comes from, you can't even raise hay without added water. You get what, twelve inches a year?"

"In a good year. We've been having drought lately." It was painful to say "we." It was my mother alone, or with the occasional hired hand, who had endured this latest catastrophe.

"I've about got it all here on my screen. . . ." said Nigel.

Jenny was not yet done with her stump speech. "The Krehbeils do not want to sell out to a subdivision, but neither can they afford to remain on the land the way they're going. They need cash influx, and there are two programs here in Lancaster County—one county-based, one private—that have funds to purchase their development easements. The programs purchase development rights from the farms, paying cash for the gap between the farming value and the development value of the land, allowing the farms to cash in on the rise in values while simultaneously preserving the tracts for agriculture. The value of those easements is equal to the value of the land as developable land minus the value as farmland. It can be huge. And even if the Krehbeils were able to afford to keep farming while all the other farms around them are subdivided into housing tracts, the infrastructure of farm-supply stores will fold up and move away, or just fold altogether. And as developments move in, the value of the land soars, and with it, the taxes. If nothing is done, Deirdre will lose the farm just because she couldn't make enough to cover annual costs."

I said, "You say Deirdre will lose the farm. Does it belong to her?" I tried to recall what Mrs. Krehbeil had told me. My impression was that it belonged to her.

Jenny said, "No, it belongs to her mother, who obviously can't farm it anymore, and who, in fact, never did. She was a debutante who married for the life in town. Deirdre told me that they used to lived in Philadelphia, where her father had an art gallery, all very upper-crust, and this farm belonged to his mother. And much as Deirdre likes to think herself a farmer, she has little or no business sense. As I was telling Fred, the soil is not the best. And it's more complicated than that. Deirdre's father applied for the Ag easement before he died, but the application is still pending. If her mother dies before it goes through, then any one of the heirs can step in and jam the gears by saying 'no way.' "

"How many heirs are there?" I asked, wishing I could take notes without seeming conspicuously interested.

"Four," said Jenny, "if I recall accurately from my notes. There's Deirdre, the eldest; then William Krehbeil the Third; then another son named Hector; and then a second daughter named . . . I'm not sure what her name is. Everyone calls her Cricket."

"So you've met all these people?" I asked.

"No. Just Deirdre. And I forgot; Deirdre has two grown kids, Anthony and Cynthia, who live there on the farm, although, unless they're mentioned in the will, they don't count as heirs, I don't think."

"Why does it matter what the soil type is?" Nigel asked, trying to insert himself back into the conversation.

Fred said, "That's where your eye-in-the-sky GIS system needs to take a tour of terra firma, Nigel, old pal. It's no joke that Lancaster County has the best farmland in the country, but not the whole county. When the German farmers moved to the U.S., they sent scouts ahead to find the best soils, and the scouts knew to look for limestone. That soil had wonderful, thick, rich soil profiles. Of course, when the pioneers cut down all the chestnut trees that were growing here at the time, a lot of that topsoil washed right down into the creeks, but we'll skip over that part of the heritage story."

"Fred . . ." said Jenny impatiently.

Fred told Nigel, "Open your damned computer up to a general view of the county's geology, hotshot. You'll see parallel bands of rock types cutting across from east to west. The Conestoga limestone sits right smack in the middle. Flat to shallow slopes, and all that lime to enrich the soil. No need to irrigate. The Germans gobbled it up. Parallel to that to the north, you have several other limestones and dolomites; some have steeper slopes, locally. Along the north edge of the county, you have sandstones and shales, some quite steep, and nowhere near as fertile. To the south, you have granites and gneiss, less desirable yet. Way down in the southernmost bit of the county, you have the Peters Creek schist all riddled with serpentine barrens. No way you're going to make a farm out of that."

Here I cut in. "Where are the chromite mines?" I inquired.

Fred said, "They're down there in the barrens. We'll go there later today. Just the sort of field location Nigel would adore. They don't call it the barrens for nothing."

"Oh, Gawd," Nigel moaned. "That means ticks, I suppose."

Fred cackled. "Big as hubcaps. But first we're running over to Manheim Township to look at the limonite pseudomorphs, right, Jenny?"

Jenny sighed. "Actually, Fred, they paved them over yesterday."

"What!"

I turned and looked back over the seat toward Jenny. She had folded her arms across her chest as if she were cold, and was staring out the window.

"But we had an agreement that they were going to leave that land open!" Fred howled.

"I know, Fred. I'm disappointed, too."

"Disappointed? How about outraged!"

"Now, Fred . . ."

"Jenny, is that some kind of Mennonite thing? How in hell's name do you keep your cool?"

"It's not about cool. It's about saving my fire for a fight I can win."

I cut in again. "What's the story here?"

Jenny said, "The limonite pseudomorphs are a part of the county's heritage. The farmers used to bring them up with the plow and collect them."

Fred added, "They're an iron ore. Mining at its most elemental."

Jenny continued. "Fred and I had been working to preserve the last good stretch of ground they weather out of. It's the last farm to fall in Manheim Township, and we made a deal with the township government that they could cut up the farm, put in a library and all, if they kept this one field open and let the children pick up the pseudomorphs. Put up a little display in the library, even plow the ground once a year to keep them coming up." She shrugged her shoulders, suddenly looking small. "But they paved it over for a parking lot for the new soccer field instead."

I said, "Manheim Township is just south of the Krehbeil farm, isn't it?"

"It's a few miles south. But sad to say, the developments will sweep through all of those farms within the next decade if no one stops them."

Fred drove on, his jaw set. "We'll go on to Intercourse instead, then," he muttered.

"Excuse me!" shrieked Nigel. "Freddie darling, I hold you in the highest esteem, but I shall not bed thee!"

"The town, idiot," he said, his mood easing slightly. "Not your shorts."

"What mining interests are there?" I asked.

"None," he said. "But it has the best bakery in the county, and after that little 'disappointment,' I need something sweet."

◇

We continued on our diagonal through the county until we junctioned with a secondary highway that led us straight east through Bird-in-Hand to Intercourse, and I'm not making this up. Funny names or not, the scenery was splendid. Here I found the heart of Lancaster County's fabled farmlands. Great patchworks of beautifully tended fields spread out around us, undulating over softly rolling hills. My heart sang.

Fred did some classic arm-waving, drive-by geology. "This is the Hagerstown Silt Loam to the north," he said. "And to the south, the Conestoga Silt Loam. Wonderful soils, both developed on Paleozoic limestones. Over there is a log house made from the original chestnuts," he added, pointing one out to me as we zoomed past. It was a smallish structure, built of massive, squared-off logs.

"The chestnuts must have been huge," I said. "A far cry from the narrow lodgepole pines my folks' ranch was built out of."

"They were indeed," said Fred, "and they're all gone now. Jenny's noble settlers brought in the blight. Many of the old stumps are still alive, and they keep sending up shoots, but just as soon as the sapling matures enough to bloom, the blight knocks it out again, and it's back to the roots."

Jenny had a homily for this one, too. "We all do to the best of our knowledge, Fred. I'm sure those people had no idea they were carrying the blight. That's why we have to be vigilant today to make sure we aren't continuing to screw up our tomorrows."

We pulled off in Intercourse and found the bakery, which featured a confection called Whoopie Pies. They were composed of two large, soft chocolate cookies glued together with your choice of whipped filling: chocolate, vanilla, peanut butter, or maple. I chose vanilla and got a cup of coffee to go with it, figuring that Tert wouldn't miss an extra dollar, and ambled outside with the others to munch and sip in the sunshine.

The bakery was adjacent to a large parking lot filled with cars with out-of-state license plates that belonged to people who had come to Intercourse to send home giggling postcards and ogle the Amish. And Amish there were: Black, boxy, horse-drawn buggies trotted past on the main drag, driven by bearded men wearing straw hats who did their level best to ignore the gaping tourists in Cadillacs and Volvos. The local bank had not only a parking lot for its automobile-driving customers, but also a small stables block for the horse-drawn carriages. I ate my Whoopie Pie and joined the other out-of-staters in a little shameless goggling myself.

My cell phone rang. It was Faye. "I wanted to apologize for shouting at you the other day," she said.

I was flabbergasted. "That's okay, Faye. I mean—"

"No, it's not, and I wanted to say so."

I wanted to warn her about Tert, but didn't want to ruin the détente by getting in her face, so I just said, "How are things? Sloane okay?"

"A little tummy-ache."

"What?" I went on red alert.

"She's kind of cranky. She's sleeping now."

"That's, ah . . . nice. You still in Philadelphia?"

"Yeah. Taking lots of walks."

"Oh. Listen, if Sloane's stomachache gets any worse, or persists, you take her right to a doctor, okay?"

Faye came back with a defensive tone. "What, you think I can't look after my own child?"

"No! No, I didn't mean to suggest that. I've just been talking to experts about poisonous pigments, and—"

"Relax," she said testily.

I thought fast, trying to think of something to say that would keep her in communication. "Are you having a good time?"

"Tert is down at the gallery a lot, or holed up in his office here at the house." Faye sounded lonesome.

"Not much fun for you. Maybe you should head on up north and see some other friends."

"No, I made the mistake of turning in my rental car. Trying to be frugal, like you keep suggesting. But I've already seen the Liberty Bell and Independence Hall anyway."

I gritted my teeth and asked, "How's the food there in Philadelphia?"

"We're eating a lot of takeout."

I sighed with relief. "That's great."

"Huh? I thought you'd consider that spendthrift."

"Oh, no. No, no, no! Go for the pizza, the Philly cheese steak, the—"

"Em? Is something bothering you? I mean really?"

There it was, the perfect opening, and yet the moment felt infinitely delicate. If I told her that I suspected Tert of poisoning his mother—Tert, whom she trusted well enough to be his houseguest—I'd come off as a crackpot and a meddler, which in fact I hoped I was. I had not a shred of hard evidence that Tert was anything other than a privileged bit of puff pastry with an art gallery attached. So I said, "Well, it's just you say that Sloane is sick. It's just that you both mean so much to me."

There was a pause, then a surprised, "Thanks for saying."

"So keep up your strength. Eat that takeout. And stay off whatever's laying about Tert's house. He's a bachelor, you know, and sometimes they keep foods in the cupboard or the fridge way too long, and—"

"I suppose you're right. Sure, I'll order Chinese next, and then maybe Thai. Except the peppers in Thai food make my milk kind of funny, and Sloane gets gas."

I managed to chuckle. "How well I know." I stuffed another bite of Whoopie Pie into my mouth and chewed. It was great talking baby care with her again. Had I not been so anxious for their safety, I would have prescribed that they go get bored at Tert's house more often.

"So, you didn't tell me where you are and what you're doing," Faye said.

I grinned. "Oh, I'm just in Intercourse with a couple of geologists eating Whoopie Pies," I said.

Faye snorted with laughter. "Good old Em," she said. "You always know how to get yourself into something worth telling about."

"Intercourse is a town, and a Whoopie Pie is a cookie, you see, and—"

"Don't spoil it for me, Em. The image is too ripe."

I laughed. "Okay, okay. We're doing some fieldwork. Looks like I might get a thesis project after all. You were right to kick me in the butt."

"De nada."

I sighed with relief. We were on the right track again at last, and all it had taken was the consumption of a little humble . . . Whoopie Pie. "So, day after tomorrow we'll be heading home."

"Yup. So you're there in Lancaster County still?"

"Well, I'm back. I went down to Washington, remember. I saw your great uncle. Hey, I think he'd like you to call him."

"Okay . . . but anyway, I was wondering about Friday. Do you think you can maybe pick us up?"

"Sure! I'd be glad to. Maybe you'd even like me to pick you up early. Thursday night. That's tomorrow."

"No, Friday morning's okay. I can avoid the cost of a night at a hotel, eh?"

So here it was, my frugality coming back to bite me. "Okay then, give me some directions."

"It's sort of complicated. I can guide you in Friday morning by cell phone. And we'll talk again, okay?" She sounded cheered. "Oh, the baby's waking up. Good-bye!"

" 'Bye!"

I thought of phoning Mr. Carter immediately and telling him to call Faye quick while she was feeling so approachable, but Nigel interrupted me.

"Look at this," he said. He had his computer open on the hood of the field vehicle, and was tapping in commands, his peanut butter Whoopie Pie clenched between his teeth. The effect of brush mustache and soft chocolate cookies was almost too much to bear. He chewed the pie systematically, absorbing it into his body by millimeters. Suddenly, he whipped the remaining nub away from his lips and rested it on the hood of the Jeep next to his machine. "There," he said. "All the lands of clan Krehbeil, cross-referenced to both geology and soils, with tax roll overlay, for your viewing pleasure."

Jenny and I both hurried to his side. The large farm in Elm was immediately obvious, but there was also another land parcel situated in the extreme south of the county.

Fred leaned over and looked at the display. "That's interesting—they have a tract in the middle of the schists," he said. "Are you sure it's the same Krehbeil?"

Nigel clicked on that location and told the computer to zoom in. Sure enough, it belonged to William Krehbeil II, home address same as the main farm.

"Why would they have a parcel there?" I asked, knowing damned well what the family history was from Mr. Hauser. William Primus had probably kept part of the tract he sold to Tyson. But I could not tell Fred, Nigel, and Jenny what I knew without undermining my assertion that on Monday, I'd only chanced upon the Krehbeil farm. And I imagined that only I knew Primus's widow had also owned a ranch outside of Cody, Wyoming, and apparently left it to her daughter Winnie.

I glanced at Jenny, wondering how much she knew about the Krehbeils' financial situation. Who had inherited that ranch when Winnie died? Did she have children, or had the land devolved to her brother and his heirs? Did the ailing Mrs. Krehbeil now own it? And were her children eyeing it like hungry coyotes circling a fresh kill? "Would that database show lands held outside of the county?" I asked.

"No," said Nigel. "Why?"

Jenny met my gaze. She was a quick one, all right.

But my mental machinery was far ahead of her, because I knew things she did not. Tert's errand to Cody suddenly was cast in a new light: Had he gone to Wyoming to appear on the Remington committee, or was his true mission to fetch that painting from his aunt's ranch before someone else nabbed it?

I ratcheted through the possibilities this opened up. If Grandmother Krehbeil had left the Pennsylvania farm to Secundus and the Wyoming ranch to Aunt Winnie, then Tert's relationship to the painting would have slipped from heir to visitor. And he'd said he hadn't seen the painting in decades. Had he perhaps had a falling-out with his aunt? Had Winnie's death provided his opportunity to seize the painting? And if so, was it his alone, or did he owe his siblings each one-quarter of its value?

And hadn't Frank Barnes said that there was something suspicious about Winnie's death? Another doorway to possibilities opened up, and I began to wonder just how many of his relatives Tert might have poisoned.

Was he cold-bloodedly killing off his relatives to snatch his inheritance? I cleared my throat. "Jenny, why exactly did old Mr. Krehbeil apply for the easement? Was he a preservationist like you?"

"Oh, heavens no. The farm's falling down and he was a proud old coot. He wanted the bucks to fix the place up."

"And you say the Krehbeil farm is not on the best soil. How exactly does that affect the Ag easement process?"

"The County Agricultural Preserve Board system relies on annual evaluations of each property that applies for the trust. A scoring system had been devised to set the priorities for which farms get the money. Because the budget is renewed each year, the evaluations are redone annually, and the top candidates get the money. It's four years since Old Man Krehbeil applied for his easement, and each year the Krehbeil farm has scored too low. The limited county budget keeps going to farms with higher rankings."

"But you said there are two easement funds."

"Right. The other fund is privately administered. But it doesn't pay as much, and in fact relies on farmers donating their easement values as much as actually getting paid, or they get paid much less than market value."

So Tert's father had applied for the agricultural easement to gain cash needed to fix up the property and pay for the day-to-day cost of living. If he had succeeded, the land could not be developed. That would have seriously lessened its value as an inheritance, and the cash realized from the County Agricultural Preservation Board would soon be consumed making repairs. So why wouldn't Tert want to hurry Papa's descent into the grave? And why leave Mama alive? Much better to hasten their demise before the sale could go through, and lock up the sale of the development rights in probate. And what of Aunt Winnie's assets? I had to find a way to uncover that story, too.

As I mulled all this, we loaded ourselves back into the vehicle and headed south through the rolling farmlands. Fred entertained me by pointing out how I could know if a farm belonged to authentic Amish, fake Amish, or Other (authentic Amish had no phone or power lines leading to the house and instead relied on a windmill to raise water, and the clotheslines were bright with simple, solid-colored shirts and dresses in the saturated colors they preferred; fake Amish had a windmill but it wasn't turning; Other had modern conveniences). We passed schoolyards in which all the children were dressed in solid colors; they stared at us as we stared at them. "True Amish," said Fred.

"What's the difference between Amish and Mennonite?" I asked.

Jenny said, "The Mennonites are the ones with all the handicapped parking spaces at the church."

"Huh? Is there a high rate of disability?"

"Yes," she said. "A great many of us can't sing."

Fred thumped the steering wheel with glee. "That's good, Jenny. I hadn't heard that one."

"Thanks, Fred."

"I don't get it," said Nigel. "How's that different from the Presbyterians?"

"I only tell non-P.C. jokes about my own ethnic group," Jenny said, affecting piety.

Fred said, "How about a cowboy joke, Em?"

"Is 'cowboy' an ethnic group?" Nigel asked nervously. "Really, you might have warned me."

I said, "Horse goes into a bar, and the bartender says, 'Why the long face?' "

Fred and Jenny laughed.

"I don't get it," said Nigel acidly. "Let's get back to the forensics of spotting true Amish. Forensics is a topic I know and love."

Fred said, "Then you might just be interested in a little ground truth so you can see if your eye in the sky is telling you something real or not."

"Ground truth?" said Jenny.

"Direct observations of what's out here," Fred explained. "Nigel's all het up about what he can do with his black boxes, but they're really only good for extending what we discover the old-fashioned way; by getting outside and walking around over the earth, checking what rocks are where and what grows on them. Then and only then are his air photos meaningful, let alone all the layers he chunks in from God-knows-what source."

Nigel said, "You don't mean to tell me we're actually going to get out of this vehicle, do you? And . . . and my God, man, *walk*?" I could hear him tapping away at the keys. "Look here, Jenny my dear, I have the aerial photography for the entire county, strategically taken during a drought. See all these convolutions showing through from the underlying strata? And this"—he tapped another key—"is the current geological mapping of the area. Note how oversimplified it is by comparison with what the photography shows. That's because the field geologist here in Pennsylvania has less than one percent actual rock outcrop from which to discern the bending and folding these rocks have been subjected to. North America and Europe pulled apart and crashed together repeatedly over the eons crenulating this territory like a Beefeater's collar. I've seen bakers fold dough five times to make croissants and do less mixing."

"And what crop was in the fields the day that photography was grown?" asked Fred, enjoying the bantering to the utmost. "You haven't the foggiest, have you?"

"Egad, man, what difference does that make, as long as it was shallow-rooted and feeling the drought?" Nigel was grinning, his mustaches at full gallop. This was clearly a debate they had cultivated over a great many coffee breaks. "But since you ask, it was corn."

Fred swept his hand out toward the scenery we were driving past. "We just crossed from the Conestoga limestone to the Wissahickon schist. Did you even notice?"

"Of course not. There's nary a lump of limestone or schist showing for miles around."

"Not so," said Fred. "The topography changed, as did the vegetation. We've not only crossed from gently rolling hills to steep ridges and narrow gullies, but we've left behind the lushly farmed croplands with large houses, and now we're in here with the small plots with much less prosperous homes. Notice that we are in a mixed hardwood forest. No one is trying to farm down here. As we cross into the serpentine barrens, we'll begin seeing stuff that looks like the lairs of rednecks. You know; mobile homes, chain-link fences, and barking dogs that chase you down the blacktop."

"Strike three against fieldwork," Nigel snarled theatrically.

We all laughed. We were traveling now over a changeable terrain, dodging about on narrow little roads that wound through tight, steep valleys. The roads ran like a spider's web, each running only a mile or so before we'd intersect another at a stop sign, all pavements the same width and state of disrepair.

"Is serpentine a mineral?" Jenny asked.

Fred answered. "It's a metamorphic rock. It starts out as basalt that flows out under seawater. The circulating seawater alters it. This serpentine has been further metamorphosed by all the compression of the events that built our continent."

Nigel spoke again. "Speaking of ground truth and forensic work, who's this bloke that's been tailing us?"

Fred stared into the rearview mirror. "What bloke?"

"Haven't you noticed him? He's driving a bland-looking dark sedan with out-of-state plates."

Jenny and I turned and looked out the back window. Sure enough, there was a car there, hanging back just far enough that we glimpsed it only periodically as we came out of curves and into straightaways. I said, "Pull up just before the next stop sign and wait a bit, okay?"

Fred gave me a look of skeptical uncertainty, but half a minute later, he pulled up and cut the engine.

The sedan came around the curve, slowed, then sped up again, slowed, and hurried off again, making a left turn. His head was turned away from us as he passed, but I knew him in a blink: It was Agent Wardlaw.

"Why, that S.O.B.," I muttered.

"You know the fellow?" Fred asked.

"Sorry to say, I do. I'll prove it to you. He turned left. You turn right, and I'll bet we'll spot him behind us again within a mile."

Fred followed my instructions, and sure enough, along came the dark sedan. "A friend of yours?" he inquired.

"An FBI agent," I said. There was nothing to be gained by saying otherwise.

"Any special reason you get an FBI escort when you do fieldwork?" he asked.

"Well, my boyfriend's an FBI agent, so let's just say we're keeping it in the family," I said, hoping that would divert the questioning long enough for me to figure a better way to spin the situation.

"Pretty good ground truth for an eye-in-the-sky man, eh?" chirped Nigel.

"Yeah, how'd you spot him?" Fred asked, all pretense of bantering dropped in favor of frank admiration.

"As a man who's been educationally murdered four separate times and lived to tell the tale, I just know these things," Nigel cooed.

Fred eyed me askance. "So, what do you want to do? Pull over again and offer to give the man a lift? He's likely to get lost out here."

"It wouldn't be such a bad thing if he got lost," I said. "But let me think on this. You proceed on out to our destination, and by the time we get there, I'll know what to do with him."

"Is he dressed for the field?" asked Fred.

"Not in the sense that we are. He'll have street shoes on, and slacks rather than blue jeans."

"Well then, let's take him through the greenbrier," he said.

"What's that? Some sort of a bramble?" I asked. The image of Agent Wardlaw trying to extricate himself from anything involving prickers delighted me in the extreme.

"She doesn't know what greenbrier is," said Jenny. "Oh my, Em, but your life has been sheltered until this very moment."

"Is it worse than rattlesnakes and ticks?" I asked.

"You think there are no ticks out here?" she said. "And no snakes? Heavens, you've never heard of copperheads?"

"No, and I suppose I don't want to meet one," I said. "Rattlers at least give you a warning."

"The relative kindness of vipers, what a marvelous topic of conversation," said Nigel.

"And I was trying to keep the topic off of Agent Wardlaw," I muttered.

We continued down an increasingly narrow and rustic road for several minutes, then pulled up against a chain-link fence. Sure enough, on the other side of the fence was a rather decrepit-looking mobile home complete with coon dogs barking and jumping at the fence.

Fred turned in his seat and addressed his passengers. "I've pulled over here because there's a serpentine barren quite close to the road," he said. "Sad part is there are also dogs here. Right now they're on the other side of the fence, but you never know. People who live up here don't take kindly to visitors, even if you're just parking alongside the road and taking a squint at a little bit of rock. Are we armed?"

"Precisely what did you have in mind?" asked Nigel.

Fred said, "Oh, anything. Ball bats, two-by-fours . . ." He reached behind his seat and produced a hefty length of rebar. "Essential field gear around here," he commented. "Don't wander too far from the vehicle," he instructed us, as he opened the door and hopped out. "And don't lock up. We may need to remount in a hurry."

We all tumbled out and followed him, each picking up a rock as we crossed the road onto the open ground that lay beyond it. I looked around, taking in the geological ambiance of the setting. What I saw was a patch of open ground with little growing on it. Twenty feet beyond, the trees filled in again. "The trees seem stunted," I observed, as Agent Wardlaw went barreling past on the road and disappeared around the next turn. Apparently he had missed a turn a ways back and had been hurrying to catch up. I almost turned and waved to him, but was afraid I'd give him the finger instead. The dogs behind the fence had settled down, seeing that we were headed away from their homestead, but at the sight of Wardlaw's car they had activated again, hurling themselves at the fence like clods of mud.

"I hope he doesn't get out of his car," Fred said. He turned his attention to the clearing. "Yeah, the trees are stunted. That's why they call them the barrens. See what's growing here? *Antropogon scoparius*, that's this grass. That's all that can grow where the serpentine is really close to the surface, because of the thin soil and the chemistry. Too much manganese for most plants, but *scoparius* can tolerate it. That and these stunted cedars. This greenbrier here"—he bent over and grabbed at a seemingly innocuous green twig that arched out of the thin soils—"is only here because the mining has disturbed the ground enough to upset the balance of vegetation such that the deer have been foraging and dropping fertilizer." He waved a hand toward the surrounding thicket. "Over there you can see the greenbrier is much healthier. It's climbing trees, even." He pointed to a mass of interwoven vines the size of a small house.

I reached down and touched a stalk. The prickers on it stood straight out from the whip at regular intervals and were half an inch long. I tried to break the stalk. The thing was appallingly strong, and had a hefty spring to it.

"You don't want to trifle with greenbrier," Fred informed me. "It forms a bramble you wouldn't believe. If you were dropped in the middle of it, you'd lose a lot of blood and have your clothing in tatters before you got yourself out."

I grimaced.

Fred held out his hands, presenting the setting to me. "So here it is, this is where a whole network of men busy with picks and shovels dug the chromite mines. They were small features, most of them, not much bigger than a two-car garage."

"Is there a pit associated with this one?" I asked.

"No. This one has no chromite. The rocks in this area are quite old—Precambrian in age, that's six or seven hundred million years ago, in round numbers. As I've mentioned, the rocks of Pennsylvania have been through a lot of compressive events."

"What are you two talking about?" asked Jenny.

Fred stuck the rebar under his armpit so he could use both hands. "As the continents slammed together the land got all wrinkled up like the skin of a basset hound that's being petted too hard. That's what formed all the long, parallel ridges out west of here."

Jenny said, "But here we have just low hills."

Fred said, "This area is folded and faulted as well; it's older, so it's been undergoing erosion longer. And yes, as Nigel said, it's been wrung out and mashed so many times that the rocks have altered. Metamorphosis requires tremendous pressure and or heat. During Cambrian time—oh, hang on, here comes our escort." He popped the rebar into his hand with practiced speed.

I became aware of a distant howling and woofing that was growing steadily louder. A moment later, sprinting around a bend in the road ahead of a second chorus of dogs came Agent Wardlaw, moving remarkably quickly for a man with a gut. The canines were closing on him, and after he took one quick glance back, we saw his hand go around to his belt in search of his firearm.

Fred stepped out into the road with his rebar raised in the universal gesture of threat known to all dogs. "Don't pull your pistol, man! You think the dogs are bad; you don't want to meet their owners! Em, Jenny, Nigel, get back in the vehicle, and leave a seat for this fool."

We dashed to Fred's vehicle and jumped in. I stared in horror as the lead dog got a mouthful of Wardlaw's pants leg and threw on the brakes. Wardlaw kept coming, now slowed by seventy pounds of deadweight.

Fred stood in the middle of the road, his arm still raised. "Don't shoot, man! Bludgeon the thing with it!"

Wardlaw swung and bashed the dog on the head with the butt of his pistol, knocking the animal senseless, but the other dogs were almost upon him. Snatching a panicked look at them over his shoulder, Wardlaw stumbled and fell straight into a thatch of greenbrier. The dogs leapt, bit, clung.

Fred dashed to him and brought the rebar down hard on the head of the nearest cur as Wardlaw thrashed, catching himself even deeper into the briars. Fred dispatched a second dog, and a third. Those that were still conscious backed out of reach of the rebar and bared their yellow teeth at Fred, growling. "Nigel! Get me the machete!" he hollered, not taking his eyes off the dogs.

Nigel reached under Fred's seat and produced a long knife in a sheath. "Surely he doesn't expect me to get out of this vehicle," he murmured, even as he opened the door and stepped out. He crossed the distance quickly on his long legs and started whacking at the briars, dancing a two-step with Fred as they worked to keep the dogs out of reach. Once they had the agent loose, all three men dashed to the vehicle and hit it like thunder, slamming the doors behind them, a half-beat ahead of the remaining dogs. We watched as, one by one, the dogs Fred had knocked cold came back to consciousness and staggered to their feet, barking as if they had never been away. Nigel gave them all the finger. The dogs circled and growled and barked a while longer, sniffed indignantly, and then trotted away.

"I *thought* we were at the edge of their range," Fred said conversationally, fastidiously placing his rebar and machete in their stowage positions. "Well, all in a day's fieldwork. Haven't had to use my machete in quite that way since I took out a six-foot rattler while I was doing my doctorate at U.T." He was hardly even breathing hard.

Wardlaw, on the other hand, was gasping for breath.

"Good morning," I said to him. "Or is it past noon?"

Wardlaw ignored me, intent instead on the confetti that had been his pants and shirt. "Shit," he muttered, picking a length of the whiplike brier from his clothing. "I hate greenbrier."

Fred reached an arm over the seatback to offer a hand in greeting. "Agent Wardlove is it?" he inquired. "I'm Fred Petridge."

"Ward*law*," rasped the agent, ungraciously keeping his hands to himself.

"Fancy meeting you here," I said.

"Oh, this is getting marvelous!" Nigel pashed. "*Simply* marvelous. Fred, you old pebble hack, you never told me you had live entertainment on your fieldtrips. Heavens, I would have come out ages ago had I known!"

Jenny sat squeezed between Agent Wardlaw and the exultant Nigel, her shoulders pulled up tight to protect herself. "So, now, Emily," she said slowly, "perhaps it's time you told us more about your friend here. I mean, what exactly is going on? I thought I was coming out to learn some geological heritage, and now we've got—"

Wardlaw grinned nastily at me. "You mean Hansen ain't explained that she's a double agent?"

"Up your butt, Wardlaw!"

He sat back and cackled. "Oh, yes, this woman *poses* as a geologist, but in fact she's working for—"

"Enough, Wardlaw, or I'll tell your ma you've been eating Twinkies again!"

He stopped and considered the situation, the brown slime he had for brains working turgidly through a plan. I fixed a drop-dead-forever look on him, but he pulled back his lips to expose almost all of his teeth and said, "Em here is working for William Krehbeil the Third, aka Tert. So tell us, darling, what's that got to do with geology?"

How sad I was to be armed with only my mouth and my fingernails. I realized he had me. So I shut up.

Jenny fixed an indignant look on me. "You know Tert Krehbeil? But you said you'd only happened by his family farm yesterday, like it was some kind of an accidental meeting. You got me telling you their family tree, and all the particulars of their situation with trying to save the farm! Where was *that* at?"

Agent Wardlaw's grin had turned into a death's-head rictus. "I'd like to know that myself, Ms. Hansen. Why not share it with us all?"

Everyone in the vehicle was now staring at me. How I do hate being the center of attention. How I detest being caught out in a lie. How I loathe having to answer to people like Agent Wardlaw. "Show them your badge," I said, turning the heat on him.

He was more than pleased to do so. Fred and Jenny took in this information with hesitation, but Nigel yanked his identification out of his hand and took a nice, close squint. "Oh, blimey!" he cooed. "This is the real thing!"

"Yes, it is," I said. "And I am a real geologist. Am I not, Wardlaw."

"Yes, you are," he agreed.

"And my boyfriend is in fact an agent for the FBI, when he's not being a reactivated reservist in the Middle East."

"That is true."

"And I am doing nothing illegal, but you think that if you follow me, you'll find out something about the activities of certain people I might know, who shall go *nameless*," I said. "Because U.S. citizens are still, even in this era of the so-called Patriot Act, entitled to due process under the law *and* our federal constitution, and are considered innocent until proven guilty *and* are entitled to their privacy."

Wardlaw's fat lips pulled into a sassy little pucker.

Nigel said, "Quite right, Emily. Ever since the Magna Carta, things have been getting better for humanity. We've developed English Common Law, much better than Roman law, under which it is 'woes betide the accused.' Of course, your current administration is wont to play fast and loose with things in the name of fighting terrorism, but that can't be why Agent Wardlaw is following you through the serpentine barrens, can it?"

Wardlaw shifted his intimidating gaze onto him.

Nigel said, "Hell, man, quit looking at me like that! I have a perfectly valid green card, I'll have you know, and I've paid U.S. taxes to the last farthing every year I've worked here!"

Now Wardlaw turned his glare on me. "Who are these people?"

I shook my head. "Wardlaw, I think your line here should be more like, 'Hey, thanks for saving my butt from the dogs,' or, 'Would you please drive me back to where I hid my pursuit vehicle so I can hide my head in shame at having been such a lousy tracker and leave you all alone so you can get some honest work done?' "

Wardlaw closed his eyes and leaned back in his seat.

"I'll take you to your car," said Fred. He started the motor and pulled out onto the road. "I'm Dr. Petridge of the Pennsylvania Geologic Survey, and this is Dr. Iago of the same. Sitting next to you is a private citizen who can introduce herself to you or not as pleases her." His tone was pleasant but firm. I was liking him better and better.

Jenny gave Wardlaw a look that would freeze ether. Wardlaw said nothing.

A quarter-mile down the road, we found the federal vehicle. Fred stopped to let Wardlaw out. "We're on our way to the Krehbeil mine," he informed him. "It's a podiform chromite deposit. It arises from the gradual differentiation of more disseminated chrome ores in serpentine, which is a metamorphosed basalt, in this case a pillow basalt, a term used to signify the shape taken by such mafic extrusives when they cool underwater. Now—"

"Can the lecture," said Agent Wardlaw, as he climbed out of the vehicle. "I'm just interested in what Em's doin' here." He tried once more to look intimidating by planting his feet wide apart and thrusting his chest and gut our way, but his attempt was ruined by the fact that he kept glancing all about for the pack of dogs.

"That's what I've been trying to explain to you," said Fred. "We're out here doing fieldwork. This is what geologists do when they are trying to learn something about the history of the earth. It's a free country, and you are welcome to join us, but to get where we're going, your leather-soled shoes would have you sliding down some fairly steep slopes, and I don't feel I know you well enough to offer to do a tick check when we return."

"And all of this is about is paint pigments," I told Wardlaw. "You assumed that everything I was doing in the East had to do with what *you* are interested in. But no, this is research for my master's thesis. Now, if you prefer, I would be pleased to give you my cell-phone number, and you can give me yours, because I would be surprised if the reception is all that good out here, so we're going to be playing some phone tag. Or I can just call you when I get set up with a room for the night, and you can come by for a moment and I'll spill the whole day's intellectual riches to you, right down to the last podiform chromite deposit. I'll even bring you a copperhead, if we find any."

Wardlaw had found his sardonic smile again. "I already got your damned cell-phone number," he said ominously. "So just tell me where you're staying, and your dossier will be up-to-date."

I opened my mouth to say something creative, but Fred said, "Jenny booked you a room at the Cameron Estate Inn."

"It has the best heritage value within easy driving distance of the Survey," Jenny chimed in.

"Thank you," I said, through clenched teeth.

"It's in Mount Joy," Fred informed him. "Not far from Middletown, where the Survey is. We'll be back by quitting time, so Em should be there by six, if you insist on harassing her any further."

And that was it. Wardlaw shoved off, I supposed in search of a replacement for his shredded pants, and the rest of us continued on into the serpentine barrens, but my mind was already focused on spending the coming evening in the town where Hector Krehbeil lived.

23

YOU REALLY GET TO KNOW SOMEONE QUICKLY WHEN YOU DO A tick check together.

Jenny Neumann and I stripped down in the women's room at the Pennsylvania Geologic Survey, right down to our birthday suits. It seemed that she lived alone, and, as the only one who might be waiting for me at the Cameron Inn was someone I would not on a bet ask to search my hide for ticks, I was more than pleased to swap searches with her. She was very thorough, even checking my hair with a fine-toothed comb she had in her picnic basket.

As she leaned close to my scalp, she said, "So, you have an interest in the Krehbeil family."

"I'm not sure how to answer that," I said.

"That's okay," she said. "I'll talk and you listen, and we'll see where it goes from there. I'm finding them a rather difficult bunch to work with, and the thing is, I want to get them that Ag easement, whether they're with me or against me. But they're not making it easy."

"And you're hoping I have some insight into the family that might help you."

"Anything would help just now. The application was in Mr. and Mrs. Krehbeil's name, and, like I said, he's gone now and she won't be with us forever. Deirdre seemed quite interested in the idea of following through—she's lived there all but the few years she was married, and her grown children live there with her now, so it's her home, see—but lately she hasn't been returning my calls. William the Third doesn't come around to visit, so I've never met him. He lives in Philadelphia, right?"

That much I could give her. "Right. He owns an art gallery there."

"That tallies. His grandmother founded it. Then there's Hector, and I haven't managed to get through to him. And there's Cricket, but she doesn't come around much either."

"What's the story there?"

"I knew her in high school. Wandering soul. Disappears for years at a time. No one really knows where she goes or when she'll return. Deirdre said drugs, but it sounded like she was just trying to get me to think ill of her. She's the youngest by quite a stretch—it's almost twenty years between Deirdre and Cricket."

"And Deirdre's the only one who ever married or had kids?"

"That's what they say," said Jenny. "So anyway, I was kind of wondering if you might want to help me find Cricket."

"Why me?" I asked, as I shook out my underpants and climbed back into them.

"Because you're a detective."

"I'm a geologist."

She shook her head. "No, you're not. I saw how you handled that FBI guy. He's onto you because you're onto the Krehbeils, and God knows what he's got on them, but the whole idea is to make sure their farm doesn't get cut up into McMansions, regardless of what happens to the family. You see, it was William the Second's ardent wish that the farm be preserved, and—"

I held up a hand. "It's okay. You don't have to justify this to me. If that's what you want and it doesn't hurt anyone, and if even better yet it helps keep Lancaster County from being totally overrun with BMWs and burger stands, then all the better."

She seemed embarrassed nonetheless. "It's just that you seemed to handle yourself so well with that guy. I could really use some help with this file."

"That 'help-me' act may work on the guys, Jenny, but you should never kid a kidder. Besides, I like you, and I figure that helping you might be helping me. So why not? I can pose as your assistant, and that would explain why I'm so interested in the family."

Jenny clapped her hands together. "Oh, thank you!"

"What did William Krehbeil Secundus die of?" I asked.

"I don't know," she said. "He seemed healthy enough when he first applied for the easement, but then he got sick and died."

"What did he die of?"

"I don't know. I hear he wouldn't go to the hospital."

"A family trait," I said. "Perhaps they can't tell the medical ward from the mental ward. Surely they suffer a collective insanity, and they could get a bulk deal—maybe have a wing all to themselves."

"Pride goeth before a fall," said Jenny. "When people hang on to something that tightly, it's usually because they've got it confused with their own self-worth. Funny thing is such clinging tends to turn them kind of mean."

"You seem to know the Krehbeils better than you said, too."

"I knew Cricket in high school, remember? She was a nice kid. Kind of sad. Didn't have a clue how to defend herself. Girls would insult her and she'd just stand there and take it."

"So you think that's why she left?"

"Yeah, she just couldn't take any more. I've always hoped she'd learn a little emotional ju jitsu and come home, but maybe she's made a nice life for herself somewhere."

We finished knocking our clothes clean and putting them on and returned to the parking lot in the front of the building where the men had just finished unloading the gear from the state vehicle. Nigel turned and faced Jenny. "O, Vision of Post–Ground Truth Loveliness, will I ever see thee again?"

Jenny smiled pleasantly. "I'm sure you will, especially if you come out and help Fred and me with some of our heritage projects. We could really use your help with all that GIS business. You could help us in a number of ways, mapping out resources, correlating ownership patterns, showing—"

Nigel's mustaches spread over clenched teeth. "I was thinking of something involving alcohol and a slice of rare beef."

Jenny patted him on the arm. "That's lovely, Nigel, and I'd love to, really. Just this evening, however, Em and I are going to interview Hector Krehbeil."

I said, "We are?"

Jenny smiled. "Why yes, looking for Cricket, remember?"

"So where's this Hector chappie?" said Nigel. "We can knock him off over cocktails and be on to the steak house, no problem."

"Hang on a mo'," I said. "Let me see if I can whistle him up." I suppose it was showing off, but I went to my car and dug through my duffel bag for the little notebook in which I had written down Hector's phone number and dialed.

Hector answered on the second ring. "Forsooth," he declared.

"Hector?"

Jenny had wandered over to see what I was doing. When I said his name, she went on point like a little bird dog.

"Oh. Yes, who is this? I thought it must be James. But you are clearly not he."

I said, "Hector, this is Em Hansen, Faye's friend. You remember, you called me by mistake. . . ."

"Oh, yes. Well, Miss Hansen, sorry to say, I can't chat just now." He sounded excited, not dismissive.

"Something up, Hector?"

"I shall trod the boards this evening and I must get ready. Ergo, anon."

"The boards? Oh yes, that's right, you're an actor. Where?"

"Where what?"

"Where do you trod boards? I'd like to see you act."

"Actually, there will be no boards, only a pale limestone floor. It's a rather rustic theater in a pub right here in my home duchy. A bit far for you to come. So, prithee, if thou wilt excuse me . . ."

"Hector, I'm in Pennsylvania. Can we get together after the show?"

His voice sped up and the faux Elizabethan English evaporated. "I really don't know. I really am quite preoccupied. You're on a cell phone, right? Oh, wait, you're breaking up—"

The connection was broken. I stared into the illuminated face of the cell phone. The sly fox had dumped me.

Jenny looked on expectantly. "He cut you off, eh?"

"Yeah."

"Same treatment I got. Tough customer."

"No kidding."

Nigel had wandered over and was now rubbing up against Jenny like a bear scratching itself on a tree. "So . . ."

"Why don't you come by my office tomorrow, Nigel? We could discuss your GIS," said Jenny, making it sound like an invitation to cover her with whipped cream. To me she said, "Did you get anything out of him before he bailed?"

"He said he was on his way to a theater in a pub. In Mount Joy."

She laughed. "Bube's? That's not a theater, that's a brewery."

"Perhaps he's already drunk."

Still trying to worm his way into the occasion, Nigel said, "My kind of boy."

I said, "Really, Nigel?"

Jenny grabbed Nigel's arm. "It could be a double date. Me and Em, and you and Hector."

"I think I'll go for the conference in your office instead," he said reasonably, and wandered off toward his Mini.

I told Jenny, "We could meet there for dinner."

"Fine," she said. "Seven o'clock?"

THE CAMERON ESTATE Inn turned out to be a swanky bed-and-breakfast tucked into the rolling farmlands about three miles from anywhere anyone would accuse of being a town or a highway. It was quite lovely. A three-story brick job, it featured sweeping porches facing out onto a sloped lawn that led down to a narrow brook.

The innkeeper assigned me to a nice room on the second floor: I mean *really* nice; it was as capacious as my room in Washington had been tight. It must have been one of the master bedrooms back when the Cameron family held forth at that address shortly after the Civil War. Someone—Cameron's granddaughter, the brochures advised me—had spent a mid-sized fortune tarting up the place after some years of demise, and now the innkeepers were going at it advertising period antiques and things called duvets. My room had a walloping four-poster bed with more cushy pillows than any ten friends and I could have lounged upon. I stood in the middle of the room trying to decide what to do with all this luxury.

I had expected to find Agent Wardlaw skulking around the place, but he was not in evidence. No bland federal sedan lurked in the parking lot. No jerk with dark glasses decorated the front porch. And there were no messages for me at the check-in desk.

I let down my guard a quarter-inch. That opened me to a fresh flood of worries about Baby Sloane. Would Faye follow my advice? Should I call her?

I tried my best to shove these anxieties out of my mind. I would find

Hector and get him to tell me why he thought Tert was implicated in Aunt Winnie's death, and then I'd call Faye and tell her to phone her old pal Hector if she didn't believe me.

I placed my duffel lavishly on the special luggage rack and dug out a clean pair of blue jeans and a clean shirt. Then I availed myself of the bathtub for a quick soak and got spruced up as best I could, running a comb through my hair one more time for good measure. Then I hopped up onto the bed and gave it a test flop. Very nice. But I was restless. I had given myself plenty of time, figuring to listen to the missed call that registered on my cell phone. I hoped it was Faye, but presumed that it wasn't. Maybe it was Agent Wardlaw. Maybe it was a wrong number.

I lay back and felt depression settle all around me. This whole trip was not going well, not really. I was gathering loads of information, but it was not lining itself up with flashing arrows pointing toward a master's thesis. And, aside from my chat with Emmett Jones, I was kidding myself if I thought I was doing anything that justified spending Tert's money. It was weird to find myself worrying about pleasing a client I suspected of murder.

I tried to sort the information into two groups. Group one was miscellaneous information that might help me get my master's. Subgroup A was information about artists' pigments: chemistry, history, and possible sources. Subgroup B was techniques: analytical and evaluative, meaning machines to use and how to look at the results. This was all fine and good, but techniques would do me no good unless I really thought I could do something with Tert's paint chips, which was Job A, or focused on one particular artist or work for a thesis, which was Job B. I had totally missed seeing a Catlin portrait, and I was running out of days to zip back down to D.C. and try again, little that the idea even appealed next to all my worry about Faye and the baby. And the idea of using the Krehbeils' fabled art collection had surely fizzled.

Which led me to Group Two, which was, of course, all things Krehbeil. I had lots of dirt on them now, more than I could have hoped to gather in a few scant days, and in fact more than I cared to know about them in a personal sense. They were a proud family rooted in a tradition of contrariness, and they were having a few problems with their cash flow, except for Tert. Indeed, there seemed to be an uneven distribution of wealth among them, and little happiness. The only one who had dollars in his pockets was under scrutiny by the FBI, an agency that took an interest in people only when they busted federal law or crossed state lines with their mischief.

And Faye had gotten herself mixed up in this, and taken the baby into it.

I hopped off the sumptuous bed like I had been bitten by a rattlesnake, jumped into my shoes, grabbed my jacket, and headed out the door.

That put me on the front porch with half an hour to burn.

I wandered down toward the brook, hoping that the great out-of-doors would soothe me as it so often did. The creek lured me off through a grove of trees. I followed it, listening to the birds find their perches for the night, and came across a wide pool edged in stone. The spring rose just below a steep hillside. At the top of the hill stood an old church.

I waited in the gathering darkness at the foot of the pool, hoping that an idea might emerge with the waters.

After a moment, I realized I was not alone. A woman had appeared on the stone steps that led down from the churchyard. I watched her approach.

"Good evening," she said, as she reached the edge of the pool. "I was just up visiting the church. It's quite famous. It had a patriot tree where all the parishioners took a pledge. Have you seen it?" she asked, making the kind of effusive chat one sometimes makes to a total stranger.

"No," I said politely. "How interesting."

"Yes, and there's a graveyard. The stones are really old. I'm from California, and we don't have graves going back that far. Except the Indians, of course, but they didn't leave headstones. Much more civilized, I suppose. But still, you're a Euro-American like me, so perhaps you understand. Three hundred years seems so *old*."

I smiled. "Are you staying at the inn?" I inquired.

"Yes. Isn't it lovely? Where I come from, there are no houses that old. There's so much *history* here. Generations and generations. We quite forget all of this in California."

"I suppose."

"Just imagine being able to visit the graves of your ancestors. Your grandparents, and their parents, and their parents' parents. That's what it's like up there in that yard."

"Wow."

"And yet I had to laugh when I read that plaque commemorating the oath all the parishioners took. It seemed so naïve, somehow. Loyalty and all of that. How times have changed. Wars between peoples aren't so simple anymore."

"Hmm."

"Well, I suppose I have to go. My husband will be wondering where I've gotten off to. It's time to go to dinner, and I don't want to turn an ankle moving up through the darkness."

"Right."

"Nice talking to you."

"You, too."

She moved off through the trees.

I stood a while longer, watching the reflection of the darkening sky on the waters. Loyalty. Wars. Traditions. Death and dying. Graves.

And suddenly it hit me: Mrs. Krehbeil's illness was the key to the whole Krehbeil puzzle.

The question became, How could I prove what was making her sick?

24

Bube's Brew Pub was an old brick building on the main drag of the not-at-all bustling metropolis of Mount Joy, Pennsylvania. The town appeared to be a secondary hub built around the farming trades. A railroad ran through it, forming a slot through the heart of the central district. Bube's was prominent within what Mount Joy had for a semi-industrial neighborhood. It was a very old brewery. It had the ten-foot-tall oak barrels to prove it.

"I'm supposed to meet a party here," I told the hostess who greeted me inside the big wooden doors.

She looked at her clipboard and said something that was lost under a loud whooping from the bar. Somewhere, somebody was doing something clever with a basketball, and a number of young fellahs were sounding pretty excited about it.

I said, "We're here to meet a party who's . . . in the theater."

"Oh. Then you'd be downstairs."

She led me through the dark, lofty reaches of the barrel room to the top of a flight of wooden steps, the kind of rough-hewn staircase that has treads but no risers. The stairs led down—I mean *way* down. It went down at least two stories into the earth. Far below, I could hear music and raucous laughter, and I could just make out the rough form of a stone floor. *A limestone floor*, I noted. *Is this what Hector meant? Oh well, in for a Jenny, in for a pound*, I told myself, and started down.

At the foot of the stairs, I stepped into a cavern in the living rock. The low ceiling arched above me. Running the length of the room were wooden tables and benches, arranged in a U that opened to a curtained passageway at the far end of the cavern. On the benches were twenty or thirty men and women howling with mirth and swilling from tankards filled with beer. Clearly, they'd been at it awhile. At the near end of the cavern sat two minstrels—there was no other word for it; they were dressed in tights and funny slippers with curling toes, and they sat on low stools and were playing lutes. Candles burned all around them, wax dripping down the natural ledges in the rock.

I glanced up and down, trying to understand what I had just walked into. The chief waitress—or head harlot, I wasn't sure which was more appropriate—was dressed in full skirts and a peasant blouse gathered in close to her ribs by a tight vest emphasizing her comely breasts. Her blonde hair hung to her waist. Addressing the crowd was a man dressed as an Elizabethan street beggar, a study in burlap rags and grease-paint dirt. He held forth with a steady harangue designed to loosen the diners from their usual senses of propriety. They were dressed in modern clothing, but were drinking out of what appeared to be pewter tankards and eating their salads off of what appeared to be pewter platters. I hoped for their sakes that the metal in those implements was in fact something modern—aluminum or tin, perhaps—instead of pewter, which had fallen out of favor because it contained lead.

One of the diners at the near table stumbled to his feet. "Hey, here you are!" He said. "We were wondering if you were coming!"

I wasn't quite sure how to volley this. "Uh—"

Sloshing his tankard, he said, "You're Sylvia Piorkowski from Cleveland, right?"

"Uh, no. . . ."

He roared with laughter. "No worry! You join us anyway. If you're not Sylvia from Cleveland, then you're somebody else from somewhere else, right?"

"Must be. Or last time I checked."

"Well, then, you take Sylvia's seat."

"Well, that's quite a temptation, but I have to meet Jenny."

As if on cue, Jenny popped off of the bottom step behind me. "Em," she said. "Where are we?"

"In Cincinnati, it would appear. How'd you find me?"

"I described you, and the hostess said you were down here. How did you get here?"

"Same thing. I asked for you."

Another man was on his feet. "Oh, great, you're both here now. Hey, everybody, we're all here now!"

"Hurrah!" shouted a chorus of looped Midwesterners. "May the hangings begin!"

Jenny and I looked at each other and shrugged. "Do you think we ought to go upstairs while our necks are still short?" she asked.

"Give it a moment," I replied. "I have a funny feeling about this."

The velvet curtains at the far end of the cavern split open, and more waiters in medieval garb stepped through it, pushing carts with food. One carried a baron of beef. My mouth started to water.

"Wonder what it costs to join them?" I asked Jenny.

"Sit down!" roared the woman to my right. "You're gonna get us in trouble with the Feastmaster!"

"Who's that?" I asked, bending near her to hear over the jollity.

The man to my left yanked me onto the bench next to him. "Get down! Here he comes now!" he bellowed, about bursting my eardrum. Another man got hold of Jenny and pulled her onto a bench between himself and me.

I stuck a thumb into my ringing ear and looked up just in time to see the curtains swish open around another man in tights. This one was about six feet tall and very chesty, especially with all the padding in the black velvet doublet he wore under his black velvet cape, and inside the black tights covering his otherwise not-very-shapely legs. His hair was greased back with brilliantine, and his eyes were liberally outlined with makeup, like a spoof of a bad production of *Cleopatra Queen of the Nile*. Around his neck, he wore a pewter boar's-head that brandished tusks the size of carrots. Under his arm he carried a heavy, leather-bound book. Staring glassily to the far end of the room in a splendor of affect that would have put Sir Laurence Olivier to shame, he pronounced, "I am thy Feastmaster, and *this*"—he held high his volume—"is *The Book*!"

"The Book!" howled the assembled masses, raising their tankards high.

"Oh. My. God," whispered Jenny, in the brief of silence that punctuated this explosive call and response. "This is nuts!"

I said, "No, Jenny, it's crazier than you think. Do you know who that is?'

"Who?"

"The Feastmaster."

"Some nut who flunked out of theater school. I don't know, how'm I supposed to know him?"

"That's Hector, Jenny. I know the voice. Not to mention the sense of drama." The heavy makeup could not eclipse the color of his eyes. They were a cool, pale gray, just like his brother's.

"Prithee quiet, ladies," the Feastmaster ordered of us. "For thou art unsettling the nerves of those who wouldst consume my feast."

"He's talking to us, Em."

"Yes, Jenny, he's looking right at us, too."

"Don't let him get away."

"He's not going anywhere, Jenny. This is his finest hour."

"Omigosh."

"Wench!" cried the Feastmaster. "Giveth thee names to these who wouldst speak when told of silence!"

The bosomy woman with the long blonde hair came over to us and planted her fists on her hips. She pointed at Jenny. "This one be Purple Claws," she said, and of me, she declared, "and this one shall hereby be known as Blue Jeans!"

"Be it so!" roared the Feastmaster.

"Purple Claws!" howled the merrymakers, pounding their tankards on the table. "Blue Jeans!"

The Feastmaster drew himself up in a vampish impression of a Veronica Lake pinup and began to sing, falsetto, "I dream of Brownie with the light blue-oo jeans. . . ."

The man next to me just missed my shoulder in a last-ditch effort to avoid laughing himself clean off the bench. He lay on the floor with his legs still up beside me, gasping for breath. His friends shrieked and pointed at him.

Jenny twisted her lips into an evaluative look as she viewed the upended male. "Darwin was right," she said.

Over the next hour and a half, we were treated to a fine repast and the very finest in in-your-face dinner theater. The Wench and the Beggar played tag team down the rows of increasingly jolly Ohioans, giving shoulder and neck rubs for tips while the Feastmaster coached the women on the fine art of lying across the men's laps and reaching for proffered grapes with their tongues. I watched in fascination, feeling like little more than a voyeur until the man next to me slung an arm around me and purchased the attentions of the Beggar for me. I wasn't sure I wanted anyone with that much dirt on his hands to touch me, but as he moved up behind me and extended a hand to either side of my face, I realized that the palms were freshly washed and smooth with scented oils. He spoke to me softly and touched me with utmost kindness and care, and told me to rest against him. For the first time since Jack had left, I leaned against a man and relaxed.

When all was said and done and the drunkest of the drunk had slopped back up the steps to the main level, the actors who had played our heckling Wench, the Beggar and Feastmaster joined the crowd at the hostess's station. After one or two last rounds of hugging and singing and final swapping of jokes and slipping of tips, the Ohioans got their coats and began to depart. One man came by and pressed a hug on me and said how glad he was that I'd been able to make it and to please not be such a stranger. I assured him that I'd see him back in Ohio and sent him on his way out the door.

The Wench patted Hector on the back. "You did great tonight," she said. "I hope you stand in for Gary another time."

Hector bowed with a dramatic flourish which caught the Wench's hand to his lips for an eloquent but chaste kiss. "Would that he need not fall ill that I could be of assistance, madam."

Jenny whispered into my ear. "Working for heritage has never been like this."

"Now's when we really get to work," I assured her. "And I think the outrageous approach is in order."

I stepped forward and slipped my arm through Hector's. "Oh Feastmaster," I crooned, "prithee let a lonesome wench purchase you a drink."

Hector rolled his expressive gray eyes and cocked a hip, sending the message that he was thirsty but not my kind of guy. "I never turn down a drink," he said. "The bar's right over here."

We were quickly settled and, in the time-honored fashion of those who are truly devoted to being hammered, Hector was soon drunk. After that, it was no trouble at all getting him to talk about his family. All I had to ask was, "Are there more talented artisans like you in your family?"

"Father liked to paint," he told us mournfully, slipping down another

Mai Tai as full beers lined up in front of me and Jenny sipped a raspberry lemonade. "He was a wonderful painter, in fact; studied in Philadelphia, and even New York. *His* mother painted, you see. . . . It's a family tradition, art. We like to think we're like the Wyeths."

"You mean like N. C. Wyeth?" I indicated that I was very impressed. "Was he from around here? I've seen some of his paintings in a museum." I didn't mention that the museum in question was near his aunt's ranch. I wasn't supposed to know that yet.

"Why, yes, my dear woman. The Brandywine School, you know."

Jenny chimed in, "The Brandywine School of art refers to a wonderful bit of heritage. It's—"

I held up an index finger, shushing her. "Hector was telling us about his father and grandmother," I told her.

He was in fact dramatically arching his neck and staring up into the beams of the ceiling, warming to a tale that would assure us that he was related to a noble tribe. Jenny nodded and fell silent again.

Hector crooned, "Just one county east of here, you'll find lovely Brandywine Creek, and its banks are fairly *littered* with men of artistic flair." He took a capacious swill of his drink. "*And* a few women, I hasten to add. Grandmummy was able to persuade Granddaddy to let her study painting with Howard Pyle of the Brandywine School."

"Tell me more," I said.

Hector rolled his eyes, quite a show with all that mascara and eyeliner. "Heavens, my dear woman, the Brandywine was a regular mecca for artists, always has been . . . or at least, since its founding in the 1800's, which by local history is really *not* all that old, but just the same . . . N. C. Wyeth was of the Brandywine School, and of course you'll know his son, Andrew. And I think Andrew has a son, though I wonder at his sexual orientation . . . but Pyle was a very important illustrator of books."

It seemed time to sink the first probe. "I've seen some of his work in the Whitney Gallery in Cody, Wyoming."

"Ah, Cody . . . cowboys . . . Indians . . . and the domain of Miz Whitney and her royal court. She took Grandmummy under her wing. Whitney had a summer home there, you see, and she'd have all her artistic friends come out, and they all built homes nearby. So you see, Grandmummy eventually realized her girlhood dream and went west. She had the house here in Lancaster County *and* the ranch near Cody."

Hector's monologue suddenly took a left turn. "But *I* did not inherit the family gene for the visual arts. No, I find the expression of my own dark soul in the *theater*."

"Does anyone in your generation paint?" I inquired, tossing the question in like I was only making polite conversation.

Hector's gaze was fixed in space some inches over my head. It seemed he found less resistance to his fantasies there. He pressed his lips together to silence a belch. "Precious *William*," he drawled. "*He* went to art school, and learned all those brushy things, though he was *never* as good as father. *Never*. Father could paint as well as *anyone*. And Cricket, though what she's done with it I cannot say. We never *see* her anymore. Little miss cutesy pranced away and left the rest of us with the *work*," he whined, tipping his head from side to side in a burlesque of one child taunting another. I wondered whom he was imitating. "Or you could say she *escaped*," he said more darkly. He took another sip. "More power to her if she did."

"Escaped what?" asked Jenny.

"The family *curse*," said Hector, with a flourish of his drinking hand. The Mai Tai slopped like a bathtub in an earthquake.

I wanted to groan. He was talking, all right, but self-pity was a tedious topic.

Jenny said, "Where did Cricket go?"

Hector gazed briefly at Jenny from under veiled eyelids. "We don't talk about Cricket," he informed her coolly. "She *left*."

I signaled the waitress for another round of drinks, eliciting an indulgent smile from Hector. I asked, "Did you ever get out west on vacation when you were a kid?"

Jenny gave me an inquiring look. I blinked my eyes to say, *Just roll with this*.

"Yes," said Hector. "Cowboys. Buffalos. It was up near Yellowstone National Park. My first love was a horsie named Gertrude. Ah, here's my sustenance."

The waitress brought the drinks. I took tiny sips out of one of my beers while Hector got after it with his fourth Mai Tai.

I said, "It's cool that your family could afford two places like that."

"It was *Grandmummy's* when we still went there. She gave Daddy the *farm* because it was close to *Baltimore*, and he was supposed to carry on the *business*. And dear Winnie liked the *West*, I suppose. . . ."

"So you'd go and visit her during your summer vacations?"

Hector lay a wrist across his forehead, smearing his greasepaint. "Oh dear, I'm getting a headache. . . ."

Jenny signaled for the waitress. "I'll get you another drink," she said. Mai Tai Number Four was already almost gone.

"Oh, that will help *nicely*," said Hector, finishing his drink in one gulp. "They always mix them leaner when I start to put them away."

"What happened to the ranch?" I asked.

Hector leaned forward onto his elbows, arching his back like the caricature of a fop that he was. "Oh, Winnie lived on and on. Outlived Daddy, even. Then suddenly . . . *ooof!* . . . she's gone, too." He put a hand to the corner of his eye, as if to brush away a tear.

"What killed her?" I asked, emphasizing the second word ever so slightly. I hoped he was drunk enough now to pick up where he had left off on the phone the night he thought I was Faye.

I had guessed wrong. He raised his eyebrows as if to express his horror at my asking such an indecent question. "Old age, I suppose."

"Was she good at art, too?" I asked, struggling to herd this sheep into the pen.

Hector laughed unkindly. "She preferred puffy pink poodles," he said, really laying into the *p*'s. "She was the only one in the family who adored things like Pennsylvania Dutch slogans painted on little plaques to hang in the kitchen. I always thought that Grandmummy sent her away in *embarrassment*. We used to think she was someone else's baby who got switched with the real Aunt Winnie in the hospital. Except Grandmummy had her at home, and . . ."

"And what?"

"She was every bit as stuck to this damned family as the rest of us. Perish the thought any one of us should truly escape. Cricket tried. . . ."

"She came back?"

"Deirdre worked on her until she felt so guilty she had to come back." He seemed to forget where he was for a moment, and then said, "And, having lured her back into the web, Deirdre sent her to live in the barrens. Our family gulag. She may as well have gone. I haven't seen her in forever."

The new drinks arrived. Hector had to grope for his.

"You can't split the fortunes any finer," I said.

"No, you can't," said Hector, icing his words with bitter irony.

Jenny gave me a *What are you talking about?* look. I turned to her and said, as if I were an old family friend who of course knew all this, "Hector's family had a collection of very valuable paintings. Worth millions."

"Long gone," said Hector. "Daddy sold them to pay for his . . . I'm so glad Grandmummy didn't have to live to see it. I loved my grandmummy *soooo* mush. . . . She was a *lovely* woman. Art all around her and art within her." He turned to Jenny. "You see, *Grandmummy* got to know all the artists, and began to trade in it, though you'd never hear her call it a *gallery*. She star' out swapping pictures with *friends*, and before long, she was making *stacks* of money." He swung out an arm to indicate grandeur, but it fell precipitously into his lap.

"She built up quite a collection," I said.

"Yes. It wasn't the land with her, it was the art. The land was *Granddaddy's* obsession. E'cept the *ranch*. That was *her* thing. She bou' it affer he died."

"It must break your heart to see their estate fought over like this."

"Yes it *does*."

"How is Deirdre going to manage Cricket?" I floated this question past him ever so delicately, a butterfly of logic for him to follow with what was left of his heart.

Something very dark passed across Hector's eyes. "*Deirdre* . . ." He drawled the word, suggesting a deeply held rancor that was best expressed through innuendo, ". . . says she can *handle* Cricket." He looked away across the room, and this time the emotion was not the deceit of self-pity, but a very deep, abiding hurt. It was naked. It was raw. It required medication. He lifted his drink and swilled mightily.

"I'm sorry, Hector. This must be very painful to talk about."

He was beginning to wobble.

Jenny caught my eye. She mouthed the words, *You're good!*

The waitress came by to see if we needed more drinks. I shook my head. Hector certainly did not need another. He was the kind of drunk who got blotto all at once, providing only the narrowest interval of candor, and he would soon collapse. It was a pattern I had seen in many of the men who had sat near my mother in the bars she frequented before my father's death forced sobriety on her.

Hector's was a sickening kind of drunkenness, but not as horrifying as my mother's. She had grown meaner with every drink, moving toward cruelty, not honesty. She'd spit out judgments that could kill.

But Hector's lash was hardest on himself, and even in the depths of his decay, he still clung piteously to the defense of family. He wasn't going to tell me anything that would hang his brother. I decided to use the last few moments before he passed out to see if, through ignorance, he might say anything that would indicate that Agent Wardlaw was on the right track. "Art," I said. "So your family's still in the business?"

"Oh, yes, William carried on the tradition."

"Has he been successful?"

"Oh, yes, *very*," said Hector, momentarily bragging on anyone to whom he could claim relation, but he as quickly retreated to the vein of poison that so limited his soul. "He wiggled his way under the wing of all of Daddy's *friends*."

Daddy's friends. Were they the kinds of people Wardlaw had told me about? Cutthroat fancy boys who saw themselves above the law? "And Tert took over the gallery."

"In no time at all," said Hector, his voice going into a lilt, as if he were telling a fairy story. He tried to snap his fingers. He missed.

"So, your grandmother, your father, and now Tert—uh, William . . ."

"Tert, Tert, Tert," chanted Hector, demonstrating that he had been accurately named. "I don't want to talk about Tert!"

Okay, on to Jenny's concerns. "Why hasn't your mother seen a doctor?" I asked.

"Deirdre says she won't go," he said dismissively, as if that explained everything.

"What's her diagnosis?"

Hector sniffed and averted his gaze. This was clearly something one did not discuss in public. Drunks may not be able to keep track of whom they're talking to, but they do have their standards.

"And Aunt Winnie?"

"We don't *talk* about Aunt Winnie's little problems," he scolded, his voice rising to a falsetto of the old woman on the porch.

Hector certainly was an actor. In the past few minutes, I had heard the voices of half the women in his family. Too bad he didn't know that their castrating values had come to live in his head.

I turned to Jenny. *Any questions?* I mouthed.

She thought for a moment. "That's quite an estate you're telling us about. A farm here, a ranch in Wyoming. Who will inherit the land when your mother dies?" she inquired, straightening the saltcellar and lining it up with the mustard and ketchup, as if she were asking his preference among condiments.

"Share and share alike," he said, floating one hand up and away to evoke the diaphanous. As his hand floated down again, his face darkened with rage. "Mum-mums has not changed the will; just let it ride from Daddy's take on reality." He took a gargantuan gulp of his drink, then tried to set the glass down demurely, as if it were made of fine crystal. His pinkie even went up. I had to reach out and catch the glass before it tumbled. Almost whispering, he said, "The will was made so long ago that Cricket and I are listed as minor children."

Jenny said, "Is there a living trust, something that would spell out whether the farm should be kept a farm? The way land values are rising, I'd think that they'd have put in some sort of guidelines."

I shot her a cautionary glance. She was sounding too hopeful, her fishing line baited for too specific a catch.

Hector made a dismissive gesture. "Oh, Daddy wan' it kep', sure. He applied for one of those developmen' things . . . agricultural easements . . . wha'ever you call it." He hiccuped, or perhaps it was a belch. "Cash on the barrelhead, and you get to keep your lands, or at leas' your fucking *pride*!" He whipped his hand up suddenly, this time succeeding in knocking over his drink. It was no loss. He did not need another drop. Then he leaned forward and put a finger to his lips to indicate silence. "I can tell you this because I'll never see you again, and you don't give a *shit* who I am."

I said, "That covers the farm property. Who got the ranch after Winnie died?"

"Taxes, mostly. She lef' the res' to charity. The poodle fanciers' society, I suppose. Precious *William* went out to fetch the last few remaining *family* items."

"How *sad*," I said, trying to match his mawkishness. "What was left?"

"Oh, just some things that Grandmummy wanted to have stay in the family." Suddenly he pressed his lips together to suppress a smile, but could not contain a snigger that burst forth, erupting fully into a guffaw.

"What's so funny?" asked Jenny.

Hector squeezed his mascara'ed eyes shut. He was now cackling with laughter. "I c-can't tell you!" he roared. "We have our little secrets!"

I watched him snort and gasp, wondering if what amused him so was the knowledge that Tert had gone in search of a Remington but had come home with a fake. Did he resent his siblings as much as Deirdre did? Or did he simply resent being Hector?

Jenny said, "Share and share alike. That's not taking a whole lot of responsibility for how the estate gets divided, is it? That's just leaving it for your generation to duke it out."

Hector's laughter evaporated. He tried to focus his polluted gray eyes on her. It was a weird effect, seeing those eyes peering out of a face owned by such a different personality. "Tha's wha' Cricket said," he informed her. "She kept telling Daddy, 'Fix the will, or we'll fight.' But no one ever lissened to Cricket."

"So you're fighting," I said.

"Not *really*," Hector drawled, imbuing his words with a sloppy sarcasm. "Darling *Deirdre* is the executor, after all, so she parcels out the *cash*, don't you know . . . or what little there *is*. . . ."

Now I got it. Hector was getting a dole from Deirdre, and that bought his loyalty. He was under her thumb and willing to sell out his brother if that's what it took to stay in good with his sister.

He put his face into the crook of his arm and blubbered. "It's hard, being . . . who I am."

Hector was about my age, and he had been a minor when his father had made his will. Tert was five or six years older, and had been in his majority, at least eighteen. That meant that the will had been drawn up, say . . . twenty-five years ago. What had happened about that long ago that prompted Secundus to write his will?

A loud thump brought my attention back to Hector. I knew instantly that I wasn't going to get any more information out of him: He was collapsed facedown on the table, snoring like a bear settled in for a long winter.

The man who had played the Beggar—now showered and dressed in a shirt and chinos, his hair combed back to frame a surprisingly handsome face—moseyed over from the bar and got a hand under Hector's armpit. "Come on, old lad, time to take you home." I caught a noseful of the Beggar's wonderful scented oil and looked up at him. He gave me a very sober wink.

"Thanks again for the shoulder rub," I said.

"It was my pleasure," he said. "You ladies okay driving?"

"She's drinking lemonade and I've had about a quarter-ounce from each of these bottles," I said.

"Smart women. Hope to see you again."

"You, too. Who do we owe for the dinners?"

"No one. You took the seats of two no-shows. Food may as well be eaten."

"Thanks."

I helped as he got Hector to his feet and spirited him out through a back door. It was just like old times with my mother.

My mother. The ranch. For a moment, I considered settling in for a little bit of drinking, myself.

Jenny reached across the table and put a hand on my shoulder. Without looking me in the eye, she quietly ran her other hand through the air in front of my face and chest. Like a paramedic working quickly over a fallen patient, she ran deft fingers down the inside of one arm to my pinkie, then reached around and touched a bottom rib just above the crest of my hip and nudged a toe up against my big toe. Then she reached out and yanked something unseen away from my heart, as if removing a thorn. Instantly, I felt better.

"This next one is more difficult," she said, reaching out to touch my temple. A sense of rage suddenly surfaced in me, and I found I needed to take a deep breath. She traced her fingers back and forth over the top of my head, then down the back of my neck, zigzagged down my side, and continued down the outer side of my leg to my second-smallest toe, ducking her head underneath the table to hold it for a moment, as if tacking it to the floor. Then she bobbed up and looked at me, her face lost in concentration. "You ready to let go of her?"

"Who?" I asked.

"Your mother. Or at least that's what I'm getting. Wait, I need to run triple warmer, too. There's a sense of betrayal." She reached out and touched the outer corner of my eye, ran a finger around behind my ear, down my neck, along my shoulder, and down the outside of my arm to my third finger. "Yes, betrayal."

"I'll say," I said. "She sold the damned ranch. What are you doing?"

"Just a little Chinese medicine. Your meridians were blocked. There's more, but that's what's right at the surface. Are you ready now?"

"Yes," I said, surprised to hear myself saying so. A great charge of anger seemed to have dissipated.

Jenny reached up and moved her palm toward my forehead until it rested there.

I felt an odd shift inside my head as if an argument had just ended. "Thanks," I said, not at all sure what I was thanking her for.

"Where was the ranch?"

"Chugwater, Wyoming. Beautiful little spread up along a creek with short-grass prairie leading up to the foot of the Laramie Range."

"Just what the developers love," she said tiredly. "You might have some odd dreams tonight. That's normal. Well, tomorrow is another day, not to mention another cause to be championed. Here's my phone number." She slipped me a business card. "Give me a call if . . ."

"Right. Here's mine."

She got up and left.

I sat a while longer, not quite sure what to do with myself. The temptation to drink had passed, but I was not yet ready for all the turns on the dark roads between the inn and me.

A shadowy shape slithered by the table and a hand with short, stubby fingers slid another card onto the table. It spun as it skidded to a stop next to Jenny's, lining up exactly so that it could be read easily. It read, FEDERAL BUREAU OF INVESTIGATIONS, and below that, AGENT BRUCE WARDLAW.

I looked up. He was halfway down the aisle toward the door already. He gave me one backward look and waved. "See you at the inn," he said.

25

"Chrome yellow occurs in nature as the rare mineral crocoite, a red lead–bearing ore. Vauquelin (1797) reported his discovery of a new metallic substance in the mineral and suggested that the metal be named chrome (Greek for *color*) owing to its ability to impart color."

—*Artists' Pigments, Volume 1*

—*from the notebooks of Fred Petridge*

FULL DAYLIGHT PLAYED UPON THE DUST MOTES IN THE KREHBEIL farm kitchen. Deirdre sat at the table, staring at the phone that was mounted on the wall to her right. The cord still swung slightly from the call she had just made to Hector.

She drummed her insensate fingers on the frayed old tablecloth. Eight-thirty in the morning and Hector was still drunk from the night before, a state that typically made him especially unpleasant. At such times, he typically took his latest screwups and threw them in her face, managing to make a bludgeon out of his failings. The news he had coughed up certainly fit into that category: Two women had accosted him in the bar at Bube's Brew Pub the evening before and had bought him enough liquor that he had told all sorts of tales about the family. He was sorry, or so he had said. Would she forgive him?

Not precious likely.

She stopped drumming. Her thick, numb fingers contracted, pulling the tablecloth with them, slowly toppling the saltcellar and pepper shaker and the plastic gadget that held the thin paper napkins.

Like a viper striking its prey, she shot out a hand and snatched the receiver off the hook. She dialed. The phone rang once, twice.

A woman answered. "Hello?" At first, Deirdre thought she must have misdialed. But no, the voice was saying, "Um, this is Tert Krehbeil's residence."

"This is Tert's sister. To whom am I speaking?" The words were polite, but she barked them out with as little kindness as a Marine Corps sergeant addressing a recruit who could not do push-ups. It was alarming to discover that a woman was visiting him.

"This is Faye Carter. I'm a friend of Tert's."

"Oh. How lovely," said Deirdre, her tone indicating the opposite. She heard a baby fussing now. Her pulse quickened with alarm. Was Precious William not only picking up on a woman, but one who already had offspring?

"I'll get him for you," Faye said. "He's just come out of the . . . um, here he is."

"Hello?" said Tert.

"Tert, dear brother," Deirdre began, her voice dripping with rancor. "Darling Hector has gone and spilled some family stories in a bar again. Don't you think it's time we did something about this?"

"You mean time *I* did something," Tert observed. "You're calling me to ask *me* to pay to dry him out again."

"It's the least you can do!" Deirdre said viciously.

Tert said nothing for several seconds, then, "Why? Because I am not as impoverished as you? Because you look after Mother? I've told you I can put her in a home, but you—"

"It's time you came to see her! *Today*, Tert. She's not getting any stronger."

Tert let out an exasperated sigh. Several more seconds passed. Then he said, "Why not? Hey, I have guests here, and a business to run, but why *not* just drop everything and run up to Lancaster to see what disaster Deirdre is imagining this time? Sure, put on a can of beans for lunch, darling sister. Or better yet, let me bring a hamper and we'll have a picnic. We'll sit around the lawn in those lovely old wicker chairs and pretend we are still so grand."

"I'll expect you by eleven."

"Heavens, Deirdre, I wouldn't think of inconveniencing my guests by pressing them to get ready that quickly."

Deirdre bared her teeth at the phone. "You'll come *alone*!"

Tert let out a sardonic laugh. "No, no, no, Deirdre darling, I wouldn't *think* of leaving them behind. Mother will be delighted to meet my friend Faye. And Faye has the most adorable little baby, just the right size to sneeze some virus into Mother's face and give her pneumonia! But I must not hurry my guests. They are not *dressed*. We have not yet *breakfasted*," he said, letting the implications of his statement sink all the way in: *A woman has stayed the night at my house, Deirdre; I am a grown man having relations with women, and you know what that will mean to Mother! She'll think I'm getting married at last, and with a ready-made family! And I'll sire more children, and they'll be charming and perfect, not ugly slugs like you made. You'll no longer be unique, no longer the only one who made grandchildren. You'll be usurped, you hopeless bitch!*

The hole in Deirdre's soul where self-worth had never grown erupted with the hot rage of jealousy, that terror that whispers all the thousands of lies, like, *You're not happy because he's got what you want;* and, *They don't love you because they love him instead*. It kept on spewing until it got down to her central, most visceral fears: *You can be replaced*, and, *You are not loveable*.

Screaming inchoate hatreds to guard herself from these fears, Deirdre slammed the phone into its cradle.

I LAY IN THE BIG, COMFY BED AT THE CAMERON ESTATE INN TRYing to decide what in hell's name to do. I had slept much later than I had intended. It in fact surprised me that I had been able to sleep this long: Generally, when I am this far into a case, sleep is something I am lucky to acquire in three- and four-hour chunks. In fact, I had to force myself awake to escape the scenery that sleep was conjuring.

I had dreamed I was lost in a jumble of tall houses in a city somewhere, having crossed a bridge from a neighborhood of smaller houses. I was having a long talk with Tom. He was telling me that Faye was okay, and that I should go my own way and have a good life.

But Tom was dead. Did that mean I was dreaming of my own death? Or had something inside me died?

And why hadn't Tom asked me about his tiny daughter? He didn't seem worried about her. Why?

I got up off the enormous bed with its opulent furnishings and lurched into the bathroom, where I took a freezing-cold shower to yank myself the rest of the way out of the dream. Agent Wardlaw would no doubt be waiting for me downstairs, and I did not want to face him half-asleep. I dressed and headed off in search of the breakfast that came with the bed.

The innkeeper greeted me and showed me out onto a long sunporch lined with tables set for breakfast. They were all empty. "Am I the only one staying here?" I asked, looking around for the FBI agent.

"Our other guests rose early," he said diplomatically. He pointed out the side table with its big flagons of steaming hot coffee. "I'll have your breakfast up in a jiffy."

My cell phone tweedled at me. I said hello in a flat tone, expecting it to be Wardlaw, but it was Fritz Calder.

"You okay for takeoff tomorrow morning?" he asked.

"Sure," I said, not sure of a damned thing. "How's it going?"

"Um . . ."

"Tough connections with the money guys?"

"Well, that looks positive," he said.

"How about your military-hardware guys?"

He said nothing.

"What's up, Fritz?"

"Not much, Em. In fact, I was wondering if you guys might be ready to leave today instead of tomorrow."

"Uh . . . sure. Just let me get hold of Faye and we can meet you anytime. Why, are you done already?"

"Yeah. I'm just sticking around to have lunch with an old buddy, and then I'm good to go."

"Something go wrong, Fritz?"

He was silent for a moment, then said fiercely, "Since you ask, something went entirely right." His voice was filled with something I hadn't heard in it before: earnestness, and a tinge of rage.

I imagined him sitting in a hotel room all by himself, his guts full of something that had wound him up tighter than a watch spring, with no one to tell it to until his buddy met him at noon. "Fritz?"

"I told them I wouldn't make the parts they wanted. I'm done with it, all of it!"

"All what? The military stuff?"

"The military, war, the whole shot. I'm just done. I'm going home to Utah and I'm going to build myself a life. No more 'going along to get along'. If my ex-wife doesn't like it, well then she can divorce me!"

I fought to suppress laughter. His words were funny, but his meaning was not. Something had happened, some slender thread of reality had snapped, moving Fritz closer to his own center. "This sounds good, Fritz."

"Well, it is, and it's high time. So, if you and Faye are ready early, give me a call, okay?"

"Will do. And, Fritz?"

"Yeah?"

"How do you know when you've got a target you don't want to bomb?"

He said, "You have to listen to your heart," and rang off.

I looked around the empty room feeling like I had just woken from that dream about Tom all over again. I had a heart, but it felt like a wound that had dried shut around something as hard as a steel bolt.

I dialed Faye's number. I got a recording saying that the party was not available at this time. That meant she had her phone switched off.

I ended the call and settled in to shock my system with a good dose of caffeine while I stared down the lawn toward the little creek that led out of the spring. Ducks took off and landed, going into their lively skids. The water wasn't steaming this morning, which suggested that the day was already warm. I searched out the sun and did a rough calculation of its angle. It was higher than I had expected, which meant I had slept later than I thought. I finally chanced a look at my watch: It was already a quarter past nine. Where was Wardlaw?

The scene outside the window was idyllic, a harsh contrast to what was going on in my heart and in my head. Hector was in there stinking of drink, and his phantom sister Cricket was running into a thick fog. The image of his mother falling out of her chair played in slow motion, and her face turned into that of Leila Bradstreet Hansen, the woman who had borne me. . . .

I pulled out my cell phone again and called Mr. Hauser, who answered on the fifth ring. "Mr. Hauser, good morning," I told him. "This is Emily Hansen. I have another question or two for you."

"Certainly, my dear."

"Tell me, did the Krehbeil family fortune take a nosedive during the environmental cleanup campaign of the late 1970s and early 1980s?"

"Oh, yes," he replied. "They held a healthy block of Chromex until 1970, when the old girl died and the board of directors finally formally excused the second William Krehbeil from the corporate presidency. The old girl had run the company until she was well into her nineties, setting her boy up as titular president, but when she died, things rather began to fall apart. It was just a few years later that the environmental cleanup was mandated, and the stock plummeted, and slid even further when the company reorganized to avoid bankruptcy. It's doing all right now, but I hear that the family sold its block long ago."

So, the board had bucked Secundus out of the saddle, and he had to live off of capital instead of income. And there the money started to dry up. The cleanup order certainly would have gotten him talking to his lawyers, and they would have forced him to get his affairs in order.

I did more mental math. By the 1970s, Deirdre would have been through college, and soon after, so would have Tert, who had enjoyed sufficient cash flow to become part of the wealthy set that Faye had run with. Hector would have been vulnerable, but Grandmummy had left money earmarked for his education. *At least she knew how to divide up a pie*, I decided. *The last successful personality in the clan.*

"That's very helpful," I said. "May I call you again if I have more questions?"

"Certainly, my dear. And keep me posted about those heavy metals you're studying. It's a means of demise," Mr. Hauser said cheerily. Then he signed off.

I sat a while holding the phone, trying to decide what detail to pick at next.

The innkeeper appeared just then and delivered my breakfast: "Ramekin of baked oatmeal with brown sugar and top milk," he informed me. "And here are some seasonal fruits, and your muffin. Can I get you anything else? Some juice?"

"O.J.," I said uncouthly. I had never seen oatmeal served up as a gourmet treat before. "And can you answer a question?"

"Surely," he said.

"Has a man with . . . a paunch . . . and maybe conservative business clothes . . . but cheap cut and fabric . . . been asking for me this morning?"

"I haven't seen a man of that description," he said. "Can I get you anything else?"

"No, that will be all."

I took a bite of the oatmeal. It was incredibly sweet, clearly from the same cuisine that had produced the incomparable Whoopie Pie. On an empty stomach, the sugar kicked like a mule, but it was delicious, all toasty and warm. I began to think I could get used to spending Tert's money.

Tert's money. I pulled the cell phone back out of my pocket and punched in a number I had not dialed in a very long time, but which I remembered by heart.

My cop ex-boyfriend answered on the second ring. "Raymond here," he said drowsily.

I remembered too late that it was two hours earlier in Salt Lake City. "Oh, I'm sorry, is it your day off?"

"Em?"

"Yeah."

"I was on night shift. Just drifting off."

"Sorry. I'll let you go back to sleep."

"No, it's okay. Is there something—"

"I'm calling from . . . the East Coast. That's why I forgot. But I'm working on a case, and . . . well, I was wondering if you could give me some advice."

Ray's voice immediately sounded much clearer. "Sure. Fire away." He sounded pleased, in fact. Had I just restarted something I did not know how to finish?

"Well, the client is this guy who sells art. My task is really, in fact, quite limited, but I'm out here looking at the . . . well, the family because, um, Faye's involved, and it looks like there's a lot more to this."

"And . . ."

"The *federales* are down my collar about him," I said. I had not intended to tell him this, but now that I had, I felt a huge relief.

"*Federales*? You mean the FBI?"

"Yeah. Some guy named Wardlaw. One of the ones who gives the other ones a bad name."

"I don't know him."

"Of course you don't. He's out of Washington. Dang it, Ray, I didn't sign up for this. I was just supposed to authenticate a piece of art. The idea was to use the geology of the pigments in a painting to figure out . . . Now I'm finding that the family has . . . Well, I wonder if someone's been feeding them to Grandma."

"The what?"

"The pigments. A lot of the older ones are highly toxic. Most of them have been replaced with synthetics during the last century, but the family made its money longer ago than that, manufacturing paint pigments, and then in the chemical industry that grew up around it, and my client is an artist so he knows these things, and now Granny looks like she has heavy-metal poisoning. So, I'm thinking my client might—"

"Have you told this to the local sheriff? Or the police?" Ray asked.

"No. I was really wanting your advice."

The innkeeper came and cleared my dishes. I thanked him and waited for him to get out of earshot. "Hi," I told Ray. "I'm back. What I'm wondering is, is there a way to check out this guy's financials without—"

"No," Ray said firmly. "That's a job for people who can get warrants. Tell the feds."

I let out an exasperated sigh. "Wardlaw is a real asshole."

Ray paused. Then, matter-of-factly, he said, "Sounds like a standard Em job."

"Thanks for nothing," I said.

"I don't mean that unkindly," he said. "Em, you're a very smart human being. You have a way of getting right to the nub of things. So all I was suggesting is that you're probably right."

"Any other tips?" I asked resignedly.

"Not a one. I'd suggest you quit, but I won't waste my breath."

I said good-bye and broke the connection and went back to finishing my coffee, wondering why I even cared about the Krehbeil puzzle anymore. Faye was finding Tert a bore. If I could reach her on the phone, I'd have her and the baby out of his house in a matter of hours, and I could fly home to Utah and analyze the paint chips and send my final bill to Tert and wash my hands of the whole mess.

I tried Faye's number again. Still no answer. I left a message this time, asking her to call me just as soon as she could. Where was she? Out to breakfast with Tert?

Tert. He had gone to Wyoming expecting to bring home an extremely valuable painting, but had found a fake. He had hired me to establish beyond a doubt that it was a fake. Why? Had Deirdre and he made a private agreement that she would take the land and he would get the painting? Did he need to prove it was a fake so he could reassert his claim to a portion of the 'share and share alike' division? Why not just kill her, too? Or had he already tried, and managed only to leave her with damaged nerves in her extremities? Or were her rages symptomatic of deeper neurological damage?

I simply did not know the answers to these questions, and I lacked the authority to demand them.

I took the last gulp of coffee. *The main thing is to get Faye and the baby out of Philadelphia alive*, I decided.

Where was Wardlaw? *Maybe he's gone home to Washington, I thought. Or maybe he got enough from eavesdropping last night to get a warrant, and he's down in Philadelphia raiding Tert's home. Shit. That could be why Faye has her phone switched off!*

With a brisk shake of my head to clear the ghosts from my brain, I rose from my chair, returned to my room to pack my duffel, paid my bill at the desk, and headed out to the parking lot behind the inn. *I will drive straight to Philadelphia and get Faye and the baby and we will go home to Utah*, I told myself. *I will crunch out some analyses of the paint chips Tert gave me, then I can give ol' Wardlaw a call and tell him what little I know, and be done with it. And thesis or no, I will get a job and go on about my life.*

As I loaded myself into the car, it occurred to me that, for the first time ever, the prospect of going on about life seemed like a nice option. Faye would move on to some other man, hopefully Fritz. My relationship with Jack would continue to collapse under its own weight. My mother would enjoy life in town, and I would build a life for myself, too. Where, and with whom, I was not sure, but it seemed reasonable to think that I might find some nice guy someday, and if I was too old by then to conceive a child of my own, then there were always too many war orphans. I had learned that I loved holding a child in my arms and that it did not matter if she was of my own flesh. I could relax. There was no hurry. Maybe I'd even get such a great job that I could afford to adopt on my own.

I thought all of these thoughts as settled myself into the rental car and buckled up the seatbelt. I turned the key in the ignition and started down the long drive toward the road that was the first few miles of the way home. But as I reached the towering gateposts that framed the entrance to the Cameron Estate, I spied a dark sedan, and even before I pulled abeam it, I knew who was at the wheel.

I stopped the car and waited. Agent Wardlaw got out of his car and came around to my window. I rolled it down.

He said, "Nice phone calls, Hansen. I particularly liked the chat you had with that cop in Salt Lake City. Does Jack know about him?"

27

I SAT IN A CAFÉ IN DOWNTOWN MOUNT JOY WATCHING AGENT Wardlaw stuff glazed doughnuts into his face. "You kept me waiting a long time," he said. "I was starving."

I said nothing. I was too mad at myself, and at my overweening capacity to charge off in one direction or another and always find trouble. If it was a nice, serene life on the land I wanted so much, why hadn't I married that boy from the ranch next door? Not that I'd ever stuck around long enough for him to ask. No, I'd been sent east to prep school, and then south to college; by then going somewhere else was a habit, and I'd run off into the oil patch and then to Denver, and the next time I stopped by to say hello, he was married and on kid number two or three with a nice girl he'd met in 4H. Now I had made an art form out of running away and living nowhere, jumping from one crazy cause to another that took me anywhere but where I'd told myself I wanted to go.

There was nothing like the adrenaline boost of thinking that some FBI agent had been listening in on my private phone calls to make me think more clearly. During the ten-minute drive into Mount Joy from the inn, I had redialed Ray's phone number and roused him a second time from his much needed sleep. And asked him if he'd dialed up Wardlaw the moment we'd finished our conversation an hour earlier.

Ray had given a sleepy, "Yes . . . but what did you expect? I'm going to let someone I care about get into worse trouble?"

So no, Agent Wardlaw was not breaking some anti-wiretapping law. This case wasn't so hot that he could get a warrant to listen into my line; he was just messing with me. But I had switched off the phone and put it away just in case. I didn't want to have to discuss plans in front of Agent Brucie if Faye phoned back while he was grilling me.

Now, as I sat watching Wardlaw chew, I could see that Tert had been right; the pigments in that painting were the key to the whole thing. Hector had told me that his father could paint as well as anyone, and from there it was a short hop to the likelihood that he had painted *like* other artists as well. Who better than he to forge the family Remington that had accidentally wound up with his poodle-loving sister? She had no eye for art. If he swapped a close copy for the original, she'd never notice. She'd still have something to stare at, and he could sell the original to some hopped-up megalomaniac who would covetously hide it from all other eyes. His crime would go unreported, and he wouldn't even see it as a crime; he was simply generating cash flow out of family goods.

I stared at Wardlaw. This man knew all about crimes of deceit. He was one of those law enforcement individuals who was hard to distinguish from the crooks he was chasing. As he dumped a third packet of sugar into his second coffee, I fantasized an island somewhere where all the crooks and all the bad cops could just chase each other around and around and leave the rest of the world out of their mania.

His cell phone tweedled and he answered it, grunted twice, then signed off. A bolt of anger shot through me. This man—this annoying, execrable man—had been able to get Jack to phone me when all I could get out of him was e-mails. I was back to being mad at Jack, and that was a whole lot easier to feel than guilt over wanting to go on with my life without him.

Wardlaw was watching me. He took a big, noisy slurp of his coffee. "Penny for your thoughts," he said. He picked up another doughnut and chewed, his jaws going like a cow working her cud. He fluttered his eyelashes at me. "Hm? You're thinking mighty deep ones today."

My distant boyfriend, my joke of a thesis project, the ranch—I wasn't sure which bugged me the most. I stared at him defiantly and said, "What's our deal with the land, anyway? We seem to get unnaturally stuck to it."

Speaking through a mouthful of doughnut, Wardlaw said, "Sounds like one of those thinky deals Tom Latimer used to get into."

I stiffened at the thought of this man even bowing to the ground in front of Tom, let alone working with him. I looked away.

He said, "Okay, I'll bite: What's the connection between land and Krehbeil?"

"Which one?" I asked unkindly. This guy was so focused in on the art dealings that he had failed to take a look at the bigger picture. Checking the family stresses was the first thing Tom would have done.

"There's more than one?"

"He has a sister. Deirdre. She's dug into that property like a tick, which is nuts, considering that there is no way she could afford to bring it back to its original glory. And it isn't the joy of farming she's after—there are crops in the fields, but judging by the unused look of the barn, I'd say she's leased out the land. So what holds her to the place?"

"Deirdre," he said. "What property?"

"The family farm. Right here in this county," I said, "not far from the fanciest suburb of Lancaster. The developers keep pushing outward, looking for another big farm to subdivide. They're moving right toward the Krehbeil homestead, did you know that?"

"Nope. Should I care?"

"Yes, you should, because it's an asset your quarry might soon inherit."

"But his sister's sitting on it. He'll never get her off." He grabbed a paper napkin, wiped it across his mouth, crumpled it, and tossed it onto his plate.

"The funny thing is, I suffer from this mania myself: It's a matter of self-definition. 'I am of this land, and therefore I am.' "

Wardlaw rolled his eyes. "You sound more and more like Latimer every minute. Naw, you got it all wrong. Land doesn't own you, you own it. It's power. Whoever gets the land gets to kick everyone else off."

"So you think Deirdre's a control freak."

"I never met the lady, but if she's like *my* sister . . ." Wardlaw broke off and stared out the front window of the café. For a moment, his eyes were bright, but then he closed them and took another slurp of his coffee.

"You grow up on a farm, Wardlaw?"

"West Virginia."

"What happened? Your sister get the place?"

Wardlaw put down his cup and leaned back in his chair and stared at me. "This Deirdre the oldest?"

"Yes."

"They're a contemptuous lot. I know, you'll think that's a big word for a guy like me, but I went to college. It was the only thing I could do, if I didn't want to go work in the mine that bulldozed my parents' farm away. I'm just glad they didn't live to see it happen. My old man died in the mines that ate the neighbor's farm, and then my ma went, too, from emphysema from all the dust. That left the eight of us kids. The only way for any of us to get a piece of it was to sell the farm to the mine owners. I took my chunk and ran for it. End of story."

"But your sister made the decision."

"She was the oldest. I wasn't yet eighteen. She kept extra because she said she'd earned it nursing Ma."

"She kicked your ass into college so you wouldn't die in the mines."

"She didn't give a shit where I went. She kicked my ass clear out of West Virginia. Damned state never was big enough for the both of us."

I finally took a sip of the cup of coffee Wardlaw had purchased for me. "Do you ever go back?"

He stared into his oversweetened brew, looking for something in its hidden depths. "There's nothing back there to visit. You get it? They bulldozed it away."

I almost envied Wardlaw the finality of his situation. I couldn't go home anymore either, but "home" was still there, it just . . . belonged to someone else now. Suddenly, I saw the Krehbeil debacle from a slightly different angle, and looked on Deirdre not only as the bullying older sister, but also as a human being who was afraid of losing her roots. *Is that why Deirdre holds on to that land so hard? But the others left long ago. Why do they keep hanging on? Is it a matter of identity, or is there something in that family worth sticking to? Even Cricket came back. Why? And where is she now? Hector said she was in the family gulag. Did he mean the property down in the serpentine barrens?*

Cricket. She was the one tiny bit of the puzzle that eluded me. There was something important about her, but I couldn't quite put my finger on it.

I focused on Agent Wardlaw. "Bruce . . . May I call you Bruce?"

"It's my name."

"Yeah, well, Bruce, I need to make a phone call, all right?"

"Who?"

"It's really not your business, but if you must know, I'm going to call a woman friend."

"You mean Faye, wife of the late, great Tom Latimer, who now hangs out with art thieves?"

"Come on, Wardlaw, she's just staying there. She doesn't suspect a thing."

"Then she'll be glad to let me in when I knock on the door."

"Oh, go to hell, Wardlaw."

"And I thought you were gonna call me Bruce."

"Do you think you could be just one degree less nasty?"

"Not after yesterday."

I couldn't control the smile that burst across my lips. "Hey, where's your sense of humor? Those mutts didn't break the skin, did they?"

He spread his sticky fingers across his chest. "It was your attitude that most offended me."

My smile widened. He was actually trying to be funny. I said, "Well, here's a thing you can ponder: Maybe you won't even have to get Tert on tax evasion, or whatever it is you're hoping to prove."

"Tell me more," said Wardlaw, starting his third doughnut.

"His mom is sick with what looks like heavy-metal poisoning. I think he might have fed it to her."

"That's disgusting, Hansen! Matricide?"

"Ooo, another big word for you, Brucie."

"So why would he want to bump off the old dame?"

I gave him my reasoning.

Wardlaw said, "So if Tert can get Mom dead and the property into probate before the development rights get sold into this Ag thing, then he can make a mint selling his quarter to a developer. That's good," he mused, his thick lips spreading into a sugar-crusted grin. "That's real good. But we don't got probable cause until the old lady croaks."

"All right, so you can't do anything there. So please excuse me while I go and do something about it myself."

"What you got in mind?"

"I was thinking about a little trip into Philadelphia."

Wardlaw smiled like a frog that has just caught a bug.

But first I gave Jenny a call. As I switched on the cell phone, it bleeped, indicating that I had an incoming message, but I went ahead and dialed Jenny first. "Can you get on your jungle telegraph and see if there's anything new about Cricket Krehbeil?" I asked her. "I mean really dig. It's important."

"Sure. I can ask, anyway. Like I said, she's kind of a gypsy."

"Hector said she was in the 'family gulag.' I'm thinking that might be the barrens property."

"I'll check. If she's there, someone in the old gang's got to be hearing from her."

As I ended the connection, I switched over to the message menu in search of what had bleeped me. After I punched in my pass code, I heard, "Em, this is Faye." There were background sounds as well: road noise. The baby fussing. Tert saying, "Why are you calling her?" Faye's voice continuing. "Listen, I'm . . . we're . . . on our way to Tert's mother's place. We're, uh, going to have lunch or something. We're supposed to be there at eleven. Tert promised we'd be back in Philadelphia by three or four. Just . . . ah, wanted you to know where we'll be." She sounded anxious, uncertain. Then a click. End of message.

I dialed back immediately, but got one of those messages that told me that the party I was calling was out of their service area or blah-blah-blah. "Shit," I said.

"What? So, which car shall we take to Philly?" Wardlaw was asking, as he dumped some change out of his pockets to leave the waitress a tip. "I sure ain't lettin' you take off by yourself. You might give me the slip, or lead me into another pack of dogs."

"We don't either of us have to drive," I said. "They're coming to us."

We decided to take both cars to Elm. Jenny rang back as Wardlaw followed me there, staying so close to my back bumper I started to think that he'd hitched his car to mine. She said, "I have more information than I could have hoped for, but it's rather sad."

"Cricket?"

"Yeah. Well, it wasn't drugs; it was some sort of psychological trauma that made her so . . . such a disappearing act. I could go into detail, but let's just say she didn't want to play her part in the family drama. So she'd wander off for months and years at a time and they wouldn't hear from her. Then finally she came back; she said to stay."

"So she's still here? Where?"

"In fact, I don't know. I was talking with my friend Janice, who heard from Cricket eight or nine months ago. She said that Cricket was really trying to sort things out with them this time, but it was uphill work. Proud families don't like it when one of their number can't follow the script."

"So they were getting kind of rough with her?"

"I don't know what you mean by 'rough.' When one member of a family tries to do things differently, not follow the script, the others can feel . . . er . . . rejected. Abandoned, even. I work with this all the time as I'm trying to help families sort out what they want to do with their assets."

"It becomes a power play," I said, thinking of Agent Wardlaw's bullying older sister.

"I suppose. And 'drama' is the right word. They get to playing roles. You get your martyrs who think they've earned their place in heaven, so to speak—think they deserve more than their siblings. And then there's the lost child who never quite measures up, and the victim who's supposed to absorb all the crap."

"Sounds like Hector's vocation as an actor was well chosen. Too bad he got cast in the role of the lost child. Or is that Cricket?"

"No, Cricket was the victim, the hold-still-and-take-it cute thing—or that's what Hector told us, anyway. And she had the audacity to take off and try to make a life separate from the tribe."

"That's quite a mouthful coming from a heritage freak. Isn't heritage all about family?"

Jenny laughed. "That, and it's a good rallying-cry to use when I'm trying to do business with family-oriented people. Between you and me, what I really like is open space and the natural world. To each her own."

"So Cricket came back," I said, getting back to the point. I was turning off the highway onto farm roads, and wanted to get both hands free to steer as soon as possible.

"Yeah, something just under a year ago. Thing was . . . Well, she was pregnant. It had prompted her to try to . . . I think Janice said 'reintegrate.' She'd been out in California. God knows what kind of ideas she picked up out there. But it sounded to Janice like Cricket was looking at family from a new angle and wanted to try one more time. Or maybe she just needed the money."

"Is she still there?"

"No. Janice said Deirdre sent Cricket to live in a mobile home down on that family property in the serpentine barrens. Janice phoned her once or twice, but then she quit answering phone calls. Janice went down there to see her over Christmas but she wasn't there."

"Where'd she go?"

"Janice didn't know. Some other family was living there, and they set their dogs on her. She figures Cricket hopped off somewhere else to have her baby and raise it in peace."

I didn't like hearing about another woman put in the position of raising her child alone. And there was something about Cricket's story that did not fit. If she had a baby coming, why didn't she stick around and pick up her inheritance? But perhaps she was in touch in some way, and preferred to have it sent to her. An inheritance, but not a heritage.

"Anything else you need?" Jenny asked. "This is kind of fun, using my networking skills for detective work."

"Yeah. What color were Mr. Krehbeil's eyes?"

"Deirdre's father's? Gray. Why?"

"Oh, nothing. Just sorting out a little genetics puzzle." I thanked Jenny and ended the phone call. Wardlaw and I were just reaching our objective, namely the last turn Tert would make as he drove Faye and the baby home to the farm. It was a beautiful place surrounded by nice, old farmsteads. A tractor growled halfway across the nearest field, turning over the soil for this year's planting.

I parked the car, got out, and wandered over to where Wardlaw was picking himself a blade of grass to chew on. I said, "Murder. Not your gig, right?"

"Not on the whole, unless it's on federal land. It's usually a local jurisdiction thing. People have to defraud the federal government or cross state lines to get me interested."

"What if someone managed to pull the trigger in Pennsylvania and the bullet struck in Wyoming?"

"Now, that's a firearm I'd like to see," said Wardlaw. "What are you thinking?"

"Aunt Winnie. What did she die of?"

"Give me the particulars," he said.

"Give me a sec." Thank God for cell phones. I got onto Directory Information and called Frank Barnes. Luckily, he was in. "I'm sorry I left Cody without getting together with you again," I told him. "But something came up."

"That's my Em," he said evenly.

"Yeah, well, I've got a favor to ask of you. You remember you told me about the Krehbeil ranch out west of Cody there?"

"Yeah."

"And the owner died recently?"

"Winnie Krehbeil. Yeah."

"What did she die of?"

"Lung cancer," said Frank. "But you know . . . I mean, you know how people talk. . . ."

"Yes I do, Frank, and that's what I'm asking you to do."

"Well, my sister's kid's a nurse up at the hospital these days, and she said the X rays looked real funny. Blank spots, like she'd been inhaling metal filings. But she was real sick by the time they diagnosed, so they just did what they could to keep her comfortable as possible. And then, well, there wasn't no autopsy, because everyone knew it was the cancer, y'know?"

"Right . . . Anything else?"

"She got real batty toward the end."

"Let me guess," I said. "She thought someone was poisoning her. She made accusations."

Frank made a small chuckling sound. "You always were a smart 'un, Em."

I rang off and turned back to Agent Wardlaw, who had taken a seat on the trunk of my car. "Lead chromate," I told him. "It's a paint pigment called Baltimore yellow, the same color as the Krehbeils' front door. It's what the family's fortune was built upon."

"And you say it does what?"

"Inhaled, it's a carcinogen. Causes cancer and leaves radio-opaque spots on the lungs. Ingested, you can deliver the dose over a long time, and you get lead poisoning. The first symptoms are fatigue and loss of appetite. Eventually it causes nerve damage, even mental illness, and, finally, death."

"And it would be hard to prove that the dose had been maliciously administered," he pointed out. "So, how you gonna prove this?"

"We're usually not exposed to it anymore. Baltimore yellow was a color of the nineteenth century. One hundred fifty years ago. A private citizen couldn't get it anymore, not even as artists' materials. It's just not used, precisely because it's too toxic."

Wardlaw's face bent into a nasty grin. "But if it was the family heritage, you might have a sack of it lying around. . . ."

"You got it, Brucie. He could have mailed it to Aunt Winnie as a Christmas present. He could put it in a nice box of talcum powder for the bath, or something. She goes in for her daily ablutions and puff-puff-puff, she gets her daily dose. And sending it in the mails puts it in your jurisdiction."

"But you say she's already dead. What if she was cremated? And do you really think anyone'd be dumb enough to leave a dose like that lying around after she was gone? Nah, they'd toss it down the toilet when they came around for the funeral."

I laughed and pointed at a row of gravestones that rested against some trees at the edge of the nearest field. "Look over there: These people bury their loved ones right out here in the field. Dollars to doughnuts says she's planted in some nice graveyard out there in Wyoming, maybe right next to her last five poodles. And the really good news is that heavy metals stay with a corpse longer than poisons. You can test for them in the hair and fingernails. Hell, the bones turn from calcium phosphate to lead phosphate."

A cloud seemed to have settled over his face.

I said, "Sorry to call you Brucie. Is that a sensitive matter?"

He shook his head, not looking at me. "No. I was just thinking of my father and my uncles working in those mines. Their lungs . . ."

"Yeah."

He straightened up and stretched, pushing his gut out even farther over his belt. "So, you think your pals'll come right past here." He glanced at his watch. "Won't be long. Eleven o'clock. Kinda early for lunch."

"Yeah, and I wonder what's going to show up in the cuisine."

"You think he's sprinkling it on the canapés?"

"Well, Deirdre said her mother always seems to get sicker after 'Precious William' visits. Poor old dear, she won't go to the hospital. He must be counting on that. Either that, or maybe he doesn't know that it would leave a blank spot on X rays."

Wardlaw made a face that suggested that he had glue on his teeth. "So we got us a serial killer. Dad, Mom, Aunt Whosie, and who else?"

"His sister Deirdre: peripheral neuropathy. Can't feel her hands or feet. It's another symptom of lead poisoning. Maybe he put it in the homemade jam."

"Lovely. And Hector's just gonna drink himself to death. He got any more brothers and sisters?"

"Cricket."

"What's he got in mind for her?"

"Well, she's gone missing, but no one thinks anything of it because it's a habit of hers. But last time she showed up she was pregnant. We don't want another heir, do we? So she's easy. She'd been sent to live out there where your pals the pooches live. You don't even have to do it slowly with her; you can just walk right up to her and get it over with and bury the body somewhere out in the greenbriers. Everybody will figure she just wandered off again."

Wardlaw sucked his teeth. He looked at his wristwatch. "They'll be along any minute now, so I should get out of sight. So, come on, tell me: What's your plan for getting a confession out of him?"

"I don't have one," I said.

Wardlaw jumped to his feet. "Wha'? Then what the fuck are you going to do!"

"I don't know. Not much, probably."

His brows came together in a knot. "I been willing to go along with you this far because—"

"Because you thought I was going to finger my own client. Sorry, Wardlaw. I've given you everything I have, but I don't have a magic wand. I have no idea what's going to happen. You think Tert's going to drive up and see me and just throw up his hands and say, 'Ya got me'? Or you think I'm going to invite myself to lunch where they've got guess-what on the menu? Or maybe they're going to dispense with the daily dose and just stand in a circle and point at the killer? Huh? If they're anything like the family I come from, they're going to clam up around any strangers. To tell you the truth, I got hardly anything out of Deirdre the other time I was here, and when she sees me again and finds out my name isn't the one I gave her last time, she's going to shut up tighter'n a tick."

He leaned toward me, his face strained with anger. "What am I supposed to do, then?"

"That's your problem."

"You could blow a year's work for me, Hansen!"

"I'll do what I can for you, but I've got my priorities."

He threw up his hands, his fingers hooked with rage. "Then I'm gonna put you under arrest! You're not going in there and mess up my—"

"Mess up what? I'm just going to crash a luncheon party and get my friend and her baby out of there; that's all the messier I intend things to get."

"Shit, I should have known better than to go along with some chick Jack Sampler came up with! That asshole always was too full of tricks!"

Now, that was getting personal. I leaned into his face and roared, "I don't answer to you and I don't answer to Jack Sampler!"

Wardlaw's face popped with surprise. His mouth closed. He said nothing.

My ears echoed with the words that had escaped my lips.

A flight of blackbirds rose from a tree and decorated the sky. Somewhere a dog barked.

I turned and walked a ways down the road. I felt the breeze against my cheeks. I smelled the first scents of spring. After a moment, I returned to where Agent Wardlaw waited. He was leaning on the hood of his car with both hands as if he had just collapsed onto it after a long run.

I said, "Listen, I want to jail William Krehbeil the Third because I am concerned that he's got the bad habit of murdering his relatives, sure. But mostly I want him out of action because I don't want him trying to fill Tom's shoes. I'm sad for Faye—*really* sad—because there never will be a replacement for Tom Latimer. And I'm almost thirty-nine and not married because I keep picking men like Jack Sampler, who can only love a woman from the other side of the world where she can't bite him. So I keep finding rodeos to ride in to keep my mind off my loneliness, and this is just the latest. Shit, I don't know why I'm telling you all of this!" I wrapped my arms around myself and looked away in embarrassment.

Wardlaw grunted, "So this has all been a sham. You don't have a plan to collar my guy."

"Nope, sure don't. I'm no help to you."

Wardlaw gave me what he probably thought was a seductive look. "You could be good, Hansen. You could be one of the best."

I raised both hands to my head in exasperation. "Wardlaw, get it straight! I can't prove a dang thing! I'd need a warrant so I could exhume the bodies and analyze hair and fingernail samples for heavy metals, or something like that. And you know what? It's finally occurring to me that I don't have to solve—or resolve—every bit of chaos that gets tossed in front of me. All I really have to do is what's good for me and for the people I care about. Small, simple actions, like making sure the baby doesn't bite into a poisoned cookie." I spread out my arms, palms up, and stared into the sky. "And that, Mr. Wardlaw sir, is the whole and only reason I am here!"

Wardlaw snapped away from me and stared off into the distant fields for a while. He fiddled with the change in his pockets, his jaws working like he was chewing steel. Bit by bit, he seemed to relax. Then he swatted me on the shoulder. "Time to get going," he said. "Don't worry about it. I'll get the little shit one way or another. I always do. Keep your nose clean. Give me a call if you learn anything you want to tell me." And with that, he got into his bland-looking sedan and drove away.

It was another ten minutes before a silver BMW carrying a man, a woman, and a child came down the road. I threw down the stalk of grass I'd been chewing on and moved to the edge of the road, where I stuck out my thumb. The BMW came to a halt. The window on the passenger's side slid down silently. Faye's astonished face peered out at me. "Em?"

"It's me, all right."

She opened the door and jumped out. She threw her arms around me in her good-old-buddy way, and, through clenched teeth, whispered, "Is there something wrong with your car?"

"No."

"Then, quick, help me get the baby out of the backseat and get us out of here. Tell Tert there's some kind of an emergency and we'll come by Philly later to get my bags. Tell him anything—I don't care; I'm just so sick of this precious, self-centered jackass, I could puke!"

28

Now that I had Wardlaw off my back, I could get down to work.

I found Jenny sitting in the backyard of her little cottage in the Lancaster suburb of East Petersburg, making a watercolor painting of a flower that was just beginning to bloom in her garden. Sunlight played across its brilliant anatomy. The subtle shadows it threw on its own interior formed a delicate composition of inwardly spiraling curves. "Hello, Em," she said, obviously pleased but not particularly surprised to see me.

"Come meet my friend Faye. And her baby. They're waiting in my car out on the street."

"I'd love to. Just let me finish this blossom before the paint dries."

I settled in to watch, and after a few moments asked, "How do you stay so relaxed? All day you deal with the encroachment of development and mediocrity on land that you love, and yet it doesn't seem to get to you."

Jenny shrugged her shoulders. "Sure it does. It just doesn't stop me."

"But how? I'm sorry, I sound just like Fred Petridge."

She smiled. "Remember those chestnut trees Fred was talking about? Look at my house. It was built of chestnut logs two feet square hundreds of years ago. It's been stuccoed over, but those logs are in there, just as good as new, because it does not rot. Like Fred said, chestnuts used to be the main tree around here, but they got the blight. You never see even those sprouts anymore unless you walk deep into the woods, but you know what? All the old stumps are still there, and they're alive and impervious to rot. And the roots just keep on sprouting again." She shrugged, then dipped her brush into a lovely shade of yellow paint and laid it lovingly on the paper. "As soon as the sapling gets big enough to bloom, the blight kills it back again, and that's very sad, but who knows? Maybe someday we'll figure out a cure for all of this. Nothing lasts forever in this world, not even blight. So I think I'll just honor my roots and keep on sending up my sprouts."

I sat with her awhile, watching her paint. Jenny was not a Remington or a Charlie Russell, but her little painting was better than George Catlin's landscapes, a nice integration of the tension between darkness and light, and vibrant in its portrayal of color. And she was happy, a woman at peace in the job of embracing the disharmonies of human nature. I wondered if I could ever be as comfortable with myself.

I said, "In all of your travels around this county, have you gotten to know anyone who drives an ambulance?"

"Sure. My cousin, in fact. He's with the fire department. I am a Mennonite, you know, so I'm related to half the county, if not three-quarters of it." She lifted her brush and nibbled at the end of the handle. "Why, what's going on in that busy mind of yours?"

"I think Mrs. Krehbeil needs to get to a hospital where someone can take an X ray of her lungs. I'll bet you doughnuts to Whoopie Pies that they'll find the shadows of lead. Then she'd be kept in the hospital and properly treated, and might just survive long enough to get that easement you want her to have."

"An ambulance to save the Krehbeil farm, you say? Now, there's a metaphor."

"Try tomorrow. If it's a nice day, I wouldn't be surprised if you wouldn't find her out on the front porch in her wheelchair enjoying the air, and I'll bet also that it wouldn't be long before she falls out of that chair."

Jenny nodded. "There's no one who could keep the fire department from loading her into an ambulance and getting her to town, now, is there?"

"No one. Not even her doting children. Her doctor is named Abrams. Make sure she gets someone else."

"Oh, that old sawbones? Heavens, I'd thought he'd retired. He still thinks babies come from storks."

"I thought it was something to do with toadstools. But don't wait any longer than tomorrow, okay? The old girl's probably getting dosed again today."

Jenny gave me a lovely smile. "It's a pleasure knowing you, Em Hansen. Here, have some celery," she said, lifting a dampened tea towel off of a very stubby bunch of that vegetable. "It's grown right here in Lancaster County. I go to Root's farm market every Tuesday and get some, not only because it's the most delicious celery you can find anywhere, but because Lancaster County is still a place that has farm markets like Root's. It's only open Tuesdays. Staying open daily would be like trying to be a part of the rest of the world, and that's not their point. But on Tuesdays, you can get any kind of pastry or confection made in this county, you can buy pigs, and horses, and arrowheads. . . . Everywhere you'll see men wearing flat-topped straw hats and women in plain clothes and delicate white caps, and not a lick of makeup. Not a one of them has ever seen the inside of a beauty parlor. And they don't even speak English if they can avoid it."

"In this world, but not of it."

I took a stalk and bit into it. Jenny was right. It was delicious. It had more flavor than I had ever imagined a stalk of celery could have.

Jenny said, "You can't get celery like that from a factory farm. It takes *love* to grow it, not machinery. I bought this from a little old lady who lays out her produce on velvet."

"Wow. Why try to keep up with the Joneses when the material world isn't really making the Joneses all that happy? And I thought the Amish were simply quaint."

"The lady at Root's is a Mennonite, but close enough. No, they've got their troubles and their own brand of foolishness, but they also have something to teach us."

Jenny saw me out to the street and met Faye and the baby. Jenny showed each of her colorful fingernails in turn to Sloane, who shrieked with amusement. Faye let Jenny hold the infant, and I saw that good, strong woman soften with pleasure.

When we were ready to leave, I said, "I have one last little favor to ask: When you and your cousin take Mrs. Krehbeil to the hospital, would you please relieve her of just a snippet of her hair?"

"Her hair? Why?"

"Because the main symptom people will treat will be pneumonia, but it's probably lung cancer. But perhaps the dose was given only orally. If the lead isn't in her lungs, it'll show up in her hair and fingernails. It's a bit more of a chore for you, but get those samples and make sure you have a witness. Stick it in an envelope and seal it and get your cousin to sign across the seal. Then get it to Fred Petridge. He'll know what to do with it."

Jenny tipped her head, musing. "Van Gogh used to lick his brush," she said. "How are we going to prove she didn't do it to herself?"

Faye said, "Mrs. K doesn't paint. She married into the family. Her son says she hasn't a lick of talent, and no real interest in it."

I said, "There are some paintings in that house—some truly bad paintings—"

Faye said, "The word is that Deirdre painted them. I just spent four days listening to Tert cuss about what Deirdre 'presumes to call art.' "

We were all buckled up and ready to leave when Jenny tapped on my window. I lowered it.

"One thing," she said. "I almost forgot. I phoned a friend at the Nature Conservancy and had him look up your mother's ranch. Em, there's something you need to know. Have you been back there recently?"

"No. . . . It's been a couple years, actually."

"Well, then, you need to know what's happened, and why your mother chose to sell rather than leaving it to you. You ready to hear this?"

I took a deep breath. "Okay . . ."

"It's because the ranches were being bought up by developers. It's too close to Colorado, Em. He said that folks from Denver used to go up to Fort Collins to go fishing—"

"The Cache la Poudre River," I said. "Great trout-fishing."

"Yes, but then Fort Collins grew into a city, too. It's huge now, my friend said. So everybody from there is looking for the next-farthest get-away, and guess where that is?"

"My part of Wyoming?" I asked.

"Yes, you're just over an hour from Fort Collins, right? So the developers are buying up the ranches and selling off your creek bottoms in chunks as ranchettes. They're fencing off the riparian corridor and calling the prairie on the benches 'the Commons.' "

"Shit! That'll ruin the place! The grasslands and the creek bottoms are one ecosystem! The animals need both to survive, and you've got to graze heavy, sharp-hoofed animals in order to break up the soils so the grasses reseed, or the grasses give over to brush!" I bent my head over the steering wheel, embarrassed at my outburst. "That whole ecosystem grew up around the buffalo and the antelope; that's why it was important to keep the cattle grazing!"

Jenny waited for me to calm down a bit, then she said, "So your mom had a choice: She could leave the land to you and watch you lose it to inheritance tax, or she could sell it now to a coalition that's going to keep it a working ranch, and not subject to the turnover of families."

I turned in my seat, still holding on to the steering wheel to orient myself in time and space. "But either way I can't live there," I said, my voice coming out like a tiny child's.

Jenny put a hand on my shoulder. "I know it's hard to let go of owning the land, Em. We need it so deeply. It's part of our identity, our security. In loving it, we feel loved. That must be why your mother wrote in into the bill of sale that you'd always be allowed to stay in the ranch house," Jenny said. "I think you're a lucky woman. I think your mother took responsibility for what she wanted, and did the best she could for you, too."

29

"WHAT DO YOU WANT TO DO WHILE WE WAIT FOR TERT TO COME home so you can get your gear?" I asked Faye, as we headed into Philadelphia.

She grinned. "No need to wait," she said, producing a key from her pocket.

"Does he know you have that?"

"He didn't ask, and I didn't tell him. I found it in a drawer in the kitchen. How else do you think I was able to take the baby for walks?"

"He wouldn't even give you a key?"

"Nope. A real piece of work, that boy. He's so tight I could hear his asshole squeak. When I saw you standing by the road, I all but tore the steering wheel from his hands to get him to stop."

"Sorry you had such a lousy visit."

Faye sighed. "I thought it would be good because he had so many things in common with Tom," she said longingly. "The problem is he has all of the *wrong things* in common with him!"

That was good enough for me. Somewhere in Chester County, after I had phoned Fritz to say that we'd see him in Baltimore by five, and he'd said he'd go one better and pick us up at the General Aviation terminal in Philadelphia at four, and when Faye had finally finished venting her spleen, I told her that I was sure there was a man out there who was worth her time and attentions. From there I segued into the plans I had, now that the baby was more or less sleeping through the night (as she put it, " 'Sleeping like a baby' means in fits and starts"), I would be looking for a job that would make it possible for me to afford my own place while I worked on my thesis at night. Faye allowed as how she'd miss me, but trusted that I would not move very far away.

About five miles farther down the road, she asked, "Are you mad at me?"

"For what, Faye?"

"For not figuring out how to tell you more gently."

I sighed. "I probably wouldn't have listened."

"I thought if I found you a job . . ."

I couldn't help smiling. "Thanks, Faye. But next time you find me hiding under my bed, why not just say, 'Em, you're hiding under your bed.' "

"Em, you were hiding under your bed."

"No shit I was hiding under my bed. Can we talk about Tom now?"

She took in a breath and let it out. "Do I have to?"

"No, not really. Not until you're ready. But it's okay to love me and hate me at the same time."

"I didn't say I blamed you for Tom's death."

"You didn't have to."

She looked out the opposite window for some time. The baby slept.

As we crossed the Schuylkill River into Philadelphia, I said, "If it's worth anything to you, I feel guilty as hell about Tom's death, and so does Jack. I have to believe that's a big part of why Jack went away to play soldier again, and why I've been hiding under my bed."

"Let it go, Em. We all have to let it go. Let *Tom* go." She reached out and patted me on the shoulder.

"Thanks," I said. "I love you, Faye. You're the best friend I've ever had."

"I love you, too, Em."

◇

WHILE FAYE PACKED her bags, I took a stroll through Tert's house and out into the garden, where a large forsythia bush was in full, screaming bloom, a shower of . . . well, Baltimore yellow. Sloane Renee rode on my hip, giggling and smiling as if we'd never been apart.

Tert had a pretty classy place, all right; all polished brass doorplates and eighteenth-century brick, with slate pathways leading into the fenced privacy of the yard. Amazing what you can buy with ill-gotten gains.

Within this tightly manicured splendor, my interest quickly settled upon the toolshed. It was just a hair too rickety for the rest of the show. As fastidious as Tert was, I couldn't imagine he would leave it like that. And sure enough, Faye's key got me into the shed, and I found the weather-proofed and sealed room inside. I was careful not to leave any fingerprints as I peeked inside to make sure it was filled with paintings. I borrowed Faye's digital camera and took a couple of artistic snaps.

Then I let myself into his office (the lock to the office door was appallingly easy to pick; I did it with a credit card, for heaven's sake) and dug until I found those notes he'd had with him in Utah. I duplicated several pages. Feeling pretty chipper, I "borrowed" an envelope with KREHBEIL GALLERIES letterhead and mailed the copies to Agent Wardlaw at the address printed on his business card. The artistry of the digital photographs I pumped through Faye's laptop on an Internet connection, figuring that dear old Brucie would enjoy having them to greet him upon his return to the ugliest building in Washington. I copied a few of the file entries into the e-mail just for spice:

> Hey Brucie:
>
> Your boy is fond of making notes. His handwriting is tiny and cryptic, so I can't make out every word, or should I say, every term of his code, but maybe you can do better with the copies I've sent you. Putting asterisks for each letter or number I can't make out, and trying to get the spacings between the bits of information accurately, they look like this for the past year:
>
> *May 3rd*
>
> *Rem to H**
> *Wyo/UPS (spec.)—SAC/will call*
> *O/*—ridge/hoc*
> *Pd./ck+cash*
>
> *June 8th*
>
> *orange—no. 26*
> *223,000 profit*
> *split/50.50*

Aug 12th

Big One—10% to [ ]
new frame—Rocetti/Boston
Denver—van/cash
*Split w/GRR/London a/**

I imagine you'll have fun comparing these with something like, say, a tax audit for the gallery. Keep your nose clean and I'll bet you were a real pain in the butt in Kansas City,

Em H.

P.S. You're right, I'm one of the best.

30

WE HAD A NICE FLIGHT BACK, CHASING THE SUN AS FAR AS Greenfield, Iowa, where we tucked in for the night. It's a fun little airport; you have to phone the fire department to come pump the gas, and the lady who rents rooms nearby makes absolutely killer cinnamon rolls in the morning. As we crested the Rockies, I flew for a while, but mostly I slept in the back with the baby cuddled in my arms while her mom sat up front and traded off the controls with Fritz. It had been a long four days for each and every one of us.

Like I said, I wasn't done with the Krehbeil project yet, but it's first things first if you're trying to have a life. The last weeks of school went by like a stampede of stallions, and before I knew it, I was writing final exams. Next, I took the ten-day short course on stable isotopes offered at the U, because I had an idea it was going to help with the analysis of Tert's paint chips. That done, I signed up for time on the scanning electron microscope and the electron microprobe and got to work examining those chips.

I heard from Jenny, Fred, and Nigel frequently. They'd found lead in Mrs. Krehbeil's hair and fingernails, all right—*lots* of it—but darned if the medical authorities could figure out where it was coming from. So it seemed that a bit more . . . er, *digging* was in order. It was my excellent luck that Fritz happened to be flying back to Baltimore again, and was willing to drop me off at Harrisburg, so I invited Agent Wardlaw to pick me up at the airport and drive me to the Pennsylvania Geologic Survey. When we walked into Fred's office, Nigel, who was lounging in a side chair, whipped his feet off the desk and stood up, crossing his index fingers in the sign against enchantment. "What ho!" he said. "I was expecting you, Em, but what chimera is this? Have we dog food on the hoof?"

"Knock it off, Nigel," I said, grinning. "Wardlaw popped for doughnuts just now, so you could say we've kissed and made up."

"Oh. Well. Bully. In that case, to what do we owe the incomparable honor?"

Just then Jenny arrived, and from the way Nigel ran his hands through her hair, I'd say they'd been getting better acquainted. It was hard for me to feature at first, but I noticed that he'd taken to wearing shirts that matched the colors of her fingernails.

I said, "Nigel, how tight did you say that new color IR coverage for the county was?"

"One to twenty-four hundred," he replied.

"Can you pull up that funny little Krehbeil parcel down in the serpentine barrens again? And show me any disturbed ground?"

Nigel gave me a lascivious grin. "That would show up on the IR right and proper. The new growth of vegetation wouldn't match the signature of the old." He led us down the hall to his office, sat down, and tapped away at his keyboard for a while.

This time he was on a big desktop computer, and the resolution was magnificent. As Nigel zoomed in on the properties, I could all but count the dogs lined up by the fences barking at passing cars. He narrowed the view down to the Krehbeil parcel, and sure enough, out behind the dwelling structure, about three hundred yards back, tucked in behind a screen of trees, there was a patch of ground that did not match the rest. It was oblong, and approximately three by eight feet.

Nigel looked at Wardlaw and said, "A nice bit of digging for a man on the eve of his middle age, but not insurmountable. You say Dad and Auntie are already gone, Mum's on the way, and Elder Sis is having trouble feeling her hands and feet? Well then, this is number five. How many more do we have to go?"

"One more brother, a nephew, and a niece."

"Oh, jolly," said Nigel. "Serial killing, right here in Lancaster County. And I had feared this would be such a sleepy little corner of creation."

Wardlaw got on the phone to some well-placed colleagues, and by dinnertime we had a warrant and several burly sheriff's deputies with stunners to help deter the dogs. The raid turned up one very irritable tenant with a bright-red neck who spouted slogans concerning what it would take to get him to give up his arms, but Wardlaw pointed out that our interest lay in activities predating his six months' residency. And the tenant's common-law wife was only too pleased to point out where the dogs had found Cricket's little car, deep within a shroud of greenbrier.

The inquest was scheduled for less than a week later, so I used what was left of Tert's money to buy a commercial ticket for the return trip and stuck around. By the time the inquest began, there were lab results on Cricket's bones. Mrs. Krehbeil was still frail, but gathering strength. She was put on the witness stand first, to avoid undue stress, but not surprisingly, she could or would tell them nothing. After she was done testifying, she was shown from the room and returned to the nursing home where she now resided.

Agent Wardlaw sat in the back of the courtroom with me. "I hope this nails the S.O.B.," he said, "because he saw that warrant coming, and there was nothing in that little shed back in the garden."

"No kidding." I wasn't surprised. Faye had insisted on leaving her "borrowed" keys by a note on the dining room table, and if I were Tert, I would have moved my camp, too.

"Oh, this is good," he said, as Deirdre took the stand to testify.

She looked older than the last time I had seen her, as if her fires were banked low, but she held her head up with patrician rigidity the entire time she gave testimony. She won few points for sympathy. There was a bit too much condescension in her tone as she said, "She seemed worse after each of my brother William's visits. I had become quite concerned. But of course, I thought she was merely pining for him. He so seldom comes around."

I'll bet you thought that, I mused.

My testimony was requested toward the end. I was sworn in and asked to state my bona fides and how it came to be that I was present the morning that Mrs. Krehbeil first fell out of her wheelchair. I was more than pleased to answer, because it put the evidence in the public record, right where I could access it for my thesis project. "I was there because Mrs. Krehbeil's older son, William, had hired me to analyze paint chips from a painting he had collected at his aunt Winifred Krehbeil's ranch outside of Cody, Wyoming," I said crisply, speaking into the microphone.

The judge asked a few questions about how I had come to notice the symptoms of lead poisoning in Mrs. Krehbeil, then seemed ready to excuse me.

"Wait," I said. "I have a few more points which I think might have some bearing on the case."

The judge nodded, indicating that I should go ahead and make my statement.

I then explained the rest, about Tert's suspicion that the painting had been copied and switched, and his assertion that there would be more paintings stored at the house.

"How does this relate to the case?" asked the judge.

"It goes to motive," I explained. "After all, my client is a prime suspect."

The corner of the judge's mouth crimped at my use of terms. I suppose he thought I'd been watching too much TV. "And had the painting been altered?" the judge inquired.

"If those samples are representative of the entire painting, then it's my belief that it is entirely a forgery," I stated.

"And what is your evidence for that conclusion?"

I leaned closer to the mike. "First, the green paint used was incorrect. It should have been Hooker's green, which is a mixture of Prussian blue, a synthetically produced pigment, and gamboge, which is an organic resin from Asia. The Prussian blue was present, all right, but the gamboge was not. In its place, I found a mixture of lead chromate, which is a much paler, less brownish pigment, and several other pigments meant to shift the yellow to the classic mustard tone. While Remington occasionally used lead chromate, his Hooker's green was purchased premixed, and the yellow used was gamboge."

"So from this you concluded that the painting was a forgery?"

I could tell by his tone that he was not going to be persuaded by one point of evidence. "No, I am a geologist, not an art conservator. I would not presume to suggest that I know Remington's work in such detail. But a geologist is trained to examine the relative ages of materials. So I analyzed the lead in the lead white to see if there was much silver in it. While the cyanide process used today to separate those two elements was in widespread use by 1900, I thought that, if there were a significant impurity of silver in the lead, it might indicate that the pigment used was old. However, I found it to be quite pure."

"And did you find anything else at variance with the paints Remington would have used?"

"Yes, and this last item was the most compelling. I recently took a short course in stable isotopes at the University of Utah, and I applied what I learned there in the analysis of the paints. You see, the pigments didn't clinch the case, so I turned to the oil in which they'd been emulsified."

"And what oil was used, Ms. Hansen?"

"Well, I don't know. I imagine it was linseed oil. I have no reason to suspect otherwise, and that is what Remington would have used. But I wasn't interested in the exact provenance—or origin—of the oil, just its age. You see, if the painting had been copied and switched between 1972, when the elder Mrs. Krehbeil died, the family fortunes began to slip, and the ranch where the original painting was stored was passed on to her daughter Winifred, and this winter, when my client went to fetch it, then it would be a matter of looking at the carbon isotopes present in whatever oil was used."

"So, am I to understand that you analyzed the oil for a carbon-fourteen date? You stated that the sample was only a chip; was there enough present to establish this?"

"No, that wasn't what I was doing." I got out of the witness box and crossed to a chalkboard that had been set up for just such contingencies. I drew on it two lines: a vertical line, which I notched to indicate the ration of carbon-14 to carbon-12, and then I crossed it with a horizontal line, which I notched to indicate the years between 1700 and the present. I put my finger on the line with the dates. "Consider this line a baseline. Carbon-fourteen, the radioisotope, exists in our atmosphere at a steady ratio to carbon-twelve, which is stable. The way carbon-fourteen dating is done is by comparing that steady-state number with the amount found in the item tested, any organic item such as wood or a bone which was once alive. The isotope decay clock is set at the time of death of the individual, because, at death, it is no longer taking in carbon, and the unstable radioisotope continues to decay into carbon-twelve at a standard rate, called a half-life."

I stopped to take a breath. I looked out across the courtroom at William Krehbeil III, who was staring back at me like I was a statue he did not quite like.

I said, "But there's a glitch in our steady-state situation, and that's why I've set my timeline back to the 1700s. At the beginning of the Industrial

Revolution, here"—I put my finger on about 1750—"the amount of free carbon in the atmosphere shifted. It became bound up in combustion products from the burning of fossil fuels, such as carbon monoxide. So the ratio shifted slightly over the next two hundred years." I ran the chalk horizontally almost to the 1950 mark, slowly letting it sink below the baseline. "It's not much, but it's easily measurable. At that time, something else happened technologically: We split the atom." I zigged the chalk high above the baseline, forming a sharp peak. "Above-ground testing of nuclear devices released masses of carbon fourteen, dramatically shifting the ratio. Then here—I put my finger at the top of the peak—"we banned above-ground testing. The year was 1969. The ratio once again began to decline, until now—I drew a slope leading to the present year—"it's almost back to baseline, but not quite. The point is that, in any organic material, we can measure this ratio and plot it on this graph."

I pulled a folded page out of my pocket and opened it in front of the judge. "In the Krehbeil samples, the oil in which the pigments had been emulsified displayed a dramatically elevated ratio. As you can see, there are two places where that level can be found on this chart." I pointed at that level on both the rising and falling sides of the peak. "But either date is long after 1909, when Remington himself died and therefore ceased to work. So whoever mixed that paint did so after Remington's death."

There was a restless shifting in the chairs beyond the rail. I saw perplexed reporters trying to figure out how to make notes on what I'd said. The judge asked, "And how do you believe this bears on the case?"

"Because I believe that it proves your prime suspect's innocence."

Tert's eyes widened with surprise. The courtroom broke out in a rumble of conversation and the judge called for silence.

I said, "Look, I know what the evidence is against him, because I proposed it myself. But it's all circumstantial. His mother got sicker each time he visited. That doesn't prove he was dosing her. He would benefit financially if she died before the land was sold into an agricultural easement, but benefit does not prove guilt, either. All the other points can similarly be tossed, because not a single bit of evidence has his fingerprints on it. And I think his interests show he in fact expected to get the painting as his inheritance, not the land. He in fact didn't have to wait for his mother to die to get the painting. Aunt Winnie was dead, and he trooped on out there to Wyoming and collected his prize." I realized that I had dropped several notches in the formality of my speech. "Well, you get my point," I said. "Tert told me how much he loved that painting when he showed me the fake. At the time I didn't want to believe him, because I wanted to hate him. He was paying attention to my best friend Faye, and I did not approve."

The judge's shoulders moved slightly, suggesting that he was suppressing laughter. "Go on," he said. "So, who do you suspect of poisoning Mrs. Krehbeil and murdering her younger daughter?"

I took a deep breath and said, "I'll bet you dollars to doughnuts it's Deirdre."

Excited whispering arose throughout the room. The judge said, "But she's been poisoned, herself."

I locked eyes with Deirdre. Her hard gray eyes bored into me, glinting with hatred, but not the slightest attempt at feigned innocence.

"Maybe that's how she figured out how to do the job. Lead chromate is the basis of the family fortune, so I'd be surprised if they didn't have a sack of it still sitting around in that barn. There's a bad yellow paint job on the front door of the house. Mrs. Krehbeil as much as told me it was traditional to paint it that color. Deirdre might have tried to mix that paint herself and gotten herself a nasty dose. Even the best hunters sometimes shoot themselves in the foot."

Nervous chatter broke out in the courtroom, and the judge dropped his gavel three times to quiet it. "Continue, Miss Hansen."

I counted things out on my fingers. "Point one: opportunity. She could have done it to any of these people just as easily as her brother, and timed her mother's progression by his visits just to frame him. And she'd have the same access as anyone else to the poisonous pigment, in fact, better access: Her father's studio is a locked room in the upstairs of the house, and I'll bet that's where she found the sack of lead chromate in dry form. It's what her father would have used when he tried to make Hooker's green to fake the painting."

Loud discussions broke out, and the gavel fell again. "Order! Order!"

I said, "I talked to Hector. I realize this is hearsay, but you can ask him yourself. Mr. Krehbeil the Second 'could paint like anyone.' He was a mimic, but he had no ideas of his own. Heck, it was even fashionable a hundred years ago to have paintings copied. You gave them away to your friends, or you had one for the city house and one for the country. I've been reading up on this for my thesis. And most of Remington's works that were reproduced in the magazines were copied one way or another. It was what they had for Xerox machines back then. So it would have seemed almost traditional for Krehbeil the Second to copy the painting, and he needed the bucks, so he sold the original. Besides, he inherited the good-old-boy network with his mother's gallery, and he could swear to the provenance. The only question in my mind is when he pulled the switch on Winnie."

The judge said, "That is speculation, Miss. Hansen. Please confine your testimony to your direct experience of matters brought before this inquest."

In my mind's eye, I could see through to the place where the shattered members of the Krehbeil family cut into each other like jagged pieces of glass. Deirdre's rage and jealousy and guilt were almost palpable. I had to bring the judge to the point of my vision. In mounting frustration, I said, "There was something that Deirdre said to me after I helped her put her mother back in the chair. Or more accurately, something she *didn't* say. When I asked her about her siblings, she cussed about Tert and Hector, but never mentioned Cricket. It was as if Cricket already didn't exist to her."

"The law is interested in evidence, Miss Hansen, not the interpretations of someone barely acquainted with this family," the judge informed me, the lines around his mouth hardening.

I could feel Deirdre's eyes burning into the side of my skull. I had begun my accusation in a mood of righteous anger, but now fear sat like ice in my intestines. I was attacking a woman I suspected of systematically murdering her parents and siblings in cold blood, but suspicion was not proof. What if she walked away free and came looking for me, or someone I loved?

I focused on the judge's mouth, mesmerized by his contempt. Taking a quick breath, I said, "Right, but there's one last thing: Cricket's car. Didn't the Sheriff say that duct tape was used to jam the accelerator pedal to the floor?"

The judge nodded.

"Well, even if there are no fingerprints on that duct tape, the tape itself can be matched, and I'll bet you'll find the rest of the roll in the trunk of Deirdre's car. She's so frugal she'd never throw out even an inch."

The judge's eyebrows ratcheted up a tiny increment.

I chanced a look at Deirdre. She had bolted halfway from her seat, but now descended back into it, her exit suddenly blocked by a large, muscular bailiff. Her gaze slid back my way, and the look she gave me was pure poison.

◇

MY MASTER'S THESIS was a snap to write once I got home. I was able to put my analytical data together with Nigel's GIS analysis and—*voila*—one master's thesis, or more precisely one more lap around the track with the judges watching.

The chubby underbelly of human enterprise loves to watch a proud family fall, and the print and television media had a grand time boosting their ratings and sales with every last grisly detail as first Aunt Winnie and then William Secundus were exhumed and joined Cricket's and her unborn child's remains in chemical analysis. Once that was out, it came out, too, that the family's wealth in art was long gone, sold by Secundus to maintain the appearance of continued grandeur after his mother died. The publicity didn't hurt a bit when I went to apply for a job. The Utah State Geological Survey said they needed someone to work with stable isotopes, and to address the occasional forensic case that crossed their desks.

One day my Internet server popped out the following e-mail, which was a portion of one I had sent, copied back to me with embellishments:

<u>May 3rd</u>

*Rem {ington} to H{ussein}**
{shipped from} Wyo/UPS (spec. {labeled "velvet painting"—the nerve!})—SAC {=switch at counter} / will call
O/—ridge/hoc*
Pd. / ck + cash {stupid ass, check was easy to track, hope he had fun with the cash}

<u>June 8th</u>

orange—no. 26 {=stolen Renoir}
223,000 profit
split/50.50 {with other suspect, here to go nameless until I tighten the noose}

Aug 12th

Big One—10% to [{another damned drug smuggler with delusions of grandeur}]
new frame—Rocetti/Boston
Denver—van/cash {yeah, meet me in the middle of the bridge at midnight, Bucko}
Split w/GRR/London a/ {this links us nicely with Interpol, thanks}*

Send you the rest as I crack 'em, and that thing in KC I swear it's all lies.

Brucie

The thesis write-up, rewrites, and defense occupied me from June through November—no small effort, considering that in late June I took that part-time job with the Utah Geological Survey and moved into a place of my own, with the understanding that the job would become full-time once I'd finished my degree.

Graduation that December was bittersweet: At my invitation, my mother came to watch me turn my tassel and don the master's hood, and it seemed she was really quite proud of me. Why she hadn't said so earlier, I'll never know, but perhaps it was a new sensation for her. The feeling was, in fact, mutual: My respect for her bloomed in contrast to Mrs. Krehbeil. It was nice to have a mother who at least took responsibility for what she wanted, and looked after herself so that I wouldn't be shackled with the job unnecessarily. And, it seemed, she really did have a realistic notion of what was best for me: With the master's and a real job, and the pleasure of good friends around me whom I knew cared for me, I had never been happier.

And getting my master's and the job and the new place to live wasn't everything that had gone right during that half-year.

Faye's great uncle invested funds so that she and Fritz could open what's called an FBO—or "fixed base operation"—out at the Salt Lake airport for general aviation customers who needed aircraft sales and rentals, instruction, and service. Faye was finally able to run down to Florida to pick up her plane (leaving the baby with me for the weekend, to my immense joy), and Fritz moved ahead with his prototype. The investors he found in Baltimore came through for him. Between these investments and the business they were able to bring in at the FBO, Fritz was able to drop his remaining contracts with the military.

As the air grew crisper, I got to thinking of the days six months before the whole fracas with the Krehbeil fortune had started, and I got in a mood to sweep out the last few grains of turmoil that had blown in on that storm.

I telephoned Ray. I asked him to meet me.

"Where?" he asked, surprised to hear from me after so many months. "When?"

"How about right now?" I said. "We can meet on the roof of the city library. I like the view."

"That sounds good. I'll be there in about fifteen minutes."

The air was bright and clear when I got there, and I could see my breath. I took the long way up, walking up each and every step along the long curve that led to the roof garden. It took a long time, because Sloane Renee was with me for the afternoon, and she kept wanting to get down from the backpack and take some steps herself. She'd make it up four or maybe five and then reach up to me, her little hands fluttering with an unspoken request to lift her up once again.

She was getting big: a whacking twenty-four pounds at sixteen months, but then, her mama and daddy were no shrimps. And it felt good to carry her, her little legs swinging, her little voice softly singing, "Ma-ma-ma." It felt good to work my legs, and my lungs, and to sing along with her. And I listened to the sounds of the city I had adopted to be my home, and admired its colors, from the dark gray twigs of every tree to the warm sandstone-reds of the City and County Building across the way, to the rich cobalt dance of the Utah sky.

Ray was waiting for me at the top, his cheeks rosy in the brisk air. The hood of a gray sweatshirt lay open around his neck, its cool gray setting off his wonderful coloring, from the healthy warmth of his skin to the rich dark lashes around his indigo blue eyes. He had a foot up on a bench so he could stretch a hamstring. He had taken the steps at a run.

"Hi, Ray," I said.

He rewarded me with a contented smile. "Em, it's nice to see you. Is this Faye's baby?"

I nodded as he played "Uncle Ray" to the little hussy I was carrying. I said, "It's nice to see you. So. I bet you're wondering why I called you here today."

He stood with his hands in the pockets of his sweatshirt and waited, smiling.

I said, "I thought it was time that we officially broke up."

His smile stiffened. He waited.

"Well," I said, beginning to stutter as my self-confidence wobbled, "it occurs to me that we never did break up, really."

"Em, it was over a long time ago."

I waved a hand as if to dispel a cloud of confusion. "I know that. The thing is, things ended rather abruptly between us, and—"

"Rather!" He tried to make a joke of it, but he began to blush with the humiliation of memory.

"And we never got to talk about it. And I know, you're really not a talker, even now that you've been working so hard on yourself. But I am. So here's what I want to do: I want to tell you what was good about us, and what I miss, to honor what we had. I want to say also what wasn't good, so that can be part of the past, not the present. I just don't want to be thinking about all this every time I see you."

Ray thought about this for a moment. "That's fair," he said. "I'll go first. I miss—" He stopped abruptly, and looked away.

"Let *me* go first. Then you'll know what I mean. Ray, I thank you for all your kindnesses, and all your caring. That was huge for me. I thank you for the honor of being asked to be a part of your family. I miss our walks together, and all the time we spent just being together, saying nothing. I grieve the loss of possibilities." I had to stop, and take a deep breath. Ray's eyes grew wet with tears, and he opened his mouth to speak, but I loosened a hand from the grip I had on the baby and put my fingertips almost to his lips. "Please wait," I said. "I know I'm a terrible chicken, but if I don't finish now, I'm going to make things a whole lot worse. Ray, there were things that weren't right. I lost myself in that relationship, so I don't want to go back there. I resented your insistence that your way was the right way, because while some parts of it were fine and good, other parts were not what I could do."

"I know," he said. His voice was thin and husky, like a lost child's.

"I'm doing this wrong."

"No, you're doing fine."

"And all the time, I didn't want to lose *you*," I said. "That's a great mystery to me. How could I want the man but not want what he was offering?"

Ray smiled. It was a smile that began slowly and widened at a stately pace; a smile of relief, an opening of something that had been locked away.

I cuddled the baby close—not from the cold, but from a sudden sense of exposure that had nothing to do with the weather. Sloane Renee nuzzled her little face against my neck. It felt wonderful. I said, "I care about you, Ray. Caring is something so much bigger than the both of us, and it's got nothing to do with whether or not any two people should be together or be apart. It's got to do with being human, or just being on this planet."

"Amen to that." Ray looked away at the mountains. "It feels like we should be jamming ourselves into some role our culture predicts, but we don't fit."

"No, we do not."

"We'd have driven each other mad."

"Yes," I said. "And that would have been a terrible shame. So, Ray, can we be open about this, and let it grow in the wild, and not try to make it part of anything else? I mean, I want to marry and have children, but not with you. It—it just couldn't work."

His grin was happy now. "How right you are. But we can love each other."

"And we do."

He shot me a saucy look. "It'll be hard to avoid . . . er . . ."

"Yeah, well, we can savor that part of the connection. The attraction part. And that will be a great challenge. When we get married—to other people—we'll have to bow to each other when we see each other, instead of hug."

"Bowing's good."

"This is a challenge, huh?"

He brandished his grin at the sky. "A big one. But I'd expect no less from you, Em."

Later that day I wrote a similar confession to Jack. He was still in the Middle East, so I sent it in care of his mother, figuring that she would know what to do with it. It was a moot point anyway. Jack's e-mails to me had dribbled down to one-liners, and I couldn't remember the last time I'd written back about anything more personal than the weather.

That evening, I went for a long walk with Faye and told her I'd broken up with Jack. Sloane Renee slept in the jogger as we strolled along through the avenues district of Salt Lake City, crunching over the dry leaves that were falling as the city bedded down for the winter. I asked her how things were going with the FBO.

"Fine," she said. "I got to fly a brief charter this morning, which felt really good. Thanks again for taking the baby."

"Anytime. Or at least anytime I'm not at work or . . . I don't know, out on a date, out kicking rocks across the desert. There are so many things to do in this life."

"Thanks, Em."

"How are you and Fritz getting along?" I asked. I gave the question just a little extra oomph.

Faye glanced sideways at me. "No way," she said.

"Aw heck, I thought by now, with you guys working together and all . . ."

She began to laugh. "I'm not his type. And he's not mine."

"Drat. What's he looking for? Another general's daughter like his first wife? She was a straitjacket!"

Faye looked sideways at me again and wiggled her eyebrows. "Quite on the contrary."

I stopped.

She stopped.

"No," I said.

"Yes." Her face split into a wide grin.

"Me?"

"Yes. Can't you see it? It's been obvious to me right from the beginning. He never wanted that with me. It was always you, but he respected the commitment you had to Jack."

"Yeah, well, I'm still otherwise occupied. No, *really*!" I said, as Faye began to cackle lasciviously. "Listen, I'm just now learning how to live my own life! I don't want a relationship right now!"

Faye was laughing so hard by now that she had to sit down on the edge of the nearest lawn. "I'm about to pee my pants," she said.

"No, Faye, I'm serious," I said, realizing to my delight that it was true.

"This year I've learned something, a very simple thing: I like my life. Just being alive is pretty damned fine. I'd like to have a nice relationship with a man someday, and I'd like to raise a child, but . . . but . . . I'm tired of meeting everybody a hundred-fifty percent of the way."

"Ooooh, Emmy's got a boundary!" said Faye, flopping onto her back, really whooping it up with the laughter.

"Yeah. I'm me. I'm complete. I don't have to convince anyone of anything. And I'd just like to leave it like that for a while, okay?"

Faye hitched her way up onto her elbows and smiled at me. "Fine. I'll tell Fritz to hold off on that trip to Cancún he was threatening to ask you on. He's got a charter to fly, and . . . you know . . . moonlit walks along the beach. . . ."

I reached down and walloped her with my hat. "I hate water, Faye! Didn't you tell him that?"

"Oh, I thought maybe for the right man—"

"You tell him I'm on my own brand of R and R for the near future, okay?"

"Okay, okay. Does that mean maybe in the springtime?"

I reached out a hand to help her up. "I'm not even going to think about such things right now."

She straightened up and brushed herself off. "I'm impressed, Em. And I'm happy for you. And for me. I was afraid you wouldn't need me as much if you got something nice going with him."

I gave her an elbow in the ribs. "Yeah, well, you're safe for a while, anyway. Like maybe until you're ninety, and you're so senile you can't remember who I am."

"That'll never happen, I'll need you sitting beside me on the front porch of the nursing home, helping me whistle at the young fellows passing by."

"Hard to whistle with no teeth," I said.

"We'll think of something."

"Uh-huh," I agreed. "Want me to take a turn pushing the baby?"

"Always," she replied.

"Always," I echoed, and we headed down the sidewalk in the evening light.

Author's Note
(A Pentimento)

I am interested in art for the same reasons I am interested in geology, and in fact the art came first. My dad was an artist, as was his mother before him. Tutelage began even before I could hold a crayon, because the creative process was right there in front of me, happening on a grand scale.

My grandmother, Dorothy Warren Andrews, studied art at Yale and with Howard Pyle at the Brandywine School. She was an excellent portraitist and could draw splendidly. When she married, she set aside her oils, and did not pick them up again until she was widowed. She was an aesthete who arranged all objects around her harmoniously. She and her sister lived in New York City during the spring and fall, kept a cottage in the Bahamas for the coldest winter months, and, during long summers at the family farm in Maine, painted trays, sewed, braided and hooked rugs, and kept the aging woodwork in perfect nick. She was also a wonderful cook who brought beauty to the science of baking deep-dish blueberry pies.

I recall one moment with her that is worth telling a thousand times. I was perhaps eleven or twelve, and visiting her at the farm. We sat in the kitchen at opposite ends of the old wooden table at which three additional generations of our ancestors had sat. A peaceful afternoon light played through the room, and the air was pervaded with the scent of applesauce and the patient tick-tock of the old regulator clock. I was drawing a picture of a lovely young female with a beautiful dress, and my grandmother, who dressed better than about any woman I knew, looked right past that and saw that I had drawn the hands way too small.

"Sally," she said, getting me to look up. I did. Keeping her face completely empty of any judgment or criticism, she raised one of her fine, artistic hands and placed it against her face, putting the heel against her chin and showing me that the fingertips reached clear to her hairline. I had her lesson at a glance and got at it with both ends of my pencil, starting with the eraser. And loved her even more deeply.

Dad—Richard Lloyd Andrews—painted in oils, and he sometimes let me watch as he paced up and back in front of his big wooden easel. He was a big man, six-foot-five in his stocking feet, handsome with his dark hair, blue eyes, and lantern jaw, and given to a mischievous, dramatic air, so the show of watching him enthralled in his creative process was exactly that—theater. He worked his jaw muscles as he paced, and occasionally picked up a small mirror and stood across the room from his painting to squint at it from another perspective. He studied at Black Mountain College (he is one of its few graduates) with Josef Albers, and after his stint as a sergeant in the U.S. Army Air Corps during the Second World War (during which he paid visits to such artists as Georges Braque), he studied with Hans Hoffman at the Art Student's League.

I was Dad's sidekick. He often took me with him into New York, where I took pride in walking beside him down the sidewalks—he had the great, rhythmic stride of a dancer, and wore a great coat, Stetson, and tartan necktie, and smoked a pipe upside down in the rain—as we systematically hit the art shows he had marked in his copy of *The New Yorker* as we rode in on the New York Central Railroad. He always carried a clipboard, fat drawing pencils, and later calligraphic pens, and he'd put the magazine on the clipboard and fish drawing and writing instruments out of his inside coat pocket as needed, sometimes placing those instruments inside the cardboard case his pipe cleaners came in. As we made the rounds of the galleries and museums, he'd tell me stories about the artists, many of whom he knew from school, and when I saw the movie *Pollack* many years later, it was old home week.

Dad was a brilliant eclectic. Not only did his paintings comprise a fine and legitimate body of work, but he also built model railroads (he and a friend developed ON2 gauge and he served the Model Railroad Society as gauge specialist. Many will remember him as the author of countless articles for *Model Railroader*, *Railroad Modeler*, and *The Narrow Gauge Gazette*) and designed and built multi-hull sailboats (there his outlet was *The Journal of the Amateur Yacht Research Society*). I accompanied him on a great many of his sailing trips, on water spring through fall, and ice boating when the Hudson River froze over in winter, and rode narrow-gauge railroads with him on two continents.

Always on these outings, he carried that clipboard, and brought one along for me, too, and we sat drawing together, he sketching landscapes that would grow into paintings, and I dreaming on paper. I got pretty good at drawing. Very early in life I was anointed She Who Will Carry On the Tradition, and applied to art schools. I got into a very good one. And I did not go. Why? My grandmother's sister was Constance Warren, who, as president of Sarah Lawrence College, built it from a two-year finishing school to the Seven Sisters wonderment it became. She took me aside one day and said, "Sarah, it's all very nice that you wish to develop your artistic talent. But what will happen if you go all the way through your training and discover that you have nothing to say? Wouldn't it be better if you first get a good liberal-arts education and then go to art school?"

I pounced on her idea. On the face of it, it was unassailable logic, but I will here admit that there was more to my decision than that: At eighteen, I was quite intimidated by the idea of being around nothing but really talented artists, and at the same time, felt oddly done with all that. I had put together a portfolio that was complete and accomplished enough to get me into art school, and that was indeed enough. I was ready to learn something else.

That something proved to be geology. I had shown a precocious knack for it in fifth grade, when my teacher, Miss Lucas, took us on field trips looking for minerals and had us draw—yes, draw; geology uses the same parts of the brain as art—folds and faults and the innards of volcanoes. My uncle Jack Ferry took me "rock hounding" as well, scrambling over the mine dumps that dotted Maine's pegmatitic granites. And I had gone looking for big micas with Dad, which he used, peeled into thin sheets, as the glazing in the windows of the parlor cars on his model railroads. But when I got to Colorado College—that good liberal arts joint that had a late enough admissions application deadline to serve as a good landing spot after Great-aunt Con nudged me off my original path—I still thought that "girls" could not study science (yeah, 1969 was back in the Pleistocene, and there were woolly mammoths eating daisies in front of my dormitory). I had to take a couple of science courses to qualify for that liberal arts B.A., so I signed up for geology that first term to get it out of my way, and . . . that was my only A that semester. The rest is history.

I have now also earned an M.S. and have enjoyed three decades working in the rock trades. Where did the writing come from? Well . . . as a product of that "good liberal arts education," I see no real boundaries between the disciplines, and so found no reason not to start writing mystery novels about geology when the creative itch struck for about the fifth time. I must credit my father (in his eclectic brilliance also a storyteller of the first water) and my great-aunt's master plan, not to mention my mother, Mary Fisher Andrews, who read aloud to me, and, as my sixth-grade English teacher, taught me the structure of language with all the trimmings (essay writing, sentence diagramming, and *Gawain and the Green Knight*), and her father (Stephen Joseph Herben, Professor of English Philosophy at Bryn Mawr College). All of these fine family teachers taught me one lesson above all: There are no boundaries or limits to what I could do. That bit about girls and science must have come from someone else.

This is the ninth Em Hansen forensic geology mystery novel. So, why did I write about art? The obvious reason is as a salute to a family tradition. It was darned lucky for me that they were there, because I am dyslexic, and in a great many other families I would have been labeled stupid. In mine, I was called various other things (underachiever, ornery . . .) but never stupid. Dad, Granny, and Aunt Con were always there beaming their approval and interest in everything I did, and Mother always expected me to dive headfirst into whatever career engaged my mind.

Geology has certainly done that: It is in fact an intellectual playground for me. I was born with the talent for four-dimensional thinking (a geologist thinks in the three dimensions of space and projects it forwards and backwards through time. My dyslexia, or trouble decoding linear/sequential text, is on the flip side of being able to take in discontinuous—often ambiguous—data in random order and build space-time models from it. Not a bad trade, if you ask me).

But I found other reasons to write about art. First, art and science are, to me, parts of a whole, and I prefer my universe as fully integrated as I can make it. Second, all the while I was whacking rocks with a hammer, the love of art for art's sake was in my heart. And third, deep down inside I was a chicken. That other reason for not going to art school really had to do, among other things, with color: I could not handle it. I could draw, but I could not paint. Not really. Not like my dad and grandmother could. Yes, they studied with the masters to develop their skills, and if I had gone to art school I might have gotten there, too. But I did not, and it has always bugged me. So a couple of years ago—yeah, after Dad died and was no longer there to notice if I did it badly—I took up drawing with pastels, kind of a hybrid between drawing and painting. And I noticed that I was holding geology in my hands, all ground up and compressed into sticks that I could rub onto a piece of paper to create art.

With love,

Sarah Andrews, still a student
www.sarahandrews.net
November 11, 2003